Kingston's Promise

Carrie Beckort

Carrie Beckort (signature)

For my readers
Without you, this would not exist

CHAPTER 1

"Has he spoken since you've been here?"

"He hasn't spoken since it happened. Except for his freak-out, but that was understandable."

They became silent, but he could hear their soft sighs. He'd come to recognize it as the universal sound of disappointment. It was almost as if they thought he couldn't hear them. Lack of speaking didn't always equate to a lack of listening.

"What time is it?"

"Just after four."

He swallowed past the lump in his throat.

I'm usually dancing at this time. But I can't. I'm not sure I'll ever be able to set foot in the studio again.

"Has he eaten?"

"Not since I've been here." Another sigh.

He heard someone shuffle up behind him.

"Sweetie, you need to eat something." He wasn't sure how they could expect him to eat. He remained quiet, and there was another sigh. "Marcus, I know you're hurting, but you need to be strong for your family right now. You need to eat something." Instead of speaking, he closed his eyes. Of course he should eat. Of course he needed to be strong. But he couldn't. He couldn't do anything but fight the pain.

He opened his eyes again and looked at her pale, still face. Instantly his stomach wanted to erupt. It was only one of the reasons he wouldn't eat. If he didn't eat, there would be nothing to purge. He felt a tear fall but didn't wipe it away. He just hoped they wouldn't turn into sobs. As long as they remained quiet tears, he wouldn't be forced to accept the comforting arms of someone else. He didn't want anyone else to comfort him.

"I still can't believe what's happened. I'm worried about how they will make it through this." The comment was followed by a choked sob.

He wanted to tell them to go away, but that would require him to speak. And they did have a right to be there. He forced his mind to tune out their voices. It worked for a while, until one comment finally broke through.

"When I think about how they met—that whole 'love at first sight' thing—I don't know. It just seems like it would make this so much more difficult."

"It's difficult under any circumstances to have this happen to someone you love."

"I know, I just... it just seems like it would be harder."

"It's going to be tough on everyone for a while, but they'll pull through. We just need to have faith."

He wanted to scream at them. Tell them he could hear every word they were saying, and it wasn't helping. Instead, he closed his eyes again. The comment about needing to have faith brought to mind a conversation he'd had with his mother—the one that had turned out to be their last.

CHAPTER 2
March • 1993

"Marcus? Is that you?"

He didn't respond. Instead he ran up the stairs and into his old bedroom—slamming the door in his wake. He threw his bags on the floor and himself on the bed. There was a light knock before the door opened. He didn't need to look to see his mother's reaction. She'd be standing in the doorway, one arm across her middle with her hand clutching at her shirt. The other hand would be covering her mouth in an effort to restrain her emotions. She would stand there quietly for a few seconds before walking over and sitting on the bed.

He felt the mattress shift behind him, and he would have smiled at her predictability if he hadn't been hurting so much.

"Do you want to talk about it?" She placed a gentle hand on his head, finger combing his hair. He knew coming home meant he'd have to answer questions. It was clear there was something wrong—not just because he was upset, but because he was there at all. He should have been enjoying Spring Break with his friends.

"What happens when the person you love drives over you with a cement roller?"

He heard her let out a sigh. "You get flattened."

Despite the circumstances, he smiled. He loved talking to his mother. She never tried to make things seem like something they weren't. No platitudes. No pep talks. Just honesty.

"Based on your question, I assume that means Rachel won't be joining you on this surprise visit home?"

"Nope."

"Since she hit you with a cement roller rather than a bus, I also assume that means this is a permanent break-up?"

"Yep."

"What happened?"

He took a deep breath, wiped his face, and rolled over to a sitting position.

"She cheated." He took another deep breath and pushed past the lump in his throat. "With Patrick." He snuck a glance at his mother and was satisfied with the fury in her eyes.

"So, you've been betrayed by your girlfriend and your roommate. Come with me." She stood and walked out of the room. He was too intrigued not to follow. She went downstairs, straight to the bar used for entertaining guests, and pulled out a bottle of whiskey along with two glasses. He eyed her suspiciously when she handed him one. "No need to raise that eyebrow at me. This kind of situation calls for a drink. But just one—it won't do any good to start using alcohol to mask your problems."

"I'm not twenty-one."

"I won't tell if you don't. Besides, it's not like you haven't had a drink before. I may be your mom, but I'm not an idiot." He smiled as he took the glass she offered. He then followed her to the family room, sitting next to her on the couch. She studied him over the rim of her glass, and he was mesmerized by her eyes. Eyes that were a brilliant shade of blue and perfect replicas of his own. She sat in silence, waiting for him to tell his story of betrayal.

"It was Tuesday, last week. My dance instructor let us out of class early. Something about her kid getting sick at daycare... anyway, we weren't going to complain. I decided to swing by Rachel's as a surprise. I knew Tuesdays were her study days, and I thought maybe she could use a break. I knocked but no one answered. I tried the door and it was unlocked. Just as I turned down the hall, she came out of her room wearing a man's shirt. It wasn't mine, but I recognized it as Patrick's. I wondered if I had left it there once. Or if she took it when she was at our apartment, assuming it was mine. It's amazing how much stuff can fly through your brain in a fraction of a second. Because that's about how long it took for Patrick to walk out behind her, sans shirt, and buttoning up his pants."

He took a drink and winced as the liquid burned a path down to his stomach. He'd had the slightest amount of hope it would travel in the opposite direction—burning away the image of the two of them walking out of her room together.

"I knew I never liked that bitch." He smiled again, feeling very grateful for his mother in that moment. "Did you punch Patrick?"

"Yep."

"Good for you. How'd you survive the week living with him?"

"He stayed away, and I exacted revenge on his favorite CDs. He showed up this morning to pack some bags. I guess they decided to join the group for break after all. That's when I left and drove up here." He'd made the drive from Denver to Boulder so many times he usually felt like he was on autopilot. This time, it had been the longest drive of his life.

The phone rang and his mother stood. "I wouldn't answer, but it might be your father." He watched as his mother hurried into the kitchen. "Hello?" She suddenly turned, and he could tell it wasn't his father from the hard look on her face. He shook his head no. "He's not ready to talk to you, and neither am I." She hung up with a hard slam that felt as good for him as it must have for her.

A silence fell over them as he watched her move about the kitchen. She was so graceful, even when doing something as mundane as making a snack. Her long dark hair was pulled back into a ponytail, and she was wearing a wrap over her dancing clothes—a clear indication that she would be leaving for the studio soon.

"Did you bring your dancing gear?"

"Of course." He answered hesitantly, afraid she was going to make him dance with a bunch of giggling teenage girls.

"Good. I have two classes tonight. While I'm gone, I want you to go downstairs and dance it out. Take everything going on inside of you, and put it into movement."

He didn't respond, and she turned to look at him. When she placed one hand on her hip, he knew he had no choice. He tried anyway. "It would be one ugly dance."

"No, it will be a beautiful dance about ugly feelings. Pain is often one of the most inspiring emotions. When we embrace it, brilliance can be achieved. I like to think of it as God's consolation prize for suffering."

As much as he didn't want to, he knew she was right. Dancing had always been the best way for him to work out his feelings.

"Mom, is that Marcus' car in the driveway?" Marcus glanced in the direction of the front door that had just slammed shut.

"Leanne, you can slow down. I've asked you at least a million times not to slam the door."

"I've got a lot of work to do." Leanne entered the kitchen and dropped her backpack on the counter before turning to face Marcus. "What are you doing here? I thought you were supposed to be someplace warm right about now." Her eyes suddenly grew wide and she rounded on their mother. "And why is he drinking? You won't let me drink!"

"He's five years older than you and almost of legal age to drink."

"Whatever." Leanne walked over to the refrigerator and pulled out a drink and a snack. She grabbed her backpack and walked toward Marcus. She leaned down and sniffed his glass. "I don't like that stuff anyway."

"How would you know?" He raised an eyebrow at her statement, but she just shrugged her shoulders.

"Why do you look like crap?" Leanne took a bite out of her apple and studied him through narrowed eyes.

"Bad week."

"Where's Rachel?"

"Not here." Marcus finished his drink before standing, causing Leanne to take a few steps back. "And I didn't come home so you could badger me with questions. Don't you have some test to study for or something?"

"How would you know? You don't live here any more."

"You always have a test to study for."

"Yeah, well, I am trying to get into the best business schools."

"You know Dad's going to hire you even if you don't get a degree, so why torture yourself?"

"I am not going to get a job based on being a daddy's girl! I prefer to earn my way, thank you very much."

His sister was always so serious, but he had to admire her work ethic. She'd make a great apprentice for their father some day. Not only had she inherited their father's strong business sense, but also many of his physical traits. The only thing she seemed to have inherited from their mother was her shorter stature. While Marcus looked a lot like his father, he had gotten his intense blue eyes and his personality from his mother. And his dancing.

He patted Leanne on the head before he walked off.

She swatted at his hand in return. "Where are you going?"

"Apparently, I have some dancing to do." He gave his mother a peck on the cheek before heading toward the stairs to change. Before he was able to clear the foyer, he heard the door to the garage open. He internally cursed and quickened his steps.

"Marcus? What are you doing home?" Marcus closed his eyes at the sound of his father's voice, disappointed that he hadn't been quick enough to escape. He reluctantly turned to face his father.

"I decided to come home for break."

"I thought you were looking forward to your trip south?"

"Things change." Marcus held his father's gaze. He could feel a small glimmer of hope that his father would press him for more information. That he would open the door to communication that seemed to forever be locked between them. He felt that hope fly away as his father turned toward the kitchen. He looked past his father and noticed his mother standing quietly at the back of the foyer, watching their exchange with sorrow. His father walked over to her and pulled her close.

"Lena, dear. I'm glad I made it home before you left."

"Me too." She gave his father a kiss on the cheek before turning back to Marcus. His father had already walked off toward the kitchen, and his mother nodded her head slightly in that direction. It was silent encouragement for Marcus to try again. He simply rolled his eyes and turned back toward the stairs.

Marcus dropped to the floor in exhaustion, drained both physically and emotionally. He'd spent the week pounding out his feelings on the dance floor. His mother had been right, as he knew she would be. When he first started, he'd listened to every song he owned that was the epitome of breaking-up. The emotions ranged from devastation, to anger, to relief. He listened to the songs, looking for the one that captured his feelings, and then he danced until there was nothing left.

He'd ignored his family for most of the week—keeping to his

room when he wasn't in the basement studio. His father watched him quizzically, but his mother understood. He had always been more like his mother than his father.

He took a deep breath and pushed off the floor. He was momentarily startled when he saw his mother standing in the open studio entrance. She smiled and wiped away a tear.

"I told you pain could create something beautiful."

"I never doubted you for a minute. You're the only one I can count on to give me solid advice." He walked over to his towel and ran it over his head.

"Your father could offer some pretty sound advice if you'd let him."

"Sure, if I needed help with financial planning or starting a business. He fell in love with you over the span of five seconds. He's not exactly an expert in the wounded heart department."

"And I am? I was there during those five seconds too you know."

"I think those were the only five seconds of his life that he acted based on emotions rather than detailed analytical reports."

His mother smiled at the comment. "That very well may be true. Best five seconds of my life though." She paused a moment to study him before sitting down in the middle of the dance floor, wrapping her slender arms around her bent legs. "It seems you finally settled on an emotion."

He took a drink of his water before sitting down across from her. "Yeah, it seems hurt has won out over anger." He paused a moment, not wanting to talk but needing to anyway. "I thought we were happy. I thought she was the one."

"Now what do you think?"

"I don't know."

"Then she's not the one."

"I don't understand."

"If she were the one, you'd feel like you needed to do anything and everything to get her back. There would be no question in your mind. You would still be hurt and angry, but you'd eventually forgive her."

"Is that how it was for you and Dad?"

"We never had a falling out to test our commitment. But I know neither of us would have betrayed each other the way she did you. That's the other reason she's not the one. Even if she were the one for you, you're not the one for *her*, or this never would have happened. If you're looking for that kind of love—the kind that exists from the moment your eyes find her—then it has to be reciprocated for a relationship to work."

"So what happens if my 'one' doesn't reciprocate?"

"Then you have to find an acceptable alternative. You either accept a different kind of love with someone else, or you live your life alone."

"Neither sound like acceptable alternatives to me."

"Love takes work, Marcus. Even the kind that's destined to be."

He took a deep breath. He'd thought he had worked at it. He'd committed over a year of his life to making Rachel happy.

Maybe I don't know anything about love after all.

"What are you thinking about?" He focused back on his mother when she asked the question.

"That maybe I don't know much about love. I thought growing up with parents who had the fairytale kind of love would make it a simple concept."

His mother smiled. "You know more than you think." He rolled his eyes and was about to protest, but she cut him off. "You do, you just can't see past the hurt right now."

"Yes, I'm hurting because I fell in love with a bitch who screwed my roommate. I think that automatically gives me a failing grade in the subject of true love."

It was his mother's turn to roll her eyes. "Alright, fine. You don't know anything about love. But if you want to learn—just keep dancing."

He looked at her for any sign of jest. There was none. "Now I really don't understand."

"Everything needed to truly love someone can be learned through dance. Faith, trust, endurance, pain, joy, humility, surrender, commitment, patience. If you want to be able to love someone the way they deserve to be loved, keep dancing."

He thought about his mother's words. He had felt each one of those emotions through dance.

"And what if the woman I love doesn't dance?"

"Then you teach her. And even though you're an amazing dancer, it doesn't mean you don't learn from her as well. In love, you have to give it everything you've got and take everything it has to offer in return."

He remained quiet. The feelings his mother's words evoked told him that someday they would have a hand in changing his life. He wanted to etch each word into memory.

CHAPTER 3

"Marcus?" The sound of his name came from far away, pulling him into the present. He didn't want to leave the comfort of his mother's care, even if it was nothing more than a memory.

"Marcus?" The voice was soft and uncertain. It sounded like her voice. He hated his pain in that moment. Hated the way it would sometimes transform sounds into her unique voice—giving him hope only to rip it away the moment he turned in that direction.

"Oh my God! She's awake! Call for the doctor."

Marcus finally snapped his eyes open—bracing himself for the moment his reality caught up with his twisted imagination. However, this time it was real. Her eyes were open, and he leapt to her side.

"Sarah?"

"Marcus?" She looked around the room until her eyes settled upon his. Her eyes fluttered shut, and he worried she was slipping back under.

"Sarah, honey, stay with me." His voice sounded frantic, pleading.

"Not... going... anywhere. Just need... rest."

After a few agonizing minutes, the doctor entered the room and pushed Marcus out of the way. He was about to force his way back to her side when he felt hands settle on his shoulders.

"Let him help her, Marcus." He pulled again, but James dragged him to the other side of the room.

"Marcus?" Sarah's voice was strained, and he could tell it took every ounce of her effort. He lunged again, but James had been prepared.

"I'm here, Sarah."

"Mrs. Kingston, do you remember where you are?" Marcus watched as Sarah slowly turned her attention to the doctor.

"Yes."

"Do you remember why you are here?"

If Marcus could have punched the doctor, he would have. "Why the hell did you ask her that? You know how it upset her the last time, and then she was out of it for over eighteen hours! She just woke up for fuck's sake!"

"You're... in trouble... now. He said... the f... word." Sarah's attempt at humor in the situation caused Marcus to lose the strength in his legs. It was a good thing James was still holding on to him or he'd have landed on his ass. "Yes... I... remember." Marcus hung his head and allowed James to settle him into a chair. He waited for the doctor's conclusions, fighting to breathe.

"Mr. Kingston?" Marcus looked up at the doctor. "Do you want to talk outside?" Marcus shook his head. Her family was going to want the details, and he wasn't sure he'd be able to relay the information in his current state. "Very well." The doctor proceeded to give him a medical dissertation on Sarah's condition. He was trying to follow along, but he couldn't process the information in his current state.

"Dr. Vikrant, I'm barely able to form a coherent sentence at the moment. I need you to put it in simple terms, please. Is she going to be all right?"

"It is not yet clear. Her vitals are stable, but she has lost a lot of blood. The fact that she woke up and remembers what happened is at least a step in the right direction. We will run more tests, but we just have to wait and see. She might wake up periodically and remain awake for a few minutes. Just try to keep her calm."

"So no more asking her about how she got here?"

The doctor gave him a level stare. "You know I had to assess her state of mind. But yes, no more talking about the events that brought her here until she has recovered."

"Dr. Vikrant, will she be allowed more than three visitors at a time now?" For the first time in several hours, Marcus looked at his mother-in-law. She looked tired.

"Normally, we would only allow two at a time." Again the doctor leveled his stare at Marcus. He understood the comment to be not only a rejection of the request, but a warning that privileges would be revoked if he acted out again.

"What about—"

"Catherine, don't." Marcus loved his mother-in-law, but at that moment he wanted to throw her out.

"Marcus, you need—"

"I said don't! Not in here. I don't want to hear about it. If you need to know, go somewhere else to ask your questions." He turned and went to Sarah's side. He took her limp hand in his and waited until she woke up again.

"Marcus?"

His head shot up at the sound of Sarah's voice. She still sounded so weak. He quickly leaned over and kissed the exposed side of her forehead.

"How are you feeling?"

"Tired."

"Are you hurting?" They had her doped up on meds so she shouldn't be feeling anything, but he had to ask.

"No." Relief washed through him. "You... look tired."

"I'm fine. I'm better than fine now that you're awake." He brought her hand to his mouth, and she closed her eyes. He was afraid she'd slip back under, but she opened her eyes again.

"Have you... seen—"

"I can't talk about that right now. Besides, you need rest." He stroked the side of her cheek with the back of his fingers. She closed her eyes and tears formed in the corners. His stomach clenched in response to her pain.

"You... need... to..."

"I can't, Sarah." He felt his tears fall with the same quiet pace as hers.

"You... have to. Promise."

"I'm all out of promises right now."

"You... always make... me promises. You... keep them too."

If only that were true. You wouldn't be lying in this hospital bed if I always kept my promises.

"I know... that look. Not... your fault."

His tears were flowing harder, and he was bordering on another breakdown. He lowered his head to her bed, and he could feel her try to touch him. She was too weak to even lift her hand.

"Marcus... talk to me."

He took a deep breath and wiped his face. "What do you want me to talk about?"

"I just want... to hear... your voice. Tell me... about when... we met."

"You'll be asleep again in about two minutes."

"Don't... care. Please."

He took her hand in his again and started talking.

CHAPTER 4
December • 2012

"You're a grown man, hiding from your father."

"I'm not hiding, I'm avoiding. Big difference." Marcus took a sip of his drink and looked over at Heather. Her disapproval was clear, so he turned his attention back to scanning the crowd. His nerves were on edge, but he didn't know why. He was about to spend an evening with his family, and he'd be surrounded by dancing—both of which made him extremely uncomfortable. It also would have been his mother's birthday if she were still alive.

But it was more than all of that. It was as if his body was trying to warn him that something significant was about to happen.

"You still have never told me why you hate your father so much."

"I don't hate him. We just don't get along." With each passing second, Marcus further regretted having brought Heather as his date. She was a nice girl and hot as hell, but she was also beyond annoying with a severe lack of a verbal filter. Despite all that, he thought she would enjoy the dancing—she was a dancer after all—and he'd needed a date.

"Kingston, there you are man. What are you doing hiding out in the corner?" Marcus watched his friend approach.

"See, you *are* hiding." Marcus shot a warning glance at Heather.

"Maybe I'm trying to avoid you, Van."

"Yeah, right. More like your father." Van paused for a moment to inspect Heather. "Who's this lovely creature?"

"Van, this is Heather Lowe. Heather, this is Brandon Vanderlink."

"Damn, why is it the Kingston men get all the beautiful women?"

Marcus studied Van with suspicion. "Kingston *men*? That would imply my father as well."

"Yep." Van took a sip of his drink. "Have you seen his date? A little young for him, but I respect that. I'd love to land a smokin' hot chick that's half my age." Van swept his eyes over Heather once more. Marcus and Van would both turn forty in the following year, and Heather looked like she was half that. She was petite with killer legs, and her beautiful gray eyes could practically bring a man to his knees when she looked through her lashes. The only thing he'd change was her hair—it was a nice blonde, but it was way too short for his taste.

And her personality. She really is annoying most of the time.

Marcus looked toward the front of the room, curious about his father's date. He never brought a date to the gala. It was to raise funds for the Marlena Throsen Dance Foundation, which was founded by his mother about thirty years ago. When she died, his father continued the tradition not only to support the foundation, but also to honor his mother. For as much as he disliked the things his father did, he had to admit admiration for his loyalty with regard to his mother. Theirs was a love story that sounded like it was taken right out of some romance novel. His father had dated a few women after his mother died, but never anything serious.

It must be that project manager Leanne told me about.

Marcus' sister had called him in a fit of rage about a month ago. Leanne had stopped by their father's house to pick up her son, Ollie, and walked in on their father in bed with some woman he'd hired to manage a personal project. Leanne had said she was young, probably the same age as his sister, and was likely just trying to land a sugar-daddy. The woman had somehow gotten his father to bring her to the gala, so there might be some merit to Leanne's concerns.

"So, Brandon, do you know why Marcus won't dance?" Heather's question pulled Marcus' attention away from his search for the mystery woman.

"You've not told her?" Marcus glared at Van with a look that made it clear he needed to keep his mouth shut.

"He told me he used to dance some, but not any more."

"He told you that he danced *some?*" Marcus could hear the irritation in Van's response.

"How much I used to dance doesn't matter. What matters is that I don't dance now."

Van shook his head in annoyance and looked away while taking another sip of his drink. "Whatever."

Being products of parents that ran in the same social circle, Marcus had been friends with Van for as long as he could remember. Even though he didn't often admit it, Van was more like a brother than a friend. They enjoyed goading each other, but they shared a bond that was unbreakable.

Van may not agree with his reasons for not dancing any more, but he understood what they were. And Marcus had no desire to relay those reasons to Heather. She was a social friend—the kind he chatted with at parties and occasionally called when he needed a date. She wasn't the type of friend he'd confide in.

"Well, if you're not going to dance with me I might have to find someone else." She ran her hand slowly down Marcus' arm. It sounded dangerously close to flirting so he shifted his stance, putting his arm out of her reach.

"That's an excellent idea. I'm sure Van would love to dance with you." Marcus slapped his friend on the back, causing him to choke on his drink. Van recovered quickly and smiled at Heather.

"I'm more than happy to fill in for this chump. My date flaked at the last minute, so I'm all yours after a required dance with my mother." Van looked over his shoulder. "Speaking of my mother... I'll have to catch up with you later." He gave Heather a peck on the cheek before slapping Marcus on the shoulder and walking away.

"You really aren't going to dance with me?"

Marcus closed his eyes and let out a sigh. "Heather, I told you when I asked you to come that I'm not dancing tonight. I'm not going to change my mind." He looked at her and could see the pout behind her wine glass.

Great. Now I feel like a jerk.

He finished his drink and set the empty glass on the table. He looked for a waiter, but none were nearby.

Heather set her empty glass next to his. "I need another drink."

He needed another drink—he couldn't survive the impending encounter with his father without it. However, it didn't look like she needed one.

"Are you sure? Maybe you should wait until dinner."

She giggled. He knew that giggle. It meant she certainly did not need another drink.

"So protective of me." She ran her hand down his arm again.

"Right."

More like protecting my sanity.

For a while she would be a happy, giggling drunk. Then, her already too thin verbal filter would completely disappear, pissing off not only him but everyone around them. And finally she'd turn into a crying mess, complaining that she didn't have a good man in her life.

"Well, if you won't get me another drink then I'm going to the ladies' room." She flashed him a coy smile before walking in the direction of the bar. Which was in the opposite direction of the restrooms.

He groaned and started off after her. The way she swayed her hips as she walked told him she knew he was following. They were just friends, but he was aware that she'd take the benefits if he'd be willing to open that door. She cut through some tables and the gap was instantly filled by other guests, causing him to turn and go another way. He glanced across the room and stumbled as the room faded from his focus.

Everything disappeared, except one woman.

She was standing alone at a table, nursing her glass of wine. He could only see her profile, but he could tell she was struggling. She wasn't sad, but she looked haunted. Her wavy, brown hair—pulled to the side in some sort of ponytail—shimmered under the lights of the room. She suddenly shifted, bringing her back into view. Her gown cut low, and he felt a sudden urge to run his hand along her spine. He blinked rapidly, trying to get a grip.

What the hell? My heart's racing a million miles a second.

He scrutinized his reaction. He could tell she was good looking, but she wasn't the type he was normally attracted to. For one, she was taller than the women he normally dated. He was aware some of that could be the heels she was wearing, but she still had to be tall. He normally preferred blondes, and she was not. And this woman was way too thin. His mother had suffered from severe anorexia in her younger years. It did damage to her body, and the doctors believed it had been the underlying cause that killed her. He also spent a lot of time around dancers who had eating disorders. It was a deal breaker for him. This woman obviously had some sort of issue.

So why am I still standing here, staring at her? It can't just be a physical attraction, even if she is cute, because she's not my type.

She turned to say something to the woman behind her, and he saw her face.

Oh, holy hell. She's the one.

He'd been waiting for this moment for nearly half his life. Waiting for the moment he would find the woman who owned his heart. For most people it sounded like insanity. He knew this because his friends, namely Van, had told him on numerous occasions it was. But he saw how it had been with his parents, and he knew it was his fate as well.

He was debating if he should approach her or wait until after dinner, when his eyes landed on someone he most certainly didn't want anywhere near her. His feet were moving before he fully thought through what he was about to do. As he reached her she stepped back, bumping into him. He instantly felt a flash of heat spread through his body. He ran his hand over the small of her back to her hip and pulled her to his side. She looked up at him in alarm, and he had to struggle to keep breathing.

I was wrong. She's not just cute—she's beautiful.

He felt lost in the flecks of green that danced in her brown eyes. He somehow tore his eyes away from hers to look at the asshole standing in front of her.

"Mark. I didn't think you'd show this year after the spectacle you made at last year's gala. I suggest you walk away before we have a repeat of that unfortunate situation." Mark stared back at him with pure hatred and then darted another look at the woman before walking away. Marcus looked back down at her. She had gone pale and looked like she might pass out.

"Are you all right?" He slowly removed his arm from around her back and placed his hand on her arm. He tightened his grip when he felt her wobble. He could feel his anger toward Mark growing.

"Sarah?" Marcus turned when someone approached.

How does Miles know this woman?

Miles nudged Marcus, and he reluctantly let go to step aside. "Sarah, are you all right?" Marcus watched as she focused her attention on Miles.

"Yes, I'm okay. I... I think the wine went to my head a little too quickly." She glanced shyly at Marcus. "Thank you."

The sound of her voice resonated through him, causing a slow ripple of excitement. He couldn't stop the smile from splitting his face. She suddenly gripped Miles' arm and paled a few shades. He felt panic grip his chest and was about to reach for her again, but someone beat him to it. He watched with confusion as his father placed a hand on her arm.

"Sarah, is everything okay?" At first Marcus couldn't breathe, the pain acute from realizing who she was. It quickly transformed into anger, and he glared at his father.

His father turned to Miles when Sarah didn't respond. "Miles, what happened?"

"I don't know, I came back and she looked like she was about to pass out."

"Marcus, do you know what happened?" Marcus watched as Sarah turned in his direction. She looked even more stricken than before.

"I think I need some air." Her voice was whispered and full of desperation, causing the three men to react quickly.

They ushered her through the crowd of people and out to the back terrace. She took a few deep breaths of the cold air while his father took hold of her elbows, searching her face. Marcus could clearly see the concern in his father's eyes, causing another flash of anger. She looked at Marcus for a moment before turning her attention back to his father.

"Sarah, can you please tell me what happened?"

"I... I'm not sure really. Like I told Miles, I think the wine went to my head too quickly—"

Marcus couldn't contain his reaction any longer. "That asshole Mark was pouncing on her. I could tell from across the room she was trying to get him to leave, but as usual that man has no respect for boundaries. I stepped in and told him to leave."

"Where the hell were you?" His father turned his angry gaze to Miles.

"Elijah, it's fine. Miles had to step away for a moment. I don't need to be watched—"

"Apparently, you do. Mark is relentless and no matter your progress I don't think you're up for the likes of him." Marcus didn't understand the comment, but his anger kept him from lingering over it for more than a second.

"Why the hell haven't you fired him by now?" Marcus pinned his father with a hard look.

"It's not my job any more. You can take it up with your sister."

"You should have fired him after the incident last year!" The previous year Marcus had returned from the bathroom and caught Mark harassing his date. He'd put his hands on her, and Marcus had let him know just how unwelcome it was.

"Yeah, well, he kept it in his pants at work so what was I supposed to do? You punched him, I put him on notice, and I thought that was good enough. He's—"

"Stop! Mark's not the problem. Yes, the guy's an ass, and he should probably be fired based on his general lack of integrity and respect for others, but can you not argue about that right now? I'm fine, really. I probably shouldn't have anything else to drink tonight. I didn't have lunch today, and I should've known even one glass would have been too much." Sarah's outburst startled them all. Marcus had never seen anyone put his father in his place.

If I didn't think I was in love before, I know I am now. Which is highly inconvenient since she's here with my father.

"Well, it's obvious you two have already met but given the circumstances I suppose a more formal introduction is appropriate. Sarah, this is my son Marcus. Marcus, this is Sarah Mitchell." Marcus looked at Sarah for several seconds before speaking.

"The same Sarah that Leanne has mentioned?" Marcus already knew the answer, but he had to ask anyway.

"She's the only Sarah I know, so I assume so."

Marcus stared at Sarah, trying to figure out how he had gotten into this situation. He'd always assumed the woman he loved would love him back just as instantaneously. 'The one' wasn't supposed to be his father's date. And not just any date. She's the only woman besides his mother he had ever brought to the gala. That was significant.

"That's too bad." He hadn't realized he'd said it out loud until he turned to go back inside. He joined Heather at the bar and ordered another drink.

"Marcus, where did you disappear to?"

"I had a chat with my father." Heather placed a hand on his arm in sympathy. He instantly noticed it was nothing like his reaction to Sarah's touch. He was still reeling from the encounter and tried to shake the emotions surging through his body.

Maybe I'm wrong and she's not the one.

However he knew she was. He knew it for one simple fact.

She made him want to dance.

Marcus led Heather through grand ballroom, eyes searching for Sarah the entire time. As they approached the center table, he saw her sitting next to his father and reaching for her glass. He couldn't resist getting close to her, so he leaned in to whisper in her ear.

"I hope that's water." As he pulled away he could hear the hitch in her breath. It caused him pause for a second—hoping he had heard correctly. He guided Heather to her seat and pulled out her chair before sitting next to her.

He had a direct line of sight to Sarah. He studied her, trying to put the pieces together. Based on what Leanne had said, she was sleeping with his father. However that didn't seem logical now that he'd met her. In the brief interaction he'd had with them on the terrace, he could tell there was more between them than a professional relationship, but he wasn't sure it was romantic.

I swear she's having the same reactions to me as I am to her. I heard the hitch in her breath. I see the way she blushes when she catches me looking at her.

"Hello, Earth to Marcus. Aren't you going to introduce me?" He reluctantly pulled his attention from Sarah as Heather whispered in his ear.

"Everyone, I'd like you to meet my friend Heather. This is my brother-in-law, Brad, and that's my sister, Leanne. Next to her is Miles Morgan. Miles is my father's attorney as well as a friend of the family. His wife, Tina, is the director of the foundation and she'll join us shortly." He looked at Sarah and paused for a moment, deciding what to say. "This next lovely lady I've just met tonight. Her name is Sarah Mitchell, and she's my father's... friend?" He scrutinized her and was rewarded with a blush. He reluctantly turned his attention to his father. "And of course, last but never least is my father, Elijah."

Heather offered her adorable smile. "Hello, everyone."

The lights in the room dimmed and the conversation dropped to whispers. Marcus watched as Tina walked to the podium, until he noticed movement out of the corner of his eye. He looked over in time to see his father lean in to whisper something to Sarah. She looked at his father with curiosity and leaned in to whisper back. He watched their silent communication with growing irritation. He wasn't sure what they were discussing, but it looked almost as if she were scolding him. When Sarah turned her attention back to Tina, she locked eyes with Marcus instead. Suddenly, she closed her eyes and took a deep breath. His irritation turned to curiosity when she quickly wiped away a tear.

She finally opened her eyes and glanced at Marcus again before focusing her attention on Tina at the front of the room. He was completely caught in her spell and couldn't take his eyes off her. He wanted to know everything about her—especially why she was with his father and what had just made her cry.

It had better not be because of that asshole Mark. I won't stop at just one punch this time.

Brad shifted in his seat next to him, and when Marcus looked in that direction he saw Leanne sending him the classic Kingston death glare. Their father had patented the look and Leanne was his carbon copy, so it wasn't a surprise that she'd adopted 'the look' as well. Marcus ignored Leanne and turned his attention to Tina, who was finishing her speech.

Tina walked to the table and pulled Sarah to her feet. Marcus watched as they complimented each other's gowns. He wasn't fully paying attention to their exchange—Sarah had smiled and it wiped all thoughts from his mind. He was glad he was sitting, because if he had been standing he wasn't sure his knees would have been able to keep him from crashing to the ground. He continued to watch her as the first course of dinner was served.

"So, Sarah, I understand you're from Indiana. Is this your first time in this area?" Marcus was grateful for Brad's question. The more he could learn about her the better. He wanted to ask questions but couldn't seem to find the ability to form a coherent word.

"Yes, this is my first time here, and I'm really enjoying it. The scenery is so much different than back home. There's something so calming about the mountains. Don't get me wrong, Indiana has some very redeeming qualities but picturesque scenery is not one of them."

Marcus flinched as his father put his hand on Sarah's shoulder, and he hoped no one noticed. "You'll have to put that present to use and take some pictures..." His sentence trailed off and once again Marcus' anger transformed into confusion. A look of silent understanding passed between his father and Sarah.

"You bought her a camera? What, early Christmas present or something?" Marcus noted the accusation in Leanne's comment.

"No, it wasn't a gift from Elijah. I—" Sarah stopped abruptly and looked uncomfortable.

"Heather, tell us about you. How do you know Marcus?" Tina's sudden shift in topics caught Marcus' attention. It seemed that she had intentionally guided the conversation away from Sarah. He knew he should stop looking at Sarah, but he couldn't. Not only was he captivated by her, but the way his father and Tina seemed to be protecting her caused his curiosity to surge.

Sarah looked in his direction and crossed her arms when she saw him watching her. He finally looked at Heather when she not so gently nudged his leg with her knee.

She must be waiting for me to answer Tina's question.

Heather was smiling at him and he couldn't help but smile in return. He didn't want to share the details of how they met. She had been drunk and hitting on him at a party. He had a moment of weakness when he contemplated hooking up with her, but fate had stepped in—she puked the entire night while he held a cold cloth to the back of her neck. The next day he took her to lunch and realized the mistake he had almost made. They agreed to be friends, and he never looked back.

"We met through mutual friends." It was all the information he was willing to share of his past with Heather. Especially with Sarah present.

"What do you do, Heather?" Leanne's tone was more suspicious than curious.

"I'm a dance instructor."

Marcus was sure his family wouldn't find it surprising she was a dancer. He may not dance any more, but somehow he gravitated to women who did.

I wonder if Sarah dances.

The urge to dance with Sarah consumed him, preventing him from remaining focused on the children who had moved onto the dance floor for a short performance. He'd avoided dancing for twenty years, and from the moment his eyes found Sarah it was all he could think about. Instinctively, he ran his hand along the left side of his torso.

Throughout the second course, Leanne continued to ask Heather questions. Marcus tried to keep his attention off Sarah but was unsuccessful. He wanted to know every one of her features, her nuances, her conscious and subconscious movements. He didn't want to creep her out by staring, so he tried to hide it by taking quick glances as he ate. His thoughts were interrupted by the sound of his father's voice.

"Are you dancing again, Marcus?" He hesitated—still distracted by Sarah and also surprised that his father had asked him a question.

"No." He heard Heather give a disappointed sigh next to him.

"Sarah, you must be a wonderful dancer." His eyes darted to Sarah with an assessing look at Leanne's comment. She locked eyes with him before turning to Leanne.

"No, not really."

"Oh? I'm surprised given you'll be performing the spotlight dance with my father."

Marcus about dropped his fork at the statement. He wanted to ask what the hell Leanne was talking about, but there was no pause in the conversation.

"Yes, well, you're not alone in your surprise. Luckily I had a patient teacher."

"Patient? That must be the first time anyone has ever described my father as patient." Leanne's laugh was bitter.

His father sat forward and looked down the table. "Leanne, can we please not do this tonight."

He was trying to process the conversation when Tina interrupted and redirected the conversation yet again. He could tell Sarah was uncomfortable, and he was growing irritated with his sister for being the cause. Tina and Miles guided the conversation throughout the rest of the meal, but Marcus only half paid attention—his thoughts refused to leave Sarah alone. And he wanted clarity on Leanne's comments.

Once the plates were cleared and the second performance of the evening was complete, people started to mill about the room. There would be a brief break before dessert was served and the auction winners were announced.

Sarah suddenly stood. "If you will all excuse me, there's something I'd like to bid on before the window closes."

He was about to offer to join her when his sister beat him to it. "Sarah, wait. I'll go with you."

Sarah turned around and smiled at Leanne. He could tell it was forced. "That would be great."

He watched as they walked out of the room. He stood to follow, knowing Sarah would need some sort of buffer from Leanne, but he needed an answer from his father first.

"What was Leanne talking about when she said Sarah was doing the spotlight dance with you?"

"Exactly what it sounds like."

Marcus felt like he was about to explode. Since the start of dinner, his reaction to Sarah had only confirmed she was the woman he'd been waiting to find. Unfortunately, the obstacles were growing.

Marcus could feel Van watching him as they waited for Heather to return from the restroom.

"Seriously, Kingston. What's up with you tonight?"

"I already told you. My family irritates me."

"And I know you better than that. You looked pretty intense when I saw you talking with your old man's woman." Marcus thought about his brief encounter with Sarah a few minutes ago. He just wished it could have lasted longer, but Heather had pulled him away before he had a chance to fully engage her in a conversation.

"Let it go, Van."

"Fine." Van crossed his arms and looked down as he shifted his stance. "So, you really wouldn't mind if I danced with Heather?"

"You can go home with her for all I care. We're just friends."

"You certain she knows that?"

Marcus wasn't sure why Van's comment annoyed him as much as it did. He couldn't really fault him for pointing out the obvious. In a way he felt bad for bringing Heather. Even though he'd told her they were just going as friends, he knew there was a risk of her hoping for more.

But I couldn't have faced this night solo. I needed to bring a date for the distraction from my family. If only I'd known ahead of time that I was going to meet Sarah. I would have spared Heather and came alone.

Marcus was about to issue a reply when Heather finally emerged. Hoping to direct some of Heather's attention to Van, he let them lead the way to the ballroom.

When they reached the table, he instantly noticed Sarah wasn't there. Neither was Leanne. He looked around the room and wondered if he should be concerned. Leanne's behavior toward Sarah had been distinctly cold, even bordering on hostile, all evening.

"Mr. Kingston, it's nice to see you again." Van offered his hand in greeting. Marcus noticed his father's hesitation before responding.

"Hello... er, Dan. You keeping Marcus in line?" Van looked at Marcus in confusion.

"Usually I'm the one keeping *Van* in line." Marcus watched his father closely. He had always called him Van like Marcus did. If Van hadn't looked at Marcus in confusion, he would have assumed he'd heard his father incorrectly.

"You two were always up to no good. I suppose it shouldn't change now that you're older." His father looked slightly uncomfortable, but beyond that he acted as though he didn't get the name of his son's best friend wrong at all.

"How's your retirement going so far? Do you miss the chaos and action you had as the CEO of Kingston Enterprises?"

"This project I have has been keeping me busy, so I've not yet settled into full retirement."

"I hear good things about Leanne as the new CEO." While Van worked in an entirely different industry, their social circle was full of gossip. Marcus' family had always tried to stay out of the spotlight, but a change in leadership was too good to pass up. It seemed everyone wanted to voice their assessment of how the transition was going. He knew it pissed Leanne off to be under the microscope.

His father opened his mouth to respond but paused as he looked past Marcus. A smile that boarded on sarcastic slowly appeared on his face. "As long as she continues to make decisions based on the right reasons, she should do fine. Isn't that right, Leanne?"

Marcus turned so he could see his sister. The way she glared at their father made it clear there had been some sort of hidden meaning in the comment that only the two of them understood.

"It's the only way I know how to make decisions."

"Right." His father looked past Leanne, clearly annoyed. "Where's Sarah?"

"What's the matter, Dad, can't go a few minutes without her?" Brad gave Leanne a warning look. "What? I promised I wouldn't say anything more to *her*. I never promised anything about *him*." Leanne inclined her head in the direction of their father.

"Well, I had better get back to my table. Kingston, I'll catch up with you later. Heather, I'll come for that dance." Van shot another questioning glance at his father before walking off.

The lights dimmed, indicating the start of dessert, and everyone took their seats. Marcus was about to go in search of Sarah when she walked through the doors, looking flushed and disjointed. She quietly took her seat, eyes locked on the table in front of her and rubbing at her arms. His father noticed as well.

"What's wrong? Are you cold?" His father reached over and touched her arm, causing Marcus that now familiar spasm of irritation. "Christ, Sarah, you're freezing. Were you outside?" He stood up, took off his jacket, and draped it over her shoulders.

"Not for very long. I needed some air."

"So, Sarah, what part of Indiana are you from?" Sarah smiled at Brad, and Marcus decided she needed to smile more often.

"I live in a small town not far from Indianapolis."

"Do you still have family there? It must be hard to be away from them during the holidays."

Marcus could have sworn she cringed at Brad's question. "My parents and two of my brothers live near Chicago, but no family at home."

"Well, after meeting you I'm certain you've left a trail of broken hearts behind." Marcus held his breath as he waited for her response. He didn't believe she was in a romantic relationship with his father, but he found it hard to believe she was still single. Instead of answering she blanched, causing Brad to backpedal. "I'm sorry; I hope I haven't said something to offend you."

"That's all right, Brad. When it comes to Sarah, I can see Leanne has chosen to only share details that best paint her accusations as true." The warning was clear in his father's voice. Marcus wasn't sure which emotion was growing quicker—irritation or confusion.

"I felt those details weren't relevant to the situation and were certainly too personal for me to share." Marcus was about to pull Leanne out of the room and demand an explanation when Tina addressed him with a question.

"Marcus, are you hoping to win one of the auction items?"

Still confused he looked to Sarah. She closed her eyes and appeared to be trying to control her emotions. He was having a hard time doing the same. When Heather nudged him, he realized he hadn't yet answered.

"I put my name on a few items, but I'm hoping to win the package for a ski weekend in Vail."

"I love skiing in Vail!" He looked at Heather and had to concentrate in order to remove the look of annoyance from his face.

I have no intention of taking you to Vail. Or anywhere else after tonight.

He knew his irritation with Heather wasn't fair. She was a nice girl, just not the woman he wanted to be with. Before he invited her, he'd suspected this was the way the evening would go. But he asked her because he knew there would be no temptation. He wasn't looking to start up a new relationship, and Heather seemed like the perfect solution to his need for a date. That was all before he met Sarah.

They continued to talk about the auction items while eating dessert. Except for Sarah. She sat quietly—not eating and not participating in the discussion. He wanted to change that.

"Sarah, how about you?" She looked up confused, like she was uncertain who had asked the question or what the question even was. He saw clarity enter her beautiful eyes just before she responded.

"I bid on one item, a golf and spa package. I'm hoping to give it to my parents as a Christmas gift."

"You should have let Elijah bid on it for you. I noticed the items he bid on didn't have a single name after his." Heather seemed proud of her observation, and Marcus cringed, realizing her filter was gone.

"Yes, well, I suppose that would have been a strategy to use, but then he would have insisted on paying for it as well." Sarah looked over to his father and smiled.

"You know me too well."

Heather giggled. "I just assumed he'd be paying for it anyway. From all the conversation I've gathered tonight you two are together, right? I mean, what's the point of having a super rich older boyfriend if he's not paying for everything?" Marcus was impressed by the look Sarah used to silence Heather.

"Marcus, I suggest you control your date." His father's warning was unwelcome. Marcus had been intending to silence Heather, but his father's comment just pissed him off.

"Well, Dad, in a way I have to commend Heather for having the capacity to state the obvious. You two say you're not together, but your actions speak otherwise. Why should she feel embarrassed about making light of your relationship with Sarah?" He wasn't sure why he'd said it. He was convinced they weren't in a relationship, and Heather had been out of line. But as usual, he let his father get the best of him and he spit out words he didn't intend to say. His father started to respond, but Sarah stopped him.

"I have something to say and I *hope* this is the last of it." Sarah settled her gaze on Leanne before looking around to the others. "Two and a half years ago I lost my husband and two year old son in a car accident. My world shattered into a billion unrecognizable pieces. When I was certain there was no way out of that darkness, someone reached out to me." Marcus' heart dropped at her declaration. It dropped even further as he watched her turn to his father and grab his hand.

"Elijah has not taken advantage of me, nor I of him. He saw my pain and my struggle, and he offered me a lifeline. He has helped me emerge from that darkness and live my life again. Yes, I consider Elijah to be more than my boss. He's my friend. My catalyst. You say our actions contradict what we say, but do they really or are you only able to see what you want to see? What you should see are two people who care about each other. Two people who are helping each other not be afraid of their ghosts and make the most out of the life they have been given. So, if you don't mind, I would appreciate it if you would all keep your snide comments to yourself from now on."

Sarah shrugged off his father's coat and handed it back to him. Marcus watched as he stood and leaned down to kiss her on the top of her head.

I'm a goner. She's the one who has my heart. I'm not certain yet if she's going to crush it or cuddle it, but I can't wait to find out.

In that moment Marcus made a promise to himself that he would do everything in his power to lessen her pain. And make her smile more often.

CHAPTER 5

Marcus studied Sarah's face. Her eyes were closed again. Just when he'd convinced himself she was asleep, she slowly opened her eyes and looked at him.

"You're still awake."

"It was... a good... story." Her eyes fluttered shut but reopened a couple of seconds later. "That was... a good... promise."

"I'm not doing such a good job of keeping it right now."

"Not... in... pain. Smiling... inside." He almost smiled at her comment.

"You should rest." She closed her eyes in response. He was about to pull away when she opened them again.

"You... could have... left out... Heather."

This time he did smile. "But you're so cute when you're jealous."

He saw the corners of her mouth try to lift before settling into a slight frown. "Van—"

"I'm not ready to talk about Van. Rest now. I love you." He leaned over and gave her a soft, lingering kiss. She didn't have the strength to reciprocate, and it crushed him.

The door opened, and a nurse walked in. "Mr. Kingston, I need to take Mrs. Kingston down for some tests."

He was about to insist on going with when he felt James squeeze his shoulder. "Why don't you join us in the cafeteria for a few minutes? If you don't eat something, I'll tell Sarah the next time she wakes up."

Marcus gave his brother-in-law an irritated look. "What's she going to do about it? She can barely speak."

"True, but she'd be worried and disappointed. I know you try to avoid causing her both of those emotions. Especially in her current condition."

Marcus let out a frustrated sigh. "Fine." He gave Sarah one more kiss before following James and his mother-in-law out of the room.

As he had feared, the cafeteria held more family and friends who immediately pounced on him—Tina leading the pack. She hugged him and cried on his shoulder. He could offer no words of comfort, so he just hugged her back. Miles approached him after his wife finally pulled away and offered him an awkward hug. Sarah's brother Peter closed out the hug-fest. Suddenly, Marcus was ushered to a chair and food materialized before him. He studied the faces around him. He didn't need to ask where Sarah's father and eldest brother, Tom, were.

"Is he still not speaking?" Tina looked from James to Catherine.

"He wouldn't shut up while Sarah was awake." James' tone was lighter than the slap he delivered to his shoulder with the comment.

"You realize I can hear you, right?"

"Thank God. Your silent brooding was starting to become scary." Marcus was about to respond to Tina with an equally biting rebuttal when they were bombarded by a small, blonde tornado.

"The nurse told me you were all down here. They said she woke up. Is she going to be okay?" Marcus stood to greet Sarah's best friend, Maggie.

"We don't know yet. They're running more tests."

"Can I see her?"

"Maggie, dear." Catherine walked over and gave Maggie a long hug. "You can go in when she gets back. Until then we—" Marcus shot her a warning glance.

Maggie looked frantically between Marcus and his mother-in-law. "What's wrong? Did something happen—"

"Don't." Marcus didn't take his eyes off Catherine, ensuring she got the message.

"Marcus won't let us talk about... anything really." The disappointed look in his mother-in-law's eyes finally pushed him past the breaking point.

"You all have a right to be here. I know Sarah appreciates you being here. But if you don't shut up about all that's happened, I swear I'll drag you out the door myself!" He stormed off in the direction of Sarah's room before anyone could utter a single word.

Marcus sat alone in the waiting room, hoping Sarah's tests would be over soon. He'd thought getting away from everyone and their relentless comments would help him stop thinking about the events from the last few days.

He was wrong.

The silence of the room only seemed to amplify the rampant thoughts in his mind. He knew he shouldn't have reacted so strongly to his mother-in-law's comments, but his world had turned on its axis and he couldn't seem to find his footing.

The door opened, and he stood to greet the nurse. Instead, James walked in—carrying Marcus' uneaten sandwich. Marcus rolled his eyes and sat back down. He knew what was coming, and although he deserved it, he didn't want to hear it. "Don't start with me, James."

"I'm not. I just wanted to bring you your sandwich." He held it out but Marcus looked away. James sighed and sat down next to him. "You know, I'd like to think we became friends as well as brothers when you married my sister."

Marcus hung his head. "We are friends."

"Then I have a right to say what I'm about to say. I know you think I don't understand. But I do. You're hurting. You're angry. I get it and I might have even reacted the same way if I were in your position. I know right now it feels like it's the right thing. Like it's the only thing you can do. But it's something you will regret later. At some point, you're going to change your mind. Just don't wait until it's too late." James patted him on the back and placed the sandwich in his lap before leaving the room.

Marcus stared at the closed door long after James had left. His head knew James was right, but his heart couldn't get there. He knew there would be a turning point—a moment when his actions would irrevocably damage relationships that were important to him. There were many fears surging through his mind, but after James' comment, only one called out loud and clear.

What if it's already too late?

Marcus waited outside Sarah's room while Maggie and James visited. He had to resist the urge to push the others aside. He reminded himself that he wasn't the only one who loved her, and they needed to be able to talk to her too.

"Hey."

Marcus looked over to his sister. "Hey."

They stood under a cloud of uncomfortable silence for a few seconds before Leanne spoke again. "Are you still refusing to talk or listen?"

"You're not going to start in on me too, are you?"

She let out a frustrated sigh and looked away. "No. I stopped pretending a long time ago that I understood how you and Sarah operated. I just wanted to see how you were doing. How she was doing."

"She's been waking up, but she doesn't have the energy to sustain it for very long. They ran some more tests."

Leanne leaned against the wall and looked into Sarah's room. "Catherine told me. She also said she was calm when she woke up. That's good."

Marcus felt tears sting his eyes and his chest tighten. "I'm not so sure I agree. It almost seems like she's giving up. Before she slipped into unconsciousness, she was angry and... frantic. It sucked, but at least she had an emotional reaction. Now she just acts resigned."

"Sarah's never pegged me as the type to give up on anything."

"Yeah, well, she's never been assaulted to the point of fighting for her life before. To the point of losing everything. She lost everything once before and she had a difficult time recovering from it, remember? It was Dad who helped her overcome her pain. What if she's given up again?"

"She hasn't lost everything, Marcus. And, as I've been told *repeatedly*, there was nothing romantic between her and Dad. So if he was able to pull her out of it the last time, then I imagine you'd be able to do a hell of a lot more for her this time around."

He contemplated his sister's words as he watched James and Sarah through the room's open door. Of course he'd help Sarah fight to come back. He'd give anything to make her whole again. But it was hard to do when he felt guilty for everything that led them to this point.

"I don't know how to get past the guilt."

"Well, you'd better figure it out—quick." She patted his arm and walked away. Just then, James and Maggie exited Sarah's room.

"She's asking for you." Marcus nodded and quickly went to her side.

"Hey, honey." He gave her a kiss and sat next to the bed.

"James... told me." Tears instantly stung his eyes.

"I just can't, Sarah."

"Understand. For now." She closed her eyes for a second. "Talk... to me."

"What do you want to hear this time?"

"When we... danced. At the... gala."

CHAPTER 6
December • 2012

Marcus listened to his father speak from behind the podium. He was completely on edge, not wanting to watch Sarah dance with his father. He felt a tap on his shoulder and turned to find Miles. He motioned for Marcus to follow him to the back of the room.

"Something came up, and Elijah needs you to dance with Sarah." Marcus stared at Miles in shock.

"I don't dance any more."

"You need to make this one exception."

"No. You can do it, or Leanne can dance with Brad."

"The musicians are set to play your parent's wedding song. You're the only other person here who knows the dance. Elijah's about to announce that you're going to dance with Sarah. Do you want to leave her up there alone?"

Marcus looked over at Sarah standing next to the dance floor. She was looking at him, and he held her gaze. She looked terrified. Even if she wasn't 'the one,' he wouldn't be able to leave her up there alone and embarrassed. He turned back to Miles, ran his hand through his hair, and pointed in the direction of his father on stage.

"You enable him too damn much, Miles." He walked off in the direction of Sarah before Miles could respond. He was so furious he was shaking. And he was scared. Dancing reminded him too much of his mother, and that was too painful. He stood behind Sarah as his father finished his speech. He locked his eyes on her back and a sense of calm washed over him.

Why am I so pissed? I've wanted to dance with her since the moment I saw her. I should be excited.

But he knew it was because his father had ambushed him into it. This was a big moment for him and while he only wanted to share it with Sarah, he'd wanted to ask her. He wanted the anticipation. He wanted to watch her reaction after he asked. He wanted to feel the joy in the moment she said yes. And she would have said yes because he wouldn't have accepted any other answer.

There was a round of applause, and Marcus realized his father must have ended his speech. Sarah remained still and Marcus started toward her, gently placing his hand on her back.

"Smile, Sarah, or people will assume you don't want to dance with me." His father came down to meet them as they walked onto the dance floor. Marcus exchanged an awkward hug with him. "I can't believe you did this to me. A little warning would have been nice."

"If I would have told you, I'm sure you would have found a way to get out of it." His father turned to Sarah. "I'm sorry. We'll talk about it later. You'll do great." He gave her a hug and a kiss on the cheek before walking off the dance floor and out of the room with Miles. The irritation of watching his father put his lips to Sarah's cheek was almost enough to distract him from what he was about to do.

Pushing past the painful pounding in his chest, Marcus took Sarah's hand and led her to the center of the dance floor. He felt her shudder as he pulled her into position and tried to let go of his anger. He wanted to enjoy this moment and wanted her to enjoy it just as much. He pulled her close to whisper in her ear.

"Sarah, relax. You'll do fine, just follow my lead. I won't let you fall or even step on my toes." The music began and so did their movement across the dance floor.

Even though he knew he would, he was still surprised he'd remembered all the steps. For a moment a lump formed at the back of his throat as he was reminded of the times he danced with his mother. He took a deep, steadying breath and smelled lavender. It brought him back to the present and the fact that Sarah was in his arms. He held her closer than the dance required, but he couldn't resist. The contact with her kept him grounded in the present. He suddenly felt her falter, and he tightened his grip. He pulled back enough to look in her eyes while he whispered encouraging words.

"Look at me, Sarah. Keep your eyes on me and we'll get each other through this."

He felt her relax and it was all he needed to fully let go. He guided her through the movements, and it felt like he was soaring. He held her close except for the couple times he had to release her for a spin. He forgot about everything around him. All that existed was Sarah and the music. When the music ended he couldn't let go. He had never felt more alive than in that moment.

I vow that I will never stop dancing again, as long as Sarah is by my side.

He looked into her mesmerizing brown-green eyes and was lost. He was about to give into the desire to kiss her when he felt her go limp in his arms. He pulled her into a gentle hug.

"Don't faint on me now. We're all done and you did great." He kept his arm around her, holding her to his side, as he walked her off the dance floor. He focused only on getting her out of the room. She was struggling, and he needed to provide her with an escape.

Marcus strode with purpose to the bar in the reception area. It had been far too long since his last drink. The bartender handed him the glass and he put it to his lips, but he paused before the amber liquid entered his mouth. His mother's words reminded him of a boundary he didn't want to cross again.

It won't do any good to start using alcohol to mask your problems.

Knowing he'd already had more than a few that evening, he set the glass down and asked the bartender for water instead. He turned away, coming face to face with Heather. He could see her struggling with a reaction. It appeared she was equal parts pissed and hurt.

"I thought you said you weren't going to dance tonight. And where's your jacket?"

"Heather, don't start."

"But you told me you wouldn't, and then you danced with that woman, and you're *so* good! You didn't tell me you were that amazing! I don't understand—"

He shoved his untouched drink in her direction. He shouldn't encourage her to drink more, but he needed a reprieve from her whining.

"My father forced my hand. I didn't want to dance. I meant what I

said. You'll be dancing with Van soon enough. Come on, let's go sit."
He needed the music of the ballroom to drown out her protests. She
reluctantly followed him back to the table where she sat down with a
huff. He trained his eyes on the dancing couples and let his thoughts
wander over the last hour of the evening.

Once he had finally let go of his frustration over his father's
actions, he'd felt more happiness than he had in a long time. Dancing
with Sarah had been more than he'd imagined. He wanted to do it
again and never stop. After the dance, they'd had an enjoyable
conversation on the balcony. He'd even go so far as to say she had
flirted with him a little. He smiled at the memory.

Everything was going great until my father showed up.

The instant his father had made his presence known, Sarah had
rushed to his side and forgotten all about Marcus. It was beyond
infuriating. He still didn't understand the nature of her relationship
with his father. She insisted there was nothing going on romantically,
and he believed her, but there was something more to their
relationship than they were letting on. He could tell there was a strong
bond between them. He had hoped to get the answers he was looking
for while he was alone with Sarah, but he had botched his question
and upset her. Then his father showed up before he could fix the
situation. He wasn't sure he'd get a chance to be alone with her again
to ask for clarification, and it wasn't like he could talk to his father
about it.

There were times when Marcus wished he had a closer relationship
with his father. He often wondered if things would have been
different if he and Leanne had changed roles. If she had been the
dancer and he had been the business successor. For as much as
people praised him about his talent for dancing, he couldn't help but
feel his father viewed it as some sort of flaw.

Heather shifted next to him, bumping his shoulder, and he turned
his head slightly to look at her. She was staring at the dancers with a
pout. He let out a sigh and ran a hand through his hair.

"Do you want to leave early?" He wasn't interested in leaving, but
he felt he owed her the option.

"I want to dance."

"Van will be here soon, and you can dance until your stilettos form
an indentation in your heel."

"I want to dance with you."

"We've been over this, Heather."

"Come on, Marcus."

"Heather, for the last time, I don't want to dance."

"It didn't stop you from dancing with *her*."

"I told you, I didn't have a choice. It was a result of my father's usual lack of consideration for anyone but himself."

Where the hell is Van? If Heather doesn't stop bugging me about dancing I'm going to lose it.

"But you're *so good*. I mean, I knew you said you used to dance, but you never told me you were *that* good. I don't understand; it's such a waste of talent. Can't you imagine the two of us out on the dance floor? We'd make a spectacular couple."

Marcus cringed internally. He really needed to put a stop to this. "Heather! Please, I don't want to dance. You can sit here and keep me company, or you can go back to your hotel." He turned to look for Van and saw Sarah standing behind them.

"I hope I'm not interrupting, I wanted to return your jacket." He stood and walked over to accept his jacket—Heather already forgotten.

"So I guess my father has left you alone for the rest of the evening after all."

"Yeah, well... you know your dad when it comes to business. But he promised me the night off, so I guess I get to stay and enjoy myself." He was about to offer to get her a drink but was cut off by a rather excited voice.

"Sarah! You're back." Tina pulled her into a tight embrace. "My God, you and Marcus on the dance floor, what a sight! You did a wonderful job. I swear I couldn't stop the tears for at least ten minutes after it was over. I'm so proud of you." Sarah laughed and it was a wonderful thing to hear. "Come with me, I need a drink."

"Are you sure? It seems you've already had quite a few." Marcus could hear more laughter than challenge in Sarah's voice.

"Nonsense. My job for the evening is done, I don't have to drive, and I'm not the lightweight you are. Maybe my husband can carry *me* up the stairs instead of you for a change."

"Fine, but I'm not drinking. Miles may be in fine shape for a man of his age, but I doubt he could carry us both upstairs."

"Marcus can carry you." Tina smiled at Sarah and winked at him as she pulled Sarah over to the bar in the corner of the ballroom. He had adored Tina before, but she just became his favorite person ever. After Sarah, that is. He made a mental note to figure out why Miles had the pleasure of carrying Sarah up the stairs.

"Marcus."

Shit.

He turned to face Heather, prepared for his punishment. The look on her face told him he should take her some place more private. And that he should get a drink. Not counting his year of rebellion, he always heeded his mother's warning about drinking, but the night was proving to be beyond his tolerance level.

"Let's get out of here for a minute." He walked in the direction of the doors without waiting for a response, heading straight for the bar in the reception area. With most of the people dancing, the room was nearly empty.

"Why did you bring me if you don't want to be with me? And why did she have your jacket?" He paused to think before responding. She was teetering on the border of her crying phase of drunkenness, and he didn't want to deal with it.

"Heather, I'm sorry. Of course I want you here. It's just that my family is all kinds of messed-up, and it's put me on edge."

"And what about *her*?" He didn't like the way the word 'her' sounded bitter on Heather's lips. He didn't want anyone speaking badly of Sarah, even if it was only due to irrational jealousy and drunkenness.

"What about Sarah?"

"You like her don't you? You'd rather be with her than with me."

"Heather—"

"It was obvious when you danced with her, Marcus. It was like you were trying to devour her with your eyes right there on the dance floor! I was humiliated." Her tears started to fall.

He took a deep breath before responding. "Heather—"

"Now look what you've done! My mascara's going to run." She turned and quickly walked in the direction of the restrooms, passing Van on the way.

"What the hell did you do now, Kingston?"

"Don't start with me, Van."

Van let out a sharp breath and looked away for a moment. "Look, I know this evening is always difficult for you. But seriously, you seem much more on edge than usual. What gives? I'm just trying to help."

"If you want to help, you can dance with Heather."

Van studied him for a moment. "Alright. I mean, it will suck—having to dance with a beautiful woman—but I can take the hit for my best friend."

Marcus gave up a reluctant smile, and he could see the triumph in Van's eyes. "She's a good dancer, so you'd better bring your A-game."

"How would you know? You don't dance any more. Or is it that you don't dance with anyone except your father's girlfriend?"

"She's not his girlfriend."

"You two looked pretty intense on the dance floor." Van watched him for a reaction but he refused to give one. He knew he'd spill to Van soon enough, but it wasn't the right time or place. "Right, fine. I get it. But tomorrow we're doing lunch before you bounce."

"Noon? The usual place?" Marcus knew there was no point in trying to get out of it.

"Yep. Now, I'd better go find Heather before she drowns in her sorrow of unrequited love." He turned but stopped after a step and turned back to Marcus. "You really don't care if I go home with her?"

People always accused Marcus of being the playboy. He was nothing compared to Van.

"No, I don't. Just don't be a dick to her. She's a nice girl, and even though I don't like her in that way, I don't want to see her get used."

Van's face broke into a confident smile. "I promise to be all dick till dawn, and then I'll turn into a gentleman..." He turned on his heel and strode in the direction of the bathrooms.

"I mean it, Van!" He turned and gave Marcus a mock salute without even breaking his stride.

Marcus waited until Van had Heather occupied on the dance floor before returning to the ballroom. He was relieved to find Sarah alone at the table. His heart rate quickened with each step closer to her. She looked at him when he sat down, and her brows pinched together in the center. It was adorable and he wanted to kiss her right in that exact spot. And on the lips. And everywhere else.

Get a grip. She's not some one-night-stand you can seduce on the dance floor. Although the thought was tempting.

"What happened to Heather?"

"She decided to find someone who was willing to dance with her."

They sat in silence. While he wanted to know everything about her, he'd prefer to do it in private. He was consumed with the sensation of being near her—the sound of her voice, the lavender smell that must have been from her soap or shampoo, the way her hands were constantly looking for something to hold on to. He was trying to etch everything about her into his memory.

His observations were cut short when Sarah started asking him about dancing. He loved everything about dancing. It wasn't just a passion; it was a part of who he was. He was thrilled to share that side of himself with her. They talked for a long time while the music played and people danced before them. He loved the way she looked at him intently while he talked. For that small moment in time, he could believe that he was the only person that existed in her world. That his father wasn't hovering somewhere in the background, waiting to take away her attention again.

He was disappointed when Tina and Miles approached the table. He was about to ask Sarah if she wanted to take a walk when Miles pulled her out of her seat.

"What are you doing?" There was a slight panic in Sarah's voice.

"We're going to dance."

Sarah drew her arms away in protest. "No, I can't dance remember? Not like them at any rate." They all laughed as she waved her hand across the crowded dance floor. "What's so funny?"

"Sarah, you dance just fine. Besides, I promised Elijah I would make you dance at least one more time. I don't want to tell him I failed, do you?" Miles gave her a pleading look.

"But I only know the one dance."

"If you can do that one, the basic waltz will be a piece of cake. I'm sure Miles will go easy on you." Marcus gave her an encouraging smile and was happy to see her blush in return. It was becoming obvious to him that she reacted as much to him as he did to her.

Maybe those obstacles won't be so difficult after all.

He watched as Miles led her around the dance floor, eventually coaxing her into relaxing and having fun.

"You okay there, lover-boy?"

"Hmm?" Marcus turned his attention to Tina, who now occupied the seat where Sarah had been sitting. She was watching him closely.

"You seem quite smitten with Sarah." Marcus had always admired Tina's blunt nature.

"That obvious?"

"Yep—except to her probably."

Marcus closed his eyes and sighed. "She's had a rough time of it. You seem to be pretty good friends with her. Do you think she's ready to move on?"

"So you don't share your sister's belief that she's involved with your father?" Marcus shook his head. "I always knew I was crushing on you for more than your good looks—that mass of hair women just want to sink their fingers into, your killer bod, and your eyes... Those gorgeous aqua blues are so striking it's like getting hit with a jolt of blue lightning. But you've got brains too."

Marcus laughed. "Blue lightning?"

"The most dangerous kind of lightning there is. That's how your eyes work—all it takes is one flash for you to strike a woman down. Damn near killed me the first time you looked at me, my heart was racing so fast."

"Don't let Miles know."

"Oh, he knows. But he's confident in the fact that you have no interest in me. Especially now that we've seen you with Sarah. I do believe there are hearts breaking all over the Rockies." Marcus gave her a playful nudge, and she laughed. "Okay, seriously. I believe there could be something real between you, but I'm not sure she's ready to move on. She's had a difficult time letting go of her grief. Elijah's been helping her, but she still has a long way to go."

Marcus was quiet for a moment as he watched Sarah dance with Miles. "My father's really helping her?" He wasn't sure he was able to hide the sorrow from his voice. While he was happy Sarah was getting help, he wanted to be the one to give it to her.

"Yes, he is. Just be patient. With both of them." They sat in silence for a few moments, watching Sarah and Miles dance. Tina stood when Miles eventually led Sarah over to the bar area. "But if you break her heart, I'll beat the ever-living shit out of you."

The look she gave him before walking away convinced him she'd be able to do it. He smiled, happy that Sarah had such a good friend. He watched as the three of them chatted off to the side of the room for a moment. When Miles and Tina walked off leaving her alone, he stood to join her. Unfortunately a short, stubborn obstacle appeared before him in the shape of his sister.

"Marcus, what do you think you're doing?"

"I can honestly say I don't know, but I'm sure you will enlighten me."

"You seem to have taken a strong interest in Sarah."

"So?"

"So? She's with Dad! You can't be serious."

"I'm very serious, and I suggest you stay out of it. Actually, on second thought, maybe you could clear something up. Explain to me the situation when you found them in bed together."

"What's to explain? I walked into Dad's room and they were in his bed sleeping."

"Were they naked? Were they in each other's arms, or lying next to each other?"

Leanne crossed her arms over her chest and he watched as her face hardened. "I don't see how any of that matters. Regardless, it was inappropriate for him to be in bed with his employee—and with his grandson on the floor a few feet away!"

"Just humor me, how did you find them?"

"Fully clothed, but in each other's arms."

The answer gave him a small measure of relief. He would have felt even better if they had been on opposite sides of the bed, but at least he could accept fully clothed. For the moment. He looked in the direction where he last saw Sarah, hoping she hadn't left. What he saw boiled his blood.

"Marcus—" Leanne called out after him, but he didn't slow his pace.

He reached Sarah just as she cried out in pain from the grip Mark had on her arm. Marcus grabbed him by the neck and pulled him away. He delivered two quick punches to Mark's face before the man even had a chance to register what was going on.

"Don't you ever touch her again!" He reared back to deliver the third—and what he intended to be the final—blow, but his forward momentum was stopped. He turned to see Brad holding his arm.

"That's enough, Marcus. We'll get him out of here." Brad motioned someone over to help, and they hauled Mark toward the doors.

Marcus quickly went to Sarah who was having her arm inspected by Leanne. He gently took her arm and looked it over. There would be a mark. He had to resist the urge to chase after Mark to finish the job. Without thinking, he took Sarah's hand in his and entwined their fingers.

He turned his heated gaze to Leanne. "Two years in a row. His ass had better be fired by Monday. Dad didn't have the balls to do it last year, so you'd better step up." He walked past Leanne without waiting for a response, gently pulling Sarah with him.

"Where are we going?" He could feel her gently tug on his arm as they walked.

"To dance." He felt her stop in response, causing him to come to a halt as well. He turned and looked at her in confusion. "What's wrong?"

"I don't want to dance."

"Sure you do." He turned and tried to move forward, but she stood her ground. He turned back to look at her. "Why aren't we moving?"

"I just got manhandled by some jackass who was insisting I dance with him even though I didn't want to, and now you're trying to do the same thing. Although, I admit your approach is much more gentlemanly. I said I don't want to dance."

Shit. I'm an ass.

"You're right, I'm sorry." He let out a quick breath and gently squeezed her hand. "Sarah, will you please dance with me?"

"No." She pulled her hand away and crossed her arms.

He opened his mouth to respond, but nothing came out so he closed it again. He narrowed his eyes and looked at her, still confused. He hadn't expected her to resist.

"Look, I don't feel like dancing. Besides, I thought you said you didn't want to dance. Several times in fact."

"That was with Heather." He paused to let out another breath and run his hand through the side of his hair. "Look, I can't fully explain it. It's just that seeing Mark harass you, *again*... it beyond pissed me off, and to calm down I want to dance. With you. It doesn't make any sense seeing as dancing is the one thing I've avoided the most over the last twenty years, but it's the way I feel. Besides, if you recall I already asked you to dance with me a second time when we were outside. You never answered my question, so I'm asking you again. Will you dance with me?" He held out his hand, praying she would take it. Relief washed over him when she did, and he smiled before leading her to the dance floor.

A song was already in progress, but he swept her up and they moved smoothly in sync with the other couples. He had relaxed by the time the song ended, but he refused to let her go. Luckily, another song began immediately and he continued to move. He closed his eyes and enjoyed being near her—the way she felt against him, the way she smelled, the sound of her breathing—everything was sending him into overdrive. He knew he should back off if he had any hope of moving slow with her, but he didn't know how.

The second song ended and she pulled back. He tightened his grip, restricting her from walking away. "Um, I hope the dancing calmed your mood."

"It did... why?"

"Because I think you might need to talk to Heather. She looks like she might be about to flip a table, and it would be good if at least one of you were calm." He turned in the direction of her gaze and his shoulders dropped with a heavy sigh.

"Do you mind waiting for me at the table while I talk with her?"

"Actually, I'm going to retire for the evening." He couldn't hide his disappointment.

"Are you sure? There's a lot more dancing left in the evening."

"I'm sure. I've well surpassed the amount of dancing I thought I would do tonight." They stood in awkward silence. He almost laughed as he watched her struggle with how to say good-bye. He knew how he wanted to do it, but he didn't want to scare her off for good. Suddenly she stuck out her hand. "Well, it was nice meeting you, Marcus. Thank you for the dancing, especially for bailing out your dad and not leaving me stranded. And for getting rid of Mark, twice..."

He looked at her hand with amusement. He took it in his, but instead of giving it a shake he gently pulled her toward him until his mouth connected with her ear.

"You're welcome. I look forward to the next time we meet." He pulled back, winked at her, and walked off in the direction of Heather.

Marcus stood at the bar, sipping his water. The encounter with Heather hadn't been pleasant, but luckily Van saved the evening. It was almost disturbing how quickly she was able to shift her attentions from one man to the other. Of course, Van didn't mind. Marcus knew him well enough to know that he probably viewed it as a challenge.

He finished his water and decided to turn in for the night. He wanted to dance with Sarah, but she had gone to bed. With no one left to keep him company, there was no point in staying up. He started toward the stairs and was stopped by a pretty, young blonde. It was the same woman who had showed him his room when he arrived, but he'd forgotten her name.

That's odd. I think I even remember thinking she was sort of hot when I first met her.

The only thing that had changed in that time was meeting Sarah. He wondered if she had already blinded him to all other women.

That didn't take long.

"Mr. Kingston, retiring so soon?"

"Yes, I've decided to call it an early night."

"Mrs. Troupe had insisted on turn down service, and I was just ensuring it had been done. Would you like the same for your room?"

"No, thank you." He shook his head, but it was more in response to Leanne's absurd request for turndown service than to emphasize his response to the question. While the estate was huge and offered a lot of space for events, there weren't many guest rooms. The only other people staying in house were his family, the Morgans, and Sarah.

I wonder if she's asleep by now.

He climbed the steps to the third floor, turned in the direction of his room, but stopped after only two steps. He turned and looked in the direction of Sarah's room. He shouldn't go see her, but he was tempted.

Maybe I could just go down and have a listen. If she's awake, I can knock and tell her good night.

He was already going through withdrawal. He wanted to knock on her door and ask her out on a date, kiss her—do something. Anything. But he knew he couldn't. She was struggling, and he needed to make sure she could trust him and feel comfortable with him. He didn't want just a knee-buckling kiss in the heat of the moment. He wanted a lifetime of earth-shattering moments with her. He turned and reluctantly went to his room. Just as he closed the door behind him, he heard what sounded like a scream. He yanked open his door and stood in the hall, listening. When he heard it again, he took off in the direction of Sarah's room.

He reached her door and was ready to pound on it when he heard something coming from his father's room. Confusion momentarily replaced his panic, and he quickly went down to the next door. He listened closely, but could no longer hear anything. His heart was still beating rapidly, but his anxiety was abating.

Maybe I imagined it.

He listened for a while longer and was about to leave when he heard the water turn on in the room's bathroom. He put his ear to the door, trying to figure out what was going on. There was silence for a few seconds and then he heard his father's voice. He couldn't make out what he was saying, but he could hear enough to know his father was talking to someone. Then he heard Sarah's voice.

He nearly broke down the door to demand some answers. She had said nothing was going on and he'd believed her.

Then why is she in his room?

He took a few deep breaths to calm down, playing back the evening in his mind. There was no question that he'd had some sort of an effect on Sarah. He was confident she could feel a connection between them just as much as he did. He was also certain there was nothing romantic between her and his father. There had to be an explanation for why she was in his room. Tina's reminder to be patient echoed through his mind. With both of them.

Whatever that means.

He had lost patience with his father a long time ago. But something was going on, and he was determined to get to the bottom of it. His future with Sarah might depend on it.

CHAPTER 7

Marcus watched as tears pricked at the corners of Sarah's eyes.

Damn. I probably should have left out the parts about Mark.

A chill raced down his spine as an idea tried to formalize in his mind, but Sarah's voice interrupted his thoughts.

"You vowed... to keep... dancing."

"Yes, I did."

She looked at him for a few seconds before continuing. "I know you. You can't... stop... dancing."

"I'm afraid that every time I set foot in the studio I'm going to be reminded of this moment. Or more specifically, of my failure."

"And you think... not dancing... will make... you forget?"

He opened his mouth to speak, but a sigh replaced his words. He knew she was right. There wasn't anything that would make him forget this time in their lives.

"Not dancing... will only... make it... worse."

"I'll make a deal with you—I'll go back to the studio when you feel up to dancing with me again."

"Your classes."

"Kelli's been there long enough to run the place while I'm out. She's going to bring someone in to help."

She closed her eyes and nodded slightly. He thought maybe she was drifting off to sleep when her eyes opened again. "Did I... ever tell you... I thought... someone... was listening... at the... door?" He shook his head. "His... hallucinations... had started."

He didn't like to think about his father's fight with Creutzfeldt-Jakob Disease—or CJD since the actual name was a mouthful. The gala had been when he'd first noticed his odd behavior, but he hadn't known his father was sick. He certainly didn't know he was dying. It was an ugly, rare, and fatal disease. There was no cure. Unfortunately, it ran in his family.

He had mixed feelings about his father's death. He missed him, and he wished they'd had a better relationship. It was painful witnessing what his father had to go through. No one should have to suffer through CJD. However, if his father hadn't been sick, Marcus never would have met Sarah.

He shook off his thoughts, not wanting to think about any of that at the moment. He turned his attention back to Sarah. "It was hard for me not to break down the door and pull you away. The idea of you being in his room—at night, alone—damn near shattered me."

"But it... caused you... to come and... check things... out."

"Really, I showed up early that Christmas to check you out. Finding out what was going on with my father was just a side agenda at that point."

"I know. I'm glad." She paused and he could see another attempt at a smile. "Again... you could have... left out... Heather."

"Well, since I included her the first time I thought you'd appreciate hearing about her leaving with Van."

"Good point." She held his gaze and he knew what was coming. "Van—"

"No, Sarah."

"Yes... Marcus. You... have to."

"I can't."

"Not his... fault. Not your... fault. Only one... person... did this."

"Yes, and he's still out there, somewhere!" He ran a frustrated hand through his hair. They weren't supposed to talk about it. He couldn't let her get worked up thinking about it. The only way to avoid it was to relent on his stubbornness.

"Why don't you rest, and then I'll talk when you wake up again?"

"Tell me... about your... talk with... Van. After... the gala. It will... help."

"You need to rest."

"I will. After... you talk."

He got up and paced the room. In a rare moment of fate, they were alone. He knew she was right, knew that James and everyone else was right. He needed to let go of his anger and fear. Somewhere, deep down, he knew Van wasn't to blame. That in reality he owed Van his eternal gratitude for keeping things from being worse than they were.

But admitting it meant that he'd have to absorb all the blame himself. He could only handle so much guilt at once. Right now, he only had the strength to shoulder the guilt he held for Sarah being in the hospital. He just couldn't take on anyone else. It was a weakness he was embarrassed to possess, but he didn't know how to overcome it at the moment.

He looked back at the bed, hoping she had fallen asleep. She was awake and watching him. With a resigned sigh, he sat back down.

"What do you want to hear?"

"The highlights... following... the gala. The things... that brought... you to me."

"I was yours before we met." This time she actually did manage a smile. It wasn't much, but it was the best smile he had ever seen.

"Tell me... anyway."

CHAPTER 8
December • 2012

Marcus sat in the foyer, sipping his water. It had been a long night with little sleep. Visions of Sarah kept dancing around in his head. He'd gotten out of bed early in hopes of seeing her before he left. Two hours had passed, and not a single person emerged from their rooms. Finally, he heard footsteps on the stairs and sat forward in anticipation. He sat back at the disappointment of seeing his sister.

"Marcus? What are you doing sitting there?" She paused for a moment and then threw her head back in disgust. "You have got to be kidding me! You really want to torture yourself by sitting there, waiting to see her come down the stairs, after she spent the night with Dad?"

"She had her own room."

"With a connecting door to Dad's! Come on, Marcus, you're not as gullible as that. You have to see the obvious here."

He ran a hand over his face in frustration. "I'm not talking with you about this, Leanne." Even though he was convinced otherwise, the more she talked the more his confidence faltered. Especially after having heard Sarah in his father's room last night.

"Fine. But don't come crying to me when she breaks your heart." Leanne stomped off out the door. Brad offered him a sympathetic look as he followed.

Theirs was a relationship he would never fully understand. Anyone who didn't know them would assume Brad was a beaten puppy who followed Leanne out of equal measures of obedience and fear. In reality, he was the foundation of their relationship. He was the one who held Leanne in check and grounded her irrational control issues. He just wasn't sure how Brad could put up with it all the time.

He must really love her.

The thought made him remember the last conversation he'd had with his mother before she died. He could see how her words played out with Leanne and Brad. He instinctively ran his hand along his left side. He heard more footsteps and sat forward again.

When his father came into view he took a deep breath and stood. He physically deflated when Miles appeared where Sarah should have been. His father stopped when he saw Marcus.

"Good morning, Marcus."

"Morning. Get all your business taken care of last night?"

His father looked at him in confusion. "What are you talking about?"

"You know... the urgent business that caused you to back out of the dance with Sarah and throw me into your place?" His father looked to Miles in confusion and Marcus was instantly suspicious.

"Right, that. No, it's not all worked out, but we made some progress." His father ran a hand through his hair. Marcus knew it was a sign of frustration.

"Did Sarah help you?"

"I thought she went back down with you?" Again, he looked to Miles for support. Something wasn't right.

His father had spent many years as the head of Kingston Enterprises—a family business that was extremely profitable. He was the kind of man who took what he wanted and didn't leave leftovers. His father didn't question or second guess, he never conceded on anything, and he never allowed any vulnerability to show through. He had always been tough and arrogant, but more so after Marcus' mother had died. His looking to Miles twice for confirmation in the span of thirty seconds was irregular.

"She did. I meant after she went up to her room."

His father's jaw tensed, and his face suddenly settled into a hard look. "Why do you have so much interest in Sarah?"

"Isn't she a part of your life now? Doesn't that give me the right to ask questions?"

"No."

"'No' she's not a part of your life, or 'no' I can't ask questions?" Marcus couldn't resist goading him.

"Sarah's off limits to you." Marcus pulled back as if physically pushed by his father's words.

"What the hell's that supposed to mean?" He took a step closer, his fists clenched at his sides. He would never strike out at his father, but it had been a long time since the urge to do so was so strong.

"It means she's in a vulnerable state, physically and emotionally, and she doesn't need you sniffing around."

"You make it sound like I'm a dog."

"Yeah, well, the way you treat women implies they're the female version of a dog so what's that make you?"

Marcus took another step closer, his anger hitting the surface. "What the—"

"Hey, let's not do this here." Miles stepped up between them. Marcus took a few deep breaths and backed away.

"You're right, Miles. Dear old Dad has formed his opinion of me, and I can see that's never going to change." He turned, grabbed his bag, and walked out the door.

Van was late and Marcus was tired of waiting. He was about to send him a text to cancel, when someone grabbed him from behind and planted a kiss on his cheek.

"What the hell, Van?"

"Afraid of a little man love?"

"What's got you in such a good mood?"

"I had a *really* good night. Thanks to you."

Marcus groaned. He didn't want to hear about his night with Heather; although, he hoped whatever had happened would keep her from pursuing him.

"I'm happy for you, but I don't need to hear about it."

"Why, jealous? I would be if I were you. I still can't believe you passed on her. As impossible as it sounds, I've never had sex with a dancer before. Now my sexual appetite is forever ruined for all other professions."

"No, I'm not jealous. We hang in the same set of friends, and I really don't want to know. I passed because I wasn't interested, but

I'm glad it worked out for you. Are you going to see her again, or was it a one-time thing? I'd like to know what to expect the next time I see her."

"I'll probably call her. We left it open. I'm not ready to commit."

The waitress materialized with their water and shamelessly flirted with them both before walking away with their orders.

Marcus was constantly reminded—whether he wanted to hear it or not—that he had been blessed in the looks department. Van hadn't been as lucky. It wasn't all bad—his brown hair was stylishly messy, his dark eyes were framed by long lashes, and his neatly trimmed goatee suited his face. However, he was somewhat short, his nose was a little big for his face, and his ears stood out if he looked at you in a certain way. But what he lacked in physical appearance he made up in sex appeal. At least that's what his female friends told him. Many of his gay friends too.

"Kingston, what the hell was up with you last night?"

"It was a night full of unexpected surprises. Some good, some not so good."

"Start with the good."

"I found her."

"Who?"

"*Her.*"

Van paused with his water glass suspended in mid-air. He placed it on the table and sat back in his chair. "Seriously? Who is she? I only saw you with Heather and your father's hot piece of—wait, don't tell me you fell for your father's girlfriend?"

"First, don't ever call her a 'hot piece of' whatever it was you were about to say. Second, she's *not* his girlfriend. Third, yes, that's the not so good part of it."

"Shit. And I thought my love life was screwed up."

"You don't have a love life. You have a sex life."

"True. So what are you going to do? She's really the one? I mean, I was surprised to see you dancing again, but I thought maybe that was all a result of your father."

The waitress reappeared with drink refills, even though only a couple of minutes had passed and their glasses were still mostly full. She flirted with Van a few minutes before finally walking away to take another table's order.

"I don't know what I'm going to do yet. My father's just one of the obstacles in the way. Since I'm convinced they're not having any sort of intimate relationship, I don't think that's too big to overcome. Although, I'm not certain *he* wants to keep it platonic. There's just something about the way he looks at her that doesn't sit straight with me."

"What are the other obstacles?"

"About two and a half years ago she lost her husband and two-year old son in a car accident. I guess she hasn't fully recovered yet."

"Man, that's heavy. Are you sure you want to get into all that?"

"I don't have a choice."

Van shot him an irritated look. "There's always a choice."

Marcus just shook his head in return. "Not in this case. I'm telling you—she's the one. I can't walk away, it's just not possible."

"I still don't understand how this 'one' shit works."

"Admittedly, neither do I. The sensation of seeing her for the first time was exactly what I had expected. It was how my father had described first seeing my mother. He said when she stepped out onto the ballet stage, everything around him was lost and he felt more alive than he thought humanly possible." He paused to take a drink of his water. He was about to continue when the waitress showed up again.

He was used to extremely attentive service when he and Van went out and were seated in a woman's section. This resulted in leaving a tip that was usually half the amount of the bill. Not that the service was always exceptional, but he felt it was considerate to at least pay for the amount of time dedicated to their dining needs. The other downsides were dealing with the flirting and constant interruptions. He wasn't in the mood to tolerate it at the moment.

She finally walked away and Marcus rolled his eyes at Van. "Can you just get her number, or stop flirting? It's hard to have a conversation when she keeps stopping by."

"Did you see her ass? She must be new—I haven't seen her here before." Van craned his neck to find her.

"Didn't you *just* have sex with Heather?"

"That was hours ago." Van finally looked back to Marcus. "What? I told you, we left it open. She was cool with it—you don't have to worry. So, back to you and your father's not-girlfriend."

Marcus often found talking to Van exhausting. He should have known Van wouldn't be able to focus in a public place surrounded by women. He took a deep breath and forged on. If he was in need of clarity, Van was sure to give it to him.

"When I first saw Sarah, it was just like my father had described. I literally stumbled. Everyone and everything in the room faded except her—she somehow became more vibrant. At first I tried to pin it on a strong physical attraction, but—while she's beautiful—she's not the type I'm usually attracted to."

"What part's not your type? I know she's not blonde, but that certainly hasn't stopped you before."

"Mainly, she's way too thin. You know that's a deal breaker for me. And yet, that's what sealed it. Despite the fact that she wasn't my type, and that she has some sort of eating disorder, I couldn't walk away. In addition to all of that, from the moment my eyes landed on her, I wanted to dance with her."

Van finally grew serious and studied him. "You really don't have a choice do you?"

"No, I don't. But I don't know how to proceed. That's the part that doesn't match up with how I thought all this was supposed to work. I was supposed to look at her and know we were destined to be together, and she was supposed to do the same. She wasn't supposed to be my father's date, and she wasn't supposed to be broken from the last love of her life—and son—dying. What if she's not interested?" Marcus felt his chest tighten at the thought.

"When you two were dancing—I don't even know how to describe it. For one, you've been wasting your damn talent and you need to stop that shit. Couple that talent with Sarah? That was some intense dancing. She looked just as mesmerized by you as you were of her. I'd say she's interested. However, even though I don't have a love life, I do understand it. She lost her husband. That never goes away. You'll always ride bitch while his memory takes shotgun."

Even in a serious conversation Van had to throw in his unique—and usually crude—quips. Marcus opened his mouth to speak when the waitress showed up again. He'd had enough.

"Excuse me, Staci is it?" Marcus waited for her to look at him. "Do you mind waiting until after we're done eating before trying to hook up with my friend? I'm sure he'll still be interested later, and right now we're trying to have a conversation. We don't need anything, so please don't stop by again unless you have our food. Then, when it's time to settle the bill, you two can settle your other business as well."

Her face flashed red with either embarrassment or anger—possibly both—before turning and walking away.

"Damn, Kingston. Why'd you go and do that? Not only have you likely ruined my chances of scoring with her tonight, but she's probably going to spit in our food."

"Just a few minutes ago, you said you only wanted to have sex with dancers from now on."

"She might be a dancer. Don't most starving artists also wait tables while waiting for the next gig to come along?"

Marcus ran a frustrated hand through his hair. "Van, get your sexual tourette's under control and focus. Please."

"Is the new, in love Marcus always going to be this uptight?"

"I'm just frustrated and don't know what to do! I can't walk away, yet I can't go in guns blazing and tell her I love her. I'm not even sure I can ask her on a date. Given her situation, she'd likely shoot me down and avoid me. And I know the memory of her late husband will always rate higher than me. I spent most of last night thinking about it. It'll be hard, but I'll find a way to deal with it. I have to. I just need to figure out when to ask her out and how to get her to say yes."

"Spend time with her. Let her get to know you first."

"How am I supposed to do that? She's living at my father's house."

"That's perfect."

"How? I go home once, maybe twice, a year for a few hours."

"And one of those times is at Christmas—which is about a week away. Go early and spend a few days there. Certainly you can suck it up and deal with your father for a few days in the quest for love."

It's brilliant. I'll have to get Leanne to go so it won't be obvious. Wait—

"What if she's going home over Christmas? She might not be there."

"Then you'll have to endure a weekend with your family. You can spend the time strategizing a new plan while dodging your father's insults."

"See, when you focus you're kind of a genius. Now if you could just tell me how to deal with my father."

"What was up with him last night? Did he really call me Dan? Was he drunk?"

"He wasn't drunk, and yes he did call you Dan. He was acting strange this morning too. It was as if he'd forgotten all about last night. I suppose I can get to the bottom of that too while I'm at the house."

The waitress arrived with their food. She set Van's down gently with a smile before turning to Marcus. She hesitated long enough for Marcus to believe she would dump it in his lap, before she finally dropped it on the table in front of him. Van laughed.

"Check your food, man. Check your food." He was still laughing as he took a bite of his sandwich.

Marcus dropped the weights back onto the stand and ran a towel over his head. Three days had passed since his conversation with Van. He'd waited to take action, wanting to ensure he was doing the right thing. He was still certain Sarah was the one—maybe even more certain as the days had passed—but he didn't want to scare her off or cause her any discomfort. If he showed up at the house unexpected, both were likely. However, he needed to make a decision soon if he had any hopes of getting Leanne to agree to the plan. He also needed to come up with an actual plan his sister would buy into.

He showered and dressed, grabbing a quick breakfast on his way out the door. A few years ago he'd opened his own practice just north of Colorado Springs. It was a family community—not exactly ideal for a single guy, but good for business. He pulled into his parking spot and entered the clinic from the back.

May, who attended to the animals that needed to stay overnight, greeted him with a smile. "Good morning, Dr. Kingston."

"Hello, May. How are our patients doing this morning?"

"All are recovering as expected."

"Excellent. Is Dr. Harper back?"

"She's in the office."

He walked past sleeping and barking dogs, stopping to check on a few, as he weaved his way to the office. Joan was sitting behind her desk, staring hopelessly at the computer. He watched her for a moment, playing with her hair. He knew she was desperate to get it colored again, but that would have to wait. He'd always thought her natural dark blonde was fine, but she preferred a lighter shade. He knew this because she mentioned it almost nonstop.

"Good morning, Joan. How was your visit with your parents?"

"Marcus, it's good to see you! The visit home was good. It was just the break I needed. It sounds like I didn't miss much at the clinic while I was gone."

"Just your typical vet stuff. Nothing exciting to report."

"How was the gala?"

"It was eventful."

"Did you dance?" Joan was more than just his partner at the clinic—she'd been a good friend since veterinary school. She knew his history and that he didn't dance, but every year she asked anyway. He was happy to tell her something different this time.

"I did in fact." Her eyes went wide, and her mouth dropped open. She stood and rounded the desk.

"Oh, my God! Who is she?" He smiled. She knew there was only one reason why he would have started dancing again.

"Her name is Sarah Mitchell. She's from Indiana, and she's here working on a project with my father." She raised her eyebrows at him.

"It sounds like there's more to the story."

He gave her the quick version, and by the end she was crying. He pulled her into a hug and patted her back. She pulled away, wiping her eyes and nose on the sleeve of her shirt.

"Sorry, it's these darn hormones. I'm just so happy you finally found someone. But I'm so sad for her..." She started crying again.

"Are you going to be like this for another seven months?"

"Yes. And it will probably only get worse as the pregnancy progresses." He hugged her again until she was able to calm down.

"Van thinks I should go to my father's early and spend a few days there. Give Sarah a chance to know me better before I ask her out on a date."

"Okay, I think the world has just come to an end. I never thought I'd see the day I actually agreed with Van on something. But he's right; you should go and spend some time there."

"You really think it's a good idea?" He felt confident of the plan when talking to Van, but as time passed doubts started to seep in.

Van wasn't exactly the most reliable resource when looking for the best way to start a long-term relationship with a woman.

"I do. You're actually going to have to work for this one." She ran her hand over her still flat stomach. "It's going to be tough, Marcus. I couldn't imagine starting over if I'd lost my husband and baby." Her lip was quivering again, on the verge of another breakdown.

"I know, but from what I've seen from her so far she's one tough woman. I just hope she's willing to give me a chance."

"Well, just be patient with her. It might be a long road ahead for you."

That was twice he'd been told he would need to be patient. He prayed he had the capacity to do so.

"Marcus, hello. Leanne's not home yet."

"I assumed as much. I actually wanted to talk with you about something."

There was a brief pause before Brad spoke again. "You're not going to get me in trouble are you?"

"Maybe. Look, I feel bad about everything that was said to Sarah at the gala. Between Leanne, Heather, and that asshole Mark she had a pretty rough night. I was thinking it might be good to try and make up for it somehow."

Brad let out a hard sigh. "I agree. She seems like a really nice person, and I feel bad too. I was so pissed when Leanne didn't warn me about her circumstances. I felt like such an ass bringing up her family situation."

"Don't beat yourself up over it. If you hadn't asked, I was going to. Either way it would have come out since we didn't get the warning."

"What is it you have in mind?"

"We're all planning on being at Dad's for Christmas Eve dinner, but I was thinking we should show up a couple of days early and spend the weekend. We can get to know her better and show her we're not so bad after all."

"How do you know she'll be there? She mentioned her parents live in the Chicago area. It's likely she'll be visiting them over Christmas."

"It's a possibility. But you know how demanding Dad is when it comes to projects. He usually doesn't give any time off. Even at the holidays. And if she's not there, we can still pretend we all like each other."

Brad was quiet for a few seconds. Marcus knew he was considering Leanne's reaction. He knew Leanne would never have agreed to the plan. Brad was his only hope.

"You know Leanne's not going to like this."

"I know, but tell her she can use the time to confirm one way or another if her suspicions about Dad and Sarah are true. The best way to get to the bottom of the situation is to spend time there."

"When are you planning to go?"

"I thought about getting there Saturday morning and leaving on Monday after Christmas Eve dinner."

"Alright. I'll find a way to get Leanne there. But we already have plans on Saturday, so we won't get there until Sunday morning."

"Perfect. Thanks, Brad."

"Yeah, well, I do agree it's the right thing to do. However, you will probably owe me one after this."

"I'm already in your debt."

CHAPTER 9

The door opened and Sarah's mother walked in, followed by the doctor.

"Marcus, dear, the doctor wants to talk with you."

Marcus looked back at Sarah. Even though she had fallen asleep, he had kept talking. She believed that talking about Van would help. Mostly it just stirred up his guilt, so he remained lost in the memory past the point of his lunch with Van in an effort to diffuse his feelings.

"It's okay, I'll sit with her for a while." The look on his mother-in-law's face told him what she wanted to talk to Sarah about when she woke up again. He left the room quickly. He waited for the doctor and then followed him down the hall to a private room.

"Mr. Kingston, your wife's test results are back." Marcus watched as he pulled out scans and charts.

"What are her chances of a full recovery?"

"It is still uncertain. While she is not getting worse, she is not getting better either. If she does not start moving in a positive direction, there might be other permanent damage we will have to watch for. As you know she lost a lot of blood initially, but we got that under control. The injury she sustained to the head does not appear to have caused any lasting trauma. When she is awake, she is alert and aware of her surroundings. And she has not suffered from any memory loss. The puncture to her lung from the broken rib is very small, and it is likely that it will heal on its own. While she is showing signs of extreme fatigue, I do not see any evidence of serious damage from the puncture. I believe the fracture in her wrist will heal fine. She might need reconstructive surgery on her knee. We will not know if what we did so far will be sufficient until she can begin physical therapy."

Marcus felt his stomach clench as the doctor talked. He wanted to kill the bastard that did this to her. After he hit himself a few times for letting it happen. He'd have to throw Van into that mix as well.

"Doctor, as you said, her memory seems fine. However, she's been asking me to tell her about events from our past. Is that normal?"

The doctor started collecting Sarah's scans. "Everyone reacts to trauma differently. It is possible she just wants to be reminded of happy times—to be able to use them as something she can anchor to during her recovery. Try not to read so much into it."

There was a knock on the door, and a nurse poked her head in.

"Mr. Kingston, sorry to interrupt but there's a detective here to see you."

"Send him in." The nurse stepped aside and the detective entered.

"Mr. Kingston. I'm Detective Smith." He extended his hand and Marcus shook it as he eyed him up and down. He was of average height—a few inches shorter than Marcus—mostly bald, and had a narrow but stocky build. He held an eerie resemblance to a detective on one of the crime shows he and Sarah sometimes watched.

"Detective Smith, it's nice to meet you. This is Dr. Vikrant." The men shook hands and the doctor made to leave. "Doctor, you can stay if you like." The doctor nodded, and they all took a seat.

"How's your wife, Mr. Kingston?"

"She's awake and stable, but we don't know... we'll have to wait and see."

"And what about—"

"I'm sorry, but you'll have to talk with Dr. Vikrant about that after I leave." The detective looked at him with curiosity and suspicion.

"I don't understand."

"It's not your job to understand. Your job is to find the bastard who did this."

"Okay then." Smith shot him another suspicious look before typing something in his tablet. "When will I be able to speak with Mrs. Kingston?"

"You won't." Another look of suspicion. "Look, Detective. Sarah just woke up. She can't keep her eyes open for more than maybe fifteen to twenty minutes—tops. She can't speak a full sentence without getting winded. She knows she's here because she was assaulted, but she doesn't know anything. Talking to her will only upset her, and I won't allow that." The detective eyed him before turning to the doctor.

"I agree with Mr. Kingston." It was clear the detective wasn't happy with the refusal, but he didn't push the issue further.

"Have you found the son of a bitch who did this?" Marcus tried to remain calm, but his patience was wearing thin.

"Not yet. The fact that your wife went unconscious after the blow to her head was good—she didn't feel any of the subsequent hits. However, it's bad because that means she can't give us any information on her attacker. I spoke with Mr. Vanderlink a few minutes ago. He was able to give us a physical description, but admittedly it could represent over half the male population in the state of Colorado. We have nothing specific to go on. Is there anyone you can think of that would want to cause harm to Mrs. Kingston?"

Marcus had tensed slightly at the mention of Van's name, but he blocked it back out of his mind. While the latest conversation with Sarah allowed him to recognize he needed to address the situation, he still wasn't ready to talk or think about it.

"You think this was done on purpose by someone she knows? We were told it was a random attack."

"I'm just trying to exhaust all possible scenarios."

"My wife is the most caring person I know. No one would want to harm her intentionally."

"Good to know." The detective looked back down at his tablet. "The report said Mr. Vanderlink had accompanied Mrs. Kingston—" He paused for a second, remembering his boundaries. "—to an appointment. Is that accurate?"

"Yes." Marcus felt his chest tighten.

"And you were otherwise occupied at the time?"

"Yes. I was supposed to be home, but something came up."

"And that something was?"

"Irrelevant to this case." Marcus gave him a look that made it clear he should stop pushing.

I had promised her I'd always protect her. I have to live with the regret of failing to deliver on that promise. There's no point in going through the details of my failure. It won't help find the bastard.

An awkward silence hung over the room. Finally, the doctor rose to his feet.

"If that is all for now, gentlemen, I have rounds to make." Marcus and Smith stood as well.

"We should be good for now. I'll let you know if we make any progress. Call me if Mrs. Kingston should remember anything that would be helpful." The detective handed Marcus a card.

"Certainly." They stepped out into the hall and Marcus nearly ran into Van. It was the first time he had laid eyes on his friend since the attack. He was being pushed in a wheelchair by his mother. His arm was in a sling and his leg was in a cast from ankle to mid thigh. There was a bandage around his head and his face was covered with bruises and stitched-up cuts. Marcus felt the room wobble. A vice began to crush his chest. He had to look away, unable to face what had happened to his best friend.

"Marcus... uh, I'm sorry. Catherine said Brandon could visit Sarah for a moment."

Marcus turned and ran in the other direction. He just made it to the men's room before his sandwich made its reappearance.

It's dark and the street lights cast a haunting glow on the wet pavement. I'm walking then suddenly I'm in an alley. I turn again and am back on a deserted street. I see Sarah walking ahead of me. I call out to her, but she's too far away to hear. I walk faster. Suddenly someone grabs her and pulls her to the ground, kicking and hitting her repeatedly. I scream and run but the pavement's slick and I can't get traction. I'm trying so hard my legs hurt, my chest hurts from breathing so hard, and my throat hurts from screaming so loud.

Marcus heard a noise and woke instantly. The room was dark and he couldn't see. Panic gripped his chest, and he rushed quickly to Sarah's side. As he approached the bed, he stepped on something. It was the television remote. His panic was replaced by relief. She must have moved her arm enough to have knocked it out of the bed. He hoped it was a positive sign.

He put the remote on the table next to the bed and leaned down to kiss her forehead. When he pulled away, she stirred.

"You... sleeping on... that... pathetic cot?"

He looked at the clock. "You should be sleeping."

"Heard you... scream."

"I'm sorry. Bad dream."

"Talk to me."

"Honey, it's early. You should rest." When she was awake, he wanted her to rest. When she was asleep, he wanted her to wake up. It was a losing battle of conflicting needs.

"You promised... to make me... happy. I like... to hear... you talk."

"What do you want me to talk about?"

"Will you... tell me about... your dream?"

"No." She was quiet for a moment.

"Then... our first... Christmas."

"After we were married?"

"No... our first. When we... met. When we... danced."

"You kicked me."

"Accident."

"It still hurt. If I tell you, do you promise to go back to sleep?"

"Yes."

CHAPTER 10
December • 2012

Marcus stood on the porch of what used to be his home, debating if he should ring the bell or just let himself in. He was suddenly nervous that this was all a bad idea.

What if I walk in and find them in bed together?

The last time he stopped by to surprise the woman he loved it had crushed him. He took a deep breath, reminding himself that Sarah wasn't Rachel and that there was nothing going on between her and his father. Despite what Leanne said.

He turned away from the door and looked out over the mountains, trying to collect his courage. He had always loved his home growing up. The house was situated on a large space of land, surrounded by mountains. The land had been in their family for generations, and when he was about ten his parents had decided to build on it. The house was enormous, but it needed to be in order to compete with the magnitude of its surroundings. He took a deep breath and turned back toward the door, deciding to ring the bell first.

When no one answered after the second ring, he punched in the house code and let himself in.

"Dad? Sarah? Anyone home?" His questions were met with silence. He turned down the hall to the right of the foyer. If his father was home, he'd likely be in the office. The door was open and he walked inside, stopping abruptly at what he saw. Or rather, what he didn't see.

Normally, the room housed a large desk that sat in front of the built-in bookcases, a set of chairs that flanked a fireplace, and a large conference table that sat along the back wall. Of course the built-ins were still there, but they were bare of any items. The desk still held a laptop, printer, and a few stacks of files. The conference table was gone. He walked over to the now open space and looked out the back windows overlooking the mountains.

It wasn't unusual for his father to redecorate the house. He had done quite a lot of it after his mother died and Leanne left for college. However, the office had been redone only a couple of years ago—designed specifically for his father's needs. Confused, he left the office and went toward the kitchen.

He stopped short as he entered the great room. It was a huge room, designed for entertaining, that had a floor-to-ceiling glass wall in the back. At Christmas his father went all out in the decorating. He hired someone to adorn every inch of the home in festive garnish. In the early years it had been tasteful. Somewhere along the way it had become gaudy. Now the room was simply decorated with a large tree right in the center of the room. It was stunning, and it reminded him of his mother. Pushing past the lump in his throat he walked to the kitchen.

"Dad?"

Still there was no response. He turned and noticed the door to the basement was open and the lights were on. He descended the stairs and followed the sounds to the exercise room. His heart rate increased with each step, and he froze in the door when he saw Sarah running on the treadmill. Her back was to him and he could hear music coming from her ear buds, making her unaware he was there. She was wearing nothing but a sports bra and barely-there jogging shorts.

I was right. She is tall. Maybe about five-nine.

Being over six foot, it wasn't that unusual that the women he'd dated in the past were considerably shorter than him. Watching Sarah run he realized the benefits of a taller woman. Her legs looked like they extended for miles. He still thought she was too thin, but he could tell that with a little more weight her ass would look amazing. She picked up her towel from the arm of the treadmill and wiped the sweat from her face. Marcus had never before wished he were a towel.

I'd like to scoop her up, carry her to the shower, and help her wash—

Marcus shook his head and tried to clear his thoughts. He needed to stay focused. He turned his attention to her stride. He didn't run much, but he ran enough to recognize that she was an avid runner. She had a strong, steady pace. At one point he thought she was going to stop, but instead she quickened her pace. He leaned against the door frame and continued to watch. He was certain his heart rate would match hers if they tried to compare. Finally, she hopped off the treadmill and turned toward the door.

"Shit!" She clutched a hand to her chest and pulled out her ear buds. "What the hell are you doing here? You scared the shit out of me!" She let out a jagged breath.

"Obviously." He probably should have felt bad, but she was adorable when she was caught off guard.

"Seriously, what the hell are you doing here?"

"You need to work on your greeting skills. After last week, I had the impression you at least liked me enough to give me a friendly welcome when we met again."

"If you would have arrived on Monday, as *expected*, I would have given you a friendly greeting." He tried to resist, but he still swept his eyes over her body.

If she looks this good thin, she must be lethal when she's healthy.

Noticing his assessment, she used her hand towel to cover up her body. It was so absurd he almost laughed out loud. He pushed off the door frame and closed the distance between them, stopping just inches away from her. He gently took her arm and ran his thumb over the faint bruise that remained of her encounter with Mark at the gala.

If I ever see that son of a bitch again, I swear I'll finish the job I started.

He let go of her arm and leaned over to look at the display on the treadmill. Eight miles.

"Impressive. You run like that all the time?"

To his disappointment, she turned and put some distance between them by walking over to the entryway. "Not any more. My running kind of got out of control for a while, and I've been backing off. Marcus, I don't mean to sound rude, really, but you never answered my question. What are you doing here?"

He smiled in return and leaned against the treadmill. He enjoyed her feisty side.

"It's Christmas. Aren't families supposed to spend time together?"

"Most normal families, sure. However, the last thing I would call the Kingston family is normal."

"Are you always this suspicious?" Her only response was a raise of her eyebrows, and he laughed in return. "Fine, you win. Leanne and I agreed we had been too harsh at the gala and so we thought, since it is Christmas after all, we should spend more time getting to know each other. Leanne, Brad, and Ollie will be here tomorrow, and we're all staying until Christmas Eve." He noticed a flash of panic in her eyes.

"Does your dad know about this?"

"No, we thought we'd surprise him. Where is he anyway?"

"Have you ever known him to appreciate a surprise?"

"No." She didn't yet know him well enough to understand that upsetting his father was an added bonus to his agenda.

"So... your plan is to spend the weekend here to make amends with your dad over the way you all acted at the gala, and yet he doesn't know you're staying, which is something he won't appreciate. Am I the only one that recognizes this is a bad plan?"

He slowly shook his head. "I never said I was here to make amends with my father. Our plan is to get to know you better."

She buried her face in the corner of her towel while still trying to cover up as much skin as possible. Without realizing it, he closed the distance between them. When she raised her head, she jumped back about a foot. He noticed a mixture of desire and fear cross her features. It was encouraging.

"If you'll excuse me, I need to take a shower. Since you let yourself in, I assume you can make yourself at home." As she turned to leave he intended to follow, but he looked down the hall on instinct. He gently grabbed her hand.

The door to the dance studio stood open. He hadn't set foot in the room since a few days after his mother had died. He'd gone in there to mourn and ended up destroying almost everything. He was pulled from the painful memories when Sarah squeezed his hand.

"Will you do something with me?" His words were soft, hesitant. She nodded in agreement, and he pulled her with him as he walked in the direction of the studio.

He stood in the doorway for a few seconds, looking into the darkness of the room. Good and bad memories jockeyed for position, causing tears to sting the back of his eyes. He hesitantly flipped on the light. He had known his father remodeled the room, but it was still unexpected. Relief washed through him when he saw the room as it used to be, rather than still wearing the damage he'd inflicted in the height of his pain. He gripped Sarah's hand tighter and walked slowly inside to the middle of the dance floor. He sat down and patted the space next to him, wanting her close. He could feel the void when she sat across from him instead. They sat quietly for a few minutes while he tried to find his voice.

He was relieved that he was able to relax once the words started to flow. He opened up to Sarah and was pleased with each question she asked in return. Although he was pumped to have the opportunity to spend time alone with her, especially when she was wearing next to nothing, he did feel bad for dropping in unannounced. He allowed himself to dismiss the guilt, deciding instead to be grateful for the opportunity to be with her.

He continued to be surprised by the things she said. She had a unique ability to look at situations in a way he'd never before considered. His confidence in his plan for them to get to know each other better grew with each spoken word, until she'd said his name.

Nick.

The way it rolled off her tongue, with such love and longing, left no question in his mind that Nick had been her husband. The conversation had taken her out of the present with him and into the past with Nick. He tried to fight the knot of jealousy growing in the pit of his stomach.

He watched as she absentmindedly played with her music player. It hurt to hear her talk about Nick, but he had to find a way to get past it. Nick may not be a physical presence in her life, but he was still very much a part of who she was. Still a part of her heart. He couldn't take that away—he didn't want to. It would change who she was and that wasn't acceptable.

For distraction, he snatched her music player from her hands. "Let's see what kind of music you have on this thing." He brought the player to life and scrolled through her music.

"Hey, don't you know looking at someone's playlist is equivalent to reading their diary?" She tried to snatch it out of his hands but he pulled away.

"There once was a time when everyone displayed their music on CD towers for all to admire. It was a point of pride to show people your music collection."

"Yes, but you still had the option to put the more embarrassing CDs in the closet for no one to see. I can't hide anything on my playlist."

"It doesn't look like you have anything here to be ashamed of. It's a pretty admirable collection, actually. Very eclectic." He continued to scroll, and then he broke out into a hearty laugh. "Okay, I spoke too soon. You should be ashamed of this one. It can't even be called music." He showed her the offending song and she smiled.

"Admit it, when you hear that particular song it makes you want to move. I like listening to it when I run, it keeps me motivated."

"Only because it makes you want to outrun the sound of it."

His criticism came out as a mumble while he continued to scroll through her playlist. His heart stopped for two full beats when he came across a certain song. It wasn't mainstream, so seeing it in her playlist wasn't expected. It was a song he'd envisioned dancing to from the moment he first heard it. It was about a man looking for the woman he knew he already loved. He took it as a sign that she owned the song as well—not that he needed one, but it was nice to have just the same. He quickly recovered before he would have to explain himself and found another song by the same artist.

"Now this is a song that makes you want to move."

He hopped up and walked over to plug the player into the speaker. He was pleased to see her tapping out the quick beat with her foot. It was a good song to have a little swing dancing fun. He reached down and pulled up on her hands. She tried to protest, but he was too quick.

The first requirement of dancing is to remove all obstacles.

To Sarah's obvious dismay, he flung her towel across the room. Before she could protest any further, he twirled her out and back in. She stumbled over his feet, trying her best to keep up with him. Pain shot up his shin when she accidentally kicked him, and he instinctively let go to rub the offending spot. However, he quickly pushed past the pain when she tried to use it as an escape. He pulled her back in, vowing to never let go again. Happy to be dancing, but mostly happy to be holding her, he let go of all his inhibitions. To his surprise, and Sarah's amusement, he started singing. He knew he wasn't a good singer and usually didn't do it in front of anyone. But this was Sarah. He wanted to share every part of himself with her.

Near the end of the song he pulled her in close, cheek to cheek, and suddenly his humor was replaced with desire. He felt her knees weaken and was encouraged by her reaction. He was having a difficult time controlling his own reaction. His heart was racing, and he was finding it difficult to breathe. Mostly, he was finding it difficult to fight the urge to kiss her. The music ended, but he continued to hold her to his chest, not able to let go.

"Ahem." Sarah jumped at the sound of his father's voice coming from the doorway. He wanted to curse out loud. She turned and tried to step away, but Marcus planted his arm around her waist and held her tightly. He glared at his father and he returned the sentiment. Even though his father had only uttered a sound, Marcus could hear his disapproval.

"Elijah, you're back." Sarah tried to step away again, but Marcus refused to let her go. He needed her. He needed to touch her. He felt that as long as he was connected to her he could remain civil.

"What the hell are you doing here?" Marcus let out an involuntary laugh at his father's question. "What's so funny?"

"Those are pretty much the exact words Sarah used to greet me."

"Sarah, if you don't mind I'd like a word alone with my son." Marcus didn't like that plan. He wanted her there, with him. Always. He felt her pull on his arm, and he finally looked at her. It was obvious she was uncomfortable and wanted to go. Reluctantly he let her. He watched as she shared some sort of silent communication with his father before walking to the door.

"I'm going to go grab that shower. You boys play nice..."

Both men were quiet for several seconds, content with conveying all their disapproval for the other through their heated glare. Marcus crossed his arms, refusing to be the one to speak first.

"Sarah's off limits to you."

"You already told me that, but obviously I don't agree." Confusion flashed across his father's face, causing a large portion of Marcus' rage to transform into perplexity. Adding to the confusion, Marcus noticed a distinct limp when his father took a few steps forward. Something wasn't right.

"I don't care if you agree or not. Stay away. I'll not have her hurt by you!"

"What makes you think I'm going to hurt her?" Marcus was amazed at how rapidly his anger returned.

"That's what you do right? Use your looks and charm to manipulate women, take what you want, and then move on."

"I'm sorry, but that sounds a lot like you. It's not like you've been a monk since Mom died—I know you've slept with a few women since then. The only difference is that I take them out in public and attempt to have an actual relationship! Yeah, I've dated a lot of women. I'm almost forty; it's not a real shocker. But I've known all along it would stop the moment I found her." His father visibly ruffled.

"Sarah's not the one for you!"

"Why, because you have an interest in being with her? Is that why I can't get close to her? Or is it because you have so little respect for me you think that I can't possibly love her?"

"I can't let you hurt her!" Marcus stared at his father in shock. He really believed Marcus was incapable of love. Furious beyond control, he strode past his father and out the door before he said something he'd regret for the rest of his life.

Marcus sat in the family room by the fireplace waiting for Sarah to return from her shower. The encounter with his father left him both angry and puzzled. His father had been acting strange. He didn't seem to remember their recent conversation after the gala, and he was being more of an ass than usual.

He knew his father thought he used women. It's probably because in the beginning, after his mother died, he had. He wasn't proud of that time in his life. But he had been hurting and lashed out in unexpected ways. He had been desperate to find 'the one' and dropped a woman quickly if she didn't turn out to be her. It didn't stop him from taking what they were willing to offer—as long as it didn't last for very long. He had stopped his womanizing ways about ten years ago, but his father held onto his original assessment. He had always expressed his disapproval of Marcus' lifestyle, but had never vocalized it so directly before.

He heard Sarah walking through the great room and he quickly picked up the newspaper. He didn't want her to know he'd been waiting. He could feel her watching him and he savored the feeling, wanting it to last. It meant she had at least a little bit of interest in him. Finally, he put down the newspaper—which he had just realized was upside-down—unable to resist looking at her for another second.

She was breathtaking. It was the first time he'd seen her with her hair down, flowing around her shoulders. It was still slightly damp from her shower and left little water marks on the scarf she wore around her neck. She didn't have any make-up on, and he was awed by her natural beauty. At the gala he'd noticed she had a hint of green in her eyes, but he couldn't see it now. She turned away from him and walked to the coffee maker. After she finished making her coffee, she leaned on the counter separating the kitchen from the family room.

"You can sit next to me. I promise to behave." He couldn't deny the disappointment he felt when she didn't budge.

She pursed her lips and looked down at her coffee. "It's probably no surprise, but Elijah has asked me to request that you leave." He laughed at her directness.

"No, it's not a surprise. I'm sure it's equally unsurprising that I'm not leaving."

"No, I know you well enough by now to know there's nothing I could do or say to make you leave." He felt his stomach do a flip at her comment and smiled. "That wasn't meant to be a compliment."

He shook his head. "I didn't think it was."

"Then why do you look so pleased?"

"I like the idea that you know me so well after such a short period of time."

She looked like she was about to respond, but a phone alarm sounded. She looked irritated at the interruption and turned to the refrigerator. She pulled out food and then retrieved what looked like a food journal before sitting on one of the counter stools. Uncontrollable fear and anger flashed through him, and he rounded the counter to face her. "What the hell is that?"

"I beg your pardon?"

"That." He pointed to her journal. "Is that a food journal?"

"I'm not sure how that's any of your concern."

"Damn it, Sarah, answer the question. Is that a food journal?"

"Yes, it's a food journal. What's the big deal?"

"What's the big deal? The big deal is you have no business trying to lose weight!" The fear surging through him kept him from thinking rationally. He was acting like she already knew he was in love with her—that he had every right to express his concern and demand she stop unhealthy behaviors.

"What makes you think I'm trying to lose weight? And even if I were, again—how is it any of your concern?"

"Don't be ridiculous, of course it's my concern. Let me see that." He reached for her journal but she pulled it away from him. "Sarah, let me see it."

"No."

She looked angry and confused. He knew he should explain—tell her that he already lost someone he loved to an eating disorder and would do anything to keep her from the same fate. But he was too stricken to find the words. Suddenly clarity entered her eyes and her anger disappeared. She looked at him like she understood him completely.

"Marcus, I'm sorry, but my journal is private. But I will tell you I'm not trying to lose weight; I'm trying to gain it. Based on your reaction I assume you've noticed I'm... somewhat underweight. When we were downstairs, I mentioned my running had gotten out of control after the accident. In addition, I sort of forgot to eat most of the time. I've gained weight since being here, but I still have a long way to go. Elijah insisted I meet with a nutritionist and that's why I'm journaling my food and workouts. I have to review it with her a few times a week."

Embarrassment instantly replaced his fear. He hadn't even considered the possibility she was trying to gain weight. He collected his thoughts to offer her an explanation, but she spared him by speaking again.

"I won't share my journal, but I'll share my food."

He gave her a half smile, still embarrassed by his reaction, and scooped a cracker through the hummus. While eating, he reflected back on her words more clearly.

She does understand me. She somehow knew I was reacting to the pain of losing my mother. She didn't force me to explain. She didn't run away, hurt and crying, demanding that I back off. Instead, she included me. Sure, we're just eating a snack, but based on what she said this is an important priority in her life. She chose to open up to me, rather than tell me to go to hell.

The realization was powerful.

Marcus sat on the bed and looked around the room. It had been his bedroom at one point, but it no longer resembled anything from his childhood. He closed his eyes and thought about the last time he had slept in the room. It was just after his mother's funeral. He knew it was going to be a difficult night. Being in the house reminded him so much of his mother. Especially after dancing in the studio with Sarah earlier that morning.

Shit, Sarah.

He looked at the clock and realized he'd been sitting in the room, reminiscing about his mother, for over an hour. After they had cleaned up from Sarah's morning snack, Marcus decided to try to get some answers. He'd been relieved that she offered an unprompted explanation for the time when Leanne had found her in his father's bed. It had been innocent—a moment of uncontrollable sadness over her son Danny. While he believed her and it reassured him that there was nothing romantic going on, he was still bothered by something. That encounter, along with his other observations, made it clear that she and his father had a routine. She wasn't just staying at his house— they lived together. They blended their activities and functioned as a unit. He didn't like it one bit.

The other thing that had bothered him was that he knew she had lied in response to his question about why his father was limping. He wasn't so much bothered by the lie itself, but why she even felt she needed to lie.

Yet after all of that, he was still able to get her to relax and engage in some flirty banter. He'd been feeling confident in his progress of getting her to trust him. He'd even made her smile. And then his father interrupted, again. This time to tell Sarah she had a phone call—from some Travis guy who, in a fraction of a second, had made her produce the most genuine smile he'd seen since he met her.

Marcus already didn't like him.

Sarah had left Marcus alone with his father and it only resulted in added frustration and confusion. Giving up, he had left his father in the kitchen to collect his bags from the car.

Deciding he'd wasted enough time, he exited his room and looked down the hall toward his father's bedroom. On his way up the stairs, he'd noticed that Sarah occupied the room adjacent to his father. It had struck him as odd.

He wandered down the hall on impulse. His father's door was closed, but the door to Sarah's room was open. He resisted the urge to go in, but he stuck his head in and peeked around. The room was huge, and he hoped that was the reason for her occupying that space rather than wanting to be close to his father. The room looked the way his parents' bedroom looked before his father remodeled, and it was very much a representation of his mother.

Not wanting to get sucked back into the past, he turned and descended the stairs. Passing through the foyer, he hesitated at the hall that led to his father's office. The door was open, but he couldn't hear anything. Not in the mood to see his father again, he kept walking to the kitchen. He stumbled over his steps when he saw Sarah sitting by the fireplace in the family room. It looked like she was writing in a journal, her free hand playing with the end of her scarf. The sun was shining through the windows and it cast a soft glow over her. He could have been content to stay in that moment forever.

The spell was broken when she suddenly looked up at him. Unable to hide the fact that he'd been caught watching her, he just smiled and shrugged his shoulder. Embarrassment quickly spread over her face, and she looked back down at her journal before closing it and setting it aside. He walked into the room and sat adjacent to her.

"Another food journal?" He nodded in the direction of the notebook she had just set down.

"No, this one's... private. It's how I talk to Nick and Danny."

They sat there for a few seconds, an uneasy silence surrounding them. He wasn't sure what to do. He'd interrupted her in a private moment. He didn't want to leave, but it was possible she would resent having to spend time with him when she wanted to write in her journal. He decided it would be equally awkward for him to just up and leave, so he opted for a simple question and would let her lead the direction from there.

"Where's my father?"

"He went up to his room for a while."

"He's not going to come out is he?"

She furrowed her brow in frustration. "I don't think so." He could tell she was contemplating asking him a question. He hoped she would, because if she didn't then he would take it as a cue that she wanted to be alone.

"You know you can ask me anything." She looked at him sharply, as if surprised that he knew what she was thinking.

"I—I was just wondering what happened between you two."

Marcus took in a deep breath. He hadn't intended on opening up to her so soon. He knew that if he wanted a life with her he would need to tell her everything at some point, but he'd hoped to at least take her on a date first. There were parts of his life he wasn't proud of, and he was concerned she wouldn't want anything to do with him once she knew the details.

Although, I guess I can't expect her to open up to me if I don't open up to her.

"First, can I ask you what you do know?" It would help him to understand if he needed to do any damage control from anything his father might have told her.

She shifted uncomfortably in her seat. "He mentioned drinking and girls. But no details."

He ran a hand through his hair, trying to decide where to start.

"My father and I have never really been close. I don't really know why, but I suspect it has something to do with the fact that I was more interested in dancing than business. I think he had aspirations for me to take over the family business rather than Leanne. I remember moments from my childhood when it seemed he was trying to connect, but they were fleeting. And then at some point, I'm not really sure how old I was, he just stopped trying. There was this... awkwardness that existed between us and only seemed to grow over time. When my mother died, I felt like I had lost everything. My father had checked out completely, and, well, you've met Leanne— she doesn't have a very welcoming personality. So I left."

Sarah turned slightly in her chair, pulling her feet up and hugging her knees to her chest. "Where'd you go?"

"For a while I just stayed at a friend's house."

"Was he the one who got you into trouble?"

If she had met Van he was sure she would never believe what he was about to say.

"No, actually he was the one who saved me. Besides my mom, he was the only person in my life who truly supported me. I should have been able to turn to my father during that time. That's what parents do, right—support their children? But we never had that kind of relationship."

He paused, feeling the flutter of hurt that tried to surface. He'd long ago given up on the idea of having any sort of connection with his father. But sometimes the hope tried to resurface, reminding him just how much he longed for it to be different. He pushed the hurt aside and continued.

"Realizing there was nothing for me at home, I left and I turned to my friend. He liked to party and I did a lot of it with him. I sometimes wonder if I would have taken a less destructive path if I had stayed at home. Anyway, despite the fact that my friend partied a lot, he knew when to cut if off. I wasn't so smart about it. Even though my actions were destructive, they helped me forget the pain. My friend didn't like the direction I was headed, but he knew I was hurting so he let me work it out for a while. Luckily, he brought me crashing to my senses before it was too late."

"What all did you do?"

He studied her for a moment, heart beating rapidly. He didn't want to tell her anything that would give her a reason to walk away before she even took a single step with him toward the future. "I don't usually talk about this stuff on a first date."

She noticeably tensed at his comment. "This isn't—"

"Sorry, that's not what I meant. I know this isn't a date. For starters, if this were a date you wouldn't be sitting so far away from me. My point was that I don't talk about this on first dates, so I'm not sure if I should talk about it on a not-date."

She relaxed and he was relieved to have recovered from his nearly disastrous slip. "Well, that's where you're wrong. On a date there's all this pressure to impress the other person. On a not-date impressions don't matter. So talk away."

If you only knew how important it was for me to make a positive impression right now.

He ran a hand through his hair again and scratched the back of his neck. It was going to come out sooner or later.

I guess this will help me understand just how hard I'll have to work at winning her over. If she's appalled by my past, then I know I'll have some serious work ahead of me.

"It started with drinking. The night I moved out, my friend was throwing a party. I didn't drink much before that—it's a bit counterproductive to trying to be a good dancer. As a result, my tolerance was low and it didn't take much to put me over the limit. It wasn't that I liked how drinking made me feel—I liked how it made me *not* feel. I got to a point where I was drunk most of the time, so I didn't think twice when I started sleeping with random women. That then led to the fighting—most boyfriends don't like it when someone sleeps with their girlfriend."

His heart was beating so fast it almost hurt. He watched her for any sort of reaction. She just sat, studying him right back.

"Most boyfriends? Does that imply there were some who actually supported you sleeping with their girlfriend?"

He wasn't sure what emotion he felt more, relief or astonishment. "Out of all that, that's what you want clarity on?"

She shrugged her shoulders and gave him a half smile. "I know what it's like to resort to a bad vice to overcome pain. That's what my running was all about. Just like drinking and... *women*... it's not a big deal if kept under control, but too much can destroy you. So I can understand all of that. But I've never met a man who was okay with some guy sleeping with his girlfriend. I'm intrigued."

"Wow. Okay. That's not the response I expected, but I'll run with it. Yes, there were some boyfriends who didn't mind my sleeping with their girlfriends. Usually it was because they no longer wanted to be in a relationship with them, and I gave them the excuse to cut it off. Then there were the few who wanted to take it to a disturbingly different level." Sarah's mouth dropped open in shock.

"Did you—"

"No. Never. Not my thing."

He watched as her features transitioned from shock to contemplation. He waited, deciding he should let her determine the course for their conversation after the bomb he'd just dropped.

"So how did your friend save you?"

"After a year of my self-destructive crap, he'd had enough. He put me through his personal version of a rehab boot camp. It was hell, but I came out sober and with a new intent to do something with my life. I enrolled in school and started my journey to being a vet a few months later. I'd like to say that I stopped with the women, but, well, I don't want to lie to you. I was, however, much more selective—no more women who were already in relationships and it didn't happen as often."

She shifted in her chair again, and he could tell she was becoming uncomfortable hearing about his promiscuous lifestyle. Her casual approach to asking questions had held off his fear that she would be repulsed by what he'd shared. He suddenly wasn't so sure.

"I suppose I was lucky that I never got into drugs, and I was always sober enough to practice safe sex. I guess that sounds hard to believe—I mean how would I know if I were too drunk to remember? Those thoughts scared me for a while; it was one of the strategies my friend used to sober me up. I used to get tested regularly to make sure I didn't contract anything. I finally stopped it all about ten years ago, and I only became sexually involved with someone if we were in a committed relationship."

He stopped himself, suddenly realizing the words that were escaping uncontrolled from his mouth. He stood and walked to look out the windows at the back of the room.

"I can't believe I just told you all that shit. You're probably thinking that I'm a disgusting jackass." There was a short pause before he heard her speak. Not knowing what she would say, he didn't turn around.

"Marcus, I'm not here to judge you. One of the things I've learned over the last couple years is that there's no handbook for how you're supposed to handle grief. I mean, sure, there are books out there but it's not like you study ahead of time. When you find yourself in a situation where you really need a step-by-step guide to overcoming grief... I don't know. I guess usually it comes after some of the damage has already been done. I'm not going to judge you for something I can't understand."

Somewhere in the middle of her response he had turned around to face her. His determination to make her fall in love with him just tipped the scales. He was fighting hard against the urge to walk over, take her in his arms, and kiss her senseless. He remained standing across the room, fearful he wouldn't be able to control his actions if he got any closer.

"But you do understand. I'd go so far as to say your loss was greater than mine. You didn't drink and sleep around. Did you?"

"No, I didn't. The exact opposite, actually. I cut myself off from almost everyone. While I might understand your pain, I can't possibly understand what your loss meant to *you*. And you can't compare one loss to another. Loss is loss and it causes pain. How the pain transforms inside of a person is the difference, and I can't judge that."

He stood, watching her and processing her words. Somehow she'd said the very thing he needed to hear. He lived a life full of judgment. He'd let it restrict his future—choosing to stay local so he could take business classes while dancing rather than move away to attend one of the premier schools for performing arts. He'd encountered so much judgment from his father that he expected it from everyone else.

"Why are you looking at me like that?" He watched her cheeks pink as she asked the question.

"I guess I'm just trying to figure out if you're real."

I pray to God you are, because if you're not I don't know how I could ever survive without you. And after our conversations today, if I can keep you in my life, I promise to never underestimate you again.

She looked away, uncomfortable at his comment. In their silence, he heard the clock in the foyer chime the hour. It was time to lighten the mood.

"Are you hungry? We could go and grab something to eat from this restaurant in town." She looked back at him quickly.

Shit. She probably thinks I just asked her out on a date. While that's what I'm going for, this is not how I wanted to ask her.

"Remember, this is a not-date, so no pressure. We could always find something here at the house. I just wasn't sure what all you had." She relaxed and he was once again relieved to have escaped near disaster.

"I should probably stick around the house, in case Elijah needs anything taken care of before more people show up tomorrow. I'll see what we have." He watched her hurry into the kitchen and smiled at the thought that passed through his mind.

This is the best not-date I've ever had.

CHAPTER 11

Marcus leaned over and looked at Sarah's sleeping face. He was momentarily shocked when her eyes fluttered open.

"You stopped... talking."

"You stopped sleeping."

"I'll sleep after."

"Sarah, you need rest."

"I need... to hear you... talk."

"Why? You haven't lost your memory. Why do you keep asking me to talk to you about this stuff?" He couldn't tell her it felt like she was asking him to help with her 'life flashing before your eyes' moment people talk about before they die. It was as if she wanted him to provide the images because she was too weak to think of them herself. He didn't want to do it—didn't want to give her any reason to feel like she could let go when they caught up to the present day.

She hesitated and a tear escaped down her cheek.

"Because I need... to hear... about us... to hear... you talk. It's my... happiness." He finally broke and let his tears fall. She raised her hand about an inch and he took it. "My hand... your cheek. Want to... feel you." He did as she asked and watched her close her eyes in response.

"I'm so sorry, Sarah. It's my fault you're here. It's all my fault—"

"No."

"Those things I said before I left. I was angry, and I yelled at you. I wasn't there for you." He felt her thumb wipe at the tears falling down his cheek.

"I love you. People... fight. It's normal. But it's not... your fault."

He took a deep, steadying breath. He stared into her eyes and tried to find the green flecks he loved so much. They were too dull to shine through. When he spoke again it was just a whisper.

"You deserve more than I'm giving you."

She held his gaze and kept her hand to his cheek. "I deserve... to be with... the man... I love. That's you. Flaws and all."

"I'm trying, Sarah. I really am. I just can't—" A lump lodged in his throat, cutting off the rest of his words.

"You did this... once before. You told me. You let... yourself... doubt."

He looked at her in awe. She was fighting to stay alive, but her request confirmed she was strategizing at the same time. He knew he never should have told her about what he had gone through during their month of no contact after his father died. He placed his hand over hers and brought her palm to his lips before dropping their joined hands to the bed.

"I thought we were talking about happy memories. That one's not so pleasant."

"Tell me... anyway. Please."

CHAPTER 12
February • 2013

Marcus waited for the bartender to look his way. He wasn't in the mood to be out, but Van had insisted. As usual Van was running late, and Marcus decided to give him the duration of one beer to show up before he left. However the bartender was ignoring him, making his plan feel like a futile effort. After what felt like an eternity, he was finally able to order his drink. Just as he picked up the bottle, he felt a set of hands grab his shoulders.

"Kingston! Sorry I'm late. Meeting ran over, and then Mack called. He decided to join us, but I had to pick him up." Van turned his attention to the bartender who had magically reappeared. "Jake, right? How's it going tonight—are the ladies treating you well?"

The corner of the bartender's mouth lifted in a slight smile. "It's been a bit of a slow night. But now that you're here, I'm sure things will take a turn for the better. The usual?"

"What else? One for my friend Mack too, if you don't mind."

Marcus watched the exchange in silent awe. When the bartender walked out of earshot he nudged Van.

"What's up with that? I was ignored for over fifteen minutes, yet he's practically pouring your drink as you walk in the door. Do you come here on the off hours just to sweeten up the staff or something?"

"Nah, people just love me."

Jake returned with the drinks, exchanged a few more words with Van, and walked away. Mack swore softly under his breath and Marcus looked over to find him staring at his phone.

"Something wrong?"

"One night. That's all I asked for. I haven't even had a chance to take one fucking sip of my drink." Mack mumbled a few more unsavory words before walking away. Marcus turned to Van for explanation.

"The baby's been fussy. See, this is why I don't do relationships."

"Because relationships equate to fussy babies?"

"No, they equate to women who tell you one thing and then demand another. Mack was promised a night out, but what's the point if she's calling him every time the baby spews something out of one end or the other? My way is better."

"Aren't you tired of chasing women around all the time?"

"No. Not tonight. I should have made you agree to not talking about your 'one and only' during this month of solitude. Don't look so pathetically dejected. It hasn't even been a full week!"

"Sorry, I miss her. I didn't want her to go at all, and now I can't even talk to her. What if she hooks up with that Travis guy?"

"I thought you said she promised not to talk to him either."

"She did, but it's not like she can stop him from stopping by her house or something. He has the advantage of proximity. I'm in the 'out of sight, out of mind' category."

"If she can forget you that quickly, she's not worth it."

Marcus shrugged his shoulder and took a pull on his beer. Deep down he knew she wouldn't forget about him, but doubt liked to fester in his mind.

How the hell am I going to survive the next twenty-four days? My father just died, on his birthday no less. I found out I might have a fatal genetic disease. And Sarah left with no assurances she's coming back. It's been a great start to the year.

"Alright, that's enough moping. The point of tonight was to have some fun. Let's grab a table." Van led him to a table where they sat and surveyed the crowd. The music was in full swing and people were happily on their way to an intoxicated state. A woman walked by that reminded him of Sarah. He stared in the direction she walked long after she was out of sight.

"You're thinking about her again, aren't you?"

Marcus glanced at Van. "It's kind of hard not to."

Van shook his head in frustration and took a drink. "Well, at least she's hot. For that reason alone, I should let you think about her all you want. I mean, I can only imagine what—"

"Van. You are forbidden from putting Sarah into any of your perverse thoughts."

"Too late, man. Sorry. However, from now on I'll refrain from mentioning it out loud. I have a hard enough time getting chicks with this nose—I don't need to double that effort as a result of you busting it." Marcus shook his head and couldn't help but smile at Van's rubbing. "Speaking of you bashing noses, did your sister fire the asshole who harassed Sarah at the gala?"

"Yeah, he's gone. He'd better hope I never run into him though."

Their conversation was interrupted by Mack as he sat down next to Marcus. He slapped a twenty down in the center of the table. "My bet's fifteen minutes."

"Five." Van pulled out a ten and tossed it on top of the other bill.

"The bet's twenty, not ten."

"You have an unfair advantage since you're the one that talked to her and know the situation. We're betting blind."

"Eight." Marcus threw in his ten.

"Hello, boys."

"Ladies, you made it."

Marcus closed his eyes and sighed. He should have known Van had more planned than just meeting up for a drink or two. He raised his beer in greeting to Heather and her friends. He watched as Heather slid gracefully into Van's lap and whispered something in his ear. Van whispered something back, ran his hand up her leg, and squeezed her hip before sliding out from under her. He casually pushed her chair closer to Marcus before grabbing another chair from the vacant table behind him. Heather's friends shared the remaining chair, giggling as they sipped their drinks.

Marcus tuned out the conversation around the table as his thoughts returned to Sarah. He jumped slightly at the feel of Heather's hand on his thigh.

"I heard about your father. I'm so sorry, Marcus."

He studied her face for a moment and realized that she was being genuine. "Thank you, Heather."

"It just seemed so sudden. I mean, I had just seen him at the gala and he looked so healthy. What happened?"

They had chosen to keep the specifics of his father's condition quiet. His father had been well known in the area, and he and Leanne didn't feel like dealing with any more drama than needed. CJD was still somewhat of an enigma to most people.

"I'd rather not talk about it, if you don't mind." Marcus shifted, Heather's hand still on his thigh. It almost seemed as if she had anticipated his movement, enabling her to keep her hand anchored to the same spot.

"Right, of course. How insensitive of me."

Marcus shifted again and she finally pulled her hand away, nails scraping the fabric of his jeans in the process.

"So, I assume his girlfriend is pretty shaken up about it."

"Sarah's not his girlfriend. In fact, I've asked her to move out here." He probably shouldn't have told her. It wasn't like Sarah had agreed to his request. There was still a chance she'd tell him to take a hike, but he preferred to be optimistic. And given Heather's continued attention—which was disturbing now that she'd slept with Van—he felt the best approach was a direct one.

"Like, to live with you?"

"Eventually. My father left her the house, so she'll have her own place to stay initially. But my intentions would be to marry her someday."

He watched her mouth drop open in shock. "But... you've only known her, like, a month."

He just shrugged his shoulder and took another drink of his beer.

"Oh my God! You're serious!" Her voice sounded dangerously close to a high-pitched squeal. She bent over laughing and waved at her friends. "Did you just hear that?"

Luckily she was interrupted by Mack grabbing the money in the center of the table and slamming it down in front of Marcus. "Nine fucking minutes. I'm going to have to start doing shots just so I can get a buzz in between her calls." He answered his phone as he rose from his seat and walked away.

Heather was still laughing and Marcus shot Van a silent plea for help. He received a coy smile in return.

Fine. If he's not willing to help me out, I'll make him.

"So, Van, did anything exciting happen at the office this week?" As anticipated, his question turned everyone's attention to Van. He could always count on the antics Van encountered at work to captivate an audience. Given the nature of his work he couldn't divulge many details, but he could always tell enough to entertain. Mack returned to the table a few minutes into Van's second story.

With everyone's focus fully diverted, Marcus let his mind wander once again to Sarah. He thought of their good-bye at the airport and a tingling sensation surged through his body. He understood why she needed the month of solitude, but it didn't mean he liked it. With his father dying, they didn't get to spend a lot of quality time alone. Even when they had been physically alone, the cloud of his father's illness hung over them. He'd tried to ensure she knew how he felt before she left, but nothing was for certain.

"Yo, Kingston. Wake up." Van snapped his fingers in his direction. "Heather, take his lame ass out on the dance floor."

Heather started to rise, but Marcus shook his head. "No thanks. I don't feel like dancing."

Heather sat back down in a huff. "I'll bet if *she* were here you'd dance."

"Seeing as I just told you that I wanted to marry her someday, yes I'd be dancing with Sarah if she were here. Besides, I thought you were dancing with Van these days."

Her cheeks turned pink as she picked up her glass and adjusted so she was facing away from him. He didn't mean for it to come out as critical as it did. But he felt she had no business pouting over another woman in his life, especially with Van sitting next to her. Even if Van parked her in the casual sex category, it wasn't right.

He knew his friends were just trying to help him blow off steam after all that had recently happened in his life, but their plan wasn't working as intended. Needing an escape, he pushed his chair away from the table and stood.

"I'm going to get another round."

He walked to the bar and waited another ten minutes until Jake finally stood silently before him. Marcus gave him the drink orders and surveyed the crowd while waiting. He felt oddly out of place. His heart was just too heavy to have any fun. He'd felt this before—after his mother had died. He recognized it as a bad sign.

If I stay here too long I'm likely to get wasted. It would be too easy to fall back into that old pattern—lose a parent, lose the one I love, drown it all at the bottom of a bottle. I don't handle it well when I lose everything all at once.

He'd promised himself he wouldn't do it again. Getting drunk, occasionally and responsibly, during a fun night out was fine. Getting blasted to forget the pain was not. It lead to further destruction and that was no longer acceptable.

He heard Jake set the tray of drinks down on the bar behind him. He looked at his group of friends one last time before turning to face Jake. He pulled out the wad of cash he'd just won, along with another twenty, and handed it over.

"Can you have someone take this to that table over there?" He pointed in the direction of his friends. Jake nodded and then looked at the money Marcus gave him. He looked back up in shock.

"You gave me too much, man."

"Keep it. You'll likely earn it by the end of the night with that crew." He nodded in the direction of his friends. The corner of Jake's mouth twitched in the form of a smile.

"Thanks." He pocketed the money and walked off.

Marcus turned toward the exit and texted Van, explaining why he needed to leave. A text was an impersonal way to bail, but it would keep Van from trying to convince him to stay.

"Marcus, do you want this?" Leanne held out a framed photo of him with his father. He had been about fifteen when the picture was taken. He hadn't seen it since his mother died.

"Where'd you find it?"

"In the nightstand by his bed." Marcus took the photo and looked at it, trying to feel something. It should encourage him that his father had kept a photo of the two of them near his bed. However, all his mind could focus on was the fact that it was inside the nightstand rather than on it.

He haphazardly placed the photo with his other items. His nearly empty box looked pathetic next to Leanne's pile of 'necessary' items. As if reading his thoughts, she peered inside.

"Why aren't you taking more? Sarah said we could take anything we wanted."

Marcus hadn't been ready to go through the house, but Leanne insisted. She had other things she needed to focus on—a business to run, a family to raise, a father to mourn. Unchecked items on her to-do list just got in the way.

"I guess I don't feel the need to keep a bunch of things. I have everything I need. Besides, there's still a chance I'll live here again someday." Optimism was the only way he was surviving the separation from Sarah. He still had sixteen more days to go. He heard Leanne let out a disappointed sigh.

"Marcus. Please tell me you're not still serious about pursuing a relationship with Sarah."

Out of frustration, Marcus nudged the box in front of him a little too hard and it almost went crashing to the floor.

"Leanne, I get that you don't like her. I think your reasons are unfounded, but I get it. I just don't want to hear about it any more. I plan to have Sarah in my life, assuming she accepts me, and that's that. I'm not going to stand by and let you continue to berate her."

"I admit I was wrong about her intentions toward Dad. But she's still a thirty-five year old woman who's suffered significant loss. That doesn't make for a solid relationship."

"So, what, she doesn't deserve a second chance at happiness because the road ahead is unclear and a little messy? News flash, Leanne, my future isn't paved with rainbows either."

"That's exactly my point! Yes she should have a second chance at happiness. But what are you going to be able to give her?"

"Oh, so it's me that doesn't deserve the chance at happiness? Because of CJD?"

"You refuse to get tested, Marcus. What future do you see? She comes here, you get married, and then in a few years she has to nurse you through CJD just like she had to do for Dad? Don't you at least owe it to her to get tested so she knows what she's getting into?"

"She said she didn't need to know. That she would make her decision based on the fact that I could have it. That's enough for me."

"And what if she changes her mind? What if in this month off she decides it's too much and needs to know?"

"Then I'll deal with that when the time comes."

She relaxed her stance and her eyes softened. "Won't you at least see the counselor I've been going to? She's very helpful."

"I don't need to see a genetic counselor if I'm not planning to get tested."

"She could still help."

He ran his hand over his face in frustration. "I don't want to talk about this right now."

"Why is it you always want to avoid discussing difficult topics?"

"I don't avoid difficult topics, just the ones I don't want to deal with." He knew it was a lame response and only proved Leanne's point, but sometimes even grown men resort to childish behaviors when provoked by a sibling. Needing space, he turned and walked out the patio doors. It was freezing out, especially without his jacket, but he needed to be alone. He walked to the edge of the patio and looked out over the mountains. The day was gray and gloomy to match his mood.

The truth of it was that he wasn't comfortable talking about his feelings. His mother was the only person he'd ever been able to open up to. His father had made sure they never had a close relationship, and Leanne was just like their father, making it difficult to view her as someone he could confide in. Van and Joan understood him better than anyone, but it didn't occur as a result of emotional sharing on his part. They had just been a part of his life long enough to know his struggles.

Then he met Sarah. Never before had he wanted to share so much of himself with another person. But she wasn't there and he was struggling. What was worse was that Leanne's comments too closely resembled the thoughts that had been infecting his mind the last few days.

He wasn't sure pursuing a relationship with Sarah was a good idea. He loved her, and there was no question in his mind that she was the only woman he wanted to marry. But he was starting to wonder if his actions were selfish—if not getting tested for the CJD mutation meant he was building their future on unstable ground.

She had to bury her husband and son. Now I'm asking her to blindly walk into the future with me. A future that could end with a diabolical illness. She would have to suffer through not only burying a second husband, but also watching CJD destroy my mind and body. How could that not destroy her as well? Is it worth the risk for an unknown length of happiness?

"Marcus, what are you doing out here?"

He turned to face Tina. He had been so lost in his thoughts he hadn't heard the door open.

"I just needed some fresh air."

"Well, come in before you freeze." He hesitated and she smiled slightly. "Leanne and Brad just left to get some lunch. It'll be quiet in the house for at least thirty minutes."

He smiled, shaking his head, and followed Tina into the house.

"I know that smile, what's on your mind?"

"I was just thinking there were only two people left in this world that really understood me. You just proved I needed to add a third to that list."

She gave him a knowing look before walking toward the kitchen. He walked to the nearby fireplace, hoping to pull out the chill from being outside.

"I assume Sarah's a part of that now group of three?"

"Not yet, but I hope she will be soon."

"Despite the short time you've known her, I'd say she probably knows you better than anyone else."

He thought about her observation and felt the truth in her words. Sarah did understand him better than anyone. She'd proved it again when she left for home. She could have walked away giving him nothing, but she assured him she wanted him in her life. The question was if that would be as her friend or partner. Even though she wasn't sure what she wanted for their future, she knew he needed something to hold on to. He had thought the assurance of at least keeping her in his life would be enough to forge on, but now he wasn't so sure.

"I know this is a difficult time for you, Marcus. Losing a parent is always hard, even if the relationship is strained."

He pulled his eyes away from the fire to look at Tina. She had moved to one of the chairs near him. Deciding it might be good to talk to someone, he sat in the adjacent chair. He looked back at the fire, not sure how to start. He let out a deep breath and tried to speak as if he were talking to his mother.

"When my mother died, I didn't think anything could break me more than that. Not only was she the one person I trusted the most, but she was honestly the kindest person I'd ever known." He had to stop a moment and swallow past the lump in his throat. "When my father died, I didn't expect it to hurt so much. You know what our relationship was like. I knew I'd be sad—he's my father after all. But I didn't expect to feel so... hollow. I sometimes wonder if I'm mourning the loss of a potential relationship with him more than I'm actually mourning *him*. I suppose I always held the hope that we could work it out someday. Now that can never happen. Our relationship will never be more than what it was—full of disappointment and judgment. On both sides."

"Have you read the letter he left you? I imagine he wrote it for a reason—it could help put some things into perspective."

"I'm not ready to hear what he has to say."

"Why not?"

He let out a deep sigh, closed his eyes, and then looked back to the fire. "I don't know. I suppose I feel like my feelings are the only stability I have left. I was angry at him before, and I'm angry at him now. If there's something in those letters that would make me change my perspective... I'm just not ready to face that. I need to focus all my emotional energy on Sarah right now."

"And what's your worry there?"

"I'm worried she doesn't want a relationship with me. I'm trying to remain optimistic, but as the days pass it's getting more difficult."

"You know I talk to her at least twice a week, right? In every conversation, within the first two minutes she asks how you're doing. I can tell she then spends the rest of the conversation trying to not ask about you again. She's missing you as much as you're missing her. I'd say there's a good chance she's going to give it a go with you."

He didn't want to acknowledge just how much Tina's words comforted him. It was the first time since he watched Sarah walk away at the airport that he breathed a little easier. Unfortunately, it was fleeting as his other doubts crept back up.

"But she's not making her decision knowing all the facts. And what if she changes her mind? What if she demands I get tested? I don't want to know. I'm afraid I'll react the way my father did and ostracize myself from everyone. He didn't want us to see him in his final days. You saw how it was for him, Tina. If I knew I had it—I don't think I can put her through that again."

He finally turned to Tina and held her gaze for a few seconds before she looked away.

"When your father was at the height of his illness, I cracked. Miles and Sarah were by his side through it all. I had to leave and couldn't bring myself to come back. Sarah's a very strong woman. If there's anyone who can take everything life throws out and still come out standing, it's Sarah."

"Just because she's strong doesn't mean I should intentionally cause her more pain."

"No, but doesn't she deserve happiness? She knows your situation, Marcus. It's her choice. She gets to decide if she wants to take the risk. Taking away her right to choose doesn't save her from anything."

"Of course she deserves happiness. She deserves a lifetime of it! But I might not be able to give her that."

"You can't guarantee her a lifetime of happiness with or without CJD. You know that, Marcus. One look at Sarah's past is confirmation of that fact. You two are meant to be together. It shouldn't matter how many days you'll be given—just take as many as you can get. Besides, you two are stronger when you're together."

He stood and walked to the windows at the back of the room. He wanted to believe what Tina was saying. Her words had been successful at quieting some of the negative voices swirling around inside his head. He just needed to survive the next sixteen days.

Marcus sat at the kitchen table, staring at the letters from his father. He'd hoped the stress of the letters would take his mind off his stress over Sarah. It was working. He'd reached for the letters a couple of times, only to pull back sharply as soon as his fingers touched the envelopes. He started counting down from twenty, when he would make another attempt, but was interrupted by the doorbell. He hesitated long enough for his visitor to ring again and bang on the door. He knew that pattern and didn't bother to look through the glass before releasing the bolt.

"You look like shit."

"Thanks, good to see you too." He stepped aside and let Van walk past. "So did you just come by to shower me with your compliments, or is there a reason for this surprise visit?"

"Based on the fact that you've been M.I.A. for a few days and the way you look, you need help getting your head out of your ass. Ergo, you get me."

"I haven't been drinking." Marcus walked past Van and sat down on the couch.

"Didn't say you were. I said your head was up your *ass*, not a bottle." Van plopped down in the adjacent chair. "So what have you been doing?"

"I took in a few animals for a week or so. I couldn't leave them alone."

"Sure you could've. Are they still here?"

"One. A cat—she's in the other room. Her new owner will be picking her up tomorrow."

"I don't know how you can shelter animals the way you do. The constant turn-over has to be draining."

"I think the continuously high rate of turn-over in your social life would be draining."

"Touché, my friend." Van studied him a few seconds before speaking again. "Look, I know I didn't go about helping you the right way last time. I should've come over rather than taking you out to a bar, and I shouldn't have invited Heather. But that doesn't change the fact that you need to get out of your funk, somehow. So tell me what you need."

"I need Sarah."

"That's good. I can work with that."

"I thought you were tired of hearing me pine for her."

"I was, but I realized it was a waste of my time trying to get you to stop thinking or talking about her. So if she's what's needed to get you out of this, then let's call her."

"I can't. I still have two days to go."

"I think she would forgive you those two days."

"No, I promised her no contact for one month. That's what I'm going to give her."

Van studied him through narrowed eyes. "Bullshit. You're scared. You don't want to call because you're afraid she's going to tell you she doesn't want to be in a relationship with you."

Marcus looked away, not wanting to acknowledge the truth of Van's words.

"Talk to me. Tell me about Sarah. Tell me everything—what she does for a living, what she likes to eat, her hobbies, how she kisses and what it feels like when you're in bed and you—"

Marcus threw Van the Kingston death glare. "I told you, she's off limits to your perverse thoughts." His tension released when Van laughed.

"Relax, I was just trying to get you to react to something. I knew that was my best shot. Seriously, talk to me about her. Not your feelings—you know I don't do that shit—but tell me about *her*. We'll talk for two days straight if that's what you need."

"Are you sure you can handle it?"

"I might need a brain enema after this is over, but I can tough it out. Besides, if she's the one then she and I are going to become good buddies once she's here. It'll give me a head start to know all about her."

"I'm not so sure I like the sound of that."

"Sorry. The best man and the best gal always have to be friends. It's the only way we won't be jealous of each other."

Marcus smiled and released a low laugh. It felt good. "I think you just admitted that you love me."

"Dream on, Kingston. Now talk before I change my mind."

CHAPTER 13

"Van's a... good... friend."

"He's the best. I'm getting there, Sarah. I just don't know if I can handle it. When I saw him in the hall—I'm barely holding it together watching you lie in this bed. I can't add anyone else right now. Besides, I'm still mad at him. I have a right to be mad. He went behind my back."

"So did I. You... forgave... me. You can... forgive... him."

"You're my wife. I'll always forgive you."

He watched as she fought her eyes from closing.

"You called... exactly one... month later."

"I did. I think I've told you before that I actually dialed your number a few times and cancelled before I finally drummed up the courage to make the call. The second I heard your voice, all my fears vanished. I would have saved everyone a lot of annoyance if I would have just taken Van up on the suggestion to call you early."

"I wouldn't... have minded."

She fought again against the pull of her eyelids. Eventually, fatigue won and she fell asleep. He let out a sigh and sat back in the chair, running a hand across his unshaven chin. He was still mad at Van, but his guilt was starting to override his anger the more he talked through these moments with Sarah.

Not wanting to think about it, he shifted his attention to something else that had been nagging at him. He went over the memories he'd been recanting to Sarah. A thought was trying to take hold in his mind, but it wouldn't quite materialize. It was there, just out of reach. Something in the memories had triggered it each time. The door opened and a new nurse entered.

"You must be Mr. Kingston. I'm Mark Franklin, I'll be Mrs. Kingston's nurse this shift." Marcus shook his hand. It hit him like a bolt of lightning.

"Mark."

"Sure, you can call me Mark—"

"Son of a bitch!" Marcus turned and ran out the door, almost knocking over his mother-in-law in the process.

"Marcus, what's wrong? Has something happened?"

He turned but didn't stop walking.

"What's Van's room number?" He must have looked like a madman because she paled considerably.

"You're not going to hurt him—"

"The room number!"

"Three-twelve. James! Go with him. Hurry!" Marcus saw his bother-in-law run in his direction. Marcus didn't wait for him at the elevator, and James had to slam his hand between the doors to get on.

"Marcus, what the hell is all this about?"

"I'm going to kill him." Marcus took out his phone and pulled up his search app.

"Marcus, just calm down. We've talked about this. Van's not at fault—"

"Not Van." The elevator doors opened and Marcus hurried down the hall to Van's room. He was sitting up, talking with his mother. Marcus stumbled at the door. Although he had seen Van in the hallway the day before, the sight of him battered still sent a spasm of pain through his core. He pushed past it and strode to the bed.

"Marcus—"

"Is this him?" Marcus held his phone up for Van to see the image displayed. Marcus got his answer from the horror that flashed across his face.

"Yes, that's him. How..." Marcus turned toward the door, but James blocked his path.

"Move, James."

"No. I'm not letting you out of here. It's obvious you intend to go after him—"

"You're damn right I do! Look what he did!" Marcus pointed at Van. "He's shattered everything that's important to me! I'm going to kill him." He tried to shove past James but he wouldn't budge. He heard Van's mother on her cell phone, talking to Detective Smith. "MOVE!"

"NO! I'm not going to let you do something that'll land you in prison! Let the police handle it." Marcus tried again, but James turned him and locked him in a vice grip. He dropped to the ground, dragging James with him.

"I should have seen it. I should have known." He stayed there, secured in James' hold, until security arrived to take him to a private meeting room.

"Mr. Kingston? Detective Smith is here to see you." Marcus had been sequestered while waiting for the detective. His instant fury from an hour ago had settled into a rolling boil. He still wanted to rip Mark's limbs from his body, but he was at least thinking rationally.

Marcus didn't wait for the detective to fully enter the room before unloading. He tossed his phone across the table.

"That's him. I'm certain of it. Mark Tanger."

Smith picked up the phone and studied the picture Marcus had pulled up from the Internet.

"Did your wife remember something?"

"I did. She's been asking me to tell her stories from our past. Then you asked if anyone would want to hurt her. That asshole has hurt her before, and he has it out for me. Van confirmed he's the guy."

"Why would he want to hurt your wife?"

"Not my wife—me. He used to work at my family's company as the Vice President of Marketing. He's an ass and has no boundaries when it comes to women. A couple of years ago, before I met Sarah, I caught him harassing my date at a charity function. At the gala the following year, I caught him doing the same to Sarah. My sister fired him the next week. Right after it all happened, I heard he held a grudge against me, figuring I was the reason behind it all. I never saw him, so I figured it all blew over."

"That was how long ago?"

"A year ago this past December."

"And you haven't heard from him at all since then, other than the rumors that he held a grudge?"

"No."

The detective pulled out his phone. "I need you to pull anything you've got on Mark Tanger. Used to be a V.P. at Kingston Enterprises. He just became the prime suspect in the Kingston/Vanderlink assault." He pocketed his phone and turned to James. "Don't let him do anything stupid. And don't let him out of your sight. Not even to take a piss." He turned and left the room.

James slapped Marcus on the shoulder. "Looks like you're stuck with me, little bro."

"We're the same age, you dip-shit."

"I've got you by a couple months. And I should warn you, Peter's still here. He could kick both our asses, so even if you get past me, you won't get past him."

"So I'm supposed to just let him walk around out there—after he beat Sarah and Van to within an inch of their lives and—" Marcus turned and punched the wall. It wasn't as satisfying as he knew hitting Mark would be, but it worked in the moment.

"No, you're supposed to let the police handle it. He'll get justice and you'll get to live your life as a free man. That's what I call a win-win situation."

"And what if Sarah doesn't make it? What if—"

"No, we're not going there. Everything's going to work out fine."

"How can you be so certain?"

"Because you're too stubborn to let it happen any other way. And the only person I know who's more stubborn than you is my sister." James looked at Marcus' hand. "Now, let's go find someone to patch up your knuckles."

Marcus sat off to the side in Sarah's room while friends and family visited. Usually he went to the waiting room during this time, but now that he knew the attack on Sarah had been personal he didn't want to let her out of his sight. The doctor had raised the visitor limit to four since James was under orders to stay with him at all times.

He watched as Maggie and Tina fussed over the part of Sarah's hair that wasn't covered with bandages.

"We have to go to the spa when you get out of here. We'll fly Maggie back and make a weekend of it. We'll get the works and then go out for dinner. Nothing but pampering for a whole weekend." Marcus couldn't hear Sarah's response. She was able to talk longer before getting winded, but it was still mostly a whisper.

"Nonsense, I'll be back for it. My mom's been wanting grandma time, so she can stay with Andy and the kids. No way am I going to miss out on a spa trip with my girls."

Marcus looked over at James who was reading the newspaper. "So, how's Van doing?"

James put down the newspaper and studied Marcus. "So we're finally talking about this?" Marcus looked away, accepting the blow he deserved. "He'd be doing better if you'd visit him. He thinks you blame him."

"Yeah, well... he may sound like an idiot every time he opens his mouth, but he's actually a pretty smart guy."

"It's not his fault."

Marcus looked toward the ladies to ensure they were still talking. He didn't want Sarah to overhear. "He went behind my back. He knew, just as much as Sarah did, that I didn't want her to go. If he hadn't taken her, this never would have happened."

"You don't know that. Sure, I'd say that was the case if it was a random attack. But now we know it was targeted—personal. That bastard would have found his opportunity, one way or another. And if you had been with her, it could've been you in that other room rather than Van. Then what would happen?" James paused for a moment and scratched the back of his head. "He's hurting, Marcus. And not just physically. You're his best friend. He feels like he let you down. Like he let Sarah down. You're the only one who can absolve him of his guilt."

"I'm trying. I just don't know how to get there yet."

"You asked about him, that's progress."

Maggie and Tina left the room in hushed whispers. Everyone else had already visited, so he knew they were the last. He stood and went to Sarah's side. She looked at him and he kissed her lightly on the mouth, making sure to avoid the cut and bruised side. She grabbed his hand and felt the bandages.

"What'd you do?"

"I hit a wall."

"Bad wall."

He was about to respond when the door opened. Leanne entered the room and walked to the other side of the bed.

"Hi, Sarah." Leanne's voice broke and tears hit her eyes. While Leanne had been at the hospital pretty much non-stop since the attack, she hadn't visited when Sarah was awake. Theirs was a relationship that hung by a thread, and Marcus didn't expect his sister to sit vigil by the bed.

"Hi, Leanne."

"Look, I'm not good at this. But you need to get better. You're needed. I've always wanted a sister, and now I have one, and I'm not interested in losing you any time soon. I love you." Leanne quickly bent and gave Sarah a kiss on the forehead. Marcus could only stare in shock.

"Did you just... say something... nice to me?"

Leanne laughed between tears. "Yes, I guess I did."

"Take it back and... say something mean."

Leanne looked from Sarah to Marcus quizzically and then back again. "Come again?"

"You being nice to me... is like a miracle. I don't think God... gives too many of those... to one person. I need to save mine... to get out of this bed. So take it back."

Marcus could hear Leanne choke back a sob. "You bitch. Quit being so selfish. You think that just because you're lying in a hospital bed, fighting for your life, you can make this all about you and what you need? You're not the only one who suffered from this attack. You're not the only one who needs a miracle. It's not always about you. In case you've forgotten, I protect my family. So if you don't get out of that bed I might just punch the other side of your face." The actual words were more biting than the tone Leanne was able to muster.

"That's more like it." Tears silently fell from Sarah's eyes. Leanne walked out of the room and Marcus followed. Just outside the door, Leanne sank against the wall and started to sob. He put his arms around her and pulled her into a hug.

"I love you, sis. Thanks for that. All of it."

"I'm sorry I ever doubted her."

Marcus leaned forward as he watched Sarah wake up. "Who the hell's drinking coffee?" She paused, studying him. "What?"

"That's the longest sentence you've said without needing to pause between words."

"Wasn't a long sentence. And when it comes... to coffee I can move... mountains. Again... who's punishing me?"

"That would be your brother."

"Tell him to get out."

"He can't. He's supervising."

"Who?"

"Me."

"Why?"

"I punched a wall, remember?"

"And now all walls need... protection?"

"Apparently." Marcus watched as Sarah closed her eyes and took a deep breath. At least as deep as her injured lungs would allow.

"Then dump it out."

Marcus turned to look at James. "Why don't you finish it in the hall?" James gave him a sarcastic look. "It's not like this room has a back door and there's no window. Just stop tormenting my wife— stand outside the door and finish your coffee." James picked up his coffee and stood. On the way out the door, he gave Marcus the 'I'm watching you' sign with his fingers. When the door shut, Sarah squeezed his hand lightly.

"Did he sleep here?"

"The nurses told him they would make sure I didn't leave your room so he could get some sleep back at the hotel."

"Why is he watching you?"

"I told you, I—"

"Marcus."

He let out a sigh. "I'm not going to tell you because you don't need to worry about it. Get yourself out of this bed, and then I'll tell you."

"Did they find who did this?"

He contemplated his answer. "I don't know." It wasn't a lie. They might know who did it, but he didn't know if they found him yet. The line between truth and deception depended on the words chosen. But she knew there was more he wasn't saying. She also knew it would be a waste of her energy to push him on it.

"Talk to me."

"What do you want to hear this time?"

"Tell me about when... you picked me up... at the airport. When I moved here."

CHAPTER 14
Late May • 2013

"Are you sure he's going to be all right?" Sarah looked back for what had to be the twentieth time, and Marcus tried to repress his smile. She was adorable when she was nervous—hands fidgeting with the pendant around her neck.

"Honey, Max is going to be fine. Once the sedation has worn off, he'll be running and jumping and driving us crazy." He glanced at her and smiled at the goofy grin on her face. "What?"

"You called me honey."

"Is that all right?" At first he feared it was an endearment Nick had used, but she was smiling so he dismissed the concern.

"For nearly three years I have hated that word. Everywhere I went it was, 'How ya' doin', honey?' or 'Oh, honey, you don't look so good.' I came to avoid the actual food product of the same name because I was so irritated by it."

"Then what I'm hearing is that I should come up with a new term of endearment for you?" He wasn't sure why he'd called her honey. He typically wasn't one for those things, but it had slipped out without realization. Now he found he'd be disappointed not to be able to use it again.

"No, actually I like it coming from you. You are officially the only person who can get away with calling me honey."

"Excellent." He turned onto the gated drive that had once been his home.

Once Sarah and I are married, it will be my home again.

As the thought crossed his mind, he realized he was excited. The second he saw her at the airport, he couldn't believe he'd ever felt any doubt about pursuing a relationship with her. Now that they were moving forward, the only path he accepted was the one that led them straight to marriage. He wasn't sure when she would be ready for that step, but he intended to wait as long as necessary.

He pulled the car to a stop and watched Sarah look around the yard.

"What in the world is going on around here? Did I contract yard work I didn't know about?"

"Just some surprises I had planned for you. We'll talk inside." He'd hoped to have had the work finished before she got there, but the ground was too frozen to start earlier. He retrieved Max's cage from the back and carried him into the house. Max lifted his head and whined a couple of times as Marcus set his carrier in the great room.

Marcus turned to find Sarah standing quietly in the foyer, looking around with tears falling down her face.

Shit. I forgot about this being her first time back since Dad died.

He walked over and took her in his arms. "Is it too much?"

"It is, but just because it's the first time. I'll be fine." She pulled away to wipe her face. He gave her a quick kiss and then decided to give her a real kiss. Max whined again, killing the moment, and she pulled back. "Do you think he needs to go out?"

"I can see it now—that dog will always come before me."

She smiled and raised her eyebrows. "Well, he is pretty cute."

"No, no, it's fine. I get it." He gave her one more quick kiss before pulling away. "You go ahead and take him out of his carrier while I get something." When he returned from the garage, Sarah was standing by the patio doors with Max at her feet.

Now this is what I want to come home to every day. My family.

They might not yet be married, but Sarah was his family. And Max might be a dog, but to Marcus dogs counted.

"So, are you going to tell me what's going on outside?"

He walked over and knelt before Max to put on a collar and leash. "I told you, surprises. One of them is actually for Max. I had an electric fence installed so he could be outside without a chain, and you won't have to worry about him running away." He opened the patio doors and led Sarah and Max outside. "The flags show the perimeter of the fence. If he gets too close, it will give him a warning beep. If he crosses it, he'll get zapped. Once he learns the boundaries, we can take the flags out."

"But won't it hurt? When he gets zapped?"

"Just enough that he won't want to do it again." He walked Max around the yard, teaching Sarah how to train him.

"What's the other surprise?"

"First let me take Max inside." He returned to find Sarah standing by the pool.

She turned to look at him over her shoulder when he approached. "I don't know anything about taking care of a pool."

"Then it's good you have someone who will do it for you."

"Are you offering to be my pool-boy?"

"No... well, not unless it comes with the stereotypical housewife perks." She punched him lightly on the arm and he pulled her until her back connected with his chest, wrapping his arms around her waist. "Kidding. Well, not really—" She elbowed him and he laughed. "Okay, seriously. We contract out pool maintenance. And lawn care, and house cleaning, and snow removal. We've retained the services that my father used, but you can make any changes you want. Miles and I arranged for everyone to come this week so you have a chance to meet them and form your own opinions."

"I feel like I just stepped into an episode of *Downton Abbey*."

"Well, my lady, that would only be accurate if the staff were here and lined up outside the front door when you arrived." She turned in his arms and looked up at him. He forgot to breathe for a moment.

"You know what *Downton Abbey* is?"

"I do, and I know you got hooked on it while staying at Maggie's. I listen, and I'm always thorough in my research."

"You're too much, you know that?"

"I hope that's a good thing?"

"Yeah, it is. Now, what's this other surprise?"

"Come with me." He walked her over to the other side of the garden to the new gravel path.

"Was this here before?" She looked around as her feet crunched on the small rocks.

"Nope, this is the other surprise. I know you like to run outside, so I had a jogging path installed around the estate—that way you don't have to drive into town every time you want to run somewhere besides the treadmill. You'll have to lap it a few times to get the kind of distance you're used to, but at least it gives you options here at home." She turned to him with tears in her eyes. He leaned in to give her a kiss, but she was out of his arms and running down the trail.

"If you want a kiss, you'll have to catch me first!" He smiled and took off after her. He loved a challenge.

"There are so many boxes. I guess I know what I'm going to be doing for the next week." Sarah looked around the room as she pushed her plate away.

"Speaking of this next week, I took off work and was hoping you wouldn't mind if I stayed here." Marcus watched as a flurry of emotions quickly crossed her face. He didn't want to push her too fast, but he also didn't want to be away from her. The last few months they'd been apart had been agony for him. Finally her face settled, and a shy smile appeared.

"I'd like you to stay."

"I'm glad. I'll help you unpack this week. What would you like to do tonight?" He knew what he'd like to do, but he also knew she wasn't ready to take that step. The waiting was torture, but he was in this for the long haul so he found a way to deal.

"Not unpack." She reached down to scratch Max behind the ear. Marcus took the paper plates to the trash and put the rest of the pizza in the refrigerator.

"Follow me, my dear." He opened the door to the basement and motioned her forward. She eyed him with suspicion before doing as he asked. She stopped at the bottom of the stairs, waiting for his next direction. He grabbed on to her hips and walked her into the dance studio.

"Marcus, what are you doing?"

"Dancing with the woman I love."

"I don't dance, remember?"

"And that's something I vowed to change. We can start with one of your dance moves if you like. If I recall, you once promised to teach me the sprinkler."

"I promised no such thing." He was delighted to hear her laugh.

"It must have been the lawn mower then."

"Wrong again."

"Well, then I guess we'll have to start with something we both know." He retrieved a small remote from the shelf by the door and clicked a few buttons before clipping it to his pants. The music started and he pulled her into position.

"Wait a minute, how'd you do that?" He pushed a button on the remote to pause the music.

"While I was making a few upgrades for you and Max, I made one for myself."

"That's a bit presumptive, don't you think?"

"If you think this is presumptive, then I can't wait to see what you say about how much closet space I claimed. *And*, I took two drawers instead of one in the bathroom. Of course, once we move into the master bedroom I'll get my own closet." Sarah had elected to stay in the room she'd used when working with his father until the master bedroom was redecorated.

"So that's how this is going to work?" He could see her fighting a smile.

"When it comes to us, I promise to always be presumptive. Now, shut up and dance with me."

He turned the music back on and swung her out and back in. It was the same song they danced playfully to when he showed up unannounced nearly six months earlier. This time there were no injured shins. The last time he had wanted to kiss her when the song ended, but it wasn't the right moment and his father had interrupted them. This time, he did kiss her. When it started to get a little too heated, she pulled away—flushed and out of breath. He hoped it was from the kiss more than from the dancing.

"Marcus, I'm sorry. I can't—"

"It's okay."

"No, I know you understand that I'm not ready. It's just..."

"It's just what, Sarah?"

"Nothing. It's stupid." She buried her face in his chest. He lifted it back up until she was looking at him again.

"Whatever it is, it's not stupid. We're in a relationship and you need to be able to talk to me about anything. What is it?"

"I'm nervous. And, what if I'm never going to be ready?"

"Then I'm not doing a very good job of seducing you."

"I think you know that you're very skilled in the art of seduction. It's just that every time I start to feel my emotions get out of control, I panic. I've only ever had sex with Nick." She covered her face with her hands, as if embarrassed.

"Believe me, I love the fact that you haven't been with scores of men. I often wish my story were more like yours rather than like... mine. But our past is just that—in the past. There's no clock here, Sarah. When you're ready, we will. Until then, we won't. But... it's not going to stop me from kissing you..." He trailed a line of kisses down her neck. "Or touching you..." He ran his hand down to the small of her back. She let out a soft sigh and nuzzled close.

"So what kind of dance are we going to do next?"

He stopped kissing her neck long enough to punch a few buttons on the remote. A slow song started. "I kind of like what we're doing now." He rocked her back and forth to the music, never taking his lips from her neck.

"I know this one. I call it the Prom Dance."

"I like this one."

"I love this song."

"I love you."

Marcus let Max out and then took a couple of Sarah's bags to her room. She was soaking in the bath, and it took all his willpower to not go in and help. Instead, he went to the closet and changed into shorts and a T-shirt. When he exited the closet, the first thing he saw was Max taking up half the bed.

"Oh no you don't, big fellow. That's my side." He shooed Max off the bed. "First thing tomorrow, I'm going to get you a doggie bed." He pulled the duvet down and Max instantly jumped up again, thumping his tail against the mattress. "Max, down." He pointed to the floor, but Max just rested his head on his front paws, still thumping his tail. "Max, down." This time he pulled on Max's collar and settled him on the floor next to the bed before climbing under the covers. He grabbed his tablet and pulled up the latest journal he had been reading.

About fifteen minutes later, the bathroom door opened and Sarah emerged wrapped in a towel. He couldn't stop his physical reaction to the sight of her barely dressed. He could clearly see her blush, letting him know her thoughts weren't far from his own.

"I, uh, didn't know you'd be in here already. I forgot to bring in my clothes."

"It's no problem." The strain in his voice was clear even to him. He shifted in the bed, trying to shake his discomfort. She hurried into the closet and closed the door. He dropped his head back on the headboard and let out a groan.

Think of something... think of something...

He had to find a way to get rid of his predicament before she came to bed. Suddenly, a heavy weight landed right on his groin, and his discomfort was replaced with pain. He sat forward sharply and was licked in the face by Max.

"Thanks, buddy. I guess that's one way of doing it." He rolled to the side and took in a series of deep breaths. A few minutes later he heard Sarah approach the bed.

"You okay there?"

"Yep. Max was just helping me out with a particular situation."

"From the looks of it, it doesn't seem he was all that helpful."

"No, he was remarkably helpful. I just hope we can accomplish things differently next time." He groaned again and shifted.

"Do I even want to know?"

"Probably not." He tugged on Max's collar again. "Max, down." The dog reluctantly settled next to the bed with a whine.

"He's used to sleeping with me."

"Well, now he's going to have to get used to me sleeping with you." Marcus grunted and shifted back to a sitting position, the pain subsiding. "On the nights I'm not here, you need to keep him out of the bed or I'll never win the battle. And I'll be damned if I sleep in another bed while Max gets to cuddle you." Her mouth formed a little pout and she looked at the floor.

"It seems so uncomfortable."

"I'm getting him a bed tomorrow. I'll buy the most expensive, comfortable doggie bed available if that'll make you feel better."

"Would it be weird to get him a trundle bed?"

"Yes. It would."

"Fine." She bent down to nuzzle Max. When she stood, she looked nervous. "So..."

"So..." They had shared a bed a few times before. On those nights they had never done anything—not even kiss. They just fell asleep in the comfort of each other's arms. The only difference this time was that they were 'officially' starting their new life together. For some reason that made it more awkward. He pulled the covers aside and patted her side of the bed. "You know if you don't want this I can sleep in the other room. But I'd rather be with you when I'm here."

"No, it's fine. I mean, it's not *just* fine. 'Fine' makes it sound like I'm settling, or not really okay with it but will go along with it anyway because that's what you want. I want you to be here. I'm just—"

"Nervous. And rambling."

"Yes."

"You know, we've already been through more difficult times together than many couples who've been married for years. If we can make it through all of that, I think we can make it through this too. It will get easier after tonight. I promise." She took a deep breath and quickly got in bed, resting her head against his chest. He loved the way she fit next to him.

Suddenly, a wiggling intruder was lying on top of them. Sarah started laughing and based on that reason alone, Marcus forgave Max for the intrusion.

"We really need to establish some boundaries with this dog." She scratched Max's head and he licked her aggressively. She laughed harder. "Alright, that's enough. There's no way you're getting more kisses in this bed than me. Max, down." The dog went back down to the floor. Sarah's laughter finally settled, and she relaxed once again onto his chest.

"You can keep reading if you want."

"You don't mind?"

"No. Will you read to me?"

"It's just boring vet stuff."

"I don't care. I just like to hear your voice." He smiled, kissed the top of her head, and started reading. Within five minutes she was asleep. He'd never felt happier in his life. Shutting off the bedside light, he pulled Sarah close and fell into a peaceful sleep.

"Didn't there used to be a table here?" Marcus looked to Sarah at her question before setting the box he was carrying on the floor of the family room. She was standing in the far corner of the room. "I think it had a picture of your mom on it."

"Yeah, the table had been my in my mother's family for several generations. Leanne decided she wanted it. And the photo. Hope that's okay?"

"It's fine. I was just thinking I liked how it looked with a table here. I might get another one."

"Is this the box you wanted to go through?" He cut the tape and opened the box. "It said 'living room' but there was no number on it." He pulled out what felt like a picture frame surrounded in bubble wrap. He uncovered it and found himself staring at a picture of Sarah with Nick and Danny.

"Oh! I, uh, that's the wrong box. It must have been labeled wrong. I thought I could go through those later." She made to grab for the picture but he pulled it back.

"Why do you need to go through it later?" She reached for the picture again and this time he handed it to her. He pulled out another and unwrapped it. A picture of Nick with Danny. The next few were of just Danny.

"Marcus—"

"What? I don't see why we can't go through these now." Once all the photos were unwrapped, he spread them out on the floor. He looked over at Sarah. She didn't appear to be upset by seeing them, just uncomfortable. "What's wrong?"

"I just didn't think you'd want to go through them. I..." She paused, took a deep breath, and started fidgeting with her pendant. "I wasn't sure how you'd feel about the pictures. I don't want you to be uncomfortable by them."

"These are important to you, right?"

"Yes."

"Then why would I be uncomfortable by them?"

"Because, you know..."

"Because they're pictures of the woman I love with another man who she will always love, and would still be with today if fate hadn't dealt her a crappy hand?"

"Marcus—"

"What? I'm being serious, Sarah. Is that why you think these would bother me?"

"Yes."

"Well, knock that shit off. This is your past." He waved a hand over the pictures. "I've accepted that in order to be a part of your future, I have to embrace your past. You two weren't separated because of a failed marriage—there's no hate, no bitterness. That's often the baggage the second husband has to carry. I just have to help you carry a different kind of baggage, that's all. Nick and Danny will always have a special, and permanent, place in your heart. That makes them part of my family too." Silent tears fell down her cheeks and he walked over to pull her into his arms. "This is new for both of us. We'll figure it out together. Okay?" She nodded and pulled away slightly.

"I love you. I need you to know that. You're right, I'll always love Nick, but that doesn't mean I'll love you any less."

"I know, but it still feels good to hear you say it." He gave her a light kiss and then wiped her tears. "So, which of these are your favorites?" She hesitated for only a second before pointing out three pictures. He picked up one of the pictures and walked over to the wall, above where she wanted to put the new table. "How about we hang them here?"

"Are you sure?"

"I want you to know you can put these pictures anywhere you want in the house." He paused for a moment. "Except maybe our bedroom."

"That sounds reasonable enough. But I just want to hang up these three, and right there is perfect. We need to save space for new pictures in the future."

"I like the sound of that." He wanted to walk over, scoop her up, and carry her upstairs. But it wasn't the right time. Just when he felt like he might need to leave the room to restrain, the doorbell rang.

"Are we expecting anyone?" She turned in the direction of the door.

"Not that I'm aware of. Maybe it's Miles and Tina."

"I'll get it." She left the room as he looked at the picture in his hands. He hoped he was putting up a good front for Sarah. It wasn't that he didn't mean what he'd said. He did. It was just more difficult to displace the pangs of jealousy than he'd admitted. It wasn't that he felt Sarah loved him any less than she had loved Nick—it was that he was afraid he wouldn't be able to make her as happy as Nick had. And he constantly felt like he was being judged by Nick—that he was watching his every move from above.

I promise to do my best to make her happy, and to protect her from as much pain as possible.

"Marcus, there's someone here who claims to be your 'man whore.'"

He closed his eyes and cursed internally. He wasn't exactly in the mood to entertain Van at the moment. "Leave him outside."

"Too late. It seems I can sweet talk your woman just like all the rest." Van strode into the room, surveying the mess.

"He brought me flowers." Sarah wagged her eyebrows above the bouquet she held to her nose.

"Sarah, Brandon Vanderlink—most people call him Van. Van, Sarah Mitchell."

"We met at the door. I have to say, Kingston, I'm mortally wounded that you've been with T.O. for almost six months and she hasn't heard of me."

"First of all, I've known her for almost six months but we've only been an 'official' couple for seven weeks. You know that I was having difficulty convincing her to take a chance on me—no way in hell was I going to tell her about my 'man whore' friend. She might have walked away on the spot. Second, what the hell is T.O. and why are you already giving my girlfriend a nickname?"

"T.O.—you know, 'The One.' I gave her a nickname because she's far too important to just be Sarah."

Marcus shook his head and couldn't help but laugh. "What are you doing here anyway?"

"I came to meet T.O., and to finalize plans for your fortieth birthday party. I've been planning it for a year!"

"All I have to say is that I'm in a relationship now, so any plans you have will need to be changed. I'm sure they're no longer appropriate."

"I'm sure they wouldn't have been considered appropriate even before you were in a relationship."

Marcus looked to an amused Sarah in exasperation. "I'm sorry.

He's my baggage. I would have warned you, but there really is no adequate preparation—you just have to experience all that is Van."

"I can see this is going to be fun. I'm going to put these in some water. Van, can I get you anything?"

"Beer if you've got it."

"Coming right up."

Van watched Sarah's retreating back for far too long, and Marcus whacked him on the back of the head.

"Hey, what was that for?"

"You know what."

"Oh, right. She's off limits to my perverse thoughts. I forgot. Did she change anything? I mean, she was hot when I saw her at the gala but she's damn near lethal now."

"Van—"

"Yeah, okay, fine. But it won't be easy. Does she have a sister?"

"No. Three older brothers though, so you'd better watch your mouth if you ever meet them. And by the way, can't you put in some sort of filter when Sarah's around?"

"Why? This is me. If she's going to be a part of your life, then she's going to have to get used to crude."

"Or maybe I'll finally pitch you to the curb." It was an idle threat Marcus had made several times in the past. He never meant it in truth, but it was fun to annoy Van.

"Like that would ever happen. You know you can't live without me." He made some sort of incoherent sound and looked down at the pictures. "Who's this?"

"That's my someday to be stepson, Danny."

Van looked at him in confusion. "I thought you said her kid died in a car accident."

"He did, almost three years go. But he'll never stop being her son. That makes him my stepson. Or at least, after we're married."

Van pointed at the picture with Nick. "Then who's that—your stephusband?"

"I actually prefer the term husband-in-law." Van's smile faded as he studied Marcus.

"You're being serious."

"Of course."

"Why couldn't you just say he's your wife's late husband?"

"I could, but then people would ask questions Sarah might not want to answer. Or they would give her the 'you poor thing' remarks, and she doesn't need that either. If I tell people he's my husband-in-law, I'm hoping they're too damn confused to say anything else."

"So you've thought about this?"

"Pretty much nonstop for the last twenty-three weeks."

"This is just all kinds of weird for me."

"Well, if you're going to be a part of my life with Sarah, then you need to get used to weird."

Marcus looked past Van and noticed Sarah standing in the entrance to the family room. From the look on her face, he could tell she had overheard at least part of their conversation. He could also tell she appreciated what he'd said.

CHAPTER 15

"You know Nick's not... judging you." Sarah lightly squeezed Marcus' hand.

"Sure he is. I would be, and I'd give the guy a divine poke every time he stepped in the wrong direction."

She watched him for a moment. "You know this wasn't... a poke."

"No, it was a shove. Not what happened to you, but what I'm feeling now. I know I was wrong. I shouldn't have yelled at you. I shouldn't have left. I shouldn't have gotten drunk and ignored your call. Now I have to deal with the guilt of not keeping to my promise of protecting you."

"You know Nick doesn't... give guilt. He takes it away." He remembered the times she told him how Nick had always helped her let go of the guilt she harbored.

"That was for you."

"You too. You're his family... now too. Just like you told Van." She paused, her features turning from somber to humorous. "I remember the first time... you used your term... husband-in-law." She grimaced from the pain of trying to stifle a laugh.

"It was supposed to confuse and distract."

"Instead it made my mom... fall in love with you... faster than I did."

"Not possible. Remember, we loved each other before we even met." He kissed her hand.

"Yes we did." They stared at each other in silence for a few seconds before she spoke again. "You promised to always be... presumptive."

"I did."

"You need to do that now."

"I can't."

"Yes you can." She paused again to study him. "I'm going to rest. You can't come back... to see me until... you do three... presumptive things. About our future."

"You can't keep me out of here."

"No. But James can."

He ran a hand through his hair. "Sarah,—"

"Please." A tear leaked from the corner of her eye.

"Okay. Three things."

"Thank you." She closed her eyes and was asleep within seconds. He rested his head on the bed next to her for a while before feeling James' hands on his shoulders.

"Come on. Let's get some lunch."

Marcus followed James into the hall. They walked in silence a few feet before James spoke.

"I know you didn't know Nick, but I did. I know he would approve of you and the way you treat Sarah. Everyone has a bad moment. That's all this was. You have to let it go to move on."

"You don't get it. This was the first time I messed up, that I failed to carry through on my promise to put her first. It's not like I forgot to give her a card on her birthday—I walked away from her and she was attacked! That's kind of a big fuck-up. I wasn't there and she had to go through all of it alone."

"The doctors said she was unconscious the entire time—from the first blow to her head—so she didn't feel anything or really know that anything had happened. You were here when she woke up the first time and learned the truth. She didn't go through anything painful alone."

"I just don't know how to get past the guilt."

"One step at a time. Start with doing what she asked you to do. Do you already have three things in mind?"

"No."

"Well, I know you won't be able to stay away from her for too long, so you'd better get busy thinking."

Once they arrived at the cafeteria, they got their lunches and joined Peter at a table.

"Where is everyone?" Marcus figured where a few of them were, and he hoped they remembered it was still a subject that was off limits.

Peter swallowed his bite of food, but never looked up from his phone. "Tom took Mom and Dad over to the house to rest. They're going to let Max out while they're there. Leanne had something at the office that needed to be addressed. She said she needed to spend some time at home and would be back in a day or two. Miles is off interrogating someone."

That left Maggie and Tina. A knowing glance passed between Peter and James that Marcus tried to ignore. Just as Marcus took a bite of his food, his phone rang. He retrieved it quickly, hoping it was the detective. It wasn't.

"Hi, Joan."

"Marcus, how are you doing?"

"Pretty much the same as the last time we talked." Marcus stood and walked away from the table to a private corner of the cafeteria.

"Has there been any change?" He filled her in on the results of Sarah's latest tests and what the doctor had said.

"And what about—"

"Don't."

"Marcus, you're being ridiculous."

"I thought you were on my side."

"I am, but I'm also the only one besides Sarah who won't give you everything you want just because you batted your pretty blues. Sarah's too weak to call bullshit, so I'm doing it for her."

"Joan—"

"I'm not done. Based on the doctor's comments, she has a chance at a full recovery. But how can you expect her to fight for a future if you're not willing to do the same? Right now she's the only one fighting—and she's in a hospital bed after having been brutally assaulted! You should be the one fighting as hard as you can, for the both of you. Now stop sulking and feeling sorry for yourself and start fighting! I'm coming up tomorrow and I had better see some progress on your part." She hung up.

He stared at his phone for a few seconds before returning to the table. He ate in silence, thinking about what Joan had said. She was right. They all were. He suddenly remembered something he had told Sarah right before their first date.

You can't predict the future. You have to leap into it with your arms open, and trust that I'll be there to catch you.

She had taken the leap, and he'd caught her. But now he was letting her slip out of his arms.

"You okay, Marcus?" He looked up at James.

"Just thinking about my assignment."

"What assignment?" Peter finally looked up from his phone at Marcus and James, not wanting to be left out.

"Sarah won't let me back in her room until I do three things that are presumptive about our future."

Peter laughed. "That's our Sarah. Always making you work for it."

James finished his drink. "If you guys don't mind, I'm going to go... for a walk. Peter, don't let him out of your sight."

"Got it, boss." He gave James a mock salute. James walked away, shaking his head. Once he was out of sight, Peter turned to Marcus.

"So, I heard you know who did this."

Marcus relayed the story to Peter.

"That's why I have to watch you right now, so you don't go off and do something stupid?"

"Yep, that's correct."

Peter was quiet a moment before he looked back to his phone. "It's too bad no one in this family has ever been able to keep me from doing something stupid." The look in Peter's eyes told Marcus he understood the meaning of his statement just fine. Now that Marcus was thinking clearly, he was about to interject when they were interrupted.

"Mr. Kingston." The detective shook Marcus' hand and then turned to Peter. "I'm Detective Smith."

"Peter Polanski. Sarah's brother."

"How many of you are there?"

"Three. But I'm the only good looking one." Smith smiled and took a seat.

"You keeping an eye on this guy?"

"At all times, when James isn't around."

"Good." He looked at Marcus' hand. "What happened there?"

"A wall." Marcus watched Smith study him for a few seconds. He expected further questioning, but the detective must have been satisfied with his answer because he started talking.

"We've been able to uncover some information about Tanger. It appears he's been holding a grudge. While you may not have heard from him over the past year, he's certainly been keeping tabs on your family. We found evidence of him collecting information on Kingston Enterprises, your wedding to Mrs. Kingston, the opening of your new dance studio—if it was in the news in any way he had a copy. There's other evidence to suggest he'd either been following you, or he'd hired a private investigator. He knew some things he shouldn't have known. Like the date and time of your wife's appointment."

"What the hell?" Smith shot a glance in Peter's direction at his outburst before continuing.

"It appears that after getting fired, Tanger's life went quickly downhill. He'd already been divorced, but soon after losing his job at Kingston Enterprises his ex-wife was awarded sole custody of their children. Tanger was reduced to supervised visitations. He had secured another job in that time but lost it as well. There's also evidence of significant substance abuse over the last year—both alcohol and drugs. It appears the rumor was accurate—he blames your family for all his troubles and started his revenge by attacking Mrs. Kingston and Mr. Vanderlink."

"Have you arrested him?"

"He's disappeared for the moment." Marcus started to react but Smith silenced him with a raised hand. "We don't think he's gone far. He doesn't know he's a suspect. Right now, the media has been reporting it as a random attack, and that's working to our advantage. Also, based on what we believe his motives were, he'll want to come back and see the effects of the damage he's inflicted. He has family in Arizona, and we think he's gone there to lay low for a while. We'll get him." Marcus nodded and tried to remain calm. It was a lot to take in.

"I assume once you have him in custody it'll be a slam-dunk?"

Smith turned his attention to Peter. "Based on the evidence we have and Mr. Vanderlink's ability to ID him, he won't have much luck fighting it. He'll be going to jail for a long time." Marcus could see Peter's gears working.

That must be what I looked like when I first figured out it was Mark. No wonder I was put under hospital arrest.

Marcus knew that if Peter found Mark somehow, he'd make him pay. Peter was in extremely good physical condition. From the stories Sarah has told, Peter never lost a fight and he had quite a few under his belt. Sarah had said a key component of his success was that his opponent always underestimated him. He looked like a laidback frat boy with his carefully mussed hair and charming smile, rather than someone who knew how to take out a guy twice his size with just one punch.

"If you gentlemen don't have any further questions, I'm going to see Mr. Vanderlink. There are a few additional details I hope he can clear up."

Marcus instantly made a decision and spoke before he could change his mind. "If you don't mind, I'll go with you. I assume you can act as my chaperone on the way. I'm sure Van's mother will still be there so she can vouch for my presence until James or Peter can claim me once again."

"Absolutely."

"Just give us a minute, if you don't mind." The detective eyed them suspiciously as he walked away, and Marcus turned to his brother-in-law. "Be careful, Peter. If you give Mark a warning, he'll likely turn you in once the police pick him up. Even if he's not able to connect it to you, I'd be the first suspect and you'd be the second. It would kill Sarah."

"Are you telling me to back off?"

Marcus was thoughtful for a moment. He knew he should tell him just that. Tell him what James had told him about letting the police handle it. But it didn't feel like enough.

"I'm telling you to be careful."

"Don't worry, my warnings are never ignored. Nor are they ever reported." Peter clapped him on the back before walking away.

Marcus waited in the hall while Detective Smith talked with Van. He was nervous. He'd already seen Van, but now he was there to finally make amends. He'd been avoiding this moment for a reason. He leaned his head back and closed his eyes, breathing deeply in an effort to settle his emotions. He wasn't sure yet what he was going to say. There didn't seem to be any appropriate words to excuse his behavior. Heart still racing, he decided he needed a distraction. He pulled out his phone and texted Joan.

I need you to help me with something.

She responded instantly, and he texted back what he needed her to do before she arrived the next day.

"You know, we can pull phone records if necessary. That is, if anything suspicious should happen to Tanger."

Marcus looked up at Smith. "You can check them now if you'd like." He turned his phone toward the detective.

"No need. Just wanted to make sure you understood."

"Why do you assume I'm going to do something? Yes, I want the bastard to suffer for the damage he's inflicted. But that doesn't mean I'm going to hire a hit man to take him out."

"I warn you because I know how I'd feel if I were in your position. And if I feel that way, being in law enforcement and knowing the boundaries, I can only assume it feels significantly worse for you. No one hurts my family, and I get the impression it's the same for you."

"Warning heeded. I think I've let Sarah down enough over the last few days, and I'm not inclined to do it again any time soon."

"Good man. I'll keep you updated on our progress." Smith walked away and Marcus took a deep breath before pushing off the wall toward Van's room. He opened the door and hesitantly stepped inside. Van was sitting up in the bed, his mother in the chair next to him. He felt the now familiar spasm of pain when he looked at Van's battered body, but he'd been prepared and was able to push forward.

"Detective Smith said you were outside. I told him he must have been hallucinating." Van's voice sounded cautious. Considering how he'd been acting, Marcus understood Van's hesitation.

"Yeah, well, I figured it was time I stopped being an ass."

"So you didn't come to finish the job Mark started?"

"No. I—" Marcus cleared his throat and felt the sting of tears. "I came to say thank you for protecting Sarah when I failed."

"I didn't do a very good job." Van's voice was quiet, laced with regret.

"You did better than me. I wasn't there—I was getting drunk. I'll admit that I was mad at you. I don't appreciate that you went behind my back. I used it as a reason to justify blaming you."

"She understood why you didn't want her to go. She was going to back out, but I convinced her to keep the appointment." In that moment Marcus realized just how messed up the situation was. All three were harboring guilt for the actions of a lunatic that was drunk on rage and revenge.

"It's not your fault, Van. It's mine, and it's time I start accepting responsibility. It's not going to happen overnight, but I'll get there."

"That's about the dumbest thing I've ever heard. If it's not my fault, how can it be yours?"

"Has your guilt suddenly disappeared just because I told you it wasn't your fault?"

Van looked down and started picking at the strap of the sling supporting his arm. "No."

"I didn't think so. That's how it is for me. People can keep telling me that I'm not at fault, but words can't take away the guilt. Coming in here has made me realize the only defense against my guilt is action. Taking steps to overcome the situation. But I can only take one step at a time. And I suppose this is the kind of situation where we need to hold the guilt together. It's too heavy to carry alone. If we stick together, maybe we can keep the bastard from winning."

"I don't know, I've always been able to carry more than your sorry ass. You've always been a big pussy." Van smiled as he delivered his playful jest. Marcus understood the conversation had gotten too heavy for Van's comfort.

"Speaking of..., how the hell are you going to get any now? You look like a freak."

Van smiled wider. "Chicks dig guys with heroic stories. I plan to twist this to my advantage. Have you seen my nurse? I've got to figure out how to get her to give me a sponge bath. I do believe I'm especially dirty on my—"

"Brandon! Watch your mouth. There's no reason to be vulgar. And, Marcus, I'm glad you've come to your senses, but please don't encourage him."

"Look at it as a good thing, Ma. Continuing my vulgar ways just proves that I don't have any brain damage." Marcus looked from Van to his mother and smiled.

"At least no more than you already had." Van shot Marcus an appreciative look.

Van's going to be all right. And I think we're going to be all right too.

Marcus felt some of the pressure lift from his chest at the realization. "Did the doctor say when you could be released?"

"Tomorrow."

Marcus nodded and looked down at his feet. "I'll come by and see you again before you leave."

"Marcus, dear, I can stay if you need me. I know you haven't—"

"No, Mrs. Vanderlink, you should go home and take care of Van. We'll be fine. I'll figure it out eventually." Marcus looked away, uncomfortable under their scrutiny. He cleared his throat. "Well, I should get back to Sarah." He turned and left the room quickly.

It was early in the morning, but James had already returned from the hotel. In Marcus' opinion, he was taking the detectives orders a bit too seriously, but at least he left overnight. Marcus would have felt the need to give him the cot, and the idea of sleeping in one of the chairs was not appealing. He sat quietly on the other side of the room, reading the newspaper, while Marcus watched Sarah as she finally started to wake up.

She opened her eyes and looked at Marcus. "You're here."

"I'm here."

"You're done already?"

"Honey, you've been asleep since yesterday afternoon. That gave me plenty of time to complete my assignment."

"Tell me what they are."

"I'll tell you one now, and the other two later." He watched her, wishing he could climb in the bed and hold her in his arms.

"Well? What are you waiting for?"

"I just wanted to look at you for a bit longer."

"I must look like a freak."

"No, you look beautiful. Van looks like a freak."

Her eyes got slightly wider. "You went to see Van?"

"I did. We're good."

She let out a sigh and her eyes welled up with tears. "Thank you. Is that the first thing?"

"No, that was a bonus. This is the first." He handed her a piece of paper from the table.

"A spa resort?"

"I talked to Maggie and Tina and they agreed they could go the weekend after your birthday. It's non-refundable, so you have about four months to get yourself well enough to go. That should be plenty of time."

She smiled and reached for his hand. He gave it to her and she brought it to her mouth, planting a kiss on his bandaged knuckles.

"Speaking of pampering... looks like you finally... showered and shaved."

He stroked his chin. "I thought you liked my scruffy look."

"You were starting to look... like a mountain man."

"We do live in the Rockies."

"True. Did you go home?"

"No, I used your bathroom."

"Who's taking care of Max?"

"Family is taking turns. Your parents are there now. They say he misses you."

"Would it be weird to disguise him... as a doctor and sneak him in?"

"Yes. It would."

"Fine." She let out a restricted sigh. "Will you talk to me?"

"What do you want to hear?"

"How about when I asked... you to marry me." He reached for her forehead. "What?"

"Just checking for a fever. Up until now you've remembered everything accurately."

"I remember just fine. You know what... I'm talking about."

"Yes, I do."

CHAPTER 16
June • 2013

Marcus looked over at Sarah and smiled. It had been almost a week since she moved out to Colorado. They spent their days unpacking and their evenings talking. He'd be lying if he said he hadn't wanted to take their relationship to the next level in intimacy, but it was clear she still wasn't ready. Sleeping next to her every night but not being able to make love with her was an intense exercise in self-control. He wasn't looking forward to Sunday when he'd have to return to his house. The issue of separate living arrangements was the reason behind the surprise he had in store for Sarah. He looked at her once more before turning into a parking lot and stopping next to the only other car.

She looked over at him in confusion. "Why won't you tell me what we're doing?"

"It's a surprise. Besides, we're here." He jumped out and hurried to her side before she could open the door on her own.

"This looks like an empty building."

"It is. Come on." He took her hand and led her inside where Isabella, the agent he'd been working with, was waiting for them. She turned when they entered and flashed a smile he knew she'd used on many men. The only accurate way he could describe her was petite, sexy, and sassy. And bold—she tried to flirt, even with Sarah planted firmly under his arm.

"Mr. Kingston, it's always a pleasure to see you." Isabella kissed both his cheeks and he felt Sarah stiffen. She turned to address Sarah.

"You must be the lucky woman that tamed this playboy." She put her hand on his forearm and Sarah raised her eyebrows at him.

"Ms. Verdos, this is Sarah Mitchell. Sarah, this is Isabella Verdos. She's the realtor that's listing my place and helping me scout locations."

Sarah's eyebrows now came together in the center. "Locations for what?"

"Ms. Verdos, would you mind giving us some privacy?" He noticed her smile falter for a second before she recovered.

"Of course." She walked outside and pulled out her phone.

"She's pretty." Sarah watched Isabella through the window.

"Really? I hadn't noticed." He shifted and pulled Sarah to him.

"Yeah, right. She's not exactly subtle in her flirting. She might be perfect for Van."

"Oh no you don't. No scheming."

"I don't scheme. I strategize for the greater good of others."

"Well, just make sure your strategy accounts for the fact that Van drops women after taking what he wants."

"And yet the women still flock to him afterwards. Somehow, his actions only drive stronger infatuation rather than scorned fury. We could invite her to your birthday party on Saturday."

"No. Save the strategizing for after we've secured a location. Just to be safe."

She turned to him. "Fine. So are you going to tell me why I'm standing in the middle of an empty commercial building?"

"Now that you've moved here, I don't want to be an hour away. I figure once we're married we'll want to live in my old home, which now belongs to you thanks to my father, so I'll need to find work here. I considered opening another veterinary clinic, but there are too many in this area to be competitive. Besides, my first passion was dancing. So, I want to open a dance studio."

She studied him closely, no doubt analyzing her response before she spoke. "Won't you miss being a vet?"

"I would. That's why I thought I could also practice as an on-call vet. You know, fill in for Joan and at other clinics when they need someone."

"Would this make you happy? I don't want you to give something up for me, or settle for something you don't really want to do."

"All I really want to do is be with you. Don't roll those pretty eyes at me. It sounds corny, but it's true. The way I see it, this is the best possible outcome. I get to be with the woman I love and work with both of my passions at the same time."

She looked at him with suspicion. He could see her gears turning. He knew she was the type to analyze every situation, and this one would be no different.

"Sarah, honey, I'm being honest with you. This is what I want. I've given it a lot of thought in the time we were apart. I've already wasted too many years avoiding something that's a basic part of who I am. We know that the future is uncertain—I don't want to regret passing up this opportunity. My father had closed my mother's studio a few years after she died, and I had always wanted to open one if I ever started dancing again."

"What about Joan?"

"She and I talked about it. We've already started by my assuming a less active role at the clinic. Once I move here, I would drive down there at most once a week to help until Frank, the new doctor, is settled. We'll evaluate the situation after a year and make adjustments as necessary. I can always sell my half if it's not working out."

"Can we afford this?"

He couldn't help but smile at her concern. "Yes, we can afford this. Even without the money you bring into our relationship, or the sale of the clinic, we've got enough to buy this place outright, make the necessary improvements, and plan our future."

He didn't tell her the reason why he knew this so readily. He'd spent countless hours with Miles the past few weeks ensuring a secure future for Sarah in case anything should happen to him. Miles had helped his father through the same preparation. He didn't like thinking about it, but knew it was necessary.

She finally smiled. "Well, then show me around! Have you looked at other venues or is this the first one?"

"I've been looking for a few weeks. This is the fifth place—it just came on the market. It's my favorite." He walked her around the space, showing her how he envisioned the studio. At the end of the tour, he walked her to the middle of the largest room and pulled her close. "And this is where I thought I could teach you to dance." He brushed a kiss just behind her earlobe.

"If this is a part of your dance lessons, we should probably use the home studio."

He turned her around to face him. "That's a great idea." He captured her lips with his and kissed her deeply. Regardless of his restraint, it was getting to the point where he became unraveled any time he touched her, no matter where they were. His hands glided to her butt, and he pulled her as close as possible.

"Well, I must say, you two look like you're trying to test the sprinkler system." Marcus broke the kiss and leaned his forehead against Sarah's. He took a deep breath and then looked over her shoulder at Isabella.

"We'd like to make an offer."

"Excellent! Follow me, and we'll go to the office to fill out the necessary paperwork."

Sarah stretched to kiss him one more time before turning to leave. He grabbed her, and pulled her back to his chest.

"I need a moment before I can go out there, or Ms. Verdos will get to see more of me than I think you want to share."

"Wouldn't it be easier for you to recover if I weren't in the room?"

"Yes, but it wouldn't be nearly as much fun." He kissed her neck.

"I think this is counter to your attempt at calming certain things down. Don't get me wrong, I'm not complaining, but Ms. Verdos is waiting." She pulled out of his grip and walked out of the room, flashing him a smile over her shoulder as she went. He groaned and followed, trying to think unpleasant thoughts to ease his situation.

"There you two lovebirds are. I was beginning to wonder if I should leave you alone and come back later." Sarah blushed and it was as adorable as every other time she did it. He hugged her from behind and planted a kiss on her temple. "So, Mr. Kingston, will you be giving any private dance lessons?" Sarah shot Isabella the Kingston Look of Death she'd come to adopt. It was the first time he saw Isabella's smile disappear and he laughed.

"No, all my private lessons will be reserved for my future wife."

Isabella quickly recovered. "Pity." She turned on her stiletto and climbed in her car.

It was Marcus' fortieth birthday. It was a big milestone for many, and he hadn't been sure how he'd feel once his day arrived. Now that it was here, he didn't even need to search for the answer—he was the happiest he'd ever been in his life. He looked over at Sarah as he turned onto Van's street. He figured he'd make one more attempt at getting her to reveal his birthday present.

"Won't you give me even a small hint?"

She smiled and shook her head. "Nope, it's a surprise. Besides, it's back at the house, so you'll have to wait."

"The suspense is killing me. Why couldn't you give it to me before we left for dinner?"

"Because I needed help. And for it to be a surprise, it had to happen after we left."

His curiosity was piqued, but it quickly dissipated when he pulled up outside Van's house. "He said this was just going to be a small get-together."

Sarah squeezed his hand, sensing his discomfort. "Well, hopefully he canceled the strippers as promised." He turned and caught her playful smile. He shook his head, smiling in return.

"Wait here." She didn't like waiting for him to open her door, but he insisted. It was a small pleasure that he wanted to indulge in—he loved watching as she carefully maneuvered her way out of the car. She stood and he pulled her in for a kiss. "Have I told you that you look beautiful tonight?"

"Yes."

"Well, you always look beautiful, but tonight I'm going to have to keep you close. Some of my friends are opportunists, and you will definitely be tempting."

"They can't be any worse than Van."

"You'd be surprised. Van's just obvious because he doesn't hide his motives. The others practice the art of stealth." He took her hand and led her up the walk.

"Van lives here?" He nodded, understanding her confusion. It was not the typical bachelor pad. "Given the size of this place, I assume it means he has an actual job that pays pretty well. How does he not get fired for sexual harassment?"

He couldn't stifle his laugh. "First, he comes from more family money than I do, so that helps. Second, he does have a highly paid job. He's an entirely different person at work—it proves that there's a grown-up in there somewhere, and I'm hopeful for the day he emerges full-time."

"What does he do?"

"You wouldn't believe me if I told you." She stopped and he turned to face her.

"Now you have to tell me."

"Actually, I think I'll make you guess."

"I'll just ask Van."

"Good luck with that."

He turned and started back toward the house. The closer they got to the door, the more pronounced the music became. When they entered the house, he could feel the bass vibrating off his chest. There were people everywhere—most of whom he didn't know. He guided Sarah through the room, keeping her close. Their progress was stopped by a very drunk blonde.

"Marcus! You're here! Happy birthday! Do you want your present now, or later?" She leaned in and tried to pull his head down to connect his lips to hers. He pulled away sharply and she almost fell on her face, so he put a hand on her shoulder. In the movement she noticed Sarah planted under his other arm. "Who's she?"

"Trisha, this is Sarah. I'm with her. Permanently." Her mouth dropped open in shock before she turned away, mumbling something incoherently.

"One of your many fans?"

"If you want to know, I'll tell you. But I'd rather not talk about it." Even though he'd told Sarah of his promiscuous past, it didn't mean he wanted to flaunt the women under her nose. And he certainly didn't want to talk with her about the details. He wished she didn't have to know at all. But because his past was extensive, he knew the day would come when they'd bump into someone he'd slept with. He usually kept to women that didn't run in his circle of friends, but for some reason he'd broken his self-imposed rule with Trisha. He looked at Sarah, concerned of her reaction.

"Okay."

"Are you sure?"

"You have a past, Marcus. I don't like seeing women you've likely had sex with, but if you're okay with pictures of my late husband hanging on the wall, then I can deal with running into a few of your exes from time to time. She just better not touch you again now that she knows you're off the market." He smiled, relieved that she had been mostly unaffected by the encounter.

"Let's go find Van. Then maybe we can sneak out after about thirty minutes."

"Marcus! This is your birthday party. You can't sneak out!"

"I didn't want a party. I just wanted to be home with you."

"We can do that tomorrow."

He pulled her close and put his mouth to her ear. "I like the sound of that." He trailed a line of kisses down her jaw line.

"Marcus, we're in a house full of people." Someone shouted a catcall in their direction, as if trying to help prove her point.

"It's my party—I can kiss you when and where I want." He cupped her face and gave her a deep kiss before finally pulling away. He needed to stop before he lost control.

"Kingston, it may be your party, but you can't have sex in the middle of my living room. At least take it to the bedroom." He watched Sarah blush before turning to face Van.

"I thought you said this was going to be a small gathering?"

"This is small. Where the hell have you been?"

"Dinner ran over."

"I'll try to not be offended that you blew off part of your own party for dinner, even if it was with the beautiful T.O." Van clapped him on the back before turning away. "Come on, you need a shot!"

Sarah pulled Marcus down to whisper in his ear before following after Van. "Does he realize he's no longer in college?"

"I don't think so." He led Sarah through the house and joined Van in the kitchen. There were several people gathered around the counter, and he was relieved to see some people he actually called friends. He pulled up to the counter, placing Sarah in front of him. There was a round of birthday greetings before everyone's attention turned to Sarah, and he made the necessary introductions.

Van reappeared and passed out full shot glasses. "Here's to being forty! May you have twice the stamina you had when you were twenty!" Van raised his glass, and the others followed his lead.

Marcus knocked his back and watched Sarah with amusement as she contemplated the full glass before her. He wrapped his arms around her waist.

"You can drink if you want. I don't plan on drinking anything else, and I'll carry you if needed." She looked back at him before picking up the glass and taking it down with an impressive gulp. He felt her shudder, and he placed a kiss on her temple.

"Another round?" Van was already refilling the glasses before anyone responded.

"None for me."

"What? This is your party, man. You can't have just one."

"I'm driving tonight."

"No way. You guys are staying here tonight."

"We didn't bring—"

"No arguments. Ace, Mack—you know what to do." Before Marcus could react, one friend pinned his arms while the other confiscated his keys and tossed them to Van. To everyone's surprise, Sarah's hand shot out and intercepted the keys. She tucked them into the pocket of her jeans before any one of his friends could react.

"What'd you go and do that for?" Van tried to sound annoyed, but Marcus recognized the admiration in his tone.

"We have to get home to let Max out. Sorry."

"T.O., you're breaking my heart! And here I thought you were the perfect woman." Van dramatically clutched at his chest.

"She is perfect—for me." Marcus squeezed Sarah a little tighter. His friends coughed into their drinks but he ignored them, preferring to pay attention to the blush taking over Sarah's face. He decided to get her out of there before his friends started spouting inappropriate comments.

"I'm going to take Sarah downstairs."

"Come back up after you've delivered her safely to the others."

Sarah looked at Marcus in confusion as he turned to lead her to the stairs. "What's that supposed to mean?"

"The women usually hang out downstairs. I wanted to introduce you."

"You're going to ditch me?"

"No... I just thought you'd want to meet the other ladies. I'm going to go back up to appease Van for a few minutes, but then you'll be stuck with me for the rest of the night."

The basement was filled with people. A group of his friends were playing cards and he stopped to accept the birthday wishes and make introductions. He had two groups of friends—those from before he graduated college and those from after. They didn't often hang together, except when Van threw a party in his honor. Luckily when they did mix the groups, everyone got along fine. It was a perfect opportunity to introduce Sarah to everyone at once. He took her over to a group of women sitting on the long sectional couch. He was happy when they immediately welcomed her.

"Hi, Marcus. Happy birthday." Marcus cringed when he heard her voice. He took in a quick breath before turning.

Please let her be civil.

"Thank you, Heather. You remember Sarah?" He wrapped his arm around Sarah's waist and pulled her close.

"Hi, Sarah, it's nice to see you again. Would you like a glass of wine?" Heather's cheeks were pink, highlighting her discomfort.

"Thanks, Heather. That would be great." Sarah raised her eyebrows at him as she started to follow Heather across the room. Before she could pass, he quickly pulled her in to whisper in her ear.

"I'll be back in a few minutes. If you get uncomfortable, just come find me." He planted a kiss on her forehead and turned to locate Van. He found him still in the kitchen, handing out shots.

"Kingston! Seriously, man. You need to do at least one more shot. Even if you're driving, that won't be for hours and you'll have plenty of time to sober up before then."

"No, thanks. But I will have a beer." Van grumbled but handed him a bottle anyway.

"The ladies taking care of T.O.?"

"What's T.O. stand for?" Mack looked from Van to Marcus.

"That's Van's doing. You'll have to let him explain."

"It's just a nickname. I approve of her, so she gets a special name. The letters are the initials of her actual nickname because it sounds much cooler."

"You never gave my wife a nickname." Mack looked like his feelings were genuinely hurt over the realization.

"Who says I didn't? Maybe I just don't use it outside of the bedroom..." Van wagged his eyebrows and gyrated his hips back and forth.

Ace laughed at Van's rebuttal, choking on his drink in the process. "I always thought mini-Mack looked more like a mini-Van."

Now they were all laughing, and Mack gave Ace a friendly shove. "Not cool, man. Not cool."

"Okay, okay. Back to Sarah's nickname, what does T.O. stand for? Total Optimism?"

"No, I know—Take Over."

"Take Out."

"Turn Over."

"Turbulent Overdrive."

"Alright, that's enough." The guys were laughing even harder and Marcus shook his head at the absurdity of their guesses. It was clear Van wasn't going to divulge the information, and that was fine with him.

He changed the subject and soon they were laughing about a recent incident at Van's office. The doorbell rang and Van actually yelled 'come in' a couple of times before realizing the impossibility of being heard. He mumbled something about why anyone would actually ring the bell at a party as he strode out of the room.

Marcus turned to go join Sarah when someone pulled him out on the deck. He engaged in polite conversation for a few minutes and then excused himself. He decided to go down the deck stairs and enter the basement through the patio. Before his foot touched the first step, someone grabbed his shoulder.

"Kingston, you'll never guess who just showed up." Marcus turned to look at Van. Mack was standing next to him, looking around like he was trying to ensure no one was close enough to overhear the conversation.

"Since I won't guess, why don't you just tell me?"

"Rachel." The name hit Marcus like a brick. He hadn't seen Rachel since she made the mistake of showing up at his mother's funeral. He didn't remember exactly what he'd said to her that day, but he knew it hadn't been nice.

"What the hell is she doing here?"

"She showed up with Jen. Apparently, she and Patrick got a divorce and she knows you're not yet married, and well... I guess she thought she could slither back in your life like you've been waiting for her all these years. Do you want me to kick her out?"

"Only if she tries to make trouble with Sarah."

"Have you told Sarah about her?"

"No, it didn't seem important."

"Not important? Dude, she broke your heart and then you turned into a raging dick."

"That was more a result of my mother dying, and you know it. The fact that Rachel cheated with Patrick a few weeks before that was just the extra shove I needed. I don't care about her—she's not important. I've made it a point not to tell Sarah the specific details about my past because she doesn't want to know."

"But—" Just then the door to the patio below opened and Sarah's voice floated up.

"I'm sorry, what was your name again?"

"Rachel."

Marcus tensed and started down the stairs, but he was held back. "Shh, let's see how this plays out." Van whispered hard in his ear.

"I'm not going to stand here and eavesdrop on their conversa—"

"Shut up!" Van clamped a hand over Marcus' mouth.

"I hear you and Marcus just started dating." Marcus could hear the sarcasm in Rachel's voice and knew Sarah would pick up on it as well.

"Something like that."

"What's that supposed to mean?"

"We're not exactly dating." Van had finally removed his hand from Marcus' mouth and he couldn't help but smile. Sarah knew what she was doing.

"Oh, so you're just one of his many one-timers?"

"No. I'm his only full-timer." Van stifled a laugh, and Marcus elbowed him in warning. It was a few seconds before Rachel responded.

"Well, I'm sure you know that I was his first serious relationship. I wish it could have ended differently, but we were so young."

"Actually, he's never mentioned you."

Marcus heard Rachel's bitter laugh carry through the dark night. "I find that hard to believe. We had something pretty... intense. It says something that he didn't feel he could confide in you."

It was Sarah's turn to laugh. "Marcus' past is just that—his past. I don't need to know about it unless he wants me to know. He shares with me all the significant aspects of his life. I guess you didn't make the cut. However, since you seem intent on telling me all about it, how long ago did you date?"

Rachel hesitated. Marcus knew her intention had been to rattle Sarah, and she hadn't expected to be questioned in return. He wondered if she would even answer, realizing how ridiculous her actions were.

"Twenty years." He heard Sarah laugh.

"And how many times have you seen him since?" There was silence, but Rachel's expression must have given away the answer. "That's what I thought. So what exactly are you expecting to get out of this conversation?"

"I just thought I'd give you a warning. It's obvious he never got over me and has been waiting for me to come back."

What the hell? Did she become delusional over the last two decades?

"No. He's been waiting for me." Marcus' chest swelled with love and pride at Sarah's response. A couple of seconds later they heard the door slam followed by a sigh. Marcus quickly descended the stairs and Sarah jumped slightly when he rounded on her. "Marcus—" He pulled her to his chest and captured her mouth with his. He reluctantly pulled away when Van and Mack shook his shoulders.

"I think I'm in love." Van picked Sarah up and spun her around.

"I've got it—T.O. is for Totally Awesome!" Mack slapped Marcus on the back with a little too much force.

"Awesome starts with an 'a' you idiot."

"Right. I mean Totally Ohmygodthatwasfuckingawesome!"

"Did you guys hear that whole conversation?"

"I was on my way down when you came out. Van and beer-for-brains here somehow convinced me to listen in." To his relief, Sarah laughed.

She extricated herself from Van and wrapped her arms around Marcus' waist. "I think she still has a thing for you."

"You think? Huh. I hadn't noticed."

"I might actually feel sorry for her. It's kind of pathetic."

"Excuse me?" Marcus looked at her with shock that was half sincere. She laughed again.

"Not the part about her still having a thing for you. That's totally understandable. What's pathetic is that she thinks she'd even have a chance after twenty years. Has she really been pining for you that long?"

"No, she's been boning his ex-roommate since before he dropped her sorry ass." Marcus shot Van a warning look, but it was ignored. He looked back at Sarah to find her studying him.

"Well, that's good to know. I now officially have zero pity for her." He placed a kiss on her forehead and looked over her shoulder. He saw Rachel standing on the other side of the door, watching them. He locked eyes with her long enough for her to know he saw her. She didn't look much different. He knew she was the kind of woman that would rely on plastic surgery to remain looking young. Over the years he'd wondered what he would feel when he saw her again. Now he knew—he felt nothing. He turned his attention back to Sarah and hugged her tight to his chest.

"Sarah? Is everything all right?" Marcus tried to pull out of his sleep induced fog to focus. It was just after three in the morning.

"I'm sorry, I shouldn't have called. Everything's fine."

"Obviously not if you're calling in the middle of the night." There was a pause and he willed his heart rate to slow.

"I just... I'm just not used to being in this house alone. I know I lived alone for a long time after the accident, but I was familiar with that house and all its sounds. I'm just not used to this house yet. I'm sorry I worried you."

He let out a relieved sigh. "It's okay. Do you want me to drive up?"

"No, but thank you for offering."

"Is Max in bed with you?" He wanted to distract her errant thoughts and pull her out of her fears. She hesitated, and he heard her muffled voice as she put the phone to her shoulder.

"No."

He couldn't help but laugh. "Liar."

"I am not. He's not in the bed... any more."

"The first night I'm not there and he's already taking my spot. He has his own bed now."

He heard her sigh. "I know. I just like to cuddle."

"Then I'm definitely driving up."

"You have to work tomorrow—I mean today. I really should let you go back to sleep. Do you have a busy day?"

"Just a full schedule of regular check-ups." There was a pause and he could tell she didn't want to get off the phone. "Are you sure you're going to be okay there all by yourself?"

"Yeah, really, I'm fine. I guess I just thought I would miss you less once I got out here since I can actually see you every week. But when you left today I realized I just miss you more." He understood exactly how she felt.

"We'll figure it out." If he had his way he'd fly her to Vegas and marry her at the first available chapel.

"I know." There was a short pause before she spoke again. "Have you talked to Van today? He was in pretty rough shape after your party."

"I called him when I got back to my place. He had one hell of a hangover, but I'm sure it didn't keep him down for long. He wasn't alone, and it sounded like he was in good hands."

"Has he ever had a serious relationship?"

"Once—it didn't end well for him. After a few years of what seemed like happy bliss, she got a nose and boob job and basically told him that he was no longer good enough for her."

"I guess that explains a lot about his current behavior."

There was another pause and he decided to ask the question he'd been hesitant to speak aloud.

"We haven't talked about next weekend yet. Do you know what you want to do on Sunday? Do you want to be alone or do you want me there with you? This is new for me, and I don't know what I'm supposed to do."

"In a way it's all new for me too. While I've been through two of these now, this is the first year I'm actually trying to function. Normally I'd spend the day curled up in Danny's room, trying my hardest to forget the images of the accident. I know I can't do that any more. I was thinking about taking Max for a hike somewhere. I'd like it if you joined us. This will be my third marker, and I'd like for you to be a part of it and all the future ones."

"Marker?"

"I've always had difficulty calling it an anniversary. While the term is accurate, I always associate anniversaries with celebrations. I don't want to celebrate the day of the accident each year. I want to celebrate their life, but I should do that every day, not just on the day they were taken from me. In my healing I've come to think of my progress as a form of endurance. Since I'm a runner, I associate endurance with a marathon. There are mile markers along the way that remind you how far you've gone and how much more you have to endure. That's what it's like for me—each year that passes is like a marker reminding me that I made it. That I'm still breathing and moving. That I'm still running forward, toward another marker. The only difference is that I don't have a finish line. I just need to make it past as many markers as I can. It's possible I'll get fatigued, but I intend to keep pushing."

"That's why you lean on me when you need to. I'll carry you across every marker if I have to."

She was quiet for a long time and he could hear her trying to fight against her emotions. When she finally spoke, her voice was soft and full of love.

"Will you talk to me until I fall asleep?"

"What do you want me to talk about?"

"Anything. I just need to hear the sound of your voice."

Marcus stumbled through the doorway, dropping a box in the foyer. He heard Sarah call out from the office.

"Marcus, is that you? I wasn't expecting you for another hour."

"My afternoon appointments were canceled, so I left early. I'll be right back." He hurried out to his car to retrieve another box. He dropped it next to the other and turned to see Sarah standing at the entrance of the hall leading to the office.

"What's with the boxes?"

"I'm moving in."

He almost laughed at her shocked expression. "Come again?"

"I'm moving in." He turned and went to retrieve his suitcases from his car. When he returned, she was standing with her hands on her hips. She looked furious, but he decided to ignore it. "Of course I can't fit everything in my car, and we'll have to go through my place together to determine what furniture we want to keep or sell, but I brought the essentials—"

"Marcus Nathaniel Kingston! You cannot just move in here without talking to me about it."

She used my full name—she's really pissed.

He almost made the mistake of laughing out loud. "Well, Sarah

Lynn Polanski Mitchell—some day to add Kingston to that long list—I figured it was inevitable, so why wait?"

"We're not married!"

"Honey, you've called me every day this week in the middle of the night. I'm moving in."

"Fine, I'll stop calling."

"I don't want you to stop calling. I don't want you to have to call in the first place." He walked over and pulled her to him. She resisted, but eventually relented. "I want to be with you. All the time. It's that simple. Besides, I stay here over the weekend and you don't have a problem with that. Why should adding the rest of the days of the week be a big deal?"

"Because it is." She actually pouted and he had to resist the urge to kiss her. "Moving in together is a big deal. I know that we'll eventually be married and living together, but I don't know when I'll be ready."

"I don't mind waiting. However, it will be much easier if I'm waiting with you at my side rather than over an hour away."

"You can't just up and leave Joan."

"Frank's doing well, and he'll be ready to take over my schedule after this coming week. Until then, I'll make the drive every day."

"No." He pulled back slightly at the force in her voice. "No way. The more you're on the road, the more chances you have of being in an accident. No."

His shoulders sagged in defeat. "Alright. However, I'm staying until Monday and one week from today I'm moving in." She narrowed her eyes at him.

"So, you're here until Monday, then you'll be back on Wednesday for my birthday, and then you will be moving in on Friday. How exactly does that *not* equate to you getting your way?"

"I'm conceding on two days. You have to admit, that's generous of me. I'm a Kingston after all—we don't usually concede on anything." He laughed when she rolled her eyes. "If you want, we could spend your birthday down at my place. You can sleep there once before it's sold. On Thursday you can go through my stuff and figure out what you want to keep. You can drive back up on Friday morning and I'll join you after I get done with work." It was her turn to laugh.

"So really, you're only giving up one day of us not living together." He smiled and watched her melt before his eyes.

"Come on. These boxes can wait. I feel like dancing."

He pulled her toward the basement stairs. When they got to the studio, he programmed the player to repeat the same song. He stripped out of his T-shirt and kicked off his shoes. He smiled as he watched the flush take over her face. When he got close, she instinctively ran her hand along his tattoo. She traced her finger over the words, and he shuddered at the sensation. He looked up at the same words that she had added to the studio wall for his birthday present, and felt an overwhelming rush of love.

Not able to resist any longer, he pushed the button on the remote and the music resonated around them. It was the song he'd asked her to dance to with him months ago, but she had refused. A smile toyed at the corners of her mouth, and he kissed her as he pulled her to his chest. She broke away and searched his eyes.

"I don't know what to do."

"I'll teach you. Just follow my lead. And your instinct."

"What if I'm not good?"

"You're the best dance partner I've ever had, and the only one I'll ever want."

He started to guide her though the steps he'd envisioned in his mind countless times. At first he could feel her hesitation, but the more they moved the more she relaxed. It was a sensual dance and touching her was driving him wild with desire. At one point he turned her to him and pulled her leg up, resting her thigh on his hip. He couldn't resist dropping a kiss on her neck. She melted against him and he forgot all about dancing. He pulled back and hesitated long enough to give her a chance to tell him to stop. Instead, she pulled him back to her and kissed him deeply. He picked her up and she wrapped her legs around his waist before he turned for the door. He didn't want risk going all the way upstairs—afraid she'd change her mind by the time they reached the bedroom—but he refused to have their first time be on a hard dance floor.

CHAPTER 17

Marcus turned at the sound of a loud cough, irritated at the interruption.

"You okay back there, James?"

"Yep. Just wanted to make sure you remembered I was still in the room."

"You could leave."

"I'm still under orders to watch you. Besides, Sarah's supposed to be calm. She doesn't need to be worked up over... those kinds of memories."

"You do realize I've... had sex before, right?"

"That doesn't mean I want to hear about it!"

"Like Marcus said, you could leave."

"Not a chance. I can tell by that machine you're hooked up to that your heart rate is already elevated. Not going to happen. Skip past that particular part and any future that resemble it."

Marcus looked back at Sarah and gave her a wink. She smiled and he leaned in to give her a gentle kiss.

"Oh, come on! If I won't let you talk about it, do you honestly think I'll let you reenact it?"

Marcus gave her one more kiss before pulling away. "Fine. Where was I?"

CHAPTER 18
June • 2013

Marcus sat next to the pool, soaking in the warm summer sun. He turned when Max barked, playfully attacking a stick in the yard. Sarah was inside talking on the phone with Tina, discussing her new responsibilities for the regional CJD foundation she would be leading. A few minutes later he felt Max nudge his shoulder, and a slimy tennis ball dropped in his lap.

"Looks like you found your ball." He picked it up and tossed it out in the yard. Max leapt after it and brought it right back. Marcus got up and walked out into the yard with him. He tossed the ball a few times before Max gave up on it and jumped on him instead. He knelt down and scratched Max behind the ears. "Did you enjoy your hike yesterday?" Max responded with a bark and a lick to the face.

Sarah had wanted to go hiking in remembrance of her marker day. Given the significance of the day, she had been quiet for most of the hike. He'd tried to pay attention to her silent cues, giving her distance when it seemed she needed to be alone with her thoughts. It killed him to know she was in pain, but there was nothing he could do except be there for her when she needed him. Later that evening, he'd held her close in bed while she shared memories of her life with Nick and Danny.

Marcus sat down in the grass and Max instantly nestled beside him. He wasn't sure why, but he felt the urge to talk to Max. "I know Danny would have loved having you as his best friend. And you would have loved Danny. Even though I never met him, I know he was a pretty cool kid." Max whined as if he understood it to be true. "Nick was allergic, so that would have been a problem. However, I know he loved his family so much he would have probably committed to getting shots every day just to keep you around. That's assuming shots would have done the trick—if not, I'm sure he would have found something else. But I'm afraid you're stuck with me."

Max quickly scrambled to his feet and bounded in the direction of the house. Marcus stood and turned to see Sarah standing a few feet away. She was breathing heavy and tears were streaming down her face. His stomach clenched instantly.

"Sarah, is something wrong?" He stepped in her direction only to stop at her words.

"Will you marry me?"

He stumbled, unsure if he'd heard her correctly. He searched for a response but couldn't find the capacity to speak.

"We both know that we'll get married some day, but I also know you won't ask until you're sure I'm ready. I don't know if I'll ever fully feel ready. All I know is that I love you, and I want to be with you always. I don't want to waste any more days questioning my feelings. You told me once that I needed to leap into the future, so this is me leaping. Will you catch me? Will you marry me?"

He felt tears sting his eyes, and his breathing became labored. He closed the distance between them and kissed her. She pulled back and rested her forehead to his.

"So is that a yes?"

"No." She raised her head and looked at him in confusion. "That was a wonderful way for you to let me know that you're ready, but I still intend to be the one to ask. I've already got it all planned out." A smile spread slowly across her face.

"You've already planned how you want to propose?"

"Since the moment I saw you."

"How long have you lived here?" Sarah walked through the small two bedroom condo, inspecting everything.

"About five years. I purchased it not long after Joan and I opened the clinic. It's a nice place, but I'm looking forward to living with you full-time." Marcus watched the blush take over her face. He knew she was as eager as he was to be living together. She turned to face him.

"You mentioned doing something for my birthday tonight?"

"I thought we'd go out to dinner with Joan and her husband, Darrel, if that's all right." He watched her reaction, knowing she hadn't celebrated her birthday since the accident. While he'd be content to stay at home with her, he felt it would be good for her to be social since she was trying to establish new patterns in her life.

Finally, she smiled and nodded her head. "That sounds fun. I'm excited to meet Joan. I know she was at Elijah's funeral, but I didn't get a chance to talk with her." They were silent for a moment at the reminder of his father's death.

He cleared his throat. "Well, I know she's excited to meet you too. She's bugged me about it nonstop since the week after the gala. Now, go get ready."

He changed clothes, let Max out, and resumed packing boxes. When Sarah emerged from the bedroom, he forgot to breathe for a few seconds. She'd swept one side of her long brown hair up in a clip and wore a dress that stopped just above her knee. One shoulder was exposed and his eyes traveled the length of her arm up to her eyes.

"Wow. Maybe we should stay in after all."

"Tempting, but Joan might take it personally if we stand her up."

"She'll get over it." He walked over to her and trailed a line of kisses from her shoulder to just behind her ear.

"Marcus... you're not playing fair."

"You started it by coming out looking all irresistible." She cupped his face and pulled his lips to hers. He took a step toward the bedroom but she pulled away.

"We can finish this after dinner." He groaned and rested his head on her shoulder before pulling back to look at her.

"Fine. But I want to give you your present before we go." He led her to the couch where he sat next to her. He produced a small box from his pocket, and her eyes grew wide. He didn't wrap it, so it was obvious it was a jewelry box. "Open it." She took the box with a shaking hand and opened it. There was a moment of confusion on her face before she smiled.

"Marcus, it's beautiful."

"It's a charm for your necklace, to go next to the pendant my father gave you. The two stones are meant to represent Nick and Danny." She put her face in her hands for a moment, choking back a sob, before throwing her arms around his neck. He held her tight until her sobs subsided.

"Thank you. It's amazing. You're amazing." She pulled back and wiped at her eyes before letting out a small laugh. "Great, now I have to fix my make-up." He attached the charm to her necklace before she went to the bedroom to freshen up. When she returned, he stood and took her hand in his. He led her out to the car and opened her door.

Before she got in, he leaned to whisper in her ear. "For a moment you thought an engagement ring was in that box, didn't you?" She hesitated but finally nodded. "I'm not going to be that predictable." He planted a kiss behind her ear before she lowered into the car.

The drive to the restaurant was quiet. He knew there were moments when she still fought to remain in the present, and this was one of those days. He held her hand and felt surges of relief when she occasionally squeezed her fingers around his, letting him know she was still with him. He parked the car and led her into the restaurant.

"Hello—reservation for four under Kingston." The hostess checked the chart.

"The other half of your party is already at the table. Please, follow me." When they arrived at the table, Darrel was the first to greet them.

"Marcus, good to see you again." They shook hands before Darrel turned to Sarah. "You must be Sarah. Happy birthday." Marcus could see the surprise on Sarah's face when Darrel pulled her into a hug.

Joan rounded the table and hugged Marcus, whispering in his ear. "She's a knockout."

"That's just the outside. Wait till you get a chance to know the rest of her—you'll be as smitten as I am."

"I have no doubt." She kissed his cheek before turning to Sarah. His heart thudded into a rapid pace when he noticed the pallor of Sarah's face. She looked as if she was about to pass out. She recovered enough that Joan didn't notice.

"Sarah, I've been dying to meet you." He watched as Joan pulled her into a hug, contemplating if he needed to intervene.

"It's wonderful to meet you too. Marcus speaks very highly of you." Sarah's voice was strained, but he knew he was the only one who'd noticed.

"Not nearly as much as he gushes about you, I'm certain." Joan moved back around the table to her chair and Marcus gently gripped Sarah's elbow.

"Is everything all right?" She looked up and nodded at his whispered question. She smiled but he could tell it was slightly forced.

As they waited for dinner, Joan engaged Sarah in conversation. He tried to concentrate, but he couldn't stop wondering what had upset her. Midway through the meal his phone rang, and he looked at the incoming number. It wasn't one he recognized, so he slipped the phone back in his pocket. He turned his attention back to Sarah. She was clutching the charm he'd given her.

Maybe it was a mistake. I thought it would make her happy, but maybe it's too much of a reminder.

He mentally kicked himself a few times for screwing up. He should have at least waited until after dinner to give it to her. As dessert was served, his phone rang again. It was the same number as before. He decided he should answer in case it was some sort of emergency. He excused himself from the table, answering as he walked toward the door.

"Kingston."

"Marcus?"

"Yes, who's this?" There was a slight pause.

"Don't tell me you don't recognize my voice any more." He faltered for a step before regaining his footing. With that comment he knew who it was, but wouldn't let her know.

"I'm sorry, I don't know who this is." Another pause.

"It's Rachel."

"How'd you get my number and why are you calling?"

"You wouldn't talk to me at the party, so I was forced into calling. I have some things to say to you." She didn't answer the question on how she got his number.

Jen must have given it to her.

She had always supported Rachel's version of the story.

"There's nothing you have to say that I care to hear."

"Marcus, I'm sorry! I know I screwed up. I tried to tell you at your mother's funeral, but you were so mean. I understand now that you were hurting and lashing out, but I was so shattered by what you said. I thought there was no way to make up for what I'd done. I went back to Patrick, and by the time I realized it was you I wanted to be with I found out I was pregnant. I stayed with him for my daughter, but divorced him after she graduated high school. Jen's kept me informed of how you were doing. How messed up you were over our break-up and how you never got close to another woman. I know we can make this work if you could just forgive me. I've moved back here just for you."

Marcus stood outside the restaurant in complete shock. He finally recovered and resisted the urge to laugh.

"Rachel, I have no adequate words for you. I'd like to tell you how bat-shit crazy you sound right now, but I don't think you'd believe me. Besides the fact that it's been *twenty years*, how can you still think there could be something between us after your conversation with Sarah at the party?"

"She told you about that?" The anger in her voice was clear.

"She didn't need to. I heard the whole thing."

"Marcus, please, you have—"

"I don't know what kind of delusion you've cooked up over the last twenty years, but you and me—it's beyond over. I'm going to marry Sarah soon, and there's nothing you can say or do to change that. Don't call me again, and don't ever approach Sarah again." He hung up before she could respond. He ran his hand through his hair and shook his head at the absurdity of the situation. If he hadn't known better, he'd have thought he somehow stepped into the middle of a bad soap opera. Or that Van was punking him. The timing of the whole thing was just suspicious.

This had better not be Van's doing, or I'll kick the shit out of him.

He thought back to Van's reaction when Rachel had showed up at the party. He quickly dismissed the option that this was a bad joke orchestrated by Van. Taking a deep breath, he returned to the table.

Sarah took his hand as he sat down. "Everything okay?"

"It is now." He lifted her hand and placed a kiss on her wrist. She lifted her brows in question. "I'll tell you later." While he knew she'd find it amusing, he didn't want to mark her birthday with Rachel's crazy antics.

Throughout the rest of dinner Sarah remained engaged in the conversation, but he could tell there was still something bothering her. They finished dinner and said their good-byes before parting ways in the parking lot. He opened Sarah's door but pulled her in for a hug before letting her climb in. He walked to the driver's side and slid in next to her, instantly taking her hand after pulling out onto the road. He looked over and she was still clutching the charm.

"Do you want to tell me what happened at dinner? I know something bothered you. If you don't want to talk, that's fine, but I want to know what I can do to help. I hope it wasn't all too much."

She squeezed his hand before pulling it up to plant a kiss on his knuckles. "No, it was perfect. I'm just not used to celebrating my birthday, that's all."

He knew there was more she wasn't saying, but he also knew she would tell him when she was ready. He just needed to be patient.

"So, do you want to tell me who called?"

He considered telling her that the conversation could wait until the next day, but something had already affected her and he didn't need to add to her worry for no reason.

"It was Rachel." His response was met with silence and he glanced in her direction. It was too dark to make out her features. Understanding she wasn't going to respond, he relayed the phone conversation with her.

"Was she like this before, when you dated her?"

"No, well, I mean she had some obsessive tendencies, but nothing like this. It's all just so out of the blue. For a split second I actually considered the possibility that Van brought her back just to mess with me."

"Marcus! Van wouldn't do something like that!"

"Um, you forget I've known him since we were kids. Yes, he would do something like that. Not out of spite, but because he would think it was funny. The thing about Van is that he'd find a way to do it without being cruel and everyone would have a good laugh in the end. I don't know how he does it to be honest. However, based on his reaction when she showed up at the party, I know he was just as surprised as I was."

"Well, hopefully she'll get the message soon."

"I'm just sorry you have to put up with her."

"She's harmless."

"Yeah, maybe. But you've been here less than three weeks and already you have to deal with a psycho ex. It's not the best start to your new life out here." He glanced over and caught the shrug of her shoulder.

"It might be somewhat unexpected and crazy, but it's better than what my life was at this time last year. At least I know life with you won't be boring."

"I can promise you our life will never be boring."

A thought flashed through his mind that maybe their future could actually benefit from a little dose of the mundane. He hoped they would never feel complacent, but he also hoped they would never have more drama and excitement than they could handle. He knew the thought was fueled by the mutated CJD gene that might be lurking deep inside his body. He pulled Sarah's hand to his lips, letting the contact settle his fears.

Marcus sat in his car, staring at the house. He'd been waiting for this day since he first saw Sarah, so he wasn't sure why he was so apprehensive. Her surprise proposal at the start of the week made him confident that she wouldn't reject him, but he couldn't shake his nerves since the night of her birthday dinner a couple of days ago. She still hadn't talked to him about what had affected her.

On some level he also knew his hesitations stemmed from not knowing his fate with regard to CJD. Sarah had said it didn't matter. That if she made her decision to start a life with him, then it would be with the assumption that he could someday develop CJD. The fact that she moved out here, and proposed on her own, told him that she meant what she'd said.

How do I know we will survive this blind trust in the future? Do I owe it to her, to us, to find out my fate before we take this step?

He had to believe they were on the right path. Everything about their relationship felt right. If she was willing to take a walk of faith, he would walk right next to her the entire way.

He took a deep breath and opened the car door. He retrieved his suitcases and entered the house. He knew she'd still be out with Tina, giving him time to prepare everything. As he crossed the foyer, his phone rang. He dropped one of his suitcases on his foot as he answered the phone and let out a curse.

"What's wrong with you?" Van's didn't try to hide the laughter in his voice.

"I dropped a suitcase on my foot."

"Where are you?"

"Home—or at least my new home. I'm moving in with Sarah as of today."

"So your new home is your old home—you realize how weird all of this is, right?"

"Is there an actual reason for your call, Van?"

"Yes, you need to come by my place tonight. We need a fourth for poker."

"Sorry, I've got plans."

"I think T.O. can make it one night without you. Better yet, bring her along. You can drop her off at Mack's house, and she can hang with Kate."

"Not tonight."

"What are you not telling me?"

Marcus let out a resigned sigh. Van was going to find out soon anyway. "I'm going to propose tonight."

"No shit! Oh, this is huge. You sure she's ready?"

"Since she surprised me with her own proposal on Monday, yeah, I'd say she's ready."

"Well, damn, if she's already proposed why do you have to do it? Run with that, man, and come play poker tonight. We'll start planning your bachelor party since the guys will be here."

"That may be your style, but it's not mine. I intend to do this right. Besides, I have a ring that belongs on her finger."

"When did you buy a ring?"

"A while ago." He didn't want to admit to Van just how long ago he'd actually ordered the ring. He'd taken enough rubbing when it came to his presumptive nature with Sarah.

"I hope you confirmed it doesn't look anything like the one your 'husband-in-law' gave her." Marcus felt a knot form in his stomach.

Shit. I never thought of that.

"Oh, man. You didn't check, did you?"

"Damn! What am I going to do now?"

"Is T.O. home?"

"Not yet, she's with Tina."

"Okay, so you need to search through her things. Either find the ring, or see if it's in any of those old family photos."

"What do I do if it looks the same? I can't give her the same ring!"

"Then you come play poker while you figure out an alternate plan. We'll still plan your bachelor party though."

"I'm not coming, so find someone else. I've gotta go." He hung up and took the stairs two at a time.

He entered the room he shared with Sarah and looked around as a moment of panic washed over him. The room was empty. The furniture was still there, but all personal belongings were gone. He looked in the closet to find it empty as well. Confused, he walked out in the hall. When he turned, he noticed the door to his father's old room was closed. On impulse he walked over and opened the door. The room had been completely redecorated—including a new bed and furnishings. He walked over to the nightstand and picked up a framed photo of him with Sarah. He walked over to the closet to find Sarah's clothes neatly hanging in the large space and his in the smaller adjoining closet. He couldn't contain his smile.

He'd forgotten why he'd gone upstairs in the first place until his eyes landed on Sarah's jewelry box in the closet. It felt wrong to go through her things, but he needed to see what her old ring looked like. He pulled out each of the small drawers until his eyes found what he was looking for. He picked up the ring and breathed a sigh of relief before tucking it back into place. He looked around the room one more time before closing the door behind him. It was clear Sarah had intended for the room make-over to be a surprise. Now it was time for him to prepare the surprise he had in store for her. The first step was to text Tina and make sure their plan was still on track.

Marcus looked around and smiled. While he knew Sarah loved the house as much as he did and they were happy to be living there, it had harbored sadness for both of them. Much of their time together in the house had been clouded by the pain of his father's illness. He was hoping his plans would be the start of a life full of happy memories. His pulse quickened as he heard Sarah enter through the garage.

"Marcus? Are you home?" He savored the sound of her question for a moment before responding.

"I'm in here." He stood in the middle of the great room, waiting.

"Sorry I'm late. Tina spilled something all over my blouse at dinner and insisted on taking me by her house to get something new to wear." He heard the sound of her heels clicking on the tile. "Why are there candles—"

She stopped when she rounded the corner. She looked around the room that was illuminated by candles and adorned with dozens of roses. He absorbed the sight of her in the dress he'd picked out. It was a perfect fit, and he knew the color would bring out the green in her eyes. When it appeared she was too stunned to move another step, he closed the distance between them. He cupped her face and softly kissed her. He pulled away and she let out a shaky breath, her eyes still closed.

"I'm beginning to think Tina's accident was more like a calculated effort in a very intricate plan."

"You would be correct." She opened her eyes and held his gaze. He kissed her once more before taking her hand and leading her down to the basement. In the dance studio there were more candles and rose petals covered the outer perimeter of the dance floor. He led her to the center of the floor and turned her to face him.

"Are we going to dance?"

"I'm going to dance, and you're going to feel instead of watch this time." Her brows knit together in the center, and he didn't hold back from kissing the spot.

"I don't understand what that means."

"I want to show you exactly how much I love you, and the best way I know how is through dance. And the best way for you to understand it is to feel it—experience it with me. You're going to close your eyes and let me move you."

"But I like watching you."

He smiled at her response. "And I'm very happy about that, but this time it's much more important that you feel. Trust me."

He secured a blindfold around her closed eyes to ensure she couldn't see anything. Her breath hitched when she felt the fabric touch her face. He traced the line of her jaw with his thumb before lightly brushing her lips with his. He then ran his hands down the length of her body, slowing when he reached her hip, and stopping on her left ankle. He lifted her foot, and she steadied herself by gripping his shoulders. He gently took off her shoe and placed a kiss on the top of her foot before repeating the process on her right leg. He placed her shoes to the side of the room and turned on the music.

It was a slow, haunting song and it captured his feelings for Sarah in a way he felt compelled to express. He'd practiced a few times, but it wasn't the kind of dance he could perfect without her help. He hoped his emotions would carry his movement. He stood in front of her for a few seconds, committing the vision of her to memory. He slowly ran his hand along her collarbone as he walked to stand behind her. He rested his hand on her arm, took a deep breath, and started to dance.

He moved Sarah to the music, in constant contact with her body—touching, lifting, holding. She was hesitant for the first few seconds, not able to anticipate their movement with her eyes closed. His heart surged when she finally surrendered to him completely, letting him move her without resistance. Every movement was intended to show her how much he cherished her. The intensity of their connection caused a tear to escape down his cheek.

As the song neared its end, he raised her left arm and slid the ring on her finger as he continued his hand down her arm and knelt before her. He watched her closely as she removed the blindfold with a shaky hand. She looked at the ring and then to him, tears falling down her face. He took her hands in his and cleared his throat, suddenly finding it difficult to breathe.

"Sarah, practically my whole life I knew I'd someday find the woman who owned me whole. You hold not only my heart, but my entire being. We both know the future is unpredictable. I can't promise you a life of perfection, but I can promise you that I will never take a second of my life with you for granted. While I know our souls are already joined and forever will be, I want to make it clear to everyone else just how much I love you. Will you allow me to cherish you for the rest of our lives? Will you marry me?"

She pulled her hands free and placed them on the sides of his face as she sank down to her knees. She placed her forehead to his.

"I don't need the certainty of tomorrow. I just need you today and every today we will be given in the future. Yes, I will marry you."

CHAPTER 19

"I never felt more loved... than I did in that moment." Sarah looked at Marcus for a few seconds before closing her eyes. They both knew there was more he wasn't saying. That there was another reason they counted that night as special. He laid his head on the bed next to her, searching for the strength to be the man she needed him to be. "You're stronger than you think." He should have been surprised at her comment, but she knew him better than he knew himself most of the time.

"What makes you so sure?" He lifted his head to look in her eyes. They were fighting to stay open.

"I know you." She closed her eyes again.

"You look tired."

"I am." Her eyes fluttered open once more before she drifted into sleep. His worry was growing. She should be getting better by now. He stood and turned to the door, intent on finding the doctor. He didn't wait for James, knowing he would follow anyway. In the hall James stopped to take a phone call. He waved Marcus on since the nurse's station was within his sight.

"Hello, Mr. Kingston."

"Hello, Nancy. Is Dr. Vikrant here today?"

"No, I'm sorry he isn't."

"Can you call him for me? I want to discuss my wife's progress." She hesitated for a moment but then agreed to page him. While he waited, he called to check on Van.

"Hello, Mrs. Vanderlink. I'm just calling to see how Van is doing."

"He's been ornery as ever, so I suppose that means things are going well. I'd let you talk to him, but he's sleeping at the moment."

"That's fine. I just wanted to check in. I'm glad to hear he's doing well. Do you need me to send someone over there to help? Do you need to go home for a while?"

"Actually, a woman by the name of Isabella showed up. She didn't know he'd been in the hospital, and when I told her what happened she insisted on staying to help. Brandon acted like he didn't want her here, but I know my son. I think this Isabella just might be the woman I've been praying for."

Marcus smiled. Sarah had succeeded in setting up Isabella and Van. They had hit it off and dated for a short time. But of course Van resisted, reluctant to acknowledge his feelings. Marcus had wondered what would bring them back together.

Maybe something good can come out of all this after all.

"I think you may be right, Mrs. Vanderlink. Let Van know I'll check in again later." They said good-bye as James approached.

"Tom needs to head back home. The timing's not good, but someone has to run the business. I'm going to drive him to the airport, so I'll have Peter stay with you."

"I can call Thompson to pick up Tom."

"No, that's all right. He and I have some things to discuss, and the drive will give us that opportunity. I'll bring Mom and Dad back from the house while I'm at it."

"How are Juliet and the boys doing? Do you need to go home soon too?"

"She took the boys to her mother's house. She could have brought them here, but we didn't think it was appropriate. They wouldn't understand the situation. I've been able to work some remotely, so I should be good through next week if needed."

"I really appreciate your being here. All of you. I know I was a bit of a jerk in the beginning, but I'm glad you're here."

"Don't worry about it. You kind of had a good excuse for being a jerk."

"What do you need, James?" Marcus turned at the sound of Peter's voice.

"I have to take Tom to the airport, so you need to watch Marcus."

"Oh, come on. You're not still abiding by that stupid edict are you?"

"Yes. Until Detective Smith confirms they have Mark in custody, we're keeping an eye on Marcus."

"But I had something I needed to do."

"Sorry. Tom has to get back."

Peter looked from James to Marcus in frustration. "Why the hell are you still going along with this?"

"Detective's orders." Marcus shrugged his shoulders. He had a feeling James was pairing them up to keep Peter in check more than Marcus at the moment. Peter's reaction indicated that the something he needed to do wouldn't be considered appropriate.

"Man, this is bullshit."

"Is the thought of spending time with me really that awful?"

"It's been quite enlightening, actually. Sarah's been having Marcus recount most of their relationship."

"Sounds more nauseating than enlightening."

"Maybe it will inspire you to tame your wicked ways."

Peter huffed and crossed his arms over his chest as he stared at his brother. "Not likely."

"Mr. Kingston? I have Dr. Vikrant on the line." Marcus crossed the hall to take the call. He relayed his concerns to the doctor, eventually convincing him to order more tests. By the time he hung up, James was already gone and Peter was still pouting. They returned to Sarah's room to find her sleeping.

Peter dramatically flopped down in one of the chairs. "How can you stand sitting in this room all day?"

"If Sarah's here, I'm here."

"Yeah, but she's asleep. Can't we go down to the cafeteria or the lobby or something?"

"I don't want her to be alone, even if she's asleep. Your parents are still at the house and I assume Maggie and Tina are... occupied."

"Can I at least turn on the TV?"

"Just not too loud. Sarah needs her sleep." Marcus sat next to Peter and watched as he alternated his attention between the TV and his phone that was continuously buzzing with text messages. Marcus' curiosity got the best of him after a few minutes. "I know you're currently between jobs, so who's been blowing up your phone?"

Peter's fingers froze for a moment before he finished his message and pocketed his phone. "Just a friend."

Marcus wasn't satisfied with his response. "What was it you needed to do?" Peter looked at him suspiciously. "You told James you had something you needed to do."

Peter shifted his eyes back to the TV. "Just something stupid."

"Mr. Kingston?" Marcus opened his eyes and immediately closed them again, unadjusted to the bright light. He rubbed his face and sat up in the chair. He opened his eyes again and focused on Detective Smith.

"Sorry, I must have fallen asleep." He quickly looked at his watch. Five hours had passed.

No wonder my neck hurts.

"Where's Mr. Polanski?"

"Which one?"

"The one that's supposed to be keeping an eye on you."

"James took Tom, his other brother, to the airport and Peter's..." He looked at the vacant chair next to him. "I don't know where Peter is. He was here when I fell asleep."

"How long ago was that?"

Marcus sat forward, suddenly alert. There had to be a reason the detective was asking questions. He looked over to Sarah's bed to ensure she was sleeping. She was quiet but stirring.

"Do you mind if we talk in the hall?" Marcus stood and led Smith out of the room without waiting for a response. "Why are you asking about Peter?" Just then Peter walked into view carrying a couple of bags from a nearby fast food establishment.

"Detective. I didn't expect to see you here on a Sunday. Have you captured the bastard that assaulted my sister?"

"Where were you a couple of hours ago, Mr. Polanski?" The hairs on the back of Marcus' neck stood to attention.

"Well, I got tired of looking at sleeping beauty here, so I went out and chatted up a cute nurse. Then, I decided to go and get food that wasn't cooked in the cafeteria. Why?"

"What was the name of the nurse you spoke with?"

"Tammy, or Cami, or something like that."

"Detective, what's with all the questions?"

"Tanger returned this morning. We went to pick him up, and it would appear that someone attacked him. Or more accurately, his car—while he was in it." Marcus turned to study Peter's reaction. He seemed almost angry.

"Was he hurt?" The venom of Peter's question confirmed Marcus' suspicions.

He must not have done it and is angry that someone beat him to it.

"Just a few cuts from the broken glass. But he was quite shaken up." Marcus should have felt bad for being disappointed that he wasn't lying unconscious in a room down the hall. But he didn't.

"So you're here because you assume it was one of us?"

"It seems likely."

"Believe me, I wish I would have done it—"

"Peter, shut up. Did he say who did it?"

"He didn't see. Just said it was a couple of guys in hoodies with baseball bats. It seems he was too busy cowering on the floorboards to get a good look." The detective looked down at his phone. "What time was your brother's flight, Mr. Polanski?"

Peter laughed. "You seriously think Tom or James would have done something like this? They're a couple of straight-laced pansies who busted me every time I so much as even thought about crossing any lines."

"Just answer the question."

"James left the hospital before lunch to pick up Tom and my parents at Marcus' house. He brought my parents back here before taking Tom on to the airport. His flight was scheduled to leave around noon, but it was overbooked and so he offered up his seat for a later flight. He does that kind of shit all the time. He makes good money but still has to take advantage of every freebee that comes his way. Anyway, James texted me that he was going to hang out with Tom at the airport until his flight left. I got a text a few minutes ago that he was on his way back to the hospital."

"I might need to pull your phone records, to confirm your story."

"So, what, now you're more interested in who smashed the lowlife's car to pieces instead of building a solid case against him in my wife's attack?"

"I didn't say that, but he filed a formal complaint and we have to look into it. As long as the other two can confirm they were where Mr. Polanski said they were, then I've considered it looked into. However, if there is a link to any of you then it could negatively impact our case against him. I'm sure his lawyer would try to spin it in some way that makes Tanger's actions look like self-defense. Assuming you're all telling the truth, there's nothing to worry about."

Marcus felt some of the tension leave his shoulders. "You still believe it will be an open and shut case?"

"He's not talking and he's with his lawyer right now. However, the evidence against him is staggering. My guess is that his lawyer is trying to get him some sort of deal considering he doesn't have a strong defense."

"Since he's in custody, does this mean we can stop watching Marcus around the clock?"

"Yes."

"Thank God." Marcus shot Peter an annoyed look.

"Have Mr. Polanski—James—give me a call when he returns. I'll keep you informed." Smith shook both their hands and walked away.

Marcus turned to Peter. "Are you going to tell me the truth?"

"That was the truth!" Peter ran a hand over his face in frustration before turning around to make sure no one else was in the hallway. "I was going to do something. A guy I know was able to get me some information. I knew he was back in town. But James put me on lockdown with you, and it seems I've missed my chance. Besides, I wouldn't have been satisfied with just the car."

"How do you know a guy... you know what, never mind. I don't want to know. I just hope your guy didn't decide to go ahead and do something anyway. If he did, and there's any link to you, it won't end well."

"There won't be a link."

Marcus should have felt relief. Mark was in custody and nothing could tie Peter to the attack. But something in his gut told him it wasn't over.

Marcus was near the end of his patience when the door finally opened. He watched as the nurse wheeled Sarah back into the room. Once the nurse left, he resumed his post at her side.

"Hey. There are those pretty brown-green eyes I love so much." Sarah settled her tired gaze on him and smiled. "Were your tests all right?"

"Yes. I'm tired though." He tried to hide his concern. She should be getting stronger, but she just wanted to sleep more than ever. He watched her look around the room. "Where's the protector of walls?"

"I've been released."

"I assume that's a... good thing?"

"Yes, it is."

"Now do I get to know why?"

"Not yet. I told you that you had to get out of the bed for me to tell you what happened."

"You don't play fair."

"Neither do you. Should I talk until you fall asleep again?"

"Yes. First I want another one of your three... presumptive things." He contemplated refusing to give it to her just yet, but decided to comply hoping it would lift her spirits.

"I planned a trip for our first anniversary. That gives you about six months to be in perfect health."

"Do I get to know where we're going?"

"You mentioned you always wanted to go to London." He nearly cried when he saw the light enter her eyes. "It gets better. I figured while we were in England I'd take you here." He pulled a piece of paper out of his pocket and unfolded it before handing it to her.

"Downton Abbey?"

"The official name of the estate is Highclere Castle. I've already purchased tickets, and they are non-refundable and non-transferable. So, we're going on our anniversary."

"Marcus. Thank you. It's wonderful. Your surprises keep getting better. I don't know how you're... going to top this." He tried not to think about the bag sitting under the table. It would definitely be the one she would appreciate most, but he wasn't ready to give it to her. It was time to distract her before she asked about it.

"What do you want me to talk about tonight?"

She was quiet for a few seconds before she spoke. "Since you are on a roll with... the surprises, tell me something... I don't know."

"I tell you everything."

"There has to be something."

"Are you saying there are things you haven't told me?"

A small smile played at her lips. "How else do I keep you... interested?"

"You don't need to do anything to keep me interested. But I will make you spill your secrets just as soon as you're feeling better."

"Fine. But you first."

He didn't have to search for the one thing he hadn't told her. He wasn't exactly sure why he hadn't told her yet, and he wasn't sure this was the right moment. But she had asked, and he couldn't refuse. He took a deep breath and said a quick prayer that he was about to do the right thing.

CHAPTER 20
July • 2013

As expected, Marcus found Sarah and Tina in the backyard. They were walking around, planning for the wedding. When Sarah had told him that she wanted to have a small ceremony at the house, he couldn't have been happier. He walked up behind the ladies and slipped his arms around Sarah's waist, causing her to jump slightly.

"Hey, how are things coming along at the studio?"

"Everything's right on track. We should be done before the wedding. Speaking of the wedding, how are you ladies doing with the planning?"

"Considering you two only gave me a two month window, I'd say it's coming along fabulously. You know everyone's going to think this is a shotgun wedding, right?"

"That's why we're only inviting the few people we actually like. They all know the deal, and I don't give a flip what anyone else thinks." He felt Sarah shift in his arms and he twisted her slightly so he could see her face. "Will it bother you if people assume it's a shotgun wedding?"

Sarah looked back at him, momentarily confused. "Oh, no. I don't care what anyone thinks. My family was a bit concerned at the rush of it all, but James helped convince them it was all legit."

He nodded and gave her a light kiss on her neck.

"So. Vail. For your honeymoon. In the summer. You couldn't do any better than that?" Marcus reluctantly pulled his lips from Sarah's neck to address Tina's ribbing.

"What's wrong with Vail?"

"Nothing, except it's right in our backyard. A honeymoon is supposed to be special. You can go to Vail any time."

"Joan will be on maternity leave, and there's no other doctor available to fill in. Frank will be there alone, and I need to be nearby in case there's an emergency." He looked at Sarah again. "You're okay with Vail, right?" She didn't respond, silently staring off into the mountains. "Sarah?"

She snapped back to attention and looked at Marcus over her shoulder. "Sorry?"

"I was just making sure you were okay with going to Vail for our honeymoon."

"Oh, yes, don't mind Tina. She's just trying to live vicariously through us. She's been to Vail several times, so she was hoping for something different. I've never been, and I'm looking forward to it."

He accepted her answer, but he knew there was something bothering her. She still hadn't told him what upset her the night of her birthday dinner. He tried to ask a few times, but she skirted the subject each time.

"Good. And I promise to make up for it on our first anniversary." Sarah's phone rang and she pulled away to see who it was.

"It's my brother. I'll be right back." Marcus watched her walk off toward the house before turning to Tina.

"Do you think Sarah's doing okay with all of this?"

"Why do you ask?"

"We both know this is hard for her. I'm worried it's bringing up too many painful memories of her life with Nick. She says that she's doing fine, but something happened on her birthday. The evening seemed to be going fine until dinner. She tried to hide it, but I could tell she was struggling. She won't tell me what it is, and I'm hoping she's at least confided in you."

"No, she hasn't said anything to me. Are you worried she's not ready to get married?"

He ran his hand through his hair. "I don't know, maybe. I don't want her to feel like I'm pressuring her. I kind of forced the issue on moving in, and maybe it was all just too much too fast."

Either that or she's having regrets marrying someone who might suffer at the hands of a horrendous, rare, fatal disease.

He shook his head as if it could physically shake out the negative thoughts. Sarah hadn't given him any reason to believe she regretted her decision. She wasn't the type of woman to do something she wasn't one hundred percent committed to. If his possible fate with CJD was a barrier, she would have said so.

"I haven't noticed anything, but I'll pay closer attention going forward."

"Thanks, Tina. I'm glad she has you as a friend."

"Since I can't have you for myself, I had to settle for being best friends with the woman who did claim you. That way I can stare at you without it being weird."

"It's still weird." He nudged her with his elbow, causing her to laugh.

"Come on, I'll walk you through our plans so far." He followed Tina around the yard and listened as she explained their plans. He didn't offer any opinions, and she finally stopped asking for them. It wasn't that he didn't care about the wedding details; it was just that there was only one detail he found important enough to worry about. And that was making sure Sarah was happy. As long as the color of the flowers, the menu, and the location of the reception tent made her happy, then he was happy.

Max suddenly bounded noisily through the yard and Marcus turned, knowing Sarah wouldn't be far behind. There was an odd look on her face.

"Everything all right with James?"

"What? Oh, no, that was Peter. He's coming to visit this weekend. Something about it being his responsibility to make sure you were worthy of being my husband."

Marcus hadn't yet met Peter and he knew he was going to be the most difficult one of Sarah's family to win over. Peter had been best friends with Nick, and Marcus knew that it would be difficult for him to watch his sister marry someone else.

"Should I be worried?"

"Possibly."

"Because of what he's going to do to me? Or because he might be able to convince you to change your mind?"

"I'm not changing my mind about marrying you. But he might intend to do you bodily harm."

"Great. I can't wait. It sounds like it's going to be a fun weekend."
Sarah and Tina laughed at his obvious discomfort. "I'm going to let
you finish up out here without me." He turned toward the house,
deciding he needed to focus on developing a strategy for Peter's visit.

The doorbell rang and Marcus chastised himself for being nervous.
He wiped his sweaty palms down the front of his jeans and followed
Sarah to the door. They'd offered to pick Peter up at the airport, but
he insisted on driving so he could visit friends who lived in the area.
Marcus took a deep breath as Sarah opened the door. Peter stepped
forward and instantly pulled her into a hug.

"Hey, sis. You look wonderful."

"It's good to see you, Peter." Sarah took him by the arm and
practically dragged him inside. Marcus closed the distance between
them and offered his hand in greeting.

"It's good to finally meet you, Peter." He took Marcus' hand and
scrutinized him blatantly.

"First impression—you're too good looking to be fully trusted."

"Peter!"

Peter turned to look at Sarah. "What? You forget I got all the good
looks in our family, so I know how it works. Not that I'd admit it in
public, but he's even better looking than I am. I think it's those eyes."
Peter looked at Marcus again and leaned in close, as if trying to
discern if his eye color was real or fabricated.

"They're real. And hopefully by the end of your stay you'll find I'm
very trustworthy when it comes to your sister." Peter narrowed his
eyes and leaned away from Marcus.

"We'll see. It's the whole point of my trip after all."

"Alright, that's enough. Can't you at least wait to start the
interrogation until after you've had a tour of the house?"

Peter studied Marcus for a few more seconds before responding.
"Fine." He turned away and looked around the foyer. "This is one
hell of a place you've got yourself. You got the same trust that I did,
and I know you don't make much managing projects, so what gives?"

"You know Elijah left me this house. Marcus and I make enough
to cover the living expenses. Besides, I invested my trust wisely where
you only focused on the three G's."

"The three G's?" Marcus couldn't resist asking for clarification.

"Gambling, girls, and gin." Her explanation was said with more disapproval than amusement.

No wonder she wasn't surprised by the confessions of my past. It seems Peter had already primed the way for dysfunctional behavior.

"I'm off the gin and on to whiskey now. It's a much better investment. So, let's get this tour started. By the size of this place it looks like it might take an hour or more."

"Actually, it should only take forty-five minutes." Marcus couldn't help but laugh at Sarah's witty retort. Marcus allowed Sarah to take the lead on the tour. Roughly thirty minutes later they ended on the back patio. It took longer than usual simply because Peter had so many questions. Marcus often forgot Sarah's family business was in architecture, but he was quickly reminded whenever her brothers were around. She could hold her own in a conversation, but she didn't share the passion in it the way her father and brothers did.

They settled on the patio, Sarah nestled under Marcus' arm, and Peter across from them.

"So, why the need to get married so quickly?"

"Directness must run in the family." Sarah lightly jabbed Marcus in the ribs with her elbow, but he ignored the warning. He had a sister— he knew how this worked. He focused on Peter, holding his gaze. "We decided there was no reason to wait."

"Except for the whole 'get to know each other' part that usually comes before marriage."

"Sure, that's one approach. But there are some people who can be together for sixty years and never really know each other. Then there are those that know each other instantly."

"And that's you—instantly, just like that—" Peter paused to snap his fingers. "—you know each other?"

"Yes, for me at least. Although, it took Sarah some time to come to the same conclusion."

"Six months isn't that much time. You have to understand our reluctance. If—"

"'*Our?*' Did the family send you as a representative to speak on everyone's behalf?" The irritation in Sarah's voice was rapidly growing. Marcus took her hand and squeezed it, trying to reassure her.

"Not exactly. I have my own agenda here, but you can't be surprised that we all have concerns over the speed of your relationship. The only reason we've been accommodating is because James vouched for the two of you."

"Well, I'm so glad you all believe in James more than me. It's great to have such a supportive family." Sarah pulled her hand free and crossed her arms. Marcus stifled his smile. She was quite adorable when she pouted. He tightened his arm around her shoulders, trying to get her to release some of the tension.

"It's not like you can be objective in this situation. You're making a life altering decision, when not long ago you were refusing to even live your life. How could we not be concerned?"

"This coming from the guy, who at thirty-eight years old, can't even hold down a stable job or relationship."

"I could, I just choose not to." Marcus looked back and forth from Sarah to Peter, who'd locked eyes in an impressive stare down. Finally Peter sighed and ran a hand across his face. "Look, I didn't come here to argue."

"Then why are you here?"

"To see if I approve of Marcus."

"It doesn't matter if you do or not! I'm not changing my mind. Marcus and I will be married, in this backyard, in one month. I'd love it if you would be here to celebrate with us, but if you can't support us then don't bother coming." Marcus could hear the slight tremble in her voice and pulled her tighter.

"I'm not going to try to change your mind. I know it doesn't matter to you if I approve or not. I just need to know for myself if I approve. Did you forget that Nick was my best friend? I need to know if I can be okay with Marcus as your husband." The tension finally left Sarah's shoulders and she slumped against Marcus' side.

"No, I didn't forget." She paused for a moment and looked off toward the mountains. "So how do you go about figuring out if you approve of Marcus?"

"By spending time with him, of course. Alone. I thought maybe we could go for a hike tomorrow."

Marcus took a deep, steadying breath. He was good at charming people, but Peter was going to be the most difficult challenge he'd ever encountered.

"Just promise me you won't push him off the side of the mountain."

Peter smiled and shook his head. "I suppose I can at least promise that much."

Peter had been mostly quiet on the hike, and what conversation they did have was casual. However, Marcus knew better than to assume it meant he was off the hook. They reached the end of the trail, which looked out over the mountains, and sat down on a large boulder. Peter waited to speak again until the other two hikers they encountered on the trail had moved on.

"I'm sorry if I came off a little harsh yesterday, but when it comes to my baby sister I don't mess around."

"I have a younger sister as well, so I fully understand. I put her husband through quite a bit of shit when it was clear they were serious." He glanced at Peter, who was nodding while looking out over the mountains. "So you and Nick were best friends?"

Peter looked at him sharply, almost as if he was surprised Marcus would initiate the interrogation.

"He was a year younger than me, but we were on the soccer team together. He was a good man."

"That's what I hear. I'm sorry he's gone."

"Are you? I mean, no offense, but if he were still here then we wouldn't be having this conversation. You probably never would have even met Sarah."

It was Marcus' turn to nod. "I know it seems impossible to understand. There are moments when I don't fully understand it myself. All I know is that I would give anything to make Sarah happy. If having Nick and Danny back in her life would make her happier than she's able to be with me, then that's what I would want for her."

"I'm sure you're not surprised that I find that hard to believe. I don't want you to give me answers you think I want to hear. I want the truth."

"I'm not surprised, and it is the truth. Over the last few years I had convinced myself I was never going to find the woman I was meant to be with. As you said, if Nick were still alive I likely never would have met Sarah. Had I not met her, I would have continued on with my life the way it was and would have probably never married. But now that I've met her, I can't live without her."

Peter was quiet for a moment, absorbing Marcus' words. "Have you ever been in love before?"

"Once, when I was in college. At the time I was convinced I would marry her."

"What happened?"

"She cheated on me with my roommate. It kind of killed the whole 'happily ever after' theory I had going on."

"No one since then?"

"I've dated several women over the years, but none that I loved." Marcus took a deep breath and looked around at the beautiful display of nature before him. "My mom died shortly after I broke it off with Rachel. It was a difficult time for me. I became obsessed with finding the kind of love my parents had, knowing that there was one woman out there for me and all I had to do was find her. Admittedly, I could have gone about it a different way, but it is what it is."

"What makes you so sure Sarah's the one you've been looking for?"

"You know that I dance." He looked at Peter and saw the smile spread across his face. "And I know you think it somehow detracts from my masculinity, but I don't care—I got over that stigma a long time ago. Anyway, when my mom died I stopped dancing. The thought of stepping onto a dance floor caused an anxiety attack. I think that when I lost my mom I also lost a piece of my soul. I didn't know how to get it back. Until the moment my eyes found Sarah. In that instant, all I wanted to do was dance. Just looking at her made me feel alive again—feel whole. She's all that matters in my life."

"I know you're aware that Sarah told us about your father's illness and that you may have it too. Why should I be okay with you marrying my sister when there's a fifty percent chance you could suffer the same fate? If Sarah has to watch you go through that someday, it could destroy her all over again."

Marcus closed his eyes and took a deep breath. He'd wondered if Peter would ask about his possible illness. He wanted to tell him that it didn't matter, because that's what he wanted to believe himself. But he knew that in this moment honesty was the right answer. He looked out over the mountains again and searched for the appropriate words.

"I haven't yet been tested for the CJD mutation, and I'm not sure if I ever will. I had asked Sarah before we even started down this road if she needed to know. She decided to take a leap of faith and I jumped with her. I can't think about her having to watch me suffer from CJD someday." He had to pause. A lump had formed in the back of his throat and threatened to choke out his words.

"Yes, I'm worried about our future. But if I let my possible fate with CJD keep us apart, doesn't that mean I also have to back off based on all the other 'what ifs' that are out there? I could die in a car accident. I could get cancer. I could have a heart attack. The list is endless. I refuse to not reach for happiness simply because something bad might happen someday. I'm just grateful that she has a strong family that will support her should anything happen to me."

Marcus watched as Peter picked up a small rock and rolled it around in his hand before tossing it over the edge of the mountain.

"I saw the pictures hanging in the family room. I don't know many men that would be able to embrace the situation the way you have."

Marcus let out a sigh. "I'll admit, it's not easy sometimes. I think I'll always feel like I'm living in his shadow. I know they had a strong relationship, and that she still loves him. I don't think I could claim to be human if I said it didn't bother me. I guess I feel like the best way I can manage it is to integrate him into our lives in some way."

Peter studied him before pulling an envelope out of his back pocket and handing it to Marcus.

"What's this?"

"It's the reason I needed to decide if I approved of you. Nick gave me that when Sarah was pregnant with Danny. He told me to hold on to it, and if anything should happen to him, I was to give it to the man Sarah married next."

The envelope in Marcus' hands suddenly became very heavy. It reminded him of the letters his father had left for him when he died. He still hadn't opened those letters, and he wasn't sure how he'd be able to open this one either. "I—I don't know what to say."

"You don't need to say anything. You just need to read it. This looks like a good spot to read the words of your soon-to-be wife's dead husband." Peter clapped him on the back before standing and starting down the trail, leaving him alone with Nick's words. With a trembling hand he broke the seal.

To the man who loves my wife,

Let me start by saying that it's as uncomfortable for me to write this as it is for you to read it. I'm sure if Sarah knew I was doing this she would be upset, telling me there's no reason to write such a morbid letter. I don't agree, so that's why she will never know unless you choose to tell her.

Something's been nagging me lately and I couldn't figure out what it was. When I looked at Sarah's sleeping face this morning, so beautiful and peaceful, I finally found clarity. You see, she's eight months pregnant with our first child. We don't know if it will be a boy or a girl, which I'm sure you know is driving Sarah nuts. She likes to plan and organize. Not being able to decide on a theme for the nursery is her definition of the worst kind of torture. Personally, I like surprises. The more drawn out the better. However, it appears nine months is almost too long even for me. It's a good thing she's due soon, or I might let the doctor tell us!

Anyway, as I watched Sarah sleep I thought about the day ahead of us. I know she will almost instantaneously launch into her nesting activities. If you've not had children of your own, it's truly an amazing phenomenon to witness. Everything in the house has been cleaned and organized more than once. And it doesn't seem to stop the next day. Thinking about this nesting instinct pregnant women go through is what highlighted my issue. I think I'm facing the urge to nest as well. But mine has nothing to do with how the dishes are organized or how clean the closets are. It's about protecting my family's future.

I expect to be here for Sarah for many years. To be by her side for a few more children and lots of grandchildren. But I know life isn't that predictable. If you're reading this as the soon-to-be husband of my wife, then my life definitely didn't turn out as I had planned. It also means that Sarah has gone through something very painful.

Sorry, I can't think about that, so I'll get to the point of this letter.

I'm going into this with the assumption that you know just how beautiful Sarah is on the inside as well as the outside. When she commits to something, she gives herself over to it completely. If she's marrying you, that means she has given you everything she has to give. However, she is human and that means she has flaws and weaknesses. The main challenges Sarah faces are that she can't let go of guilt and she doesn't trust in her own strength.

I've tried to work with her on letting go of guilt. Unfortunately, I haven't made much progress. I think it's because of the second issue—she doesn't know how to rely on her own strength. She's always been this way. I chastise her brothers because I think it's their fault for being overprotective. With three older brothers, she never needed to shoulder anything on her own. When we started dating, I took over the responsibility and never stopped.

I messed up once, when I graduated high school. I was young and stupid. I thought I was doing Sarah a favor, forcing her to be tough through separation. I intended to win her back when she joined me at college, but it hit her harder than I had anticipated. Eventually, she did pull through and we found our way back to each other. However, knowing how that separation impacted her in the past scares me for how she will be affected if something happens to me in the future.

If she's marrying again, then something's gone right. Somehow she found the strength to move on and embrace a new life. And I probably have you to thank for that.

So that's why I'm writing this letter. To say thank you for loving and taking care of my family. I'll soon have a child and so this is about more than just Sarah. It's about my son or daughter (or children if we have more by the time you get this letter). I hope you can embrace my children as your own while reminding them just how much I loved them.

If Sarah chose you, I know you're the kind of person I would have called a friend. So as a friend, promise me you'll always love and protect my family. Until Sarah figures out on her own just how strong she is, she'll need someone to remind her.

Nick

CHAPTER 21

Marcus watched Sarah closely, waiting for her reaction. He wasn't exactly sure why he'd never told her about the letter. When he thought about it, he always felt it was because he was ashamed to claim the credit Nick gave him. Talking to Sarah about it would have forced him to admit he wasn't everything he should have been.

It was my father that helped her move on, not me. I've always hated that. I know it's petty, but from the moment I laid eyes on her I wanted to be the one person she could rely on most in the world. At least I knew I could protect her. I made a promise to myself, as well as to Nick, that I always would. And now I've failed at that too.

"Why didn't you tell me about the letter?"

"I don't know. I guess part of it is because I felt I didn't deserve his gratitude. He thanked me for helping you heal. But it was my father who did that—not me. It didn't feel right."

"Marcus. Look at me." She waited until he complied with her request. "You did help me heal. Elijah taught me to trust in my strength. But you taught me to accept hope. I needed both to heal."

"But now I failed—"

"Don't even start on the... protecting me crap again. It's not your fault. Let it go. I mean it. No more."

"It's not that easy, Sarah! You're more vital to me than breathing! How could I not need to protect you? The one time I turn my back on you, this happens. This wasn't a small slip—it was huge! How is it not my fault?"

"Even as important as breathing is... you can survive for a while... without it. Someone can breathe for you. A machine can help you." She touched the tubes under her nose to help make her point. "You can't protect me... every hour of every day. It's not possible. I didn't listen to you. I went to the appointment. If you're at fault... so am I. You have to let it go."

He didn't know what to say. He knew what he *should* say, but the words refused to form. The door opened and he was relieved at the interruption.

"Sarah, dear, you're awake."

"Hi, Mom."

Catherine looked from Sarah to Marcus, her brow furrowing in the center. "Did I come at a bad time?"

"No, Catherine, it's fine. You know you're welcome any time."

"Marcus, I want to talk... to my mom."

He felt a slight pang at her words. He wasn't making things easy for her. He was afraid she was getting frustrated with his constant self-loathing. Or that she was upset from hearing about the letter from Nick.

He gave her a gentle kiss before walking out of the room. He mindlessly wandered through the hospital, not aware of his surroundings until he found himself in an empty waiting room. He sat down by the windows and looked out over the city lights illuminating the dark night. He always loved the fast pace of the city, but now all he wanted was to go home. He longed for the peace and isolation their house offered, surrounded by the beauty of the mountains.

He wasn't sure how to give Sarah what she wanted, what she needed, and he was afraid it would permanently damage their relationship. If not worse. She was fighting to hold on to life while he was focused only on holding on to guilt.

Even though they were destined to be together, he'd always known their path wouldn't be easy. There was too much pain in Sarah's past and too much uncertainty in his future. But he'd convinced himself that he would remain strong enough to shoulder anything that life threw their way. This was his first test of that commitment, and he was failing miserably. There was a truth he could feel hovering just under the surface that he knew would set him free, but he couldn't grab hold of it.

His phone buzzed and brought him out of his thoughts.

"Hello, James."

"Where are you? I went by Sarah's room and Mom said you left several minutes ago."

"I'm in some waiting room. When did you get back?"

"Just a few minutes ago. I decided to swing back by the house and get some work done before coming here. I let Max out while I was there. I'm taking Mom and Dad back so they'll be with him overnight."

"Did you talk to Peter? Detective Smith came by and wanted to speak with you when you got back."

"Yeah, I gave the detective a call and answered his questions. It's one of the reasons I'm calling, actually. Detective Smith said there was something he needed to discuss with you. Said he'd swing by the hospital tomorrow morning."

"Did he say what it was about?"

"No. I asked, but he insisted it was best to discuss it in person. He'll be here at eight."

A knot formed in the pit of his stomach. He couldn't think about the possibility that Mark would get off on some sort of technicality. "Alright, thanks for the update." There was a long pause and Marcus waited, sensing James had something to say.

"How are you holding up?"

"I wish I could say 'the best I can,' but I'm not so sure that'd be accurate."

"Sounds accurate enough to me."

"Well, then you're an idiot. I'm failing and you know it. I don't need your gentle affirmations right now."

"Would you rather I come down and kick your ass?"

"Yes."

James sighed and Marcus closed his eyes. "Listen, I'm not judging you here and neither is anyone else. You're the only one passing judgment. I know you Kingstons have an unnaturally high regard for yourselves, but you're the only one who sees this as your fault. You have to at least consider the possibility that you're wrong and everyone else is right."

Marcus was quiet for a few seconds before accepting James' words. "Thanks. That actually helped."

They said their good-byes and he hung up, heading back toward Sarah's room. He was tired and decided he wasn't going to be able to alter his state of mind that night. Tomorrow was another day and he would try again.

Marcus lay on his uncomfortable cot, staring at the ceiling. It was just before eight in the morning, and he'd already showered and checked on Sarah. She'd been sleeping since he returned to her room the night before. It gave him a lot of time to process his actions. He wanted to be the man he promised Sarah he would be. It was time. It was as if his body could feel every second that ticked away, bringing him closer to what he couldn't bring himself to acknowledge.

He heard the door open, and he looked up to see James enter. Marcus nodded in the direction that James had just come and got up to follow him out into the hall.

"Sarah's still sleeping?"

"Yeah. She's been asleep since you left last night."

"Did you get the results from the additional tests you asked the doctor to run?"

"He said he'd review them with me today." They walked in silence for a few minutes before James spoke again.

"Is it all right if I sit in on the meeting with you and the detective?"

"Sure. Why do you think he wants to meet?"

"No idea." James shrugged his shoulders as they entered the small meeting room down the hall from Sarah's room. It was the same room where Marcus had punched the wall a few days ago. His hand tingled at the thought.

"Mr. Kingston, Mr. Polanski."

"Good morning, Detective Smith. Do you mind if James joins us?" The detective hesitated a second, as if he was going to say no, but then nodded in agreement.

"This is my partner, Detective Crass." Marcus took in the new detective's appearance as they shook hands. He didn't look like he was a day over sixteen. His blond hair was short and spiky. His tall frame was narrow, playing into his youthful look. Marcus looked down at their joined hands and noticed a trace of tattoos under his sleeve.

"Have you been working on my wife's case the whole time?"

"Yes, but I often leave the interviews to Detective Smith. People respond to him better than they do me. Probably because I look like I should still be in high school." Marcus smiled, appreciating his direct approach.

"I'm sure you're wondering why I asked to meet with you."

"Did something go wrong with the case against Mark?"

The detectives exchanged glances. "Not exactly. But, he's claiming to have had help."

Marcus felt his pulse quicken and the hairs on his arms rise. "Van said he only saw Mark."

"We're certain that he was the only one that attacked your wife and Mr. Vanderlink. However, he claims there was someone feeding him information. Remember when I told you he had access to details, such as your wife's appointment schedule, that he shouldn't have known about? It's possible that his accomplice provided him with that information."

"Who is it?"

"He won't say. He's trying to leverage the information to get a deal."

"What the fu—"

"I think what Marcus wants to ask is if you're willing to give him a deal for the information." James shot Marcus a warning look. He clenched his teeth and sat back, knowing James was right. It wouldn't do any good for him to lose control in front of the detectives.

"We don't want to—that's why we're here. We'd like a list of all the people who would have access to your wife's schedule."

"This is unbelievable. I found it difficult to grasp the fact that there was even one person who would harm her, let alone two!"

"What about you? Is there anyone who would wish to harm you that would have access to this information?"

Marcus let out a frustrated sigh. "I have no idea."

"Why don't we start by listing the people that work with Mrs. Kingston?"

Marcus looked at Crass. "This is ridiculous. I won't let you harass good people. She works with a charity organization! It's their mission to get people out of the hospital, not put them in! Can't you make that asshole talk without a deal?"

"We've tried, but he's not budging. Look, Mr. Kingston, we're on the same side here. We don't want to harass anyone, and we don't want to give Tanger a deal. But we need to figure out who could have given him the information. You've made it clear we're not allowed to talk to Mrs. Kingston, so you're our best chance of figuring this out. If you would stop resisting and start listing names, then Detective Smith and I can get out of here and make some progress."

Marcus shook his head in frustration and started naming the people who worked in Sarah's office.

"Thank you. What about the people you work with, at your veterinary practice and your dance studio?"

Marcus was about to protest again when he felt James' hand press down on his shoulder, reminding him it was better to cooperate. He rattled off the names, unable to believe any of them would conspire with Mark to hurt Sarah. The detectives asked for a few more names—friends, house cleaning staff—basically anyone Sarah had interacted with over the last year.

By the time they were finished, his mind was racing back and forth between various conspiracy theories and the possibility that Mark was lying. Marcus asked to use the room privately and waited until the others left before pulling out his phone.

"Miles, do you have a minute?"

"Marcus, did something happen?"

"No, things are still the same since the last time you were here. Tina probably mentioned that Van has been discharged and is recovering at home."

"I'm sorry I've not been there much. I'm in the middle of a case and it's taking up all my time. Tina's been keeping me informed."

"Yeah, she's been great. I know Sarah appreciates that she's here so much."

"What can I do for you?"

Marcus told him everything he knew about the case against Mark. "I was hoping this would be a slam-dunk, but it's not turning out that way. I know you're busy, but I was hoping you could do your 'lawyer thing' and look into it. Not that I don't trust the detectives to do their job, but I'd feel better if you were involved."

"It's not exactly my area of legal expertise, but I know someone who can help. I'll give him a call today."

"Thanks, Miles."

Marcus hung up and left the room quickly, no longer wanting to think about the possibility that someone they knew and trusted had betrayed them. He was stopped by Dr. Vikrant when he reached Sarah's room. He leveled Marcus with a stern glare before speaking.

"Mr. Kingston, I am going to be blunt. I cannot find any medical reason why your wife is not recovering as expected. Her wounds appear to be healing and I don't see evidence of internal trauma that was previously overlooked."

"You're saying it's a mental block?"

"Your wife went through a lot of trauma. Most people who have experienced an attack like this live in fear. They are afraid of getting attacked again. Your wife's case is different. We have established that she did not feel anything during the attack. She did not see it coming, so there was no fear before it happened. In her mind, she was outside on the street one minute and in the hospital the next. I do not believe she fears the attack, but rather the results of it. You know what I am referring to. She needs your help to get past it. That is my opinion at least."

Marcus watched the doctor walk off down the hall. It was getting harder to hide from the impact of his actions. With a heavy heart, he walked back to Sarah's room. Her eyes fluttered open when he took her hand.

"Good morning. I've missed you."

"I've been right here. Can't leave this bed... unfortunately."

"I know, but you've been sleeping for a long time."

"I'm tired."

"I know."

"I can't do this any more." Tears pricked his eyes at her words, and the tightness in his chest felt crushing.

"You have to keep fighting, Sarah. I know it's hard, and I know you're tired. But I need you. I need you to fight."

She closed her eyes as a tear fell down the side of her cheek. "I can't keep fighting... for both of us."

He kissed her hand. "You're right. I haven't been fighting hard enough. Not for the right things at least."

"It's time. Tell me about your father's... letter. And everything... that surrounds it."

He felt his throat constrict. He was sure the tightness would choke out his breath as well as his words. He swallowed hard. "I don't know if I can."

"You have to. This is it, Marcus. My last request."

"And then what happens?"

"I have to stop trying... to fix you... so I can... fix me."

He felt the blood drain quickly from his face.

That's why she can't heal. She has been fighting, but she's been fighting for me. She's spent so much energy trying to help me get through this that she doesn't have enough to fight her own battle.

It finally clicked into place. There was a purpose to her walk down memory lane after all. It wasn't just to remember happier times as Dr. Vikrant had suggested. It was to help him find a way back. Each memory she asked him to talk about was carefully considered—they were key moments in their life together. She wanted to not only remind him of the promises he'd made, but also of all that they had been through together so far. He'd been so consumed by his failure to protect her that he lost sight of how his self blaming affected her. It was time to let it go. He wasn't sure yet how to do it, but he knew the first step was to talk about it.

CHAPTER 22
Late July • 2013

Marcus glanced over at Sarah. She stood at the other end of the counter, chopping tomatoes. He smiled at her slow, deliberate slices. She wasn't much of a cook, but he didn't mind. It wasn't that she didn't know how—she just didn't like it. When he did succeed in getting her to help, she usually took responsibility for preparing the salad. He looked back to the steaks he had just pulled off the grill. As he placed one on a plate, he noticed a sudden movement out of the corner of his eye and he looked over to Sarah. She stood clutching the counter with one hand and her head with the other.

"Sarah, honey, are you okay?" He rushed over to her side and placed his hand on her back.

"I think so. I just got lightheaded all of a sudden."

"Sit down here for a minute." He helped her to a chair in the family room and knelt in front of her. She was pale and looked tired. "Did you eat enough today?" Even though she was eating regularly and was back to a healthy weight, he'd always be concerned she didn't eat enough.

"I thought so, but maybe not. I had meetings all day, and over lunch I decided to complete a few wedding tasks. I might have forgotten to eat. I probably over did it."

"If planning a wedding is too much, we can still go to Vegas." She smiled before giving him a light kiss.

"The wedding is less than a month away."

"So? We can still run off and get married and then wait a couple of months to have a party. It would give you more time to plan. I don't like seeing you so stressed."

"I'll be fine. Really. I promise to not forget to eat again, and I should probably rest tonight. That means I'll have to watch you dance, rather than dance with you. It'll be hard, but I think I can suffer through it."

He pinned her to the back of the chair with a kiss that he wanted to turn into more. Remembering that she wasn't feeling well, he pulled away. "You go get settled outside, and I'll bring the food."

He watched her walk slowly to the patio doors. She almost fell over when Max jumped up on her, excited to be going outside. He was about to go help her when she steadied herself and stepped out onto the patio. He quickly finished dinner and prepared two plates. Sarah was sitting at the patio table, staring off at the mountains. She smiled at him when he set her plate down in front of her. While they ate, he talked about the progress they were making at the studio. By the time they finished eating, she had regained some color in her cheeks and he relaxed.

"By the way, I talked to Ms. Verdos this morning. There was an offer on my house. It's actually a pretty good offer considering the current market conditions. The bonus is that they requested a closing date just before the wedding and then thirty days after to move in. I thought the timing would be perfect. Miles will act as a proxy for us at the closing, so we won't need to be there. The buyers are from out of state and won't be there either. We could stay at my house after we get back from Vail. You could work from there while I'm filling in for Joan at the clinic, and we could finish packing up my stuff in the evenings. I'd have to figure something out for the remainder of Joan's maternity leave, but at least we'd have the first month figured out."

He noticed he lost Sarah somewhere during his long winded update. She was staring off at the mountains again, her eyes vacant and her fingers clutching at her pendant.

"Sarah?"

"Hmm? I'm sorry, my mind drifted."

"Are you sure you're okay?"

"I'm fine, just tired."

He'd stopped asking her what had upset her the night of her birthday dinner, but he felt the need to try again. This time he decided to take a different approach.

"Did Joan say something to upset you?"

"What? No, why would you think that?"

"You know I'm aware that something bothered you the night we had dinner with them for your birthday. Ever since, whenever I mention Joan's name, you... become tense. I know you'll tell me when you're ready, but I can't help but wonder—"

"It was seeing Joan pregnant."

The unexpectedness of her statement caused his brain to malfunction for a second.

"I don't understand."

"I didn't know she was pregnant before we met with her."

"I'm sorry... I didn't realize that I hadn't told you."

How could that have not come up in conversation?

Marcus searched his brain for an explanation. He'd told her a new doctor was coming on board at the clinic and she must have assumed it was because he was leaving to open the dance studio. It never occurred to him that he hadn't mentioned the initial reason was to cover for Joan while she was on maternity leave. It had just worked out that the doctor could come on board full time when Marcus decided to switch professions.

He watched Sarah bury her face in her hands and he quickly went to her side, pulling her into his arms.

"Honey, talk to me. Why did seeing Joan pregnant upset you?"

"I realized we've made a lot of assumptions about our future. From the moment I decided to move out here we've been on one course. We're getting married in less than a month, but we've not talked about some of the most important things when it comes to marriage. Like having children." She closed her eyes and turned her face away.

"Sarah, honey, look at me." He waited until her eyes found his. The pain he saw about pulled his heart right out of his chest. "We both have reservations about having children—you because you've lost yours, and me because of my family history with CJD. And we do need to talk about it, but regardless of how that conversation goes I still want to spend the rest of my life with you. I don't know what the future holds for us, other than the fact that we're supposed to be together."

"But what if we don't want the same thing? It's not like choosing a paint color for the walls. This is a big deal."

"Come over here." He led her over to the seating area and settled next to her on one of the large patio chairs. "Answer me this. Are you ready to have children right now?"

"No."

"Neither am I. Are you, right now, firmly set one way or the other—do you absolutely want more children, or do you know for certain that you don't?"

"No."

"Neither do I. So as of *right now*, we're in agreement. This gives us time to discuss everything when it comes to children—our hopes and fears. I have every confidence that we will come to a conclusion together because I believe in us."

She took a deep breath and let it out slowly. "You once asked me if you having CJD would keep me from having a future with you. I told you I'd make my decision based on the possibility that you could have it someday. I still feel that way. I don't want CJD to influence our future any more than you do. However, when it comes to having children I think it's an important factor to consider. I'm not saying I wouldn't want to have children if you test positive for the mutated gene, but I feel it's something we should understand before we make a decision that would impact the lives of our future children."

He looked off to the mountains, wishing he could be pulled into the serenity of the glow from the setting sun. Instead he felt a heavy weight settle in the middle of his chest.

"I'm afraid things between us will change if I test positive for the CJD mutation. I don't want us counting down the days, waiting with bated breath for something tragic to happen. I want to look forward to tomorrow, not dread it."

"I want the same. But I've already buried one child." She paused to stifle the sob that threatened in her voice. "Although CJD is a disease that doesn't manifest until later in adulthood, I don't know if I could give my child that fate. All parents want the best for their children—want them to have a long and healthy life. I'm no different. Again, I'm not saying that I won't want to have children if you test positive. But, there's a part of me that feels like I need to know beforehand. I need to be able to prepare myself mentally before we head down that road. I'm learning a lot through my work at the foundation, but there's still so much I don't know. If we have children and there's a possibility they could have it too, I want to be able to help them in every possible way." She gently turned his face so their eyes met.

I'd do anything for her. Even face my greatest fear.

"Okay."

She looked at him a moment in silence before tracing his lips with her finger. When she finally responded, it was nothing more than a whisper. "You promise this won't break us?"

"I promise."

Marcus dropped to the floor in exhaustion and leaned against the wall. He'd been dancing for hours, trying to find the courage to do something he'd been avoiding since his father's death. Dancing always centered him, giving him the ability to see things more clearly. The conversation with Sarah a few days ago about children had unnerved him. She was asking him to get tested, but he didn't want to. It was the first time they had disagreed on an important issue.

He looked over at the envelopes sitting next to him. One had his name written in his father's handwriting and the other in Miles'. He was supposed to read them in order. He hadn't been ready to read his father's words, but now he hoped there was something in there to give him the strength to give Sarah what she was asking for. He picked up the one with his father's handwriting and broke the seal before he could change his mind.

Marcus,

It's with a heavy heart that I'm writing you this letter. It's been fifteen years since your mother died, yet I miss her more every day. I mention this first off because her being gone is the reason I'm writing you this letter. She was supposed to tell you and Leanne all of this when the time came, but fate changed that plan.

Assuming fate hasn't intervened a second time, you're reading this because I've died. Most likely at the hands of familial Creutzfeldt-Jakob disease (CJD). I know you and Leanne are probably angry at me for not telling you about my illness. It was a decision your mother and I made a long time ago, and I'd like to explain it to you now.

I've instructed Miles to not tell you and Leanne about my illness until I'm admitted to the hospital. By then, most of the worst parts of the illness should have passed. My reasons for not telling you are very simple—I don't want you to see me go through something so devastating. I don't want your memories of me to remain cemented in the horrors of this illness. Although we haven't had the best relationship, I'd still rather you remember those moments than the ones that CJD will produce.

I take full responsibility for the challenges in our relationship. You see, I had high expectations for us. I was very close with my father. When you were born, I was consumed with happiness. I envisioned a relationship like the one I had with my father. The first few years were amazing, and my dreams about us someday working together grew exponentially. However, as you got older it became clear you were going to be more like your mother.

At first, I thought it was a phase. Just a 'mama's boy' complex that would fade over time. But it didn't fade—it became more pronounced. There were a few years where I resented it. I'm not proud of that point in my life, but I was mourning the loss of a future I'd dreamed of for so long. Eventually I was able to come to terms with it, and I was determined to find a way for us to connect on a common ground.

That's when your grandfather died and I became aware of my genetic risk to CJD. Right or wrong, I decided it would be best to foster the gap between us rather than try to close it. It was painful for me to lose my father the way I did. I want to spare you that if I can. If you hate me long before I die, then maybe it won't be so hard for you after. Of course I run the risk of being wrong, and my actions may only cause you more pain. But I wouldn't be a Kingston if I spent my time second guessing my decisions.

If I have made it worse, please know that wasn't my intention. I love you, Marcus. I'm also very proud of the man you've turned out to be. I know you think I'm disappointed in your choices, but I'm not. Sure, I wished for something different when you were first born. But, surprisingly, I was wrong. You were destined for greater things.

My only regret is that I haven't encouraged you to continue dancing since your mother died. You have been given an amazing gift that should be embraced every day of your life. I hope you find it again.

It will be your decision to determine if you want to get tested for the CJD mutation. If you have questions, Dr. Holden will be able to explain the process. There are days when I'm happy I know what's likely to happen to me someday. There's an odd sort of comfort in not having to face uncertainty. Then there are days when I wish I had never been tested. This usually occurs on the days when I wish I had made a different choice in regard to our relationship. I let the test results guide certain decisions in my life, and while I'm not one to second guess my choices, it doesn't mean that I don't sometimes regret them.

I assume you will look more into this illness either way, and when you do you'll find that testing positive for the mutated gene doesn't automatically mean you'll suffer from CJD later. It may not manifest at all. However, I was never able to make that distinction in my mind. From the moment I tested positive, I've obsessively looked for signs that I was developing symptoms. So far this has resulted in a very exhausting, and lonely, twenty-plus years.

I can't tell you how to live your life—but I am going to tell you to live it. Do whatever you need to do to make that happen.

I love you, son. Don't ever question that.

Dad

Marcus didn't fight his emotions from taking over. He was angry. He was hurt. He was relieved. But more important than anything he felt was what he *didn't* feel—he was no longer confused. For so long he couldn't understand his father's actions. He'd felt it was something he had done, or had failed to do, that caused the rift between them. Now he understood it was a choice his father had made in an effort to spare him. He had felt it would be better to cause minor pain through a strained relationship in the hope of saving him from a greater pain down the road. It was misguided, but at least now he understood why his father built the wall between them.

When he felt he had control over his emotions, he picked up the second envelope. Sarah had shown him the letter his father had written to her, which was also addressed from Miles. It meant that this letter was likely written at the same time. He took a moment to remember the events from the day that had triggered the writing of the letters. Finally, he broke the seal and began reading.

Marcus,

If you're reading this it means I've died. It also means that you know I died because of CJD. Miles told me that I already wrote you a letter explaining my illness and reasons for not telling you. I don't remember, so I'll have to take his word for it. Miles is typing this for me since I no longer have that ability.

It's Christmas Eve, my last, and I'm having a good day. My mind is clear, which is something I don't think has happened for a while. Miles is nodding like a bobble-head so I'm guessing I'm right. Although my mind is clear, my words are not. Miles will edit my thoughts so you can understand what I'm trying to tell you.

I just came up from downstairs where two remarkable things happened. The first is that I saw you dance. I don't even have the words. All I can say is thank you. I wish I had the capacity to hold that moment in my mind forever, but I know it will be gone very soon. When I came back upstairs, Miles reminded me I had recorded you and Sarah dancing at the gala. I just watched it again and I'm amazed by your talent.

The second thing that happened—I discovered how much you love Sarah. I have no idea how it happened. Miles told me you met at the gala. I don't remember that. Unfortunately, Miles also told me that I've said some less than positive things to you in regard to you pursuing a relationship with Sarah, and I've gone so far as to tell you to stay away from her. I'm told that I've been somewhat of an ass lately. At least I can blame that on CJD. Regardless, I'm sorry.

Sarah is an amazing woman and having her as a daughter-in-law someday makes me very proud and happy. Even though I won't be around to see it happen, I'll hold it in my heart for as long as my memory will allow. Even in that short conversation I heard downstairs, I could hear the determination in your voice. And when I watched the video of the two of you dancing, it was clear to me that she feels the same about you.

I'm hoping that by the time you read this letter she is healed enough to let you in. If not, just be patient with her. It will be worth it.

I know you, so I also know that you're struggling with how your possible future with CJD might impact your relationship with her. I wish I could tell you that there wouldn't be an impact. But I can't. It will affect many aspects of your life going forward.

While you can't stop CJD from affecting your future, you can stop it from controlling it. You have the power to take control. I can't tell you how to do that—it's different for everyone. Figure out what works for you.

I know you and Sarah will be happy together, as long as you can both learn to embrace all the good days you have been given.

I love you and wish you a very long, healthy, and happy life.

Dad

Marcus closed his eyes and let his father's words sink in. One sentence kept cycling through his mind.

You have the power to take control.

Marcus was like his mother in many ways. But there were also many ways he was like his father. Sarah often enjoyed pointing them out. One of those would be his inability to focus on a positive future if he tested positive for the CJD mutation. However, he knew it was important to Sarah if they were to plan for children.

There has to be a compromise—a way to plan for the future without having to know my fate.

He collected his letters and quickly got to his feet.

A week had passed since Marcus had talked to Sarah about being tested for the CJD mutation. He'd done his research and was finally ready to resume the conversation. She was late getting home from spending the day with Tina—they were trying to make progress on the foundation before the wedding. He was about to call her to ask when she'd be home when he heard the garage door open.

He called out to her from the kitchen. "Hey, honey. I didn't know you'd be so late. I tried to keep dinner warm, but not sure how successful I was." She rounded the corner and dropped her purse on the counter as he left to set the dining room table. He put the plates on the table and turned to greet her as she entered the room. He pulled her into a hug and gave her a kiss. "Did you have a good day?"

"It was... an enlightening day."

"I would describe my day as the same. Sit, eat."

She sat down and started to mindlessly play with her food. "Marcus, I think we need to revisit our discussion about children."

He smiled and swallowed his bite of food. He had been concerned that she would be upset by the conversation, so he was happy she had been the one to initiate it.

"I agree. I've been doing some research this week. We have some options, Sarah. There's this procedure called pre-implantation genetic diagnosis, or PGD, which can be used with in-vitro fertilization. With this process, the embryos can be tested for the CJD mutation, and then only those without it are implanted. We'd have to work with the doctor to see which labs do this testing, but it gives us the option to have children and not worry about my passing them the CJD gene. And, I don't have to get tested. Since my grandfather and father had it the pattern has been established, and I won't have to get tested. We'll just ask the doctor to not tell us what they found in the embryos." He hadn't realized how excited he was about the discovery until he spoke the words out loud. He studied Sarah and realized she wasn't as excited as he was. She looked like she was about to cry.

What if she's already decided she doesn't want more children?

He was unprepared for the intense feeling of disappointment. "Did I say something wrong? I thought you would be excited. One of our concerns was not knowing and not having control. We have the money for this procedure, so cost is not an issue. I know there are some mixed feelings and beliefs on what to do with the embryos not selected, but we will have time to talk through all of those details with a genetic counselor. The procedure itself is somewhat invasive, but again we have time to discuss—"

"I'm pregnant."

He felt as if the air around him had been sucked out of the room. All he could hear was a ringing in his ears. All he could feel was the painful pounding of his heart.

"You mean you *want* to get pregnant—"

"No. I *am* pregnant. Right now."

I'm going to be a father? We're going to have a baby? Should I be excited? Am I excited? Holy shit, she's pregnant!

"Are you sure?"

"I went to the doctor today to confirm. That's why I was late getting home tonight."

This isn't how it was supposed to happen. We were supposed to talk about it. We were supposed to plan for it. I was going to convince her that IVF was what we needed to do. Now we won't know. What if I've passed on the CJD gene? What if I'm a crappy father? I'm not ready. How did this happen? We've only been having sex for about a month. It doesn't happen that fast. Does it?

He pushed away from the table and paced the floor. "How..."

"We haven't exactly tried to prevent it, Marcus. It's my fault really. My cycle hasn't been regular since the accident, and I just wasn't thinking. I actually had myself believing that if we did want to get pregnant that I would have problems, and we would have to use IVF. And you did all that research, and IVF would have been a great solution to our problem, but now I'm pregnant, and we don't have a choice. Marcus, we—" Her rambling was cut off by her sobs. Finally, he broke out of his stupor and went to her side.

"Hey, it's going to be okay. Everything's going to be okay." He pulled her down from the chair and sat on the floor with her in his lap. "Look at me. Honey, please look at me." Finally she raised her tear-stained face.

"I'm so sorry—"

"Why? We're having a baby. We're having a baby!" Suddenly his face broke into a wide smile and he laughed. "I love you, and we're having a baby!" She smiled despite the tears that still fell down her cheeks.

"I love you too."

"You know, Tina's going to love that this turned out to be a shotgun wedding after all." He was happy to hear her laugh. "There's my girl. Everything's going to work out, you'll see. What's meant to be will be." He pulled her into another hug and tried not to think about their baby potentially having CJD.

Don't let it control your future.

His father's advice called loudly in his head. He clung to the thought, choosing to focus on enjoying the moment he first found out he was going to be a father.

CHAPTER 23

Marcus rubbed at his eyes with the palms of his hands, trying to take out the sting. It didn't help and soon his tears were flowing. Tears of pain and shame mixed together. He looked at Sarah and the pain in her eyes mirrored his own.

"You promised... it wouldn't break us."

"I know. That's the promise, out of all of them, that I regret failing on the most."

"You didn't fail. We're not broken."

"Aren't we? Have you forgotten where you are and why you're here? All that we almost lost and still might lose? How is that not broken?"

"We're not broken."

He stared at her, anger rising quickly. He was mad at himself for making her be the one to hold all the hope for their future. He should be the one reassuring her that everything would be fine.

"I don't know what to do."

She placed her hand on his cheek. "Yes you do."

"Fine, you're right, I do know what to do. I just don't know *how* to do it."

"What would you tell me?"

"I'd tell you to trust me." There was no hesitation in his answer. He'd always told her she could trust him to help get her through any challenge.

"Then you need to trust me. Go. You know what... to do."

"I can't, not without you." His vision blurred and he roughly wiped at his eyes. When he looked back to Sarah, a knot twisted around his heart.

"I can't go and it's killing me, Marcus. It's a gut-wrenching... pain that I'm... trying to... fight. I need you... to do it for... both of us. Please."

He got up and paced her room. All of a sudden he felt confined by the space. It was a private room, but there were no windows. He wanted to scream. If his hand didn't already hurt, he'd punch the wall again. Anything to deflect the feelings of failure surging through him.

If I do this, there's no turning back. There's no more hiding. No more denial.

He was afraid he'd be crushed by the pain. Blocking it out was the only thing that had gotten him this far. He looked back at Sarah. She watched him quietly from across the room.

"It's been five days, Marcus. Five days... that you can never... get back. Five days that... I would give anything to have."

He had to look away. Unfortunately his eyes settled on the bag sitting next to the bed. The bag that Joan had brought, just as he'd asked her to do. He felt his hands start to shake.

"Marcus. Marcus, look at me." He looked back to Sarah.

"I can't. I—"

"You are *not* your father." With those five words, everything in him became still. He focused on Sarah, trying to understand what had just happened. "Elijah was a good man, and I cared about him deeply. However, he was also a man with many flaws. Especially when it came to you. But his flaws are not yours. His fate may not be yours. You are not your father." It took her a while to get all the words out, but it didn't lessen the impact.

That's what's holding me back. Not guilt. It's fear. Fear that I will continue to fail. Fear that I'll someday fall victim to CJD and hurt the people I love most. That's what my father did—he pushed me away. I don't have to be like him.

His eyes swept over the woman he loved. The bruises were healing and much of the swelling had gone down. But she was still very pale. She looked as if all the energy had been drained from her body, leaving just enough to cling desperately to the present.

That's my other fear. I'm afraid that doing this will mean I can't be here for her. She might slip away, too tired to fight any more. I've been choosing her. I would choose her every time. Now she's asking me to make a different choice.

It could go either way and it scared him. At least being by her side he felt like he was in control. Even if she was the only one fighting, he was there supporting her and making sure she knew she had a reason to keep fighting. If he did what she asked, it could make her feel like she could let go. On the other hand, it could help her fight harder.

You need to trust me.

He did trust her. And she was telling him what she needed him to do so she could heal. He slowly walked back to her side. "Will you be able to forgive me? For not being there when it happened, and for how I've been acting since?"

"I already have."

He bent to give her a gentle kiss. "I love you." Her only response was a small nod before she closed her eyes.

Reluctantly, he turned and walked out the door.

He didn't remember walking through the halls of the hospital. All he could hear was the thundering of his heart. All he could feel was panic surging through his body. With each step closer, his legs became heavier until he thought there was no physical way he could take another step. He stopped when the space around him became blurred. He put his hands on his knees and hung his head, trying to steady his breathing. There was no one there to push him forward. He had to find the strength to do it on his own. He took a few steadying breaths and moved his feet until he reached his destination. He stood immobile at the door until a nurse approached.

"Can I help you, sir?"

He opened his mouth to speak, but nothing came out. He swallowed hard and tried again. "I'm Marcus Kingston. My—"

"Mr. Kingston! We've been hoping you would come. Please, follow me."

Understanding he was having difficulty moving on his own, she gently placed her hand on his arm and guided him through the doors. She took him to a sink and instructed him to wash his hands. Once done, he turned and followed the nurse again. His mind tried to register his surroundings, but he fought to block them out. If he thought about where he was or what he was doing, it was likely he would turn and run back the way he came. He kept his eyes locked on the back of the nurse's head, focused on his breathing. The nurse led him into a private room and stepped to the side. Marcus closed his eyes and tried to prepare himself for the assault of emotions he knew were coming. With his eyes closed and nothing to focus on, he couldn't block out the sounds that penetrated past his defenses. When the constant beeping became too much, he opened his eyes and saw his sister.

Leanne immediately stood and walked to him, embracing him in a crushing hug. He let her lead him by the arm. He could barely feel his legs. His hands were shaking.

"Marcus, this is your son." His knees gave out, but somehow she caught him and guided a chair under him before he crashed to the ground.

He's so small. So fragile. So beautiful.

"Can I touch him?"

"I'll get the nurse." Just as Leanne turned, a second nurse that Marcus hadn't noticed stepped forward.

"You can hold him, Mr. Kingston. Do you want to hold your daughter too?" He looked at the tiny bundle in the nurse's arms. Not able to speak, he simply nodded his head. "Just be careful of the wires."

She helped him navigate the web of tubes and wires as she gently placed his baby girl in his arms. A choked sob escaped as he looked down on her sleeping face. He looked away only when the nurse approached to repeat the process with his son. He settled into the chair and savored the feel of his babies in his arms. He wasn't sure how long he sat there, staring at the faces of his sleeping children.

Nathaniel Eli and Lena Rose.

He said their names over and over again in his mind. He and Sarah had agreed on the names long ago. Their son to have part of his name and part of his father's. Their daughter to have part of his mother's name and part of Sarah's grandmother's. Looking at them now, he knew they were perfect.

Sarah's best friend Maggie, who's son's name was Nathan, also thought it was perfect. Sarah and Maggie were like opposite halves of the same person, so it seemed fitting they should settle on the same name for their sons.

"Mr. Kingston?" He looked up in a haze. Somehow he'd forgotten he wasn't alone in the NICU. "It's time to feed them. Do you want to help?"

"I can help?"

The nurse smiled. "Yes, we actually encourage it. Here, let me take little Eli so you can feed Lena first."

Someone must have told them that they wanted to call him Eli. The gratitude he felt for his family and friends in that moment became almost overwhelming.

When she lifted Eli from his arms, he instantly felt the void and wanted him back. He watched as she placed him in the incubator before showing him how to feed Lena through the NG tube.

"They're doing well. Eli came off oxygen yesterday and Lena this morning. Hopefully they'll make a faster recovery now that their daddy is here." The nurse smiled and patted his arm before walking out of the room. He had worked up in his mind that the NICU staff would hate him for ignoring his children for the first five days of their life. Somehow he didn't encounter any judgment. Except for what he found within himself. He looked over at Leanne who had been sitting quietly, reading a book.

"Has someone been here with them the whole time?"

"Yes. Usually they don't let friends and family in, unless accompanied by a parent. However, given your unique circumstance they've made allowances to let two people be in here."

A surge of panic went through him.

Sarah! She's alone.

It was just as he had feared. He didn't have the capacity to worry about both her and his children at the same time. When he was with her, he'd blocked them out. In the short time he'd been with them, he'd forgotten about her being alone in her room.

"Can you make sure someone's with Sarah?"

"Already done. I texted Tina shortly after you got here. She and Maggie are with her now, and her parents should be there soon. I got another text a few minutes ago—Tina said she's sleeping."

Relief washed over him. He looked back down at his daughter and then over at his son. "I don't know how to thank all of you for being here."

"There's no need. We're family and that's what we do."

"I've been an idiot, haven't I?"

"Yeah, well, some habits are hard to break." He smiled, appreciating her attempt to make him feel better.

"At first I thought I couldn't handle being in here, or talking about it, because of my guilt. Now I know that I've been afraid. I had blocked them out. It was the only way I could survive. It was too much—Sarah, Van, my babies. My whole word, shattered in one moment. I felt like I could only choose one to focus on. I chose Sarah."

"What do you think now?"

"That I never really had a choice to begin with. I just didn't want to accept my reality and I let my fear take control."

Leanne remained quiet for a moment before speaking. "Fear is a difficult emotion to overcome. It's as if it casts a shadow over everything. When you let it take over, it holds you in darkness. It cloaks the bad, but it also transforms the good—making you believe it's just another demon hiding in the shadows, waiting for the chance to overpower you. Controlling your fear, working with it to move forward, that's what will set you free."

He looked at his sister in surprise. "That almost sounded wise."

"What you got in good looks, I got in brains."

"And I and the company are thankful for that. Speaking of the company, we're not going to go bankrupt from you being here so much, are we?"

"I do know how to hire a competent staff. Besides, I'm learning that sometimes the most important things happen outside the boardroom."

"Well, look at you being all modern-day executive—demanding to have a personal life in addition to ruling your small corner of the business world. I'm proud of you."

"You don't have to look so smug about it." He laughed before turning his full attention back to feeding Lena. Once she was done, the nurse took her so he could feed Eli.

"I'm sorry about Mark. I still can't believe he did this."

Marcus tensed at hearing his name. "You don't have anything to be sorry for."

"Sure I do. Dad was going to fire him after the first time he made a scene at the gala, but I convinced him to give him another shot. To just put him on notice instead. If Dad had fired him, he never would have been at the gala the year he harassed Sarah. He never would have even met her at the board meeting a few months before that."

"This is just so messed up. You feel guilty for not firing him. Me for not being there. Sarah for going to the appointment. Van for talking her into going. All of us are trying to take responsibility for the actions of an asshole who probably doesn't even feel one drop of remorse. How does that happen?"

"I guess that's what separates the good people from the bad."

He knew his sister was right, but it still didn't take away the sting. He just hoped they could find a way to live with what had happened and not let it continue to cast a shadow over everything.

It was late by the time Marcus returned to Sarah's room. Her parents stood when he walked in.

"Marcus, dear, how are you doing? I know that must have been hard for you." His mother-in-law took his face in her hands.

"Hello, Catherine. I'm doing better. I'm sorry for the way I've acted the last few days."

"No reason to be sorry for being a father and husband who was in pain. Now, Tom and I are going to meet James and Peter for dinner. Will you join us?"

"I want to spend some time with Sarah. I'll get something later. Has she been sleeping the whole time?"

"Yes." Tears welled in her eyes and she quickly left the room, his father-in-law following close behind. Marcus turned and looked at Sarah. Everything was the same as it had been that morning when he last saw her. Except for him.

He was different. For the first time since the attack he felt in control. Like Leanne had said, it was time for him to control his fear rather than the other way around. He had never been so afraid in his life. He had never had so much to lose before. He hadn't known what to do with such crippling fear, and he let it take over.

Not any more.

He looked around the room, his mind racing with ideas on how he could help Sarah get through this. He started a mental list of the things he could do before she woke up again.

Marcus watched as Sarah slowly opened her eyes. He hadn't slept much, torn between wanting to be with Sarah and his children. He was tired, but felt invigorated with newfound strength. He smiled as she discovered the changes around her. He could tell she didn't know where to start, and it was fun watching her try to decide.

"You're lying down. Next to me. How?"

"I got tired of that cot and convinced them to bring in a bed for me. You're still hooked up to too many machines to snuggle properly, but this is better than it was before."

She smiled and furrowed her brow slightly before wincing in pain. He knew that even though her cuts and bruises were healing, they still caused her some discomfort.

"My feet feel happy."

"I swapped those hospital-grade socks with your favorite fuzzy ones."

She closed her eyes and took a deep breath before searching for his hand with hers. "Let me see your hand." Puzzled, he lifted it for her to see. "Your other one too." He complied and she inspected them.

"Looking for something in particular?"

"I have a window."

"Yes."

"It wasn't there before. Just making sure you didn't... punch out the wall."

"No more punching walls for me. I had them move you to a new room. You needed a window. And, I needed you closer to our children." She looked at him for a long time, not saying anything but searching his eyes.

"You saw them?"

"They're beautiful. Just like their mamma. And tough." He could only manage a whisper.

She closed her eyes and a tear escaped. "Did you hold them?"

"Yes. The nurses have made it their mission to teach me how to be a proper father. Yesterday I learned how to feed them and change their diapers. They also convinced me to take off my shirt while holding them. They called it 'kangaroo care' or something like that. Leanne swore it was legit." She laughed and clutched at her chest.

"Hurts... to laugh. But good... too." She finally settled and he couldn't miss the light that emanated from her eyes. "I'll bet they just wanted to see you with... your shirt off. Maybe it would... help me too." She laughed again when he instantly removed his shirt.

"Better?" She took her hand and rested it over his tattoo, seriousness returning to her features.

"Yes." He leaned in and gave her a kiss. He longed to pull her to his chest and feel her heart beat along with his.

"Good morning, Mrs. Kingst—Oh, my. Um, Mr. Kingston, that's not why we let you have a bed in here." He turned to look at the young, blushing nurse that had walked in.

"I said it was to help my wife recover. And this helps my wife recover."

"Yes, it does."

"See, she agrees."

"Right, well, um... I'll just... I'll be back in a few minutes." The nurse turned quickly, bumping into the tray table, and left the room.

"You're affecting all the nurses."

"How do you think I got you a new room and me a bed? I know when to leverage my looks and charm to my advantage."

She smiled at his joke and the pain that had been squeezing his heart the past few days started to lighten. "Tell me about our babies."

He told her about every feature and characteristic he'd already committed to memory. "They seem to like to hear me talk, just like their mamma."

"Your voice might be more... beautiful than your body."

He smiled and traced his thumb across her bottom lip. "Thank you for helping me find my way back."

"Where you go, I go. I can't be here if... you're not here too."

"Then it's time for you to come back too." He reached behind him, grabbed the bag from the table, and placed it on her lap.

"Is this number three?" He nodded as he removed the contents from the bag. She took in a sharp breath and tears fell from her eyes.

"They're size six months. Although, now that I've seen them, I think it'll be a while before they fit." She slowly ran her hand over each of the outfits.

"When did you buy these?"

"Joan helped. She brought them when she came by a couple of days ago."

"Thank you."

"They're going to be fine. You're going to be fine. Soon we will leave here as a family and enjoy life." He pressed his forehead to hers, wishing again that he could hold her close. "Yesterday you said you wouldn't ask me to talk about the past again. However, there's something I need to say. I think it would be good for me to talk about the appointment. I don't like the way I handled it before. It was wrong, and on some level it led us to being here in the hospital. I need to explain to you why I was upset."

"Are you sure?"

"Yes."

CHAPTER 24
August/September • 2013

Marcus sat in the car for a moment, exhausted from the day. It had been an emotionally draining day at the clinic. He had to put down a dog that had been suffering from the effects of old age. He closed his eyes and longed for the previous week. He and Sarah had enjoyed a wonderful honeymoon. Somehow, they had been able to put all their fears and concerns aside, and it had been the best week of his life. They were able to remain in their protective bubble for a while after they got home, but soon the pressures started to win out. Work helped provide a distraction, but as soon as he'd pulled in the garage each night his thoughts shifted to Sarah and the pregnancy.

He was starting to feel the panic return. He wasn't sure they were ready. The scars from their past wounds were still susceptible to infection—fear seeping in and transforming their hope to look like unnecessary risk. He could see the shift in Sarah too. She tried her best to hide it by talking excitedly about the progression of the pregnancy. But she didn't talk beyond the current moment. There was no looking ahead to the delivery date or to their lives after.

He took a deep breath and got out of the car. He entered his condo and found Sarah standing at the sink, draining pasta. He still sometimes marveled that this was his life. That Sarah was now his wife. She moved around his kitchen as if she'd lived there her whole life. He'd always liked his condo, but it never felt like a home until Sarah stepped into it. It didn't bother him that they were only staying there in order to pack it up and hand over the keys at the end of the month. He didn't care where they lived as long as they were together. He walked up behind her and wrapped his arms around her waist, resting his palm against her still mostly flat abdomen. She leaned into him and rested her hand over his.

I wish we could stay like this forever. It's in these moments, holding hands over the life growing inside her, when I feel like we can conquer anything. When I feel like life is perfect and always will be.

"You're just in time for dinner."

"That's good because I'm starving." He planted a kiss on the back of her neck. Not satisfied, he turned her and captured her mouth with his. He felt the familiar surge of energy that occurred every time he kissed her. Every time he touched her.

"I'm going to burn the sauce."

"I don't care. I'm not hungry anyway."

"You just said you were starving."

"Maybe I was referring to something other than food." He felt her smile against his mouth. She pulled back, but before he could be disappointed by her rejection she turned off the burner. She threaded her fingers through his hair and trailed a line of kisses down his neck.

"I like your menu better than mine."

Not one to miss an opportunity, he swept her off her feet and carried her to the bedroom.

"Cold spaghetti?" Sarah smiled at Marcus from the bed. She was wrapped in the sheets and looked irresistible. He forced his mind to focus. She needed to eat.

"Nothing but the best for my wife and unborn child." He handed her a bowl and sat in bed facing her. After a few bites, he looked up and caught her watching him. "Don't you like cold spaghetti?"

"The spaghetti's fine. You're just distracting without your shirt."

He choked on the bite in his mouth. "And you don't think you're equally distracting when I know you're naked under that sheet?" Her mouth twitched, fighting a smile.

"Fair enough." She shifted her focus to her bowl and took a bite. As he watched her, he could tell there was something on her mind.

"How was your day? Anything eventful happen?" He tried to hide the concern from his voice.

"I—never mind."

"What is it?"

"Something did happen today, but I'm not sure I want to talk about it in bed. Especially after we just... you know." She blushed. Her embarrassment at talking about sex continued to amuse him. If he wasn't so concerned about what had happened that day, he would have exploited the opportunity to tease her.

"I suppose we could get dressed and go sit in the living room, but that would delay my plans for after we eat." He couldn't resist one small tease and was rewarded with the extension of her blush as it disappeared beneath the covers. "It's okay, just tell me what happened."

She took a deep breath and set her pasta bowl on the table next to the bed. "Have you talked to Rachel lately?"

His fork froze halfway to his mouth.

I should have listened. She's right; I don't want to talk about this in bed.

"No, not since she called the night of your birthday. Why?"

"I ran into her at the store."

He felt a flash of anger. "Did she say something?"

"Do you think I would have brought it up if I just saw her putting milk in her cart?"

"You don't need to be sarcastic about it. It's a legitimate question."

She rubbed her face with her hands and sat up straighter. "You're right, sorry. It's these hormones."

He placed his nearly empty bowl on the floor and pulled her to his side. "What did she say?"

"It's not exactly what she said, but how she said it. I think she's seriously delusional. She has it in her head that you two are getting back together. She was talking all sorts of crap about how you were just stringing me along to make her jealous. 'Marcus could never love you the way he loves me.' and 'You think I'm pathetic, you're the one who can't see that he's been waiting for me all this time.' She went on and on until she saw my ring. She stared at it for a few seconds before turning and running out of the store, leaving her full cart in the middle of the checkout lane."

He leaned his head against the headboard and closed his eyes. "This is unbelievable. I've not heard a single word from her in twenty years and suddenly she's back, causing trouble." He lifted his head, looking at Sarah. He ran his fingers down her exposed shoulder. "I'm sorry she upset you."

"Oh, she didn't upset me. It was weird, but I'm not upset by it. She's harmless, and I know there's no truth to her accusations. I'm actually starting to feel sorry for her."

"But I can tell that something upset you."

She took another deep breath and stared at her fingers playing with the sheet—folding and unfolding it. "I'll admit I was a little rattled by Rachel. I do believe she's harmless, but... I don't know. I can't really explain it. Just a feeling I guess. Anyway, the encounter had confused me and I lost my focus. When I snapped out of it, I found myself staring at the cover of one of those magazines they have at the checkout. It was a women's health magazine, and the feature article was about having a baby after thirty-five. Of course I had to pick it up and read it."

He squeezed her and placed a kiss on her temple. "What bothered you about it?"

"Everything. I think the doctor tried to talk to me about the challenges when I went in to confirm the pregnancy, but I was in too much shock to register anything she said. The article reminded me. It recommended prenatal testing for certain illnesses that have a higher chance of occurrence in pregnancy for a woman my age. It also mentioned that there's a higher chance of miscarriage. I've been trying to not be scared of this whole thing, but I guess I've finally lost the battle."

"Do you want me to do some research before our appointment this week?"

"I actually think I should do it. It might be good for me. Face my fear and all."

"Well, let me know if you want help." He knew he would do his own research anyway. Truth be told, the higher risk of complications had been weighing on his mind the last few days as well.

"I will. Let's not talk about it any more right now." She picked up her pasta bowl and started eating again. He reached down for his spaghetti to do the same. He looked into his empty bowl, confused.

"I swore I still had some left." He looked over the side of the bed. Max was looking back at him, feigning innocence. "How long has he been in here?" It was as if his question were an invitation and Max jumped up on the bed, wiggling his way between them. Sarah laughed and rubbed Max on the back of his head.

"Did you eat Daddy's spaghetti? That'll teach him to leave it on the floor, isn't that right?"

"I think he needs to go outside." Marcus hopped off the bed and called out to Max. He let him out back and then secured him in the kennel for the night. They didn't always lock him up, but Marcus had plans for the evening and Max wasn't invited. Unfortunately, by the time he returned to the bedroom Sarah was sleeping. He gently took the bowl of spaghetti from her lap.

He took the two bowls to the kitchen, where he stood in the dark finishing the rest of Sarah's pasta. As he ate, his mind wandered to Sarah's encounter with Rachel. He wasn't sure what to do about the situation. If he called her with the intention to tell her to back off, she would likely twist it around and proclaim it as a sign that he cared about her. If he ignored it, she could continue to harass Sarah. What he didn't understand was why Rachel was shopping at his local grocery store. Van had confirmed that she was working and living somewhere in Denver. She had no reason to be grocery shopping near his home.

Unless she was intending to run into Sarah—or me.

He decided the situation was getting out of control, and he should do something. Van might know what to do—he had a knack for getting women to back off without causing further problems. He placed the dirty dishes in the dishwasher before walking over to let Max out of the kennel. Since his plans had been changed, he might as well let the dog hang out with him.

He sat down on the couch with his tablet, and Max settled at his feet. He pulled up the recent article he was reading, but his mind wandered to Sarah's concerns about the pregnancy. He'd been trying to not think about all the things that could go wrong. While he wasn't sure they were ready to have a child, he already loved his son or daughter. He wanted everything to go perfectly, for both Sarah and the baby. Then there were also his concerns about what kind of father he would be. He thought about the letters from his father.

I can do things differently. No matter my fate, I will ensure I have a strong relationship with my child.

Marcus woke up with a start. Sarah was thrashing beside him, soft cries cutting through the silence.

"Sarah, honey, wake up." He gently applied pressure to her shoulders. Her eyes flew open, her mouth prepared for a scream that didn't come. She looked about the room frantically, and when he noticed clarity begin to enter her eyes he pulled her close. "It's okay, it was only a dream." She sobbed into his shoulder as he stroked her hair and back.

She'd told him about the nightmares she'd had in the years after the accident. They had gone away almost entirely when she had come out to work with his father, but started again when she found out she was pregnant.

"I'm sorry." She sniffed loudly and wiped her nose with her T-shirt.

"Maybe we should ask the doctor today if she can prescribe something to help you sleep that would also be safe for the baby."

"Yeah, maybe. But I don't like taking medication."

"I know, but you need sleep. Between the pregnancy, the nightmares, the wedding, a new job, the studio—it's too much stress."

She let out a deep sigh and nestled further into his side. "We haven't talked about the appointment yet."

"By the time I get home, you're usually too wiped out." He ran a hand through his already tousled hair.

"I did some research. About the prenatal testing. While looking, I also found information on prenatal genetic testing—I think it was called chronic—"

"Chorionic villus sampling, or CVS."

"Yes, that's it. You've heard of it?"

"I did some research myself." He tensed and she shifted in his arms, studying his face in the soft morning glow.

"You don't agree with it?"

"I'd like to discuss it with the doctor before we make a final decision, but at this point I'm not comfortable with it."

"Why? It could tell us if our baby has the mutated gene for CJD."

"And what good would that do us? Do you plan to terminate the pregnancy if it comes back positive?" His heart pounded rapidly. He loved Sarah, and he knew he wanted to spend the rest of his life with her. But if they disagreed on this point, it would be a significant obstacle.

"Of course not! Do you?" She pulled back and there was a look of slight terror in her eyes. His heart rate started to return to normal.

"No, I don't. So, if we agree that we're having this baby no matter what, then what's the point? There's a risk of miscarriage in doing the test. Why take the chance for no reason?"

"The reason would be to *know*. To understand what our child will have to face someday and be prepared."

"What is there to prepare for, Sarah? CJD is not the only potential danger lurking in our future. There are so many bad things that can happen to people in life—are we going to weigh ourselves down by worrying about everything, all the time?"

"No, I don't want to spend all our time worrying about every negative thing that could possibly happen. But I've been a mother. I know that I'll worry about everything anyway. The difference is that for most dangers I can take some measure of precaution—seat belts in the car, helmets on the bike, swimming lessons, safety gates—the list goes on. I know nothing is a guarantee, but at least I can do something. With CJD, there's nothing I can do to prevent it from happening. All I can do is mentally prepare myself for the possibility."

He got out of bed and paced the room, unable to remain still for the conversation. "I don't want CJD to control our lives, Sarah."

"Don't you see? It already does! I'm constantly wondering if you're going to develop symptoms in a few years. Now, with the baby on the way that concern extends to him or her. At least with the test it gives us the chance to stop worrying if we don't have to."

He shook his head in frustration. "That's where we're different. You believe the test can offer us the possibility of a life without CJD hanging over our heads. I view it as a confirmation of my fate—taking away all my hope that it could be different. There's no cure. What's the point of knowing?"

"You sound like you already believe you have it."

"For our mutation, it's a fifty percent pass rate to children. Leanne doesn't have it. That's pretty simple math."

"The fifty percent is not a guarantee. It's an average. The last thing I'd call any Kingston is average, so you have a good chance of defying the odds."

"And that's why I still have hope. But a test would take that away from me."

"You don't have to get tested. We would only be testing the baby—"

"If the baby has it, that means I have it." Sarah was smart, but somehow she had overlooked this very simple fact. It was clear from the dawning realization on her face. Her lower lip started to tremble. He sighed and returned to the bed, taking her in his arms. "I'm not saying no. I just want to discuss it more. Make sure it's something we fully understand, and that we're willing to accept all consequences as a result of our decision."

"But the test is supposed to be done between ten and twelve weeks. That's now."

"It's not something we can rush into, Sarah."

She was quiet for a few minutes and he knew she was processing. "Maybe we could have the test but not get the results. Since it would only be for knowledge, and not for... termination... we could wait to get the results. That way we make the window for testing and can have the results if we decide to know, or we can elect to never find out. We know that for ethical reasons children aren't tested. This is our only chance and the window is closing."

It was a compromise. He wasn't sure it was one he was comfortable with, but it at least warranted consideration. "Let's talk to the doctor about it today and go from there."

Twins. How can that be possible? Multiples don't run in Sarah's family. I should be happy, but I'm freaking out. I wasn't sure we were ready for one, let alone two.

Marcus was pulled from his frantic thoughts when the car came to a sudden stop. He was grateful that he'd decided to have Thompson drive them to the appointment. He couldn't focus on anything except the fact that they were having twins. Sarah sat quietly next to him the entire drive—staring out the window, bouncing her knee, and clutching her pendant. The appointment had not only sent both of them into shock, but it seemed to firmly set both of their positions. Unfortunately, they still didn't agree.

The doctor had referred them to a different doctor, one that was more practiced in performing CVS on twins. Sarah made the appointment, stating that she could cancel if they didn't want to go through with the test. It was scheduled for next week.

Marcus got out of the car and thanked Thompson before opening Sarah's door. She took his hand, and he led her into the house. Once inside, he pulled her into a hug. "It's going to be okay."

"I'm freaking out, Marcus."

"I know." He pulled back but she didn't budge. "Hey, look at me. We'll get through this. Together. Lots of people have had twins before us and survived."

"It's not about the twins. I mean, not about having two babies at once. It's going to be difficult and it will be quite the adjustment, but I'm confident we can handle it. But that's two babies to worry about. Two more lives that I'll become dependent on. I—"

He kissed her. It was the most effective way he had of calming her down. "You're rambling. Breathe, Sarah. We're going to figure this out."

She closed her eyes and leaned her forehead to his. "I can't explain it, but I'm even more determined to get the test. I know you still don't agree, but I have to know. I have to know how to protect them."

"You can't protect them from everything, Sarah. I want to protect them too. And you. That's what matters most to me. But I just don't see how getting this test will do that. For starters, it's a risk to their lives just to have it done."

"I can't spend the rest of my life feeling this way. I feel like I'm about to snap."

"And what if you miscarry?"

"I won't."

"You can't possibly know that!"

"Just like you can't possibly know that you have CJD, but you claim to feel it in your gut that you do! Why is your gut more reliable than mine?"

He opened his mouth to respond but closed it quickly. He didn't have a valid answer. He pulled away and paced the room, trying to control his emotions while he figured out what to say.

He stopped and looked at her, trying to keep his voice level. "If we're going to go by gut, then I still don't understand why we need this test. Your gut should be telling you if they have it or not. If you're able to trust your gut enough to not worry about a miscarriage, then why can't you just trust your gut to not worry about the future of our children? I mean, that's why you said you want this test, right? To confirm they don't have it so you don't have to worry for the next forty plus years. That means your gut is telling you they don't have it. Use that to save your worry."

"My gut is not telling me that! It doesn't have an answer for their fate of CJD. That's why I need the test. Like I told you before, I need to do something. Right now I have no control in this. I can't eat differently to keep it from happening. I can't do anything but mentally prepare for the possibility. To figure out a way to accept it if this is their fate." She sank to the floor and buried her face in her knees.

I need to stop this. She's stressing out and it's not good for her or the baby. Babies. Shit.

It was still a shock every time he remembered they were pregnant with twins. He crouched down next to her and took her in his arms.

"We'll get the test next week. But, I want us to agree to wait at least four months until we decide if we're going to get the test results. We need to be certain about this, Sarah. Right now I'm not on board with knowing, but I can work with your compromise. Before our appointment, I'm going to research this doctor. If I have even the slightest doubt about his ability to do this test without risk to our children, we're canceling."

Marcus led Sarah off the elevator. He took her hand and could feel her shaking. It had been a long week. He'd tried his best to get her to relax and stop stressing out about the test. Unfortunately, he had his own concerns and hadn't been very successful at his mission. Now it was time for the appointment. He opened the door and led Sarah to the empty reception desk.

He turned to her while they waited for someone to help them. "You still sure about this?"

"Yes."

"Can I help you?" All the blood drained from his face at the sound of the familiar voice.

This seriously can't be happening.

He turned and faced Rachel. "What in the hell are you doing here?"

Her smile disappeared quickly as she looked from him to Sarah. "I—I work here."

"This is unbelievable." Marcus ran a hand down his face. "We have an appointment."

"Trying to get pregnant already?" There was a level of bitterness in her voice that he was sure she wouldn't want her boss to overhear.

"Actually, we're already pregnant."

"Oh. Oh! Right, well. I don't usually run the reception desk, but the person who does left a few minutes ago. She wasn't feeling well. Let me see what we need." She turned and quickly walked out of sight. He could hear her talking to someone in the other room. She came back carrying a clipboard. "Since this is your first visit, I need you to fill these out." She practically threw the clipboard at him and pierced Sarah with a glare.

"Hi, Rachel. So good to see you again, and so soon! I really enjoyed our conversation the other day, but you left so abruptly. Is there anything else you'd like to say?"

"I already said everything I had to say." Rachel spun on her heel and walked away.

Marcus turned to Sarah. "I think maybe we should find a different doctor."

"Marcus, he's the best choice in the area for this procedure. As long as she's nowhere near the exam room, I'm fine. We'll just tell the doctor there's a sketchy history with her, and he'll have to keep her out of it."

"I don't understand how you can be so civil when it comes to her. It doesn't freak you out at all that she happens to be working here? Out of all the possible employment options in Denver, she works here?"

"Well, we didn't know we were coming here until last week, so I don't think she planned it. We have some pretty rotten luck between the two of us, so I can actually believe it's just a bizarre coincidence." She snatched the clipboard from his hands and sat down. While she filled out the forms, he pulled out his phone to text Van.

The crazy bitch works here.

Van texted back almost immediately.

I know a lot of crazy bitches. You need to be more specific.

Marcus had talked to Van over the weekend about Rachel's stalker behavior. He said he'd look into it.

Rachel. At the doctor's office for that appt. I mentioned to you.

They were waiting to tell people about the pregnancy, but Van somehow figured it out. It was like he had an internal radar that could detect when a woman was pregnant.

WTF? I'll look into it.

"The doctor's ready to see you now." Rachel stood holding open the door to the back rooms.

"No, I want someone else." It took all his effort not to yell at Rachel.

"Oh, relax. I'm just taking you to the exam room. I'm not a nurse." Sarah got up and walked past Rachel.

Marcus stopped before passing through the door. "I heard about your little *chance* encounter with Sarah at the store. You'd better leave her alone. And if you value your job here, I suggest you keep your distance from us." He looked at her long enough to watch her face pale. Satisfied, he joined Sarah in the hall as they waited for Rachel to show them to the room.

CHAPTER 25

"Marcus?" He looked at Sarah and blinked a few times. "You stopped talking."

"Sorry, I—a thought just came to mind, and I guess I got distracted."

"What's wrong? You look upset."

"Nothing for you to worry about. Where was I? Right, the appointment. Obviously there were no complications from the test. Eli and Lena are in the NICU, but that's a result of you going into preterm labor from the attack." He had to pause. Anger flashed through him at the thought of what Mark had done and why they were in the hospital. He pushed it aside and focused on Sarah. "We agreed to not find out the results of the test, but you changed your mind."

"I shouldn't have gone. And not just because of... the attack. I betrayed my promise... to you."

"Haven't we established over the last few days that I've failed on quite a few promises? Your one is no big deal."

"Marcus—"

"Don't worry, I'm not going to start back down my path of self-loathing. I'm just trying to be honest. You can't argue with me any more about the fact that for the past five days I haven't been keeping my promises—to you or to our children. I couldn't function under the weight of it all. I know now it was fear holding me back. I'm just not sure what I was more afraid of—seeing them so small and fragile, having to see them without you, what kind of father I'd turn out to be, my possibly passing them CJD—unfortunately the list is practically endless. Blocking them out, blaming Van—it was the only way I knew how to focus on you. What I didn't realize, until you walked me down memory lane, was that I wasn't focused on you after all. I was focused on my fears. I just couldn't see them for what they were. You saved me, Sarah."

"You helped save me once. It's the least I could do."

They held each other's gaze for a moment. Tired of being so far away from her, he carefully maneuvered so that he was closer, bodies touching. He entwined his feet with hers and ran his hand down her uninjured arm.

"While I was trying to figure out how to get my head out of my ass the last few days, I realized something. While we agreed to not get the test results, we never really resolved anything. I forced your hand, feeling like I somehow had the bigger voice because it was *my* disease. I never really considered your side of the situation. I was only focused on getting you to see mine. I think that's why I was so upset that day. It wasn't entirely because you went back on our agreement—it was also because I was scared. I'm terrified at the thought of having CJD. I am. I don't want to have to think of you and the children going through that someday. I don't want to think about leaving you. Ignoring it was the only way I could function. If I hadn't ignored it, I might have done something stupid like push you away—like my father did to me. The thought that our children could have it... and it would be because of me... I couldn't face it. I didn't see how I could possibly carry the burden of all our fates at the same time." He paused and traced his finger lightly over her face before continuing.

"As morbid as it sounds, I think this whole incident is what's helped me see clearly for the first time. It reminded me that anything could happen at any moment. I've never had so much to lose before. I'm a husband and a father now. That means I'll always have a new burden to carry and many times it will feel like too much. I'm still afraid of what will happen in the future, but it's time I stop ignoring it. CJD might ultimately rob me of my mind and my body—but not my life. I won't let it. Not any more."

Her hand had been on his side the entire time they talked, resting over his tattoo. Now she gently touched the side of his face, rubbing her thumb slowly over his cheek. As she held his gaze, he was elated to see that the light was starting to register in her eyes again. He placed his hand over hers.

He took a deep breath and slowly released it. "I don't want you to hold the burden of knowing alone. I want you to tell me the test results."

"I decided not to know."

"But you went to the appointment."

"Yes, I did. But I didn't get the results. I changed my mind. Again."

He remained silent as he processed her words. "Are you certain that's what you want?"

"No." Her response was just a whisper.

We have a second chance to make this right. We can do this together, the way we should have the first time.

Relief washed over him at the thought. "I guess we have a chance to try this again then. This time, instead of us each lobbying for our own position, we work together. We make a plan—you like plans, right? You can create one of your fancy spreadsheets with all the pros and cons of knowing the test results."

Her eyes lit up even more. "We could identify what we can... control and what we can't. Determine where... the greatest risks are."

"I like it. Leanne's going to think we're nuts."

"I think she stopped... trying to figure us out... a long time ago."

He smiled. "That's almost exactly what she told me just a few days ago."

He watched as she took another deep breath and closed her eyes. Her hand slid from his face and lay limply across her chest.

"Sarah, are you feeling all right?"

Her eyes fluttered open and met his. "I'm tired."

His joy from just a few minutes ago disappeared along with her energy. "I'll let you rest."

"Detective Crass, thank you for coming by so quickly." Marcus shook his hand as he entered the meeting room.

"No problem. Detective Smith sends his apologies; he's in the middle of an interview for another case."

Marcus sat down and processed his thoughts. He'd been going over it in his head while he waited for the detective to arrive, not wanting to forget any of the important details. "Have you found out anything more about Mark's accomplice?"

Crass sat forward, resting his elbows on the table. His youthful features were still distracting. Marcus had to remind himself that he was a grown man and a competent detective. "Not yet. We've looked into the people you listed, and talked to most of them so far, but as you'd indicated none have a motive. I think there's someone we're missing."

"I agree, and I think I might know who it is."

The detective quickly flipped open his tablet. "Well, don't keep me in suspense."

"Her name is Rachel Flank—I mean Hawk. Her married name is Hawk."

"And why are we implicating her in all this?"

"She was my girlfriend, years ago. I'm talking twenty years ago. She cheated on me with my roommate and I broke it off. She later married the guy, and I hadn't heard from either of them at all. She suddenly showed up this past June. She divorced Patrick and apparently thought she could walk back into my life." Marcus relayed the encounters with Rachel since she showed up. Crass took notes in his tablet as he talked.

"She certainly has motive, and her working at the doctor's office would give her access to your wife's appointment schedule. However, how did she get connected to Tanger?"

"I figure that's your job to sort out."

"Why didn't she come up when we discussed possible names?"

"I didn't think about it. We were listing people Sarah and I see on a frequent basis. While Rachel's reappearance has always been suspicious, it never occurred to me that it could be her. At least not until I talked with Sarah earlier today about that initial appointment." Marcus studied the detective through narrowed eyes. "You don't seem surprised by this."

"Should I be?"

"You don't find it odd that she shows up out of the blue after all these years, right before I'm about to get married? That she seems to be wherever we are, regardless of the unlikely odds?"

Crass smiled. "Unfortunately, you'd be surprised at how often this sort of thing happens." He sat back and studied Marcus with a tilt of his head. "Mr. Kingston, while I'm here I was hoping we could talk about where you were the night of the attack. You're not a suspect, but it's a loose end and I have issues with those. My wife calls it OCD, I call it thoroughness. Anyway, I understand that the events from that night were very traumatic for you and your fam—er, your wife." Marcus was impressed by how everyone not only remembered his boundaries, but also respected them.

"It's okay, detective. I've come to my senses and can now talk about my family. My children." Marcus waited again for the look of judgment he expected to see when discussing his actions with regard to his children. Instead he saw only sympathy.

"Very good. I hope they're doing well?"

"Yes, they are. We're still not sure how long they'll need to be in the NICU, but they're recovering."

"I'm relieved to hear it. So, as I was saying, I understand that it was traumatic for your family. However, it would be helpful to add your story to Mrs. Kingston's and Mr. Vanderlink's."

Marcus took a deep breath and closed his eyes. He'd been opening up to Sarah and acknowledging his mistakes. This was one more he needed to face. "I assume you're aware of the reason for her doctor's appointment?"

"All we know is that it was to learn the results of a prenatal test."

Marcus nodded and looked down at his hands, splayed across the table. His right was still bruised from punching the wall. "Sarah had a lot of concerns about the pregnancy, being over thirty-five and the risks that come with it. Another concern we had was the possibility of our children inheriting a fatal family disease that runs on my side of the family—Creutzfeldt-Jakob Disease, or CJD. The appointment was for a genetic screening test. We had agreed to get the test, but to wait on learning the results. That would give us time to determine if we really wanted to know. We wouldn't terminate the pregnancy, so it would just be for our peace of mind. Anyway, we didn't agree on if we should get the results. We finally decided to not find out, but she changed her mind and wanted to go to the appointment."

"That's why Mr. Vanderlink took her, because you weren't in support of her decision?"

"Yes. I was angry and hurt, but mostly scared. I felt that finding out their fate would seal mine, and I didn't want to know. I yelled at Sarah, and then I left the house and went to the studio. I had intended to go there to dance, to sort through my feelings. When I got there, someone spilled something in the kitchenette and left it. I was looking for cleaner when I saw the unopened bottle of whiskey—a congratulations gift from our realtor from the opening of the studio. I poured a drink, intending to only have one. Then Sarah called. I didn't answer. I had never before ignored her call. I was consumed by anger and fear and guilt. Unfortunately, I let old habits take over and I got drunk and passed out."

Crass looked at him through narrow eyes. "That's it?"

"Sorry, there's no grand story of betrayal or destruction. Just drunkenness."

"And can your story be verified?"

"There's a security camera at the studio. It will show when I arrived, and that I didn't leave again until my brother-in-law Brad picked me up."

"Why didn't you want to give this information to Detective Smith when he first asked? To be honest, I was expecting something much more shocking."

"I was ashamed. I wasn't there for Sarah when she needed me. She was being beaten while I was drowning in a bottle of whiskey. She was delivering our children and nearly bled to death while I was passed out. I couldn't own up to my failure."

The detective nodded and stood up. "Just send over the security video when you get a chance." He handed Marcus a card. "We'll get in touch after we look into Ms. Hawk."

Marcus walked with him to the elevators where they parted ways. It was time to see his children. Catherine was with Sarah, so he could spend time in the NICU without worrying about her being alone. He was surprised when Peter almost knocked him over on his way out of the unit.

"Marcus, I was just coming to find you." Marcus took in Peter's unusual disheveled appearance.

"What's wrong?"

"I need to go home. I hate to leave while Sarah and the babies are still in the hospital, but there's something I need to take care of."

"Again, what's wrong?"

"Nothing you need to worry about. Just a friend who needs my help. I'm going to say good-bye to Sarah before I leave. Call me if anything changes. Actually, call me no matter what." Peter clapped him on the shoulder and hurried past him down the hall. Marcus stared after him for a few seconds, confused by his sudden departure.

When he entered their room in the NICU, he found Tina holding Eli and Maggie sitting next to Lena.

"Hello, ladies. Spoiling my children already?"

"Oh, you're going to take them away from us, aren't you?"

Marcus looked at Maggie. "Yes I am."

Maggie let out an incoherent sound as she stood, giving Marcus her seat. Tina didn't budge. He was about to tease her when the nurse walked in.

"Good morning, Mr. Kingston. I hear you'd like to hold your children. It seems Eli is occupied, so should we start with Lena?"

"Yes, thank you." He waited patiently for the nurse to place his daughter in his arms.

"You know, it's best for your babies to hold them to your bare chest." The nurse gave him a teasing wink before she left the room.

"No one's asked us to do the kangaroo care."

"That's because Marcus looks better than we do without a shirt. But I don't mind, I've been trying to get him naked for years. Why do you think I'm hanging out in here? It's not for his adorable children, I can tell you that."

"As much as I'm enjoying this stroke to my ego, you ladies can stop now." For as long as he'd known Tina, she teased him relentlessly about his looks. He knew it was all in fun, and luckily so did Miles. She claimed it was her way of trying to keep him grounded in reality. He didn't understand her logic, but usually played along. However, at the moment he just wanted to focus on his children.

"You two are hopeless."

Marcus looked at Maggie and gave her a mock look of indignation. "Don't pin this on me. Tina's the instigator. I might have to rethink my support of Sarah's friendship with her."

"This coming from a guy whose best friend is the epitome of inappropriateness."

"Give me my son, woman. You're too old for him."

He watched as Tina tried to suppress a smile. "Not yet." He didn't object. While he desperately wanted to hold Eli, he knew Tina needed the time as well. She and Miles never had children, so he could sacrifice a few minutes to satisfy her baby fix.

"How's Sarah doing this morning?" Marcus pulled his eyes away from Lena's sleeping face to look at Maggie.

"She slept a lot yesterday. I'm hoping that helped. I think the new room improved her spirits."

"I'm sure it had more to do with the fact that her husband stopped being such a big oaf."

"Yes, there's that too. Thanks for always keeping me grounded, Tina."

"My pleasure." She stared down at Eli's face and traced a finger along his brow. "I just hope, for the sake of all women, little Eli here hasn't inherited your eyes."

"Hopefully for the sake of all future boyfriends, Lena hasn't inherited his eyes either."

"You both know Sarah is gorgeous. I'm not the only one to blame if our children are blessed in the looks department."

"Yes, they are certainly doomed to be beautiful children. But those eyes..."

"Tina, is Miles not getting it done at home? You seem to be going on more than usual about the effect of my eyes."

Tina closed her eyes and rested her head on the back of her chair, a dreamy smile on her lips. "No, Miles gets everything done amazingly well. I just haven't seen him much the last few days, and your eyes are so striking. And seeing you yesterday with no shirt on..."

"Okay, you can hand over my son now. Go home. Call Miles, tell him you need to see him. You're not allowed back until your hormones are in check." This time Tina couldn't suppress her laughter. He turned to Maggie, who was also amused by the conversation. "Do you need to go back to Andy for a bit?"

"I think I can last a couple more days. But I should probably not be around when your shirt is off. Just in case."

"Then you'd better leave me alone with my children." He waved for the nurse just outside the room.

"Yes, Mr. Kingston?"

"I believe it's kangaroo care time." The nurse took Lena so he could strip off his shirt. Once she placed Lena back in his arms he nodded his head in the direction of Tina.

The nurse took the hint and stood waiting until Tina finally sighed in defeat, handing over Eli. "They won't let any of *us* hold them both at once."

"I'm their father, I get special privileges."

"Right. You know my theory, *Blue*."

He smiled at winning the battle to be alone with his children.

Marcus hadn't set foot outside the hospital for six days. It was cold, but the crisp air was invigorating. He parked James' rental car in Van's driveway and got out. Brad had driven him from the studio to the hospital the night of the attack, so he didn't have his own car. He took a deep breath and walked to the front door. Expecting Van's mother to answer, he was surprised to be greeted by Isabella. She looked different in yoga pants, a T-shirt, and no make-up. A good different.

"Marcus!" She instantly pulled him into a hug and kissed both his cheeks. Without her usual stilettos, he realized she was considerably shorter than he was. "I'm so sorry to hear about Sarah and the children. I hope they're doing better."

"They are, thank you."

"I'm glad you're here. Maybe you can get Brandon to stop sulking." She pulled him by the arm and led him into the house. A few steps into the living room she stopped and turned to face him. "The babies, Eli and Lena, right?" Marcus nodded. "How long will they be in the NICU?"

"We're not sure. We've been told that they have to be there at least until their due date, but we don't yet know exactly how long. We're lucky Sarah had made it to thirty-three weeks. It's certainly not what we wanted, but at least she was far enough along that they have a good chance at a full recovery." Isabella swiped at a tear and started speaking rapidly in Spanish. He was about to remind her he didn't have a clue what she was saying when he heard Van call out from the bedroom. She immediately turned and hurried up the stairs. Marcus followed at a slower pace.

"Isabella, what is this shit?"

"It's a vegetable smoothie. You need your nutrients."

"I need man food."

Marcus stood at the door, listening to their exchange. He could hear the edge in Van's voice. Marcus watched Isabella carefully check Van's bandages and adjust his blankets.

"You need food to make you stronger. That crap you call food is no good."

"Since when do you get to tell me what to do? We agreed to break it off, remember?"

"Since you ended up in the hospital. And *we* never agreed to anything. You decided to be a chicken-shit and stopped calling."

"When's my mother coming back?"

"She's not. You're stuck with me, so get over it. When you get out of this bed, then you can decide if you're man enough to stay with me. Until then, I'm in charge. Now, Marcus is here. I have some calls to make and I'll be back later." She planted a kiss on his cheek and walked out of the room.

Van looked at Marcus for a few seconds in silence. "What?"

"I didn't say anything."

"Your mouth may not have opened, but your eyes are yelling quite loudly. Just say it, Kingston."

"Alright. You're being an ass. As I've been one myself these past few days, it's easy to spot."

"I didn't ask her to be here. Sure, I dated her longer than any other woman I'd been with over the last few years, but it didn't stick. I told her I wasn't interested in a commitment. She can't force her hand just because I'm trapped in a bed and can't walk away."

"I just heard her say that you could decide on the future of your relationship when you were recovered."

"Right. So she can brainwash me while my mind's muddled with pain killers and... whatever that nasty shit is." He waved the hand of his uninjured arm at the green drink sitting by his bed. "She'll have me believing I can't live without her, and by the time I come to my senses it'll be too late. I'll be trapped."

Marcus couldn't stifle his laughter, which only succeeded in making Van angrier. "Is it really so painful for you to consider having a serious relationship for once?"

"Yes."

"Well, trust me. It's better to surrender to love than to fight it. You'll never win, so you might as well get over yourself and start enjoying your time with her."

"Who said anything about love?"

"Your eyes."

Van looked away. When he finally looked back, Marcus could tell he was struggling with accepting his feelings for Isabella. "Whatever. I hope you came here to talk about something other than my love life. If not, you can back your ass right out the door."

"No, I did not come here to nag you about your love life. I came to see how you were doing, and to talk about a few other things."

Van watched him as he walked to the chair near the bed. He sat down and picked up the drink, giving it a sniff and a small sip. "Awful, right?"

"It's pretty bad."

Van finally smiled and then grew serious again. "So what did you want to talk about?"

"First, have you talked to Detective Smith or Crass lately?"

"Tween called the other day. Said Mark was claiming to have had someone feeding him information."

"Tween?"

"Come on, you have to agree Crass looks like he just hit puberty."

Marcus shook his head and chuckled. There was at least some comfort in hearing Van return to his usual self.

"I think it might be Rachel."

"No shit? I guess she is a crazy bitch. It fits with her snap in sanity. But how is she connected to Mark?"

"I don't know—I was hoping you had some ideas."

"I've got nothing. Somehow I never met Mark before, even though we've attended a lot of the same functions and you've mentioned him more than once. So if I haven't met him, I don't see how she could have gotten involved with him in the limited time she's been back in town."

"That's my problem with the theory as well. I've talked to Crass about it, and he's looking into it. I'll keep you updated." Marcus sat back in the chair and started picking at his pant leg. "I also wanted to talk about the night of the attack."

"Are you sure you want to hear about it?"

"No, but I have to. It's time I stop ignoring what happened. Start with how you came to be the one to take her to the appointment."

"T.O. called me, upset. She said Tina was tied up in a meeting and I was her only option. She wouldn't tell me what was wrong, only that she had an appointment in Denver and you didn't want her to go. I figured it was about the test. I don't agree with your position. I've always been on T.O.'s side for this one. I told her she needed to go, for her sake and the babies. I was at work and had a conference call coming up that I couldn't miss, so I sent someone to pick her up."

"It doesn't sound like it took too much effort for you to convince her to go."

"She was upset, and scared. I think she had already made up her mind to go and knew that I'd agree with her. I think that's the real reason she called me and not Tina."

Marcus thought his guess was probably accurate. "If you sent a driver to take her, how did you end up with her?"

"I was able to end my conference call early. I didn't think she should get the results alone. As you know, the building where the doctor's office is located isn't far from my office. I decided to walk, knowing it would be faster. When I got to the building, I found her sitting in the lobby, clutching her phone and crying."

"That must have been when she tried to call me, and I ignored it." Marcus closed his eyes and cursed under his breath. The pain of letting her down resurfaced, and he allowed it to fester for a few seconds as a reminder of the impact of his actions. He then pushed it back down, refusing to go back to dwelling on his mistakes.

"She mentioned something about trying to call you. I couldn't really understand her though, with all the crying she was doing. It took some effort, but I finally got her to calm down. She was having second thoughts. Or would it be third thoughts since she had already changed her mind once before?"

"Focus, Van. She changed her mind, then what happened?"

Van shifted his arm in the sling and grimaced. "We sat in the lobby and talked. I'm not really sure how long we sat there. At first she tried distracting herself by talking about other things. She kept trying to get me to tell her what it was I do for a living."

Despite the heaviness of the conversation, Marcus smiled. Sarah was determined to figure out what Van did. Their friends had agreed to go along with the plan to make her figure it out on her own. It irritated her that no one ever spilled the information, despite some very clever attempts on her part.

"Did you tell her?"

"No. I let her make a few guesses though. It was fun."

"Did she ever come close?"

"Nope." Van smiled for a moment before taking a deep breath. "Anyway, she finally started talking about the appointment and how you two didn't agree. She was really conflicted. Seeing she was in no condition to learn possible life altering information, I agreed she should wait and talk with you again. See if you two could come to some sort of decision together."

Marcus nodded. "Thank you."

"I still don't understand your resistance. I've never understood why you won't get tested. I'd hoped that pushing the genetic testing would get you to change your mind and get tested yourself. I just don't understand it."

"Why don't you want to admit that you're in love with Isabella?" Van stared at him and Marcus could clearly see the answer in his eyes. "That's the same reason I don't want to get tested or know the results of the genetic testing for the children. It's just not something I can face right now. However, Sarah and I have agreed to talk through it again and come to a decision together. If I can face my fear, maybe you can too? At least allow yourself to consider the possibility of a relationship?"

Van looked away again. "You're here to talk about that night, not psychoanalyze me."

"Sorry. You're such a conundrum it's hard to resist sometimes. Tell me what happened after you and Sarah talked."

Van tried to shift in the bed but was restricted due to his injured arm and leg. He let out a string of curses and punched the mattress with his uninjured arm. Marcus instinctively got up to help, but Van waved him off.

"Don't. I should be able to at least adjust myself so my ass cheek isn't asleep!"

"Let me help you." Van tried to wave him off again, but Marcus ignored him. He placed his hands under his armpits and lifted him into a different sitting position. "How is Isabella able to help you?"

Marcus was certain her tiny frame would be no help to a man Van's size.

"She's surprisingly strong."

"Maybe you ought to rethink those disgusting drinks after all."

Van eyed the glass, considering Marcus' point. "Like I said, worming her way in. Making me believe she's my cure."

"That would imply you need fixing."

"Exactly! Beyond the obvious—" He waved his hand over his body. "—I don't need anything fixed. Glad you're back on my side."

"I'll never leave your side, but it won't stop me from trying to push you in the right direction."

Van rolled his eyes. "That's sweet, Kingston. Can we get back to other preferable topics?"

Marcus raised a brow at his rebuttal. "The topic of the attack is preferable to your feelings for Isabella?"

"Unfortunately, yes. So where was I? Right—after T.O. and I talked. It was getting late, and I offered to take her to dinner and then drive her home. I know how you feel about making sure she eats regularly, especially while she was pregnant. As I had already established, I walked to the building from work, so I didn't have my car. I started to hail a cab, but T.O. mentioned there was a bistro about a block down that she liked. She suggested we walk, saying the fresh air would help clear her head. After we finished eating, we sat talking for a while. She wanted to grill me about Isabella. I felt bad about encouraging her to go to the appointment, so I indulged her.

"When we left, there wasn't a cab in sight. T.O. suggested we walk down the block and see if any were on the next street. We were about halfway down the block when I saw a cab turn down the adjacent street. I didn't think. I jogged after it, trying to get the cabbie's attention. It kept driving, but I saw another approaching from the opposite direction so I waited. I turned to T.O. when it stopped, but she wasn't there. My only concern had been getting her out of the cold."

Van stopped talking and stared over Marcus' shoulder for a few agonizing seconds. Marcus could feel his chest tighten. He didn't want to hear what he knew was coming next, but he had to.

"I called out to her but there was no response. I walked back in the direction we came. The cabbie yelled out to me that he wouldn't wait and then he drove off. I turned the corner and panicked when I still didn't see her. A few feet away I noticed an alley. I must not have registered it when I ran after the cab. I could feel it in my core that something wasn't right. I ran to the alley and—" He stopped and rubbed his eyes.

Marcus sat forward, resting his elbows on his knees and hanging his head, unable to look at Van for the remainder of the conversation. When Van began again, his voice was strained and barely above a whisper.

"She was on the ground and he was standing over her. He kicked her in the back and then punched her in the face. The shock had me frozen for a second and I'm so sorry for that. I regret that I didn't get to her sooner. That I left her at all. I finally moved my feet, but unfortunately he heard me coming. He swung around, and I put up my arm to block the hit I knew was coming. However, I didn't see that he was holding something. I found out later it was a piece of wood the police suspected he found in the alley. He then hit my leg, taking me down. I remember screaming before he punched me a few times. I actually don't remember all the hits I took. All I could think about was Sarah lying a few feet from me. There was so much blood, and she wasn't moving."

Silence hung between them until Marcus couldn't take any more. He stood and walked to the window. If he had been with her, none of it would have happened. He would have driven her to the appointment, or had Thompson drive them. They might have still eaten at the same bistro, but they wouldn't have needed to go looking for a cab. Mark wouldn't have had an opportunity to strike.

But he would have found a way. If not that night, then he would have waited until he did see an opportunity. And what if the attack had happened after Eli and Lena had been born? If Sarah and the children had been out alone when he attacked? What would have happened then?

Marcus shuddered and tried to kick his thoughts, but they wouldn't budge until Van spoke again.

"The doctors said it couldn't have lasted long, but it felt like an eternity. I eventually heard a group coming down the street. Somehow I managed a yell for help. Mark stopped abruptly and took off. It was a group of women, so none of them ran after the bastard. Luckily, there was one woman in the group who was able to stop screaming long enough to call the police. Next thing I knew, I was in the hospital. I was told they had to do an emergency C-section on Sarah. That the blows had caused something to rupture and she was bleeding out pretty bad. Of course, they sugared it by saying we were lucky that she fell on her stomach, and therefore none of the hits were to the abdomen—"

Van couldn't finish. It was all right because Marcus knew the rest. He knew that on some level they were lucky Mark hadn't hit Sarah in the abdomen. If he had, it was likely the fate of his children would have been entirely different than just a stint in the NICU. The doctor had speculated that Sarah had braced her fall by putting out her arm, thus the injury to her wrist. She still hit hard enough to cause a placental abruption, but not enough to hurt the babies. Considering the first blow to the head had knocked her out, it was remarkable to think it was all instinct and reflex that had protected their children.

And perhaps someone who had been watching out for her from above. Someone who wouldn't let a little thing like being dead stop him from protecting her.

He finally turned back to Van. His eyes were red and he looked away from Marcus quickly. He wanted to say something to take away Van's guilt and pain. But there were no appropriate words for the situation. Instead of offering inadequate words, he walked over to the bed and planted a kiss on the top of Van's head before hugging him to his chest. He ruffled Van's hair and whispered a heartfelt thank you before stepping back. It didn't feel appropriate to just leave, but he knew Van. He knew he didn't do emotions. It was time to leave. He paused at the door and turned back to look at his friend.

"As long as you're in that bed, you have a lot of time on your hands. You should spend it learning Spanish. I have a feeling you're going to need to become fluent in it very soon." Van offered up a small, reluctant smile before flinging a pillow in Marcus' direction.

CHAPTER 26

"When can Sarah visit the NICU?" Marcus had tried to be patient, but Dr. Vikrant wasn't getting to the point quick enough.

The doctor let out a frustrated sigh. "I am trying to explain that to you. Bottom line—her vitals are improving, but not enough. She experienced significant trauma—both from the attack and from the loss of blood during delivery. I feel she should be able to recover quicker than she has, but something is holding her back, and she is still very weak. I am not comfortable having her in the NICU."

"But she's able to stay awake for longer periods of time, and she even got out of bed yesterday."

"I understand. But she is not stable enough. I do not want her to experience a set-back."

"I think it would help her, and the babies, if she could see them. Hold them. Even if it's just for a few moments." Marcus wanted to pace, but they were talking in the hallway just outside Sarah's room. He was trying to keep his voice lowered, not wanting Sarah to overhear the conversation.

"Possibly. Or it could set all three of them back."

"How do you figure?"

"What did you feel the first time you walked into the NICU and saw your children looking so small and fragile?"

Shattered. Scared. Helpless.

Marcus thought of the words that came instantly to mind and felt a chill run down his spine.

"I can see your answer written clearly on your face, Mr. Kingston. I imagine that your wife would feel those same emotions, except more because she would not be able to stay with them. It takes strength to watch your children fight for their lives—a strength she does not yet have. And what strength she does have, she needs to use to recover. I am sorry, but I will not change my mind."

The doctor walked away and Marcus let out a string of curses, rounding on the wall.

"Whoa, I thought we were done with hitting walls. This one won't give like the other, and you're likely to shatter your knuckles." Marcus shook off James' hold. "What'd the wall do this time?"

"It's been over a week and I don't know what to do to get Sarah out of that bed! She needs to be with the children. It's killing her not being able to be with them."

James scratched his head and looked in the direction of Sarah's room. "You just need to be patient. She's getting better. Eli and Lena are getting better. It will all work out."

Marcus slumped against the wall and closed his eyes, breathing deeply. When he felt in control, he looked back to James. "Are you leaving now?"

"Yeah, I came to say good-bye. I'd like to stay, but my boss claims things are about to fall apart."

"You can go in after Maggie's done. You're taking her to the airport, right?"

"That's the plan. Are you sure you'll be all right with just my parents and Tina as backup?"

"We'll make it work. I've still got Leanne, and Miles will be able to spend some time here now that his case is over. Darrel, Joan's husband, picked up Max this morning and they'll keep him at their house until we get home. How long are your parents planning to stay?"

"They're retired. I'm afraid you're stuck with them for a while. Possibly until your children reach the age of twelve."

Marcus smiled at his brother-in-law's jest. "Lucky me. I guess it's a good thing we have a huge house."

"So, have you talked to either of the detectives lately?"

"Not for a few days. They've questioned Rachel, but Detective Smith wouldn't tell me anything more than that."

"Will you keep me updated? Both on Sarah's progress and the children's, and on the case?"

"Of course. By the way, have you heard from Peter?" Marcus had received only a handful of texts since he left unexpectedly a few days ago. He'd asked Peter what was going on but didn't get a response.

"Nothing other than a text saying he was helping a friend. He wouldn't elaborate."

"Do you think it's anything we need to worry about?"

"With Peter there's always something to worry about. But I'm sure it's nothing serious. It might be something we wouldn't approve of, but not serious. You'll eventually come to learn which of Peter's 'emergencies' are truly that versus some harebrained scheme he's gotten himself into."

Marcus wasn't so sure. But James understood Peter better than he did, so he relented. "Well, at least I don't have to worry about you or Tom doing anything stupid. One out of three is manageable."

James looked back toward Sarah's door. "Yeah, well, the good thing about being responsible is that you're never suspected of doing stupid shit." James looked back and leveled Marcus with a steady glare. "No one's perfect after all."

Marcus felt the hairs on the back of his neck stand to attention. Before he could question James on his meaning, Maggie exited Sarah's room and James walked away.

"Mr. Kingston, thanks for meeting with me."

"Of course. I'd like you to meet Miles Morgan. He's a family friend and attorney. I've asked him to become more familiar with the particulars of the case. Miles, this is Detective Smith." Marcus watched as they shook hands.

"I'm sure you'd like me to get to the point, so that's what I'll do. We talked to Hawk and she claims to have no knowledge of Tanger."

"Do you believe her?"

"We haven't been able to find a link. There are no phone records between them and no evidence of physical meetings. However, Tanger's reaction when we questioned him about Hawk was suspicious. He's still not talking, holding out for some kind of deal, but based on his reaction we're not closing out Hawk."

"Have you talked with Ms. Hawk's employer?" Marcus looked to Miles with curiosity, wondering where he was going with his line of questioning.

"We talked with the entire staff. The office manager stated that Hawk is an exemplary employee. She couldn't be bothered to entertain the idea that Hawk would do such a thing. The doctor said she hadn't been working in his office long enough for him to comment."

"What does she do for the office?"

Smith pulled something up on his tablet before responding. "Mostly she helps to process insurance claims, but she does help out by filling in when people are out of the office."

"Does she have access to the patient records?"

"My understanding is that she has access to billing records and the appointment schedule. The office went digital a year or so ago, and all patient medical records are password protected."

"Have you checked to see if she could have used a co-worker's password or had someone access the information for her?"

"I'll look into it." Smith typed something into his tablet.

"What about the lab? Do you know if they use an inside or outside lab to process the results?"

"I'm not sure."

"Please find out. Also, I want copies of the information you have."

Smith studied Miles before answering. "Are you considering legal action against the doctor's office?"

"If I feel there's been any foul play, then yes. You have to understand; those test results contain very sensitive information. If Ms. Hawk was able to manipulate them in any way in an effort to cause distress to my clients, then you're damn right I'm going to take action on Ms. Hawk, the practice, and possibly the rest of the staff."

"I'll get you the information you requested."

Oh shit. I never considered that Rachel could have altered the test results. That changes everything.

"Thank you. I—"

"Wait. Back up. If there is even a miniscule chance that she could have altered the results—" Marcus ran a hand through his hair and stood. He needed to pace, but there was no space in the small room. He turned in a circle a few times, certain that he looked like an idiot, before sitting back down. He slammed his hand against the table. "We can't take the test again! If we can't trust the results, with one hundred percent certainty... this is bullshit!"

"Marcus, relax. First we need to understand how they process the results. If they use an outside lab, then there will be records on their end we can compare to. Detective Smith will get the information, and we'll go from there."

Marcus slumped back in his chair, trying to calm down.

"Mr. Kingston, we'll get the information as quickly as we can. I promise." Marcus simply nodded at the detective's assurance.

"Detective, I also wanted to understand the assault charges Mr. Tanger filed when he was attacked while in his car."

"We haven't been able to find any evidence to suggest that Mr. Kingston or any of the Polanski brothers had anything to do with it."

"Interesting choice of words, Detective. Does that mean you suspect one of them, but can't link any evidence?"

"For that particular case, I only care about the evidence. Quite frankly, there is none. It will be closed as a random act of vandalism. After all, he does live in an area where crime is currently up a few points. You can rest assured that it will have no impact on our case against Tanger."

Smith asked a few more questions that Miles answered, but Marcus had tuned out the conversation. He was roused out of his thoughts when the detective stood to leave. Once he was out of the room, Marcus turned to Miles.

"Do you have a few more minutes to talk?"

"Sure."

Marcus tapped the table a few times and cleared his throat. "You had a better relationship with my father than I did." Miles sat back in his chair, clearly anticipating where the conversation was headed.

"What is it you'd like to know?"

"Based on the letter he wrote me, it was obvious he let CJD dictate some of his life decisions. How much control do you think he gave over to his illness? How much of his life did he let it impact?"

Miles thought for a moment before responding. "In the ten years I knew your father, we became close friends. Since we met under professional circumstances, I knew about his illness from the very first meeting. It's why he sought out a new lawyer—he wanted to ensure everything was in place before the illness manifested. You want my opinion as to how much he let CJD control his life? More than he wanted."

"But I never even knew he was sick. Sure we had a strained relationship, but I would have thought that I'd have noticed if he'd given it that much control. And Leanne worked with him on a daily basis. It was as much a shock to her as it was to me."

"I didn't say he gave it full control, just more than he wanted. He was able to keep it out of his professional life. He set limits for when he would need to remove himself from the company, fearful he would make a critical mistake if he remained working once the symptoms started developing. That clear distinction made it easy for him to keep control in his professional life. It was in his personal life where he relinquished too much control. He let it determine the nature of his relationship with you. He let it keep him from getting close to another woman. He let his friendships dissolve. I think it's one of the reasons we became such close friends. I think I was all he really had in his life. Until Sarah came along. Unfortunately, that wasn't until the final months of his life."

"Do you think he would have been better off not knowing?"

"Marcus, you're not the same as your father. I can't tell you if you should get tested or not. Only you can figure out which path will let you maintain the most control over your life."

"But what about the children? Assuming the test results weren't altered by Rachel, we have a chance to understand if they have it. To me, getting the test results equates to taking away their right to make their own choice when they become adults. I wouldn't hesitate if there was even the slightest chance of a cure. Knowing would mean a chance of survival. But with CJD, knowing just feels like a death sentence."

"I wish to God there were a right answer here, Marcus. There just isn't. The only acceptable answer is the one that you and Sarah can live with for the rest of your lives."

Marcus looked away, wishing he knew what to do. He'd convinced himself it was acceptable to not know when it was just him. Even with Sarah in his life, he could justify his decision. He felt he was protecting her from his fate. But now he was a father. Even though his fear caused him to block them from his mind for the first five

246 | Carrie Beckort

days of their lives, the moment he held them in his arms he knew he'd be forever changed. They were swaddled in purity and innocence. He didn't want them to ever have to know about such horrors as CJD.

Keeping it out of their lives was a way of protecting their innocence for as long as possible. They wouldn't have to feel bad for acting like normal children—they could talk back and ignore their parents like all children did at some point. They wouldn't have to watch their father and mother sidestep certain life events because of his impending fate. If he and Sarah knew he had it, it was bound to impact their decisions—both inadvertently and intentionally.

However, if they knew their father was going to die sooner rather than later, they would feel an added pressure to be perfect. Something that is never possible to achieve. On the flip side, not knowing would mean they might later have regrets and resentment for not being able to make the most of the time they did have together.

He had felt all of it himself. There were days when he was grateful his father never told him. Happy that he could revel in his feelings and emotions without guilt. Then there were the days he nearly crumbled from the weight of the pain of not having had the opportunity to be close with his father.

There really is no right answer. Only the one we can live with while harboring the least amount of regret. It's no wonder my father made a decision and never looked back. It's the only way to focus on making sure the decision you made turns out to be the best one.

CHAPTER 27

Marcus watched as Sarah slept. He needed to do something to help her; he just wasn't sure what it was. He was frustrated because he *should* know.

She knew how to help me while she was half unconscious, lying in a hospital bed, struggling to hold on. Why can't I figure this out?

He'd asked himself the question, but he knew the answer. He'd been so focused on his own fear and guilt that he couldn't think of anything else.

He thought about Sarah's difficulty in holding on to guilt. For a while he thought that was her problem—that she'd harbored too much guilt at having gone to the appointment when she said she wouldn't.

But he'd ruled it out.

He'd come to learn how to read her guilt and he knew her cues when she was struggling with it, and he didn't see any of them in her current struggle.

He thought back over all the memories she'd asked him to replay for her. Once he had realized what she was doing, he could understand the significance of the requests. They all highlighted moments in their life together, showing him how deep their connection was from the first moment they met. They reminded him of all that they had been through to be together.

However, many of the memories were more than that. Some

contained a promise he had made that he now felt he'd failed on. Some highlighted how his relationship with his father and CJD had impacted his life. Some had both. Some even helped remind him that one of his primary flaws was his constant self-judgment and the expectation that others would judge him as well.

Each memory he recalled for Sarah contained a piece of the puzzle which he needed to help get past his fear and guilt. But he couldn't shake the feeling that there was something in there that could help Sarah as well. He ran through the memories one more time before getting frustrated.

He ran a hand through his hair and walked to the window, looking out over the dark city. After a few minutes he turned back to face Sarah, leaning against the window ledge. He studied her sleeping form. He was becoming desperate to get her out of the bed and with their children.

How the hell does Dr. Vikrant know that this is what's best? He can't know that it would set her or the twins back. He doesn't think she's strong enough, but I know her better than that. Losing Danny nearly shattered her. I know that it's killing her to not be able to see or hold them. I know she's strong enough, but I don't know how to convince him of that.

It popped in his head so quickly he blinked in surprise. He mentally scanned through the memories again and pinpointed the one he was looking for.

The letter from Nick. He'd said she didn't know her own strength. That sometimes she needed to be reminded.

It made perfect sense. After she lost Nick and Danny, she didn't know how to rely on her own strength until his father had shown her how. Now, she'd lost sight of it again.

Somehow I need to show her just how strong she is.

"Were you able to get everything on the list?" Marcus searched through the bag that Tina handed him.

"I think so, but you should go through it to be sure. What exactly is your plan with all this stuff?"

"I'm going to use it to get Sarah out of that bed." He inspected the items Tina brought, satisfied that she had everything. "Okay, now I need you to help me go through these." He pulled a stack of photos out of an envelope and handed them to Tina. She took in a sharp breath as she sank into a chair.

"Who took these?"

"That one nurse who's not in the NICU much, I don't remember her name. She's the one who accents most of her comments with a wink. Do you like them?"

"Marcus, these are incredible."

"I need your help picking out the ones that Sarah would like best."

Tina quickly shifted her attention from the photos to Marcus. "We were told not to show her any photos of the twins. The doctor thinks it might upset her to see them like this."

"Well, I'm her husband and I don't agree. I can't bypass his orders restricting her from visiting them, but I can show her pictures. You know her, Tina. It's killing her not being able to see them. I have to do something."

She thought for a minute before finally nodding in agreement. "What do you need?"

"Which photos should I show her? I think overall Winky did a good job of making the twins look as healthy as possible."

"Winky?"

"What? I can't remember her name. Like I said, she's not in the NICU all the time. When she is there, my mind is preoccupied with the twins. And she winks *all the time*. For a while I thought maybe she had some sort of twitch. I figured Winky was better than calling her 'that nurse.'"

"No, it's not. And her name is Joan. You know, like your partner. I think you can remember that. Maybe we shouldn't have encouraged you to patch things up with Van. His bad influences are rubbing off on you again."

"Okay, fine. *Joan* did a good job with the photos. Which ones should I use?"

"These. They're amazing. In this one it almost looks like Lena is smiling at you."

Marcus' heart swelled when he looked at the photo again. He suddenly had an insatiable need to hold his children. Sarah's parents were with them so he could finalize everything, but he might have to adjust his plans.

Tina must have recognized the need in his eyes. "I think the photos of the twins should be enlarged—it would have a greater impact. While I'm gone you can go see the twins. When I get back, I'll help you finish preparing everything. What exactly is the plan?"

"I've convinced the nurses on her floor to take her out of the room at a certain time. They've been trying to get her out of the bed for small excursions each day. Today's will just be extra special—I'll have all this in her room when she gets back."

Tina smiled as she stood. "I'll call you when I'm back with the photos." She gave him a quick kiss on the cheek before walking off. He grabbed the bag Tina had brought with her and turned in the direction of the NICU.

There was a knock on the door, and it opened before Marcus could respond. He cursed under his breath, hurrying toward the door. Sarah wasn't supposed to be back yet and he wasn't ready. He reached the door just as the detectives entered and he breathed a sigh of relief.

"We're sorry to interrupt, Mr. Kingston. The nurse said we could find you in here." They looked around the room, taking in the details. "I'm sorry, it looks like we might be infringing on something private."

"It's all right. Please, have a seat. Do you have more information?" Marcus sat on the end of the bed, watching the detectives study the room in silence for a few seconds.

Smith finally turned his eyes to Marcus. "Is Mr. Morgan here by any chance? I'm sorry we didn't give you a heads up before dropping by, but we recently learned some new information. We figured your lawyer might be interested as well."

"He's not, but I can try to conference him in if you'll give me a moment." Marcus texted Miles and he quickly confirmed he could join them over the phone. Marcus called him and placed his phone on speaker, positioning it on the tray table by the bed. Once Miles was on the phone, Smith got right to the point.

"The last time we talked, I told you we were still looking into Hawk. Tanger's reaction indicated he knew her, even though he stated otherwise. However, the challenge I had was that when we questioned Hawk, her reaction led us to believe she didn't know who Tanger was. The contradiction between them was suspicious." Smith stopped talking and looked at Crass.

"We looked at all possible angles, including Hawk's ex-husband and Tanger's ex-wife. We couldn't find any evidence of Hawk and Tanger interacting with each other."

Marcus looked from one detective to the other. "What does this mean? Don't fucking tell me you're here because you're giving Mark a deal!"

"Mr. Kingston, please, let us finish." Smith looked at Crass and rolled his finger in the air, indicating he should get to the point.

"Yes, sorry, I suppose I should have led with something different. Just another reason why Detective Smith usually handles the personal aspects of the cases. Anyway, I wasn't satisfied with the answer that there wasn't a link so I kept digging. And I found something. Do you recognize the woman in this photo?" Crass handed Marcus the picture. It was a still shot from a security camera and the details were somewhat hard to make out. The photo showed a man and a woman standing outside. As he studied it, he realized it was from the night of the gala when Mark had put his hands on Sarah.

"Guys, remember that I'm on the phone and can't see what's in the room. Skip the suspense and just tell me who's in the photo."

Marcus looked up at the detectives. "Was this taken from the night of the gala?"

"Yes, and we know that's Tanger based on other footage we have. The woman in the photo somehow wasn't clear in any of the camera angles except this one."

Marcus looked at the photo again. Mark's back was to the camera and the woman was looking at him. Her hand was raised and it looked like she might have been touching his face. Marcus couldn't make out any of the woman's features, but suddenly the dress caught his attention. He remembered who wore that dress. It was scandalously low cut and it would have been impossible not to notice.

"What in the hell? Is that Jen Ballard?"

"We were hoping that's what you'd say."

"Who's Jen Ballard, Marcus?"

On instinct, Marcus looked at his phone. "She's Rachel's best friend. Miles, she's the one who wore that ridiculously low cut blue dress at the gala."

There was a pause on the phone before Miles spoke again. "I remember. She wore a similar dress this past gala, right? In red?"

"That's the one." Marcus looked back at the detectives. "How's she connected to Mark?"

"Apparently she's his girlfriend."

Marcus felt his jaw drop open. "Since when?"

"From what we've been able to gather, they met the night of the gala. This image was taken after you punched him, and he was escorted out. Ballard's not talking right now, but we went back to talk to Hawk after we discovered the connection."

Smith jumped in when Crass stopped talking. "Ballard was the one who talked Hawk into returning to the Denver area. She told Hawk that you had been talking about her constantly over the last twenty years. Ballard spun a good story about how you were still in love with her. Good enough that Hawk moved back out here."

"She didn't divorce Patrick over that load of crap, did she?" After what they did to him he should have relished the idea that they had been split up by lies. The irony would have been satisfying. But he wasn't that malicious.

"No, Ballard told Hawk all this after the divorce was already final. We suspect Tanger and Ballard had been plotting together, and Hawk's divorce was an opportunity they chose to exploit. Initially, they'd simply hoped that her showing up would put a strain on your relationship with Sarah. Once they discovered you were a patient where Hawk worked, they took it to a whole new level."

"So, if I'm following along correctly, Ms. Hawk was unknowingly feeding information to Ms. Ballard, who in turn relayed it to Mr. Tanger."

"Yes, Mr. Morgan, that's correct. Hawk simply thought she was unloading to a friend—upset that she had to see the two of you at the office. We've been able to confirm that Ballard visited Hawk at the doctor's office a couple of times between the date of your initial appointment and the morning of the attack."

Marcus' head was reeling from the information. "I'm sorry, detectives. I just don't understand why Jen would do this."

"To help Tanger. She's in love with him. That much was clear when we talked to her. She believes that you ruined his life, and she wanted to help him ruin yours." Crass made it sound so simple, but it was anything but that for Marcus. He'd known Jen for years. She had been Rachel's best friend when they were dating. He knew that she'd always supported Rachel's side of the break-up story—the one that painted Marcus as the bad guy—but this went beyond the standard best friend support structure.

But if what the detectives are saying is true, she didn't even do this for Rachel. She did it for Mark.

"Detectives, what have you learned about the access to Mrs. Kingston's file?" Miles' question snapped Marcus back to attention. He looked at the detectives and felt dread seep into his core as they shifted in their seats.

"Mrs. Kingston's records were accessed four times after the test was completed. Once to log the results, once by the doctor for review prior to the follow-up appointment, and once on the day of the attack—but none of that is unusual. However, there is one unexplained instance where her records were accessed prior to the doctor reviewing the results. Unfortunately, an administrative code was used, which could be one of several people in the office. The doctor assumes it was a lab tech updating some of the results."

"What about the kind of lab they use?"

"Unfortunately, their office uses an in-house lab. We know Mrs. Kingston's test results were accessed at least once with no explanation. We also know that Ballard had been in the office more than once during that time. The doctor insists the results couldn't have been tampered with, but the reality is there's no way to guarantee the accuracy of your test results. I'm sorry. I wish I had better news."

Marcus looked at Smith and felt a vice grip his chest.

"However, the doctor said they would refund the expense of the test." Smith shot Crass a sharp look. Crass looked back in confusion for a few seconds before cursing under his breath. "Sorry. Again, this is why Detective Smith usually does the in-person interviews alone."

"Is Ms. Hawk still employed at the office?"

"No, Mr. Morgan, she's been dismissed for having let Ballard in the office. It's a shame really. She actually seems pretty shaken up by the whole thing. In a way, she's a victim in this as well."

Marcus tried to pay attention, but the fact that they couldn't rely on the test results weighed heavy on his mind. He suddenly stood.

"I need to get out of here. My wife should be back in—" He looked down at his watch. "—fifteen minutes. Please wrap up in the next five. Miles, will you call Tina and ask her to finish in here for me? I'll be back before Sarah returns." He turned and left the room without waiting for a response.

He walked briskly and mindlessly through the hospital halls, needing air and time to process the information. As soon as he exited the hospital, the shock of the cold air made him suck in a breath. He walked until he found a private bench where he sat down.

How can this be happening? Just when I think we're making progress, something comes crashing down on us.

Mark's in custody. There won't be a deal. Jen's been identified. And Rachel's not as crazy as she appeared to be.

But Sarah's not getting better as quickly as expected, and the twins are still in the NICU for an indeterminate amount of time. Now, we can't even rely on the test results. Sarah and I had agreed to come to a solution together, but now that choice has been taken away from us. There's nothing to decide.

He hung his head, feeling the mountain of pressure weighing him down. Not only did he have to find a way to get his family out of the hospital, but now he had to tell Sarah there was no choice to make.

She wasn't okay with not knowing. Maybe she would have eventually decided she didn't want to know, but she wasn't there yet. With the choice being taken away from her, she might never be okay with it. How do I keep this from crushing her?

He tried to silence his mind. He needed to go back inside and meet Sarah so he could help her get better. He couldn't afford to go back to the way he'd been acting. There had to be something he could do.

There is one thing. I could get tested. At least it would let her know what to expect. It could ease her mind.

He didn't want to get tested, but he knew it could make things better for Sarah. When she was out of the hospital and fully recovered, he would tell her about the test results and then let her decide if he should get tested or not.

Every promise I've made to her culminates to this point.

I've promised to love her.

To protect her.

To cherish my time with her.

To always be presumptive.

To not let this break us.

To trust her.

By trusting her enough to determine my fate with the test, I can give her everything I've promised.

Marcus was grateful he'd made it back to Sarah's room before she got back. Tina had finished for him and now he waited. He took in a deep breath as he watched Sarah being pushed in his direction. It was good to see her sitting up in a wheelchair, rather than lying in the bed, but she still looked so weak. Her uninjured arm was supporting her head, her wrapped leg sticking out before her. They had removed most of the bandages from her face a few days ago and the bruising was finally starting to fade. He pushed off the wall and walked to intercept them. The nurse nodded and smiled at him before walking away.

Sarah lifted her head and smiled when she saw him. "You're waiting for me."

"I'll always wait for you."

"Ever the romantic. You know what I mean."

"That's because I have a surprise, if you're feeling up to it."

"And if I said no?"

"Then I'd have to talk you into it. Because the surprise is in your room." She eyed him with suspicion, but he just smiled and gave her a quick kiss on the forehead before moving behind her. He pushed her through the open door and waited while she absorbed what she saw. He also looked over each of the items Tina had helped him set up. There were photos of their wedding, honeymoon, Max, friends, family, and their house surrounded by the mountains she loved. He included the one of his father that she had taken while she was working with him. Of course there were also photos of Nick and Danny and the twins. He also had Tina bring certain items that were important to Sarah for one reason or another.

"You did all this?"

"Tina helped. I wanted to have candles in here too, but something about hospital regulations kept that from happening. I couldn't even talk them into it while shirtless, so it must be an important regulation." His hands were resting on her shoulders, and she reached up to squeeze his fingers. She knew he was trying to steady his emotions with a bit of humor. The squeeze of his fingers told him she appreciated it for her own sake as well.

"I love it." He could hear the crack in her voice as she whispered the words.

"I thought you needed to be surrounded by people you love and who love you in return." He rounded the wheelchair to crouch down in front of her. "We're all here for you, Sarah. Even Nick and Danny." He paused and picked up a photo from the nearby table. It was one of her favorites of the three of them.

He looked at it a moment before handing it to her. She placed her hand over the photo and began to cry. He placed one hand over hers and cupped her cheek with his other.

"We're all here, Sarah. Either physically or spiritually, and we need you."

He wiped at her tears, only for them to be replaced by new, before standing and pushing her over by the bed. He picked up one of the new photos and handed it to her. It was of him holding Eli and Lena. A cry escaped from her and her hands started to shake. He gently scooped her up out of the chair and placed her in the bed, climbing into the other bed that was still next to hers. As gently as he could, he cradled her in his arms. It had been so long since he held her and the sensation caused his emotions to overflow. He held on as tightly as he could without hurting her, and she held on to the photos with just as much force.

"You can do this, Sarah. You're stronger than you think. You saved me, remember? And you did that when it took everything you had just to breathe. You're the strongest person I know. You can do this. I want to help you the way you helped me."

He reached over to retrieve something out of the bag sitting on the table next to the bed. He placed it in Sarah's lap. She was still clutching the photos to her chest, eyes locked shut and dripping with tears of pain.

"You once told me that I could read your journals. You said that you didn't want anything between us, not even your relationship with Nick. I've never read them. The fact that you offered me the option was enough comfort for me. Even though I haven't read them, I believe they will help you. I want to use your own words to show you how strong you are. Can I read them to you?"

It took a few seconds, but she finally nodded her head against his chest. He opened the first journal and started reading.

A few days had passed since Marcus had surprised Sarah with his plan to help her recover. She was much improved and the doctor said she should be able to visit the NICU in a day or two. At the moment they were expecting a visitor who, as usual, was running about twenty minutes late.

"T.O.! You're looking good!" Van hobbled in with the help of a crutch, followed by Isabella. He went straight to Sarah's side and leaned in to give her a hug. It was the longest hug they had exchanged. Marcus knew it was from the gratitude each had for the other, so he let it linger longer than he would normally. Van finally pulled away and Sarah wiped at her eyes.

She pointed to his crutch. "I might need you to teach me how to use those things in a few days."

"We can race around the halls. Winner buys the other a vegetable smoothie."

Sarah wrinkled her nose at the suggestion and Marcus raised his eyebrow in suspicion.

"I thought you were boycotting those."

"Turns out they're not so bad."

Isabella smiled at Marcus as she patted Van on the back. "Don't let him fool you. The first few days he had to plug his nose while he drank it and almost gagged each time."

"It's an acquired taste. At least I'm drinking them. Trying new things and all." The look Van shot Marcus was quick, but he still caught the meaning behind it. Van was trying to open up his mind to more than just nasty green drinks.

Isabella was the one to ask about the photos still displayed around the room, and they fell into casual conversation about the twins and Sarah's progress. It was an enjoyable visit, but after an hour Marcus could tell that Sarah was getting tired.

Van noticed as well. "You look like you could use some rest. We'll have to get together when you get out of this joint."

"Van, before you go... I just wanted to make sure you knew how much I appreciate what you did for me. If you hadn't been there—" Sarah closed her eyes and shook her head, unable to finish. Marcus moved to sit with her on the bed, but Van somehow beat him to it.

"I only wish I could have kept it from happening. I feel I owe you something for letting you out of my sight."

"Van, that's not neces—"

"Don't you even want to know what I'm offering?"

"Remember, I'm right here. Nothing inappropriate." Marcus heard Van laugh at his friendly rub.

Van looked at Marcus over his shoulder. "It's nothing inappropriate. In fact, it's something T.O.'s been begging me for since the night of your birthday, Kingston."

Marcus smiled, knowing what Van intended to give Sarah. Van was blocking his view of Sarah's face so he shifted his chair. He didn't want to miss her reaction.

"The only thing I want from you is an explanation on what you do for a living. Wait—are you going to finally tell me!"

"First I'm going to give you one more guess."

Sarah thought for a moment. "Well, I know your office is in downtown Denver. Based on the stories you tell, I know you work for a corporation. Lately I've been thinking it has something to do with human resources."

"Nope, sorry. But that's the closest you've come. You're right—I do work for a corporation. I also work with human resources quite frequently. Are you sure you really want to know? This game of guessing has been rather fun."

"Yes, I want to know now. Please."

"I'm the head of a legal division for a mining corporation. My team investigates and represents cases in sexual harassment."

It took Sarah a full ten seconds before the shock wore off. Her laughter started as restricted giggles and then she finally let go. She'd laughed harder than Marcus had seen in many months.

"You can't be serious!"

"Completely."

Sarah looked to Marcus for verification and he nodded. She laughed until it hurt, gripping her pillow for support.

Van reached out and put a hand on her shoulder. "I thought I was helping. I didn't mean to put you in physical pain."

"No, it was worth it. And here I often wondered how you managed to not get fired for sexual harassment, and you're the one doing the firing! I think this might just be the best gift ever. Thank you." She was still laughing, but it had settled into a controlled chuckle.

Deciding it was time for Sarah to have a break, Marcus walked Van out of the room while Isabella said good-bye to Sarah. "Thanks, man. That was the happiest I've seen her in a long time."

"It was the least I could do. But, damn, did she have to laugh so hard? I mean, it's not *that* funny."

"It's pretty damn funny. Ironic too."

"Yeah, well, you don't look like a dancer."

Marcus smiled and considered a rebuttal. However, given all that his friend had been through he decided to let him have the last word.

Marcus couldn't remember the last time he'd been so excited and nervous at the same time.

Maybe at our wedding, right before Sarah walked down the aisle.

He watched Sarah as she sat fidgeting with the end of the blanket that was draped around her legs. He could tell she was also equal measures excited and nervous.

"Are you sure you're ready for this?"

"I've been waiting for this moment for over two weeks. I'm more than ready." She smiled, but he could see the tears she held back.

"While we're waiting for the nurse, can I ask you something?"

"You know you can ask me anything."

"I know, but I don't want to always assume you're in the mood to be asked."

She smiled and took his hand in hers. "You can ask."

"I—" He stopped, suddenly not sure if it was the right time.

"Are you wanting to know what took me so long to get here? No need to look so surprised. Some of those times you were talking to Dr. Vikrant in the hall I could hear you."

A slight panic surged through him. "Did you hear other conversations too?"

She looked at him in suspicion. "No. Why, are you hiding something from me?"

"No, nothing like that. I've just had some conversations in the hall with the detectives, or with James, and I'm not ready to tell you about all that. I wanted to wait until you were recovered, but I don't want it to put a mark on today."

Sarah nodded her head. All she knew was that the person who had attacked her had been arrested, and he was on his way to jail for a long time. She didn't know it was Mark or that Jen had been helping him. Or that they had been using Rachel as a pawn.

Marcus knew from the detectives that Mark had finally confessed to all charges and admitted to being high on drugs the day of the attack. He'd been waiting outside the doctor's office building, wanting to see their reaction to the test results. He was angry when he saw Sarah go in alone. His rage peaked when he found out she didn't actually go to the appointment. He hadn't seen her leave, so he knew she was still in the building, and he'd waited. By the time Sarah and Van had finished dinner, he was beyond reasonable thought. He claimed to not remember everything about following Sarah and Van, much less attacking them in the alley.

The detectives had also arrested Jen and informed Marcus that Rachel had decided to return to wherever it was she came from before she showed up in their lives.

Marcus also hadn't yet told Sarah about the test results. He wanted to wait until she and the children were out of the hospital.

He was pulled out of his thoughts when Sarah touched his cheek. "It's okay. You're right. I want to know the full story, but not today."

"Good." He took a deep breath and returned his focus to their conversation before thoughts of the attack had distracted him. "But yes, I'm wondering what took you so long to get to this point. Dr. Vikrant felt that you should have recovered sooner."

She let out a small sigh and looked down at her hands. She started speaking before she looked up.

"I was so upset the day of the attack. First at you, then at myself. By the time I'd finished dinner with Van, I was hopeful we could come to a solution. Then I woke up here, weak and in pain. And without my babies." Tears pricked her eyes and her voice caught with emotion, but she pushed forward. "You were here when I first woke up and found out. You know how I panicked. My mind started spiraling out of control, and I felt as if I had lost everything again. I remember feeling the same sort of panic as when I found out about Nick and Danny, and then I blacked out. When I woke up the second time, I just felt so tired. I was suffocating from the negative thoughts of our children in the NICU, fighting without us. I was fighting for you. I was fighting the pain. Every part of my body hurt so badly—"

"Wait, I thought you said you weren't in pain? You should have said something, Sarah. They could have upped your dosage!"

"You know how I feel about taking medicine."

"Yeah, but there are times when it's kind of required."

"I didn't want to be doped up on medication. Deep down, I was afraid that if I was numb to the physical pain then I'd be numb to mental pain as well. I needed it to help me remember why I had to fight. And I was fighting, but I was just so tired. As a result, sometimes the calm of the darkness inside me was too soothing to leave. It's why I needed you to talk to me. I think you already know I picked those particular memories to help you make it through your pain, and I could have easily just reminded you of what they were. But I needed your voice to anchor me, to keep me from going too far into the darkness. That's why I felt I had to help fix you first."

Marcus moved off his seat to kneel down in front of her. "What gave you the strength to finally make it out for good?"

"Every time I thought about not being able to see Eli and Lena, a new part of me shattered. I couldn't put all the pieces back together quick enough, so I focused on you. I knew that if you found a way to get past your pain, then you would be strong enough to bring the rest of us along with you. You helped me, with all of this." She paused and waved her hand around the room. "You reminded me that I had it in me all along, I just had to trust it. Those journal entries reminded me that I made a promise to your father on his final day. I promised that I'd never go back to the way I was. No more letting the darkness consume me. I'm a Kingston now, and that means I'll do anything I can to keep my promise."

Just as Marcus leaned forward and captured her lips with his, the door opened.

"Are you ready Mrs. Kingston?" Marcus pulled back and held Sarah's gaze.

"Are you ready to meet our children?" Sarah nodded, too overcome with emotion to voice the words. Marcus stood and took her hand while the nurse took the handles of the wheelchair. As they walked and wheeled their way to the NICU, Marcus thought about their life ahead of them.

I promise to never forget this time in our lives—not because of the pain it caused, but because of the strength it gave.

EPILOGUE
November • 2030

"Nathaniel Eli Kingston! How many times have I told you not to flip over the couch?"

Marcus stopped his son, just as he was about to crash into the side table. Given Sarah's tone, he knew he should check his smile.

"But, Mom! Brody's allowed to do flips over his couch all the time!"

"Yeah, well, I'm not Brody's mom. In fact, I think it's quite possible that woman is high ninety percent of the time. She doesn't always make the best parenting decisions."

"Mom, you can't go around and accuse people of doing drugs."

Marcus released Eli with a playful nudge and turned his attention to Lena. "The woman is *always* happy. That's not achieved through natural means."

"Do you and Mom share the same brain or something? Don't you ever disagree?"

Marcus locked eyes with Sarah and they smiled at each other. "There are times when we disagree, but we agree when it matters."

"And Brody's mom doing drugs matters?"

"Yes."

"MOM! She. Does. NOT. Do. Drugs!"

"And how would you know? You're not supposed to spend time at his house."

"You know, if you're trying to set an example for why we shouldn't do drugs, you should probably reference someone who's not always happy and lets her kids do anything they want. She sounds pretty cool to me."

Marcus stifled his laugh as Sarah's brow furrowed at Lena. She looked back and forth between their children, who were starting to display looks of victory.

"You're right, Lena. I'm sure she doesn't do drugs. She must be addicted to yoga. That's why she's so happy all the time and doesn't care what her kids do."

"You're addicted to running, and I think you're happy most of the time. How come you won't let us do whatever we want?"

"Because I care."

"But you just argued that Brody's mom's addicted to yoga and that's why she doesn't care. That would imply—"

"Can we stop talking about addictions to drugs and yoga and running and get back to my flips? I need to practice."

"Eli, you're more talented than I was at your age. You don't need to destroy the furniture in your pursuit of perfection."

"Or your bones." Sarah was back to chopping the ingredients for the salad.

"But it's not the same. It's not enough to just be *good* these days. You have to have killer tricks to get accepted to the top schools."

"You have a tricked out studio downstairs, not to mention the space I added to the dance studio so you can practice there too. As your mother said, you don't need to use the furniture."

"But the couch is higher! If I can learn to clear it then I can move to the next level."

"Why did dancing have to become so complicated? Why can't a nice, traditional, contemporary routine be enough?"

"Face it, Dad, you're ancient." Marcus shot an annoyed look at his daughter.

"Fifty-six is not ancient. Your father can still dance better than half the kids enrolled at the studio."

"He might be able to still dance well, but soon enough he'll be bumping into things and forgetting our names."

"Ow, shit!"

Marcus hurried to Sarah's side. He didn't need to ask what had caused her to slip and slice her finger. They still hadn't told Eli and Lena about his possible fate with CJD. They were hoping they would never have to. They may not talk about it, but it didn't stop them from thinking about it.

For a few years after the twins were born, they had been too busy to obsess over the uncertainty of their future. They were blissfully happy in the messiness of everyday life. However as the children grew and became more independent, the shadows of doubt began to resurface. Now as each new birthday passed, he couldn't help but wonder how many more he would be able to celebrate. And each time the kids teased him about getting old, Sarah had an involuntary reaction.

"Here, run it under the water." Marcus led Sarah to the sink and turned on the cold water.

"It's fine, just a scrape."

"Still, hold it here until the bleeding stops." He held her hand under the water and pulled her to his chest. He could feel her relax into him. Just as it had since the first moment they touched, the contact of their bodies gave them the strength they needed to remain grounded in the present.

"You didn't get any blood in the salad did you?"

"Lena! You could at least try to show more concern for your mother than for your food."

"I would if it were serious. Like she said, it's just a scrape."

"Go and get your mother a bandage."

"Fine." Lena hopped off the stool and rounded the counter. She stopped to pull them into a group hug before walking off. "You know I care." Marcus watched her disappear around the corner.

"And change your clothes while you're up there!" He would never get used to having a daughter. Each year was more stressful than the last. Her head poked back around the corner.

"Are you serious?"

"Completely."

"Dad. It's just going to be the Morgans and the Vanderlinks."

"Yeah, and Mitch is exactly like his father."

Lena rolled her eyes, but he could see the blush starting to stain her cheeks. "He's like a brother."

"The way he looks at you makes it very clear he doesn't think of you as a sister." He could see the blush fully take over her face. "Please, humor your old man and change your clothes." She pulled back around the corner sharply and yelled out a sarcastic 'fine' as she walked away.

Marcus turned off the water, wrapped Sarah's finger in a towel, and led her to the couch.

"Marcus, this really isn't necessary. I need to finish the salad."

"Sure it is. And I'll finish the salad." He plopped her down and gave her a kiss before returning to the kitchen. Before he got there, Eli resumed his plea for a better dance space.

"Now that all the drama has passed, can we get back to discussing the upgrade to the studio?"

"Christmas isn't far away. If you want to upgrade your space, just put it on your list." Eli growled at his mother before turning to Marcus for support.

"Dad, do I really have to wait for Christmas to get an upgrade?"

Marcus would have scheduled the upgrade for that weekend, but Sarah liked to keep the kids from being too spoiled. It was hard to restrain sometimes, but he knew it was for the best. "Yes."

Eli groaned and stomped out of the room, pausing only to lightly tap Danny's picture as he passed. It was a tradition the children had started when they were seven. Every time they passed by his picture, they would give it a tap of acknowledgement. It was their way of honoring their brother they never had the chance to meet. Marcus knew Sarah's heart warmed with each and every tap over the last nine years.

Marcus looked back at Sarah and she smiled at him. The salad forgotten and the children upstairs, he took a step in her direction. Unfortunately, the doorbell rang and interrupted his plans. She giggled, noticing his frustration.

"Remind me again why we started this tradition."

"Because it's good to be surrounded by family at the holidays. Leanne and Brad always go to his parents' house for Thanksgiving, and my family is too far away. Besides, Miles and Tina were used to spending the day with your father."

"And Van? I swear if I catch Mitch putting one finger on Lena I'm going to break his arm."

Sarah laughed again. "Even though Van technically invited himself, I know you wouldn't have it any other way. And I also know you love having him here, despite his horny teenage son."

The doorbell rang again and Marcus groaned before turning toward the door. He opened it to find Miles holding boxes and bags. Marcus lightened his load so he could enter without tripping.

"Happy turkey-day!"

Miles smiled as he walked past Marcus in the direction of the kitchen. Tina followed and planted a quick kiss on Marcus' cheek before passing. The house quickly became a buzz of noise and activity when the Vanderlinks arrived. It didn't escape Marcus' notice the way Mitch stood awkwardly talking to Lena, or the way she slightly folded herself into a shy posture in response.

At least she changed out of that damn poor excuse for a skirt.

"It's okay. She'll always be your little girl." Marcus put his arm around Sarah and pulled her close without taking his eyes off their daughter.

Marcus was suddenly yanked away from Sarah's side, and a sloppy kiss was planted on his cheek.

"What the hell, Van?"

"I'm just excited that we'll be in-laws someday."

"He's too young for her."

"He's not that much younger, only one grade behind. Besides, isn't it 'the thing' for women to marry younger men these days?"

"Brandon, stop trying to marry off our son. I adore Lena and wouldn't want any other girl for a daughter-in-law, but they're too young for such talk."

"Isabella, as usual you're the only sensible one in your marriage."

"Alright, everyone. Into the dining room." Miles clapped his hands to get everyone's attention. They all made their way to the dining table and took their seats. Eli was bouncing slightly and Marcus smiled at his excitement.

Marcus cleared his throat before addressing the table. "I'm glad everyone was able to join us again this year. Sarah commented just this morning how wonderful it was to be able to spend this day with all of you."

"It's more likely you were complaining about the invasion, and Sarah was reminding you to be nice."

Marcus shot Tina an annoyed look. "I don't know why she would need to remind me why this is a good idea."

"Uncle Miles, why do you still use these plate covers? You make the same thing every year—it's not like it's a surprise." Lena was using her fork to try and peek under the stainless steel dome before her.

"I might change my mind one of these years." Sarah choked on her wine at the comment. She and Marcus knew he would continue to bring the same thing every Thanksgiving, and they would always use the plate covers. It was just part of the tradition.

"Okay, Eli. This is your year. What's the theme?" Marcus knew his son was bursting at the seams to get started. Eli had been excitedly planning his theme since last Thanksgiving.

Eli's face split into a huge smile. "The theme is Thanks of Torture."

The table grew quiet, trying to understand where Eli was going with his theme.

"I'm sorry, did you say 'torture'—as in pain?" Lena and Eli might be twins, with the same alluring blue eyes, but they had grown into two very different children.

"Yeah, you know, things that make you so happy it's like torture to be without them." Marcus noticed Eli's smile start to waver as the table remained quiet. Feeling the urge to protect his son's feelings, Marcus reached over and clapped him on the shoulder.

"I love it. Who goes first?"

Eli's smile was back. "I will. But first, there are two rules. One, you can't name the obvious—you know, spouse, parent, kids, siblings. Those are a given. Two, you can only give one. So, my Thanks of Torture is my newly upgraded studio."

"That's not something you already have—Mom, is that allowed?"

"It's my theme and my rules. I told you the only two rules. Besides, not having an upgraded studio *is* torturing me!"

"Honey, I hope you have the patience to listen to this non-stop until Christmas." Marcus winked at Sarah when she looked over to him.

"I guess I'll have to because he's not getting it sooner." Eli sat back in his chair and crossed his arms, a frown replacing his smile at Sarah's rebuttal.

"Go ahead, Maria. It's your turn."

"My one Thanks of Torture is for my brother, Mitch."

"You can't say your brother! There are only two rules; you'd think it'd be easy to remember them."

"Eli, if she wants to break the rules, that's fine."

"She's ten, Mom, not a baby. I think she should have to follow the rules."

"Fine. I pick my soccer ball." Maria turned and stuck her tongue out at Eli. "Your turn, Mitch."

Mitch glanced quickly at Lena before looking back down at his covered plate. "My driver's license."

"You don't have a license yet, son."

Mitch narrowed his eyes at Van. "We already established that it doesn't have to be something you already have. Besides, I'll have my permit soon."

"And then it'll be at least another year before you can get a license and another six months after that before you can have any of your friends in the car with you. So, unless Lena doesn't mind my tagging along on your dates, the license won't do you any good for a while."

"Dad!" Mitch looked at his father with mortification and Lena buried her face in her napkin. Marcus couldn't tell, but he assumed she was just as mortified as Mitch. Isabella smacked Van on the arm.

"I told you to knock it off." She then rattled off a string of quick sentences in Spanish, and Van replied just as rapidly. Marcus heard Sarah stifle a laugh as he fought to control his own.

"Lena, honey, why don't you take your turn? Those two could be at it for hours." Lena didn't look up at Tina. Instead, she spoke through her napkin.

"I pick my napkin."

Mitch placed his hand on Lena's arm and Marcus tensed. He felt Sarah place a hand on his knee, anchoring him to his seat.

"Lena, I'm sorry. Don't pay any attention to my dad. You can pick something other than your napkin."

She finally lowered her hands, revealing a bright red face. She turned to Mitch and gave him a grateful smile. Marcus' heart sank. There was no denying she was already smitten with the young boy.

"I pick my sketch pad and pencils."

"My turn." Van paused and looked down the table at Marcus. "My Thanks of Torture is for the fact that Kingston doesn't have a gun permit." The kids looked at him in confusion, and all the adults—with the exception of Marcus—laughed.

"If you're all done acting like weirdos, it's your turn, Mom."

Isabella wiped her eyes with her napkin in response to her daughter's comment. "I pick my yoga class. There's no way I'd be able to survive this clan without it."

Miles was next and didn't hesitate. "My Thanks of Torture is for my impending retirement."

"Hey, you took mine!"

Miles looked at Tina in confusion. "You're not retiring next year."

"I meant *your* retirement. I'm looking forward to having you to myself more often."

Miles gave her an affectionate peck on the cheek. "Sorry, love. Pick a different one."

"Fine. My Thanks of Torture is for my digital e-reader."

"Aunt Tina, you say that every year. No matter what the theme is! Does that dinosaur even still work?"

"Well, Eli, it's my most favorite thing ever. And yes, it still works." Tina exchanged a knowing glance with Sarah and they both resumed their laughing.

"Whatever. Mom, it's your turn."

"Mine is coffee. My life is torture without it."

"More like our lives are torture if you don't have it." Sarah smacked Marcus' leg under the table, and he grabbed her hand before she could pull it back.

He paused to look around the table before sharing his thanks. He had truly been blessed with a wonderful family and friends to match.

Sarah's right. This is how you spend the holidays. Laughing with the people who matter the most to you.

"Dad, dinner's going to be moldy if you don't get on with it."

"My Thanks of Torture is for today."

Eli cocked his head, his striking blue eyes looked at him through narrowed lids. "Your best thing is Thanksgiving?"

"My best thing is today. And every today that I'm given."

ABOUT GPD AND CJD

I would like to take this opportunity to express my deepest gratitude to Carrie for doing a sequel to Kingston's Project and helping to bring awareness to the unique challenges families' face that are at risk for, or carry, the genetic form of CJD. I appreciate and admire her selfless quest to assist in bringing awareness to a disease, that she has never experienced (and I pray she never does) nor new nothing of, until that fateful dream where CJD was presented to her and inspired her to write these books.

My prayers go out to all those impacted by GPD—remember that you are not alone!

—Deana M. Simpson

*   *   *

Although the majority of human prion diseases are caused by sporadic Creutzfeldt-Jakob disease (sCJD), 10-15% are due to genetic mutations of the prion protein gene (PRNP). Genetic prion diseases (GPD) include genetic Creutzfeldt-Jakob disease (gCJD), Gerstmann-Straussler-Scheinker Syndrome (GSS), and fatal familial insomnia (FFI). The differences in name reflect their different clinical presentations and codon mutation. There are approximately 40 different mutations that cause GPD, most of which are inherited in an autosomal dominant pattern, that is to say, the mutation risk does not skip a generation, and if one parent carries the mutation, there is a chance for each child to inherit the mutation. It is equally important to note that just because one carries the mutation, it does not mean that they will die from GPD—the penetrance (number of individuals with a mutation that develop clinical symptoms) can vary widely depending on the exact mutation. GPD can occur at any age, but tend to occur most commonly in mid-life. Illness durations can range from months to several years, depending on the mutation. Some tests commonly used to diagnosis sCJD may be unrevealing in GPD, resulting in delayed or misdiagnosis.

There are many unique challenges for patients and families affected by GPD. GPD are the only inherited infectious diseases, posing several public health challenges. Although certain safeguards must be taken to prevent theoretical transmission of prion disease in GPD mutation carriers, these are sometimes exaggerated to the point of significantly affecting the individual's own healthcare. Like other human beings, it is expected that GPD mutation carriers will develop other conditions that are completely unrelated to GPD. Because of this, care should not be denied, and typical neuropsychiatric symptoms should not be automatically attributed to the initial symptoms of prion disease and should be addressed thoroughly. Physician champions should be sought by families affected by GPD to help ease some of these burdens.

Modern medicine has allowed families affected by GPD to be more empowered. Genetic testing can be easily accomplished from a small sample of blood, but the choice of wishing to learn the result is a very individual matter, and should never be made without the involvement of a knowledgeable genetic counselor, and serious thought about its consequences.

It is never possible to predict how people will react to the knowledge of either having or not having the CJD mutation. Reactions may vary from nothing more than a healthy reappraisal of the prospects for a lengthy future life and attention to providing in advance for one's family, to a progressive state of anxiety and depression. Certainly, at a minimum, most mutation carriers find themselves becoming ultra-alert to every sign of illness wondering whether it might signal the onset of CJD. With regard to receiving a negative result it might be supposed that great relief and happiness would be experienced, but it may also be cause for intense guilt—how is that I escaped and my sister did not? These are outcomes one must live with, and some do it better than others. Specific situations need to be considered, including possible unwanted disclosures to identical twins or living parents. Reasons for choosing to be tested include life planning, participation in research, and family planning.

Dealing with the realities of any genetic disease or condition poses challenges and stressors for families that carry those mutations. Education and awareness is critically important especially given the rarity of prion diseases—not just for the medical community, but for those families impacted as well. Education and counseling can assist families to deal with the challenges, fears, and anxieties that they may experience and empower them to embrace and live life to its fullest— something we should all do regardless of our life circumstances.

* * *

Deana M. Simpson, RN

Deana Simpson received her associate degree in nursing from Ferris State University, her BA Magna Cum Laude from Oakland University and is currently pursuing her Masters in Nursing. She started her nursing career at William Beaumont Hospital in Royal Oak, Michigan caring for patients on a medical unit. As computer technology became more prevalent in the healthcare arena, she became involved in Healthcare Informatics. She currently works at St. John Providence Health System as the Chief Clinical Transformation Officer which involves setting the vision and strategic plan for integrating computer technology into clinical practice across the care continuum in order to reach optimal patient outcomes.

Ms. Simpson's involvement with CJD is one of a personal nature. Her mother died of familial CJD at the young age of 64 (1998), a brother at 57 (2012) and her family has lost 13 family members spanning five generations to the disease. Following her mother's death, she was compelled to provide support to other families afflicted with familial CJD by becoming the founder and director of CJD Insight.

Ms. Simpson partnered with Dr. Paul Brown to create CJD Insight. The objective of CJD Insight is to provide information about familial CJD and support to families impacted by familial CJD. She has corresponded with numerous families throughout the U.S. and other countries across the world. She wants to use CJD Insight to assure people that they do not have to feel helpless and alone when facing the realities of this horrible disease. As the CJD Insight logo indicates, we are "In this together."

Ms. Simpson is a member of the CJD Foundation Board, an active member of the CJD International Support Alliance, participates in fundraising activities for CJD research, and provides education to healthcare professionals and physicians through educational presentations and hospital grand rounds. She also co-authored an article with Florence Kranitz, "Using non-pharmacological approaches for CJD patient and family support as provided by the CJD foundation and CJD insight." CNS Neurol Disord Drug Targets. 2009 Nov;8(5):372-9.

ACKNOWLEDGMENTS

When I wrote my first novel, *Kingston's Project*, I wanted to make sure it was a standalone story. I did write it in a way that would allow me to publish a sequel, but it was not intended to be a two-part story. I was overwhelmed when the reviews for *Kingston's Project* started rolling in, and there was an obvious desire for a continuation to the story. I may not have written *Kingston's Promise* if not for those comments. So thank you, readers, for connecting with the story between Sarah and Marcus and asking for more.

As with my first novel, I have to give huge thanks to my M&M girls—Jaime, Phuong, Melinda, Jennifer, and Melanie. You continue to support and inspire me on a daily basis. Thanks for pushing me to be a better writer and person.

Deana Simpson extended her knowledge and support to Kingston's Promise as she did for my first novel. I am extremely grateful for her feedback, as the accuracy of my information would have suffered without her input.

Many thanks to friends and family who read the book and provided their compliments and criticisms: Kelly Babb, Kari Desnoyers, Robin Gray, Linda Kozlowski, Emily McKeon, Holle Psota, Beth Ramsey, Lara VanValkenburg, and Amanda Williams.

My husband, Jason, and daughter, Julia, continue to support me on this unexpected journey. I couldn't do it without them, and I'm honored to have them at my side.

Finally, I want to thank my cat for being a faithful writing companion. She stays with me as I write, forces me to take play breaks, and protects me from thunder storms.

ABOUT THE AUTHOR

Carrie Beckort has a degree in Mechanical Engineering from Purdue University and a MBA from Ball State University. She spent seventeen years in the corporate industry before writing her first novel, *Kingston's Project*. She lives in Indiana with her husband and daughter.

For more information about Carrie Beckort or her books, visit her website at www.carriebeckort.com or her Facebook page at www.facebook.com/carrie.beckort

Made in the USA
Charleston, SC
01 July 2014